"Combining Masonic history, mysticism, and Nordic rune-lore, Moreland's tale of a world at war is equal parts horror story and spine-jangling thriller. An adventure not to be missed!"

—James Rollins,
New York Times bestselling author of
Map of Bones and *Black Order*

"*Band of Brothers* meets *The Da Vinci Code* meets F. Paul Wilson's *The Keep* . . . Moreland weaves together the best elements of military, supernatural, and religious conspiracy genres, staking out a new territory all his own."

—T. L. Hines, author of
Waking Lazarus

"There's a solid story here—one that mixes elements of Michael Chabon's *The Amazing Adventures of Kavalier & Clay* and the fast-paced thrillers of John Saul."

—*Kirkus Reviews*

"A superbly written novel that will grip the reader's imagination and not relinquish its grasp until the end . . . Brian Moreland's exciting narrative style and exceptional writing skills make *Shadows in the Mist* an unforgettable read."

—Shane Simon, author of
The Prophecy

"A captivating tale of suspense and horror that will chill you to the bone and leave you wanting . . . *more!*"

—Ernest de l'Autin, author of
Reach to the Wounded Healer

"A rocket-paced mystery."

—Joseph P. Farrell, author of
Reich of the Black Sun

continued . . .

Shadows in the Mist

Brian Moreland

BERKLEY BOOKS, NEW YORK

THE BERKLEY PUBLISHING GROUP
Published by the Penguin Group
Penguin Group (USA) Inc.
375 Hudson Street, New York, New York 10014, USA
Penguin Group (Canada), 90 Eglinton Avenue East, Suite 700, Toronto, Ontario M4P 2Y3, Canada
(a division of Pearson Penguin Canada Inc.)
Penguin Books Ltd., 80 Strand, London WC2R 0RL, England
Penguin Group Ireland, 25 St. Stephen's Green, Dublin 2, Ireland (a division of Penguin Books Ltd.)
Penguin Group (Australia), 250 Camberwell Road, Camberwell, Victoria 3124, Australia
(a division of Pearson Australia Group Pty. Ltd.)
Penguin Books India Pvt. Ltd., 11 Community Centre, Panchsheel Park, New Delhi—110 017, India
Penguin Group (NZ), 67 Apollo Drive, Rosedale, North Shore 0632, New Zealand
(a division of Pearson New Zealand Ltd.)
Penguin Books (South Africa) (Pty.) Ltd., 24 Sturdee Avenue, Rosebank, Johannesburg 2196,
South Africa

Penguin Books Ltd., Registered Offices: 80 Strand, London WC2R 0RL, England

This is a work of fiction. Names, characters, places, and incidents either are the product of the author's imagination or are used fictitiously, and any resemblance at actual persons, living or dead, business establishments, events, or locales is entirely coincidental. The publisher does not have any control over and does not assume any responsibility for author or third-party websites or their content.

SHADOWS IN THE MIST

A Berkley Book / published by arrangement with the author

PRINTING HISTORY
Blue Morpho edition / September 2006
Berkley edition / September 2008

Copyright © 2006 by Brian Moreland.
Interior illustrations: *Map* by Brian Bodeker. *Cross and runes* by Brian Altman. *Star of David on dollar* graphics by Brian Moreland.
Cover illustrations by Eric Williams.
Cover design by George Long.
Interior text design by Laura K. Corless.

ISBN: 978-0-425-22433-5

BERKLEY®
Berkley Books are published by The Berkley Publishing Group,
a division of Penguin Group (USA) Inc.,
375 Hudson Street, New York, New York 10014.
BERKLEY® is a registered trademark of Penguin Group (USA) Inc.
The "B" design is a trademark belonging to Penguin Group (USA) Inc.

PRINTED IN THE UNITED STATES OF AMERICA

10   9   8   7   6   5   4   3   2   1

To my grandfather, Captain Henry "Hank" D. Moreland.
As a World War II pilot, he heroically flew C-47s
that dropped army paratroopers over France.
He survived to be my own personal hero.

Acknowledgments

Several publishing professionals worked with equal passion to deliver a quality book. I thank my agent Betty Anne Crawford at Books Crossing Borders as well as my Berkley editor, Michelle Vega. I also wish to thank my original editor, Karl Monger; Susan Malone; Liz Tufte; Scott "Skip" Rudsenske; Kathi Dunn; Ron "Hobie" Hobart; Les Edwards; Ed Zabel; Brian Altman; Brian Bodeker; and my publicist, Leann Garms. For German translations, thanks to Claire Hrabak-Brand.

For the invaluable WWII war stories, I wish to acknowledge the late Tex Smith, who fought as a sergeant with the 28th Infantry Division inside Germany's Hürtgen Forest. I am eternally grateful for the opportunity of touring Germany and Belgium with German historian Albert Trostorf, Dutch historian Ron van Rijt, documentary filmmaker Julian Hudson of the BBC, and the veteran German soldiers of the 89th Infantry Division, Regiments 1055 and 1056. And lastly, I thank my grandfather, Captain Henry Dawson Moreland, for sharing memories that I know were painful.

Thanks to the many friends and family who have supported me: Tim Williams, Greg "Magick" Bernstein, Mystery Lemur, Neil O. Pflum, Mary Helen Leonard, Bart Baggett, Donza Doss, Dave Gulling, Jan Marszalek, Andrea Westerfeld, Carolyn

Ash, Greta Moody, Pamela Rueda and the entire Rueda family—Roberto, Pamela, Beto, y Stefan—Val Hey, Scott Anderson, Blane Richard, and Gary Sleeper. Also, Bil Arscott, Laura Thomas, Asha Cobb, Silver Ra Baker, Eric and Jodi Kean, Brenda Kimbrough, Debbie Autin, Paula and Kenneth Chin, Mack and Carolyn Rudsenske, Paul and Dawn Richardson, Laura Moreland, David Alexander, and my niece Saxon.

My extended family at White Bluff: Jim and Dyann Smith, Toni and Ted Wilson, Madeleine and Glen Lively, Toni and Ken Wengler. The wonderful ladies of the Wild Bunch and their husbands: Bill and Betsy Torman, Dale and Luann Westerfeld, Tom and JoAnn Reedy, George and Maura Collins, Dale and Judy Moore, and Patti and Keith Moreland. I especially wish to thank the ladies of "the Bookies" book club for their support: Betsy Torman, JoAnn Reedy, Judy Moore, Luann Westerfeld, Maura Collins, Patti Moreland, Linda Watson, Sarah Torbett, Cynthia Redden, Nancy Gibson, Ann Duncan, and Pam Hughes.

I also wish to thank a very special teacher, George Klotz, and his Honors English students up in Syracuse, New York: Lauren Candee, Jackie Cavender, Alan Chargin, Meghan Coholan, Lindsey Day, Caitlyn Drumm, Amy Hegan, Leora Kenney, Kelsey Klopfer, Elissa Leathers, Tyler Massaro, Mary McAfoose, Chris Nelson, Audrey Owens, Angela Passamonte, Melissa Petti, Marc Schoeberlein, Brent Scott, Mark Seeber, Meredith Stevens, and Erin Wohlers.

My writing was greatly influenced by these mentors and fellow writers—John Saul, Mike Sack, James Rollins, Terry Brooks, Dorothy Allison, Elizabeth Engstrom Cratty, Katheryn Mattingly, Dan White, and Ernest de l'Autin. Special thanks to John Saul for his timely advice. Our conversations in Rome and Maui motivated me to complete my novel.

Finally, I wish to acknowledge my parents, Patti and Keith Moreland. Thank you both for standing behind me in my pursuit to become a novelist. I'm so happy to share this dream with you and everyone I know.

All the best,
Brian Moreland

Cult of the Black Order

During the 1930s and 1940s, the Nazis cultivated a fascination with the occult and mind control. Reichsführer-SS Heinrich Himmler, leader of the SS military, appointed several known occultists into his inner circle. One such occultist was writer and runologist Karl Maria Wiligut. Together Himmler and Wiligut created esoteric rituals for the SS ceremonies, designed the death's head ring bearing the skull and crossbones, and turned the Wewelsburg Castle in Westphalia, Germany, into a Nazi Camelot.

Studies in the occult fueled a secret obsession. In 1935 Himmler formally established an occult research division, the Ahnenerbe-SS. With over fifty departments devoted to scientific studies, teams of Nazi scientists crusaded across India, Tibet, China, South America, and Nordic countries such as Iceland to locate archeological proof of the Nazis' bizarre historical fantasy—that they were true descendants of mythical supermen known as the Aryan race.

The SS occultists, known as the Black Order, shared Hitler's vision of the Thousand Year Reich—the Nazi plan to cleanse the planet of every race not considered of "pure" German blood. Believing they were destined to become the Aryan master race, the Nazis murdered millions of Jews, Gypsies, Freemasons, and Bolsheviks, igniting the flame that would spread without control and build into the Second World War.

◆ ◆ ◆

Prologue

The castle doors creaked open for the angel of death.

Two Nazi guards yanked the leashes of their snarling Dobermans and stepped back. *"Guten Abend, mein Herr."*

Keeping a wary eye on the dogs, Manfred von Streicher entered the castle gripping a briefcase handcuffed to his wrist. The heavy doors shut behind him, sending a cascade of otherworldly echoes resounding through the stone fortress. Von Streicher shuddered.

No turning back now.

He marched alone through the grand hall of Teutonic Knights. Armored sentries wielding swords and iron spears loomed on pedestals on either side. Von Streicher hastened past them, his boots clumping across the stones. His hand, bearing the death's head ring, tightened around the briefcase handle. The handcuffs chafed his wrist. The stiff collar of his black tunic constricted his throat. Taking controlled breaths, he wound through the serpentine corridors. The shadowy reaches of the castle moaned as if disturbed by his presence.

This is madness, Manfred. For God's sake, turn back! Destroy the research.

And what? Defy the Reich? Himmler will have me skinned alive!

Von Streicher stopped before a set of colossal double doors. Voices murmured on the other side, then laughter erupted. *They're in a cheerful mood tonight. Hate to spoil a good party.* Von Streicher slicked back a few wind-blown hairs and opened the doors.

The laughter stopped. Goblets and silverware clinked on the round table. A dozen black-clad officers fixed their Aryan eyes upon the messenger in the doorway.

Von Streicher raised his arm. *"Heil Hitler!"*

Seated at the far side of the round table, Himmler scowled and checked his watch. "SS-Hauptsturmführer Von Streicher, you've missed three courses."

"My deepest apologies, Reichsführer. My plane was delayed in Norway. A storm—"

Himmler waved his hand dismissively. "Show us the designs."

"Right away, *mein Herr.*" Von Streicher set the briefcase on the table, pulled a tiny key out of his gums, and opened the case. "My expedition in Iceland has led us to a breakthrough discovery." Von Streicher removed a stack of photographs and a dossier.

Reichsleiter Alfred Rosenberg grinned from across the table. "What is it this time, Von Streicher—more Nordic cave paintings?" Chuckles circulated among the men.

Von Streicher passed around photos. "Actually, Herr Rosenberg, I combined your research with mine." The photos were received with perplexed expressions all around.

A smile spread on Himmler's face. "You actually got this to function?"

"Our testing has proven successful on one prototype." Von Streicher took the thirteenth seat at the round table, where a plate of cold lamb shanks and a goblet of red wine awaited him. He slid the plate to one side and gulped the wine.

Reichsleiter Rosenberg, holding a photo, released a nervous laugh. "But this is merely a thing of legend."

Von Streicher smiled. "Like the World Tree, Yggsdrasil, legends derive from an acorn of truth. My team discovered the acorn. Now with the powers of Odin, we can produce the tree."

Himmler said, "Not just a tree, gentlemen, an entire forest. We begin mass production immediately."

Von Streicher choked on his wine. "With all due respect, *mein Reichsführer*, we are still in the early stages. My team needs more time—"

"No more research. We've got weeks before Allies and Soviets hit our borders. We must strike now with a *Blitzkrieg* that will shake the planet." Himmler handed a map to Von Streicher. "Don't bother to unpack, Manfred. You will be overseeing the entire operation at our new base camp." On the map a red box indicated an area near the border of Germany and Belgium.

"The Hürtgen Forest?"

Heinrich Himmler grinned and raised his goblet. "Once we engage these weapons into the war, no army will withstand the might of the Reich. *Heil Hitler!*"

The Black Order raised their goblets. *"Heil Hitler!"*

Von Streicher held aloft his toast with a shaky hand. He glanced down at the map . . . from the ice fields of heaven to the forests of the Green Hell.

The angel of death is coming. And I'm bringing my demons with me.

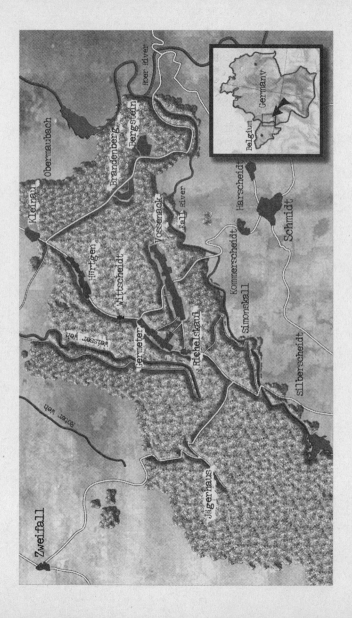

October 1944
The Hürtgen Forest, Germany

Gray fog drifted across the rain-drenched battle zone, clashing with black tendrils rising from the smoldering village. Gunshots cracked. Bullets buzzed past Lieutenant Jack Chambers's ears like swarms of angry hornets.

"This way!" he screamed at his platoon. "Move, move, move!" Chambers charged forward through the smoke and drizzle. Ducking behind the ruins of a brick building, he waved his men over.

"Krauts!" shouted one soldier.

"Take cover!" Chambers aimed his Thompson submachine gun over the chest-high wall.

Ra-ta-ta-ta-tat!

A dozen armed German silhouettes emerged from the buildings.

A metal storm strafed his platoon, chopping down several men. The ones who made it filled in around Chambers. "Base fire, everybody! Stay sharp!"

Sergeant Mahoney barked orders down the line. "You heard the man. Hit 'em with everything!"

The platoon fired over the chest-high wall. Several shadows fell backward, but more emerged to take their place. The enemy closed within fifty yards. A tank shell blasted a nearby wall. Dust drifted over the platoon, filling Chambers's mouth with grit. His men fired madly at the fog.

Ra-ta-ta-ta-tat! Ra-ta-ta-ta-tat!

Chambers hovered behind the wall, his back flat against the cold flagstones. Metal hornets chipped the stones above his helmet.

Corporal Goldstein, pressing a red cross helmet to his head, crawled to Chambers. "Got a plan, sir?"

"Round up the wounded. We're moving out."

Goldstein ran hunkered along the brick wall. Chambers studied the miasma behind them. *Which way now, Jack? Think.* He glanced at his platoon. Battered and bloodied teenagers looked to him as their savior. Bullets whizzed over the wall. One GI dropped dead, a red hole punched in his forehead. Chambers peered into the kid's glazed eyes. Blue as a spring sky.

Chambers squeezed his lids shut to the haunting memory of those vacant eyes.

Artillery shells shrieked through the village. A building one street over exploded in a spray of rubble. Sergeant Mahoney screamed, "They're closing in!"

Chambers snapped out of his trance. "Grenades!" Yanking the pin with his teeth, he lobbed a metal pineapple over the wall. "Take cover." Metal fragments popped against the bricks. "Let's roll, boys. Move, move, move." Chambers led the pack between mounds of rubble. Ahead black pines of the Hürtgen Forest stabbed upward through the fog.

Artillery screeched. To their rear, a gas station disintegrated in a fiery *whooooosh!* Flailing bodies catapulted through the air, screaming. Blasts of scorching heat knocked Lieutenant Chambers flat on his stomach. A heavy weight crashed on top of him.

Gasping, he wiped mud and pine needles from his face. Rain drenched the blaze around him. He tried to move, but a dead soldier pinned his torso and legs. Beside him lay another dead GI, his charred face staring with one drooping eye. Chambers scanned the clearing and saw only smoldering bodies. "Mahoney . . . Buck . . ."

Jesus, they're all dead!

The ground quaked beneath the metallic roar of tank tracks.

A torched GI ran past, waving fiery arms. He screamed like a punished child before being cut down by the *ra-tat-tat-tat* of submachine-gun fire.

The earth spun like a mad carnival ride. Chambers sat dazed as the drizzle formed rings in the mud puddles. *I've failed them. More casualties for Lieutenant Grim Reaper.*

Silhouettes charged through the mist machine-gunning the fallen bodies. The GIs flopped, their dead limbs and torsos animated by the onslaught of metal slugs. Bullets kicked up the mud around Chambers. *Jesus!* Grabbing his Tommy gun, he belly-crawled through the bodies. Strafing bullets snaked along the ground in hot pursuit. He rolled behind a tree, bark and fir branches snapping. Heaving, he waited for the *ra-tat-tat-tat* to end. Then he ran pell-mell through the forest, crashing through walls of sharp pine needles. The sounds of the battle zone echoed farther and farther behind.

Chambers stumbled and fell to one knee, leaning on his rifle for support. Icy rain drenched his face. Lightning jagged across the roiling black sky. He sat back against a tree, snorting a wet sigh of relief. The Hürtgen Forest was a dripping green cavern, soundless except for the occasional distant gunshot. The impenetrable gray fog ruled the trees. His hands trembled. *They're all dead. Just me now.* A mixture of sobs and insane laughter erupted from his belly. He shook his head.

Reaper. Reaper. Reaper.

Chambers glanced around at the shadowy trees.

You boys better hope you don't get Lieutenant Reaper's platoon. You get Grim, you're good as dead, chum. Good as dead.

"No, this wasn't my fault."

Chambers's mind reeled. Guilt twisted his guts. *You gonna let those men die in vain, Chambers?* It was the voice of Captain Murdock. *I didn't train you to be a quitter. You got a mission to fulfill. Now get your ass up.* Chambers's face hardened. He glared up at the bruised sky. An endless storm cloud flashed and swirled overhead. "What now? Huh! What the hell do you want me to do now!"

Distant screams echoed in the woods. "Lieutenant!"

Chambers felt a surge in his chest. "Men!" He searched the haze, trying to place the shouts.

"They're coming!"

To Chambers's right, the sound of running feet and snapping branches echoed just beyond the trees. Another sound filled the forest. Growls—rabid and doglike.

Chambers raced over the hill and followed a winding creek littered with fallen logs and slippery rocks. Freezing water filled his boots as he sloshed against the knee-high current.

Splashing sounds from around the curve just behind him. The growling grew louder.

Chambers sprinted faster. Climbing an incline, he followed a trail to a spiked wrought-iron fence covered in ivy. Beyond it stood a graveyard. He opened the gate and jogged between crosses and tombstones.

The tempest wailed through the Hürtgen like a raging thing, whipping the conifers from side to side, scattering broken branches across the cemetery. Rain angled like silver streamers in a gusty wind.

At the top of the hill a jagged roof and bell tower jutted upward above the fir trees. Lightning shattered the sky, illuminating a Gothic church with shattered windows and bricks pocked with war wounds. His soldiers cried out from somewhere near the church. "Lieutenant!"

Chambers scanned the tombstones and crypts that dotted the hillside all the way up to the church. "Mahoney! Buck! Goldstein!"

"Chambers!"

"Over here!" Chambers sloshed between tombstones.

Several voices cried out with gasping wet gurgles, "Grim Reaperrrr . . ."

He froze. "Where are you?"

"Down here, Lieutenant Reaperrrrr," a voice bubbled up from the mud.

Something pushed against the sole of his boot. Chambers jumped back. The damp soil parted. A face with pale eyes floated to the surface. Membraned eyes. Like a gray winter sky. Muddy fingers clawed outward. Another hand sprouted from the earth and gripped his calf from behind.

"What the . . ." He kicked it loose, stumbling backward into a garden of groping hands.

"Chambers . . ." Skeletal beings draped in rotted military uniforms dug themselves from the graves. "Grim Reaperrrr . . ." They crawled toward him, bony hands outstretched.

Oh God!

"You belong with ussss . . ."

Chambers lurched backward, slipping. They tugged at his legs, pulling him thigh deep into a grave. He gripped a tombstone for support, clawing like hell to break loose. The dead engulfed him, pulling him deeper into the soil till the mud rose over his hips, stomach, chest. His hands grasped a cross. He struggled against the death current.

Shadows charged from the mist. Bullets kicked up the ground. The pale hands released Chambers and sank back into the soil.

German jackboots surrounded his half-buried body. Heart pounding, he looked up at a unit of shadow soldiers. Lightning lit up the fog beyond them. Darkness cloaked their faces.

A stout soldier kneeled down, studying Chambers with eyes as cold and black as the deepest arctic waters. He looked back at his German platoon. The black-helmeted heads nodded. With a metallic hiss the stout Nazi drew a sword and drove the blade through Chambers's heart . . .

• • •

. . . Jack Chambers woke drenched in sweat.

He jolted up, searching his bedroom. The vestiges of his nightmare still moved around him, the past and present fused together. Jack clung to the bedsheets.

Outside the wind whispered, *Grim Reaperrrr.*

The dead sank back into their graves, bubbling down into the mud. Shadows of the German enemy retreated into the gloom of the past. The mist dissipated.

Just another nightmare, Jack. At eighty-three, you're finally ready for the loony bin.

A sharp pain pierced his left arm, flaring like a chain of fire up his shoulder and across the left half of his chest. Jack doubled over, groaning, struggling for air. "Eva . . ."

His wife turned on the lamp. "What is it, Jack?"

Colonel Jack Chambers held a fist against his chest. "Call 911 . . . my heart . . ."

Part 1

Buried Secrets

War brings out the best in men and the worst in men.
Several decades have passed since World War II, and
I'm still trying to decide what it brought out in me.
—COLONEL JACK CHAMBERS, *WAR DIARY*

Chapter 1

Sean Chambers ran from his rental car to the front porch of Nana and Grandpa's home. He rang the doorbell and peered into the front door's stained-glass window—a red, white, and blue lone star inside a circle. Goldie, his grandparents' golden retriever, was the first to greet him, barking at one of the foyer windows.

Inspecting the sun-baked yard and withered flower beds, Sean wiped sweat from his forehead. The merciless sun hovered at high noon, and the sweltering heat pasted his shirt to his back.

A familiar shape formed in the stained glass. Sean's heart surged as the door opened and a striking gray-haired woman put a palm to her chest. "Sean, oh thank heavens, you made it."

"Hey, Nana." As he hugged her and kissed her cheek, Goldie circled their legs, barking. "And how are you, old girl?" Sean scratched behind the dog's furry ears. He peered into the den, frowning. "I came fast as I could. How's Grandpa?"

Nana swatted at two flies buzzing around the doorway. "Recovering a bit slowly, I'm afraid. Nurse Ruby says he's stable, but you know your grandfather. He's a stubborn mule, that one. Bloody refuses to stay in bed."

"So he's awake then?"

Nana nodded, wrinkles deepening around youthful brown eyes. "Oh, yes, he's been tinkering in the war room all morning. Come in out of that heat, love. I was just making some lemonade."

Sean grabbed his suitcase, welcoming the rush of cool air. He followed Nana through the large den decorated with Texas flags, antique furniture, and mounted deer antlers hanging over a flagstone fireplace. Nana's watercolors of windmills, longhorns, and armadillos adorned the walls. Passing a well-equipped kitchen that smelled of fruit and herbs, Nana led Sean into a back study where two voices battled over that of a sports announcer.

"You're out of your league, Nurse Ruby, that's all I have to say." Colonel Jack Chambers sat in a wheelchair facing a bay window. Outside, two golfers hit long balls down the fairway.

A plump nurse with a beehive hairdo sat on a couch looking at the TV. "And I'm tellin' ya, Colonel, no one else even comes close to Tiger Woods."

Grandpa grunted. "He's way overrated. Tiger may be on a winning spree, but that doesn't make him the best golfer of all time. Harvey Penick, Byron Nelson—now those are legends."

The nurse dealt a game of Solitaire on the coffee table. "Ah, don' be such an old buzzard."

Nana tapped on the door. "Time to call a truce, you two. Love, you have a visitor."

Jack Chambers wheeled around, a paintbrush in one hand and a miniature soldier in the other. The army colonel's once muscular frame had withered. But despite his gaunt face, Chambers's green eyes were still full of spark. "How do, Sean?"

Forcing a smile, he walked into the study and shook his grandfather's frail hand. "How are you doing, Grandpa?"

"Well, I've got a zipper on my chest and my golf game's going straight down the toilet. Other than that, life's a peach."

The nurse shuffled her cards. "Colonel, that's not takin' a healin' attitude. What did I tell you about being an old sourpuss?"

Chambers snarled. "Listen here, Ruby, I dedicated four decades to the army so I could spend my golden years playing golf. I got every right to be an old sourpuss."

"Keep it up, Colonel, and you'll give yourself another heart attack."

"Ruby, make yourself scarce so I can catch up with my grandson."

The nurse muted the TV. "Don' be orderin' me round like I'm one of yer soldiers. I'll up yer dosage of prune juice."

"I can still exchange you for an army nurse."

"Mmm, boy, yer in a mood today!" Ruby waddled across the room, flinging her hands. She nudged Sean's shoulder. "Make sure the colonel stays in his wheelchair. This morning I found 'im standin' on the back lawn puttin' away."

"I'm not going to sit idle all day. Now make sure the door hits your fanny on the way out."

Ruby's voice could be heard complaining as she walked down the hall.

Sean smiled. "Grandpa, I think you've met your match."

"She's a firecracker, all right." Chambers shook his head, smiling. A golf cart drove past the back lawn, drawing his attention.

Sean took a seat across from his grandfather's wheelchair. "Think you'll get your game back?"

"Hey, I may be on the back nine, but I can still swing a club." Chambers chuckled. "So how are Meg and the kids?"

"Fine, they'll be here this weekend."

"Good, can't wait to see how Danny and Katie have grown. What's it been, two years?"

Sean looked down. "Yeah."

"Well, that's too long. Nana and I aren't getting any younger."

Sean fidgeted. Even from a wheelchair, his grandfather's steely gaze made him feel five years old. "I know. We've been busy with the move and all . . . but we're stationed in New Mexico for a while, so we'll be able to visit more."

Chambers nodded.

Sean stared around the room. The study's walls were hung with framed World War II propaganda posters; black-and-white

photos of soldiers, medals, and patches; and a gun cabinet
displaying rifles and pistols from several wars. He walked to
a large glass frame that encased two Bronze Stars, three Silver Stars, a Legion of Merit, a Croix-de-Guerre, an American
Campaign Medal, and seven Purple Hearts. "Are these from
World War II?"

"Nah, mostly from Korea and Vietnam. I'm planning on
taking those down."

"What for?"

"Just ready for a change." Chambers wheeled himself
over to his hobby table by the bay window. He picked up a
miniature soldier and, grabbing a tiny brush, painted a red
cross on the helmet. Behind him stretched a long table that
resembled an aerial view of a forest made of model trees,
rocks, hills, plastic streams, and small villages composed of
rubble. The forest was filled with hundreds of soldiers, along
with tanks, trucks, and artillery. Some soldiers had been
meticulously painted army green, others Wehrmacht gray.

"Is that one of the battles you fought?"

Chambers remained silent, positioning hand-painted soldiers in the model forest.

"Sorry, sir, it's none of my business."

"No, it's time you knew, Sean. This represents Germany's
Hürtgen Forest. Bloodiest battle I ever fought. Worse than
Korea, Nam. We called these woods the Meat Grinder because they chewed up soldiers by the thousands. Rained every
day, and the fog was so thick we could never see the enemy."
He pointed to a long chain of small white pyramids bordering
the forest and fields. "These were the Dragon's Teeth that
formed the Siegfried Line separating Belgium from Germany.
At first our tanks couldn't get through, so our infantry fought
the first wave in the worst hand-to-hand combat I ever saw."

"Amazing you got out in one piece."

"My platoon wasn't so lucky. Sean, lock the door. I've got
a special favor to ask."

"Anything, sir."

Chambers wheeled his chair over to a desk. He pushed
the desk with all his might, his bald head flushing with the

effort. The desk budged a couple of inches. He grunted with frustration.

Sean rushed to his aid. "Here, let me." The boards squeaked as Sean shoved the desk three feet down the wall, revealing a square cutout in the wood floor.

Chambers removed the square panel. "Pull out that box."

Sean reached into the hole. He pushed his hands through cobwebs and pulled out a dusty metal box. He looked at his grandfather quizzically.

Chambers wiped his brow, breathing heavily. "The combination is seven-nine-seven."

Sean thumbed the combination and lifted the lid. Inside was a German map and a black diary bound with a leather cord.

Chambers looked at his grandson, his eyes now dark and cloudy. "The map shows where my platoon was buried in Germany. The diary explains what really happened to them. Deliver these to General Briggs at the U.S. Army base in Heidelberg."

Chambers handed Sean a plane ticket.

"Germany? I don't understand."

"General Briggs owes me a favor." Chambers grabbed his grandson's wrist. "This is urgent. I'm putting a lot of trust in you, son. Just deliver the diary and map to General Briggs."

Sean stared down at the diary and ticket. "All right, sir. I'll do it."

Chapter 2

Six hours into the flight to Frankfurt, Sean Chambers sat in the first-class section, sipping a Sprite and staring down at the fold-down tray. Before him were the mysterious relics from Grandpa's past—a war diary and a laminated map of Germany. Sean ran his fingers over the diary's worn edges, the scent of old leather tempting him to explore the bound stories within.

He pushed the diary away. "It's none of my business."

Sean put on headphones and closed his eyes. Maybe Mozart could lull him to sleep. His fingers traced the leather cord that wrapped around the diary. They started to unravel the cord, then stopped. Exhaling, he yanked off the headphones and stared at the diary, rubbing his chin.

Sean unfolded the laminated map. An X indicated a region in western Germany near the Belgian border. On the back of the map, Grandpa had scribbled *Catholic church graveyard* beside an address in Richelskaul.

What could Grandpa have written to warrant a sudden trip to Germany?

Sean lifted the diary, and a black-and-white photograph slid partway out. He pulled out the photo, which showed a platoon of seven haggard soldiers. A few wore helmets. Some had smiles. One man held a cigarette clamped between his lips. Another had his arm around a buddy. A grinning, gap-toothed soldier lay lengthwise across the arms of the front soldiers, who held him up. Lieutenant Jack Chambers stood at one end of the group, his expression stoic. He was a handsome man in his day, with light brown hair and emerald green eyes. Compared to some of his compatriots, Jack looked medium built, with a slim, yet muscular six-foot frame. Even so, his piercing gaze demanded respect and admiration. Written on the backside of the photo was *The Lucky Seven*.

Sean put back the platoon photo and stared at the darkening clouds outside his window. His mind retraced the details of how he would explain all this to General Briggs. *What do I have to report really? All Grandpa did was give me a diary and a map with a list of gravesites. But what does it all mean? It's none of my damn business.*

But Sean's fingers took on a will of their own as they unraveled the leather cord. He opened the diary. The pages were stiff and yellow, like an aged newspaper. Water stains blotched the edges and speckled his grandfather's handwritten words. Sean read a passage.

> *Nearly a month now we've been fighting in this godforsaken forest. The Green Hell. The Meat Grinder. I hate the very sight of it. Endless fir trees. Brutal terrain. Steep hills and rugged cliffs border Germany like a great wall. My platoon and I have been reconning day and night, trying to map out enemy positions.*

Sean flipped the weathered pages, feeling guilty as he scanned the secret life his grandfather had always refused to talk about. What's this? Toward the middle of the book, the words changed from English to Hebrew. Sean knew his family tree was laced with Christian and Jewish lineage. His parents had elected to teach a hybrid of both faiths and let Sean decide for himself. Although he was still searching for the right path, he was well versed in biblical history and, as a young boy, had learned to read Hebrew. But it didn't make translating Grandpa's diary any easier. The letters were Hebrew, but the text was completely un-decipherable.

Interspersed amid the handwriting were crude drawings: a stylized cross, the Star of David, runes, and a complex drawing of interconnected circles. Burning with curiosity, Sean flipped to the back of the book. He encountered a drawing of skeletal figures standing in a graveyard just as a hand tapped him on the shoulder. Sean jerked. An elderly man with a trimmed white beard stood in the aisle. "Excuse me, young man. I was wondering if I could have this aisle seat?" He pointed to it with a mahogany cane. "The man next to me is snoring like a buzz saw."

Sean put away the diary and map.

Behind the thick bifocals, light brown eyes squinted as he smiled. "Ah, thank you. I am growing far too old for such long flights." He took several seconds to sit down, groaning with every movement. "My back's not what it used to be." He adjusted the knitted yarmulke on his head and pushed his glasses up the bump of his large nose.

The plane hit a patch of turbulence, shaking the cabin from side to side.

"Oy! I wish they'd get past this mess." The man buzzed a flight attendant. "Stacey, pardon me, but could I trouble you for another Bloody Mary?"

"No trouble at all, Rabbi." The blonde smiled at Sean. "How about you, flyboy?"

"No, thanks."

"How about some ice cream, then? I've got Oreo cookie."

"I'm fine."

She winked at Sean. "Well, if you need anything at all, fly-boy, just buzz me."

The rabbi watched the flight attendant saunter down the aisle. "I think she was flirting with you. Must be your uniform."

"Suppose so." Sean slipped on his headphones, pretending to watch the in-flight movie.

The rabbi nudged his elbow. "Ah, if I was your age, Sean, I'd ask her to dinner."

Sean held up his hand, wiggling the finger with the golden band.

"Yes, yes, same here." The rabbi pulled out his wallet and showed a photo of a smiling elderly woman. "Just celebrated our fifty-seventh. Six kids, fourteen grandkids—"

"Wait, how do you know my name?"

"I heard the flight attendant say it."

"No, she didn't."

"Oh, how clumsy of me." The old man blushed. "I'd make a poor spy." He offered his weathered hand. "I'm Rabbi Jacob Goldstein. Ring a bell?"

Sean kept his arms crossed.

The rabbi shook his head. "That son of a gun. Well, it's good to know your grandfather can keep at least one secret."

Sean glared as the old rabbi leaned forward on his cane.

"I served with your grandfather's unit during World War II. He and I have stayed in contact. I know about the diary. Read it yet?"

"I'm not at liberty to discuss it." Sean latched the briefcase and shoved it under the seat.

Goldstein looked down, his hands folded over the brass handle of his cane. "I was there." Behind the bifocals, Goldstein's magnified brown eyes glazed over. "Over fifty years ago, Jack and I witnessed an unspeakable horror. We made a pact to take our secret to the grave. When he told me he wrote the whole incident in his diary, I, well . . ." He pursed his lips. "Sean, you can't let the army have that diary."

Sean looked out the window.

The old man sighed. "How can I make you understand?"

"Understand what?"

"There is more to that diary than just a few missing soldiers. Do you believe in the supernatural, Sean? Do you believe there is a spiritual presence here on earth?"

Sean pinched his eyebrows together. "What are you driving at, Rabbi?"

Goldstein looked down at his aging hands. "What is buried should stay buried. Just hand the diary over to me. I'll handle it from here. Tell your grandfather you took care of it. And we can all go on with our happy lives."

Sean drew his feet tight against the briefcase.

Goldstein clamped his jaw and looked at the seat in front

of him, brooding, then turned back, his pupils dilated. "Your grandfather is not thinking straight. If you turn in that diary to General Briggs . . . it will summon a military investigation. Do you know what that will mean to your family? You love Meg, do you not? Danny and Katie? Why risk it?" He looked away, his cheeks trembling.

A rash of goosebumps sprouted on Sean's arms. "You leave my family out of this."

Goldstein's craggy face turned red. "I'm trying to *protect* your family."

Sean looked the white-bearded man square in the eyes. "Rabbi, it's time you returned to your seat."

"You're Jack Chambers's grandson, all right." He stood, rapping his cane against the aisle floor. "I just pray that between now and the time we land you will come to your senses and reconsider."

The flight attendant returned with Goldstein's drink. "Here you go, Rabbi."

Goldstein stormed down the aisle. The flight attendant looked at Sean, befuddled. Seething, he stared out the window, dwelling on the pitch night sky.

Chapter 3

The baggage-claim area of the Frankfurt airport bustled with passengers. Sean stood at a pay phone with a hand pressed over his ear, the crowd noise battling the static of Grandpa's thin voice. "Just do as I asked. Deliver the book to General Briggs."

Pinpricks covered Sean's back. He turned to see Rabbi Goldstein leaning on his cane on the far side of the luggage conveyor, staring at him.

Sean turned around. "Is Goldstein dangerous?"

"I thought I could trust him, but apparently he's unpredictable. Just be wary and don't let him get hold of the diary."

"You have my word, Grandpa." Holding tight to the briefcase, he scanned the crowd for the old rabbi. But Goldstein had vanished.

• • •

Sean went straight to the train station and bought a ticket to Heidelberg. According to his map, the small mountain city was located a one-hour train ride southwest of Frankfurt.

Just a short trip to a hot shower and a bed.

Arriving at the depot several minutes before the train, Sean sat on a bench and enjoyed one of Nana's brownies. He watched some backpackers, males and females no older than twenty, poring over a map. They laughed and spoke Dutch.

Tapping his foot, Sean leaned back against the bench. The seat suddenly shook with the weight of someone sitting down next to him.

"I see you are still going through with this." Rabbi Goldstein filled the space beside him. "I'm sorry for my outburst earlier. My intent was not to lose my temper."

"Fine. Now if you'll excuse me." Sean picked up his bags and walked to the edge of the track.

Scratching his beard, Goldstein stepped up beside him. "I don't think you fully comprehend what your grandfather is asking you to do. There are grave consequences for revealing these secrets to the army." He adjusted his long gray trench coat.

Is he concealing a gun? Sean braced himself. "Sir, with all due respect, I don't know—"

Goldstein whispered, "If the army gets their hands on that diary, they will find evidence that could incriminate your grandfather."

The train rolled in, screeching to a halt in front of them. "I have to go."

Relying on his cane, Goldstein kept pace. "Listen, Sean. You don't want to see what I've seen. I'm begging you. Burn that book. You can tell your grandfather the army has it. Jack will never know the difference. He just wants to leave this world knowing he did the right thing."

Sean clenched his jaw. "I won't lie to my grandfather."

Goldstein rapped the cement with his cane tip. "Just honor the pact between two soldiers. Keep this book out of the army's hands. I lived through one holocaust, and as God as my witness, I'll do whatever it takes to make sure we don't live through another."

Sean glared at the old man.

Goldstein shook his white head. "What if I told you that uncovering the bodies of a few dead soldiers could lead to more deaths in the future? Trust me. Some bones should stay buried."

"I've got a train to catch. Approach me again, and I'll have you arrested." Sean boarded and took a seat by a window. The old rabbi remained on the depot, his gaze seeming to burn a hole in the glass. The train pulled away from the station. When Sean tried to finish his brownie, he found he had lost his appetite.

• • •

Sean arrived at the station in Heidelberg to a brisk sunny morning and the faint clanging of church bells. He tossed his bags in the back of a taxi. "Hotel Tannhauser, please."

After checking in, Sean carried his bags up a winding staircase, passing a white statue of a nude woman on one of the landings. He entered a room furnished with fine antiques and red throw rugs on the wood floors. Latching the door, Sean dropped his bags and plopped onto the bed. He fought sleep long enough to call home. After a brief discussion with Meg about taking their two kids, Danny, seven, and Katie, five, to Nana and Grandpa's this weekend, he hung up and lay back on the flower-patterned bedspread. The ceiling tiles suddenly warped into diary pages covered with strange Hebrew text. Sean rubbed his eyes and the cryptic text disappeared. He pulled the rough-edged diary out of his briefcase, his fingers tracing the leather cord that bound it shut.

Grandpa's voice echoed in his mind: *Deliver the diary to General Briggs. On the back of that map, there's a list of soldiers and the graves in which they're hidden.*

Then it was Rabbi Goldstein's turn: *I've lived through one holocaust, and I'll do whatever it takes to make sure we don't live through another. Some bones should stay buried.*

Jesus, Grandpa, what did you and Goldstein get mixed up in that would justify burying the bodies of an entire platoon and keeping it secret for more than sixty years?

Their voices battled inside Sean's head.

Just get the diary to Briggs. I'm putting a lot of trust in you, son."

"Don't listen to your grandfather. There are grave consequences for revealing these secrets to the army.

Sean's eyelids grew heavy. Yawning, he trudged to the sink and washed his face.

The phone rang, its high-pitched foreign ring wearing on

his nerves. Sean leaped over the bed to answer it. "Hello?" The sound of breathing at the other end. "Who is this?"

There was a click, followed by a dial tone.

Feeling his stomach cramp, Sean made sure the door was locked then pushed a chair against it. Glancing down he saw a folded piece of paper wedged under the door. His heart pounding, he opened it. The message, scrawled in Hebrew, read, *Some bones should stay buried.*

Sean crumpled the paper. He placed the diary and map under his pillow, then sat on his bed watching the door.

Chapter 4

At the Twenty-sixth Army base in Heidelberg, Captain Sean Chambers followed a lanky lieutenant to an office suite with cherry wood furniture. Paintings depicting fly-fishing adorned the walls. A prize trout hung mounted over a fireplace. "General Briggs, sir. Captain Chambers here to see you, sir."

General Mason Briggs, a distinguished-looking African American with a broad chest and a shaved head, stood behind his desk with the air of a granite statue.

Sean and the lieutenant snapped to attention, holding a firm salute.

The general spoke in a husky voice. "Thank you, Lieutenant. Dismissed." Briggs motioned to one of the leather wing-back chairs in front of his desk. "Have a seat, Captain."

Sean removed his hat. "Thank you, sir."

General Briggs leaned back in his chair, the coils squeaking beneath his weight. His chiseled cheeks remained hard as he studied Sean's uniform. "It's usually a bad omen when the air force pays me a visit." Briggs's face softened and parted into an enormous grin. "Sean Chambers . . . *damn* how you've grown! Last I saw you, you were just a muddy-faced little fart running around with a jar of tadpoles."

Sean smiled. "It's good to see you again, sir."

"I've wondered about you from time to time, and look at you now. Captain in the air force. Let me guess—jet fighter."

"Yes, sir. F-16s and F-18s."

"Amazing, little Sean Chambers." Briggs folded his thick arms. "So how's Jack holding up?"

"Not too well, sir."

"Damned shame. I always considered him immortal. Saved my ass in Nam more than once." The general shook his head, his eyes entranced by the reverie. "Christ almighty. So how's Eva handling all this?"

Sean shrugged. "She never stops cleaning the house."

"Your grandmother's a strong woman." Briggs stared down at his large ebony hands. Beside his wedding band, the general wore a thick gold ring with an onyx crown. Inlaid in the onyx was a gold emblem of an architect's compass stacked above a ruler. In the center floated the letter *G*—the insignia of Freemasonry.

Briggs pressed his fingers into a teepee, the Masonic ring glinting in the light. "So what's this package? Your message said it was urgent."

"Yes, sir." Sean cleared his throat. "General, I'm not quite sure how to put this."

"Just cut right to it."

Sean's fingers felt along the seam of his hat. "As you probably know, General, in October 1944, Grandpa's platoon disappeared without a trace."

"Yeah, Jack never talked much about the war. I don't blame him. He had a tough detail in the Hürtgen Forest. His official report said Jack's platoon got lost behind enemy lines during a bloody skirmish with the Germans. He got separated from his men and somehow made it back. The rest turned up MIA."

"Well, sir, Grandpa says there's more to the story."

General Briggs lifted a thick eyebrow. "Oh . . ."

Sean placed the diary and map on the general's desk. "In truth, he knew exactly where his platoon ended up." Sean pointed to a town on the map. "Here are the coordinates of their burial ground."

"Burial ground!" Briggs's face hardened back into a mask of granite, the mirth draining from his eyes. He studied the photo and map.

Sean sat back, waiting for a response. The room was quiet—only the ticking of a clock and the general's heavy breathing. He unbound the diary and flipped through the pages.

Sean said, "He used Hebrew letters, but the words are in some type of cryptic code."

Briggs's eyes gleamed with recognition. He pulled out a folded sheet of paper. "This one's in English." He opened it and read, his eyebrows pinching together. "Unbelievable." The general dialed the telephone. "Jack! Briggs here. What the hell is this letter about? . . . Uh-huh . . . Uh-huh." Sitting with the phone to his ear, Briggs fidgeted with the diary, flipping through the weathered pages. "Let me get this straight. You're asking me to dig up an existing Catholic graveyard on German soil?" The general shook his head. "Jack, do you understand the ramifications?" Briggs tossed the diary onto his desk. He ran his hand over his shaved head. "Okay, but I'm not making any promises. I'll call you after I've read the diary. Yeah, talk to you soon. Bye."

Briggs hung up. "Christ, what a mess." He picked up the journal. "Have you deciphered this code, Sean?"

"No, sir. It might as well be in Greek."

Briggs nodded. "I have a source. Let's meet for dinner tomorrow at eighteen hundred hours. By then I'll know what the hell Jack's really talking about."

Chapter 5

In the gloom of their bedroom, Jack Chambers lay awake in bed with Eva's head snoozing gently on his chest. He clung to her, as if his wife's warm body were a lifeline to the present. But tonight, like so many nights before, he would have to battle this nightmare alone.

Against an electrical sky stood a church with pocked flagstones, jutting spires, and a cracked bell tower. Jack clamped his eyes shut.

Dear God, please give me time to make things right.

Moans arose from the foot of the bed.

Jack whispered, "Don't let them take me."

Raspy voices gurgled, "Lieutenant . . ."

Jack stared down at the floor. Stone shapes and crosses pushed up from the mud, surrounding their bed with a war-battered graveyard. Below each tombstone, damp soil parted. Skeletal fingers burrowed up from the graves like white worms.

The raspy gurgling voices chanted, "You belong with us . . ."

Jack's heartbeat ratcheted.

Muddy arms stretched upward, reaching for him.

He kicked at hands clawing the bedspread.

Shadow soldiers circled the bed, aiming bayonets and gun barrels at his chest.

An immense Nazi charged the bed, drawing a sword. A mask with dark hollow eyes stared down.

Jack backed against the headboard. "No, you're not real! Not real!"

Eva sat up and turned on the lamp. The church and tombstones had vanished, giving way to the walls filled with family photos. Jack sat against the headboard with his arms around his knees, rocking. Eva took him in her arms, rocking with him.

Chapter 6

A chilly evening breeze blew across the restaurant terrace, sending a flock of sparrows into sudden flight. The setting sun cast long shadows across the wooded hills and valleys of Heidelberg. Below, the swift Neckar River gushed beneath ancient stone bridges.

At a table at the edge of the terrace, General Briggs gulped his mug of German wheat beer. The cold liquid deluged the hot bile churning in his stomach. He controlled the muscles around his mouth, maintaining the mask of a general. Forcing a smile, he flagged down a waitress dressed like a wench. "Greta, two more beers and a large plate of bratwurst. And tell Günther to pile on the sauerkraut. Sean, you're in for a real treat."

Briggs watched the downtown district move at its evening pulse. "Peaceful, isn't it? Celia and I've lived here six years now, and we never grow tired of it. Did you get up to the castle?"

"I took a walk up there this afternoon." Sean turned his attention to the castle ruins that sat atop the mountain, looming over a sea of orange-brown rooftops.

Greta set two more beers on the table. "Here you go, General. *Der Bratwurst* vill be out shortly."

"Thank you, Greta." When she was out of earshot, Briggs leaned in. "Listen, Sean, about your grandfather's diary . . ." Briggs exhaled. "I deciphered some of the code."

"How?"

"Actually it was simple, if one understands the Atbash cipher."

"Atbash, sir?"

"It's an ancient cipher tool using the letters from the Hebrew alphabet. Your grandfather taught me how to write and decipher Atbash in Vietnam. We would send coded messages to one another. Back then I had to do it by hand. Thanks to decoding computers, I've already deciphered over half the diary."

"Anything you can share, sir?"

Briggs looked down at his hands unconsciously shredding his napkin. "Last night I read the first half and . . . I've witnessed a lot of strange shit in my day, but Jack's story tops them all. If the diary had come from anyone else, I'd think he was completely off his rocker."

Sean's expression stiffened. His neck turned red. "You don't believe him!"

"I'm afraid Jack may be suffering from a posttraumatic delusion. Not uncommon in veterans. They return to civilian life, but the war stays in their head. Eventually they can't separate the two."

"Grandpa's dying, general! He's not crazy!"

Several people glanced in their direction.

Briggs narrowed his eyes. "Watch your tone, Captain. Remember who you're talking to."

"Sorry, sir. I—"

"You know I hold your grandfather in the highest regard. I'm a general today because of him. But his diary has me convinced he's more than physically ill."

Sean stared down at the city, his jaw tight, eyes constantly moving. He turned back to the general. "Permission to speak frankly, sir."

"Go ahead."

"What could Grandpa have written to make you think he's delusional?"

"I couldn't begin to explain it." Briggs stared off toward the castle ruins. Twilight shadows began to drape the cloak of night over its stone shoulders. "For Jack's sake, it's better I think he's suffering from delusions."

A gust of wind swept along the terrace. Sean zipped up his olive fleece pullover. "Has anyone else read the diary?"

Briggs shook his head. "Jack encrypted this in the Atbash cipher because this book was for my eyes only. I did some background checking. A prewar Catholic church does exist on the outskirts of Richelskaul, matching the map's coordinates. And it has a graveyard."

"Then Grandpa is not completely delusional."

"There's more. Your grandfather wasn't the only survivor of his unit. There was a Jewish chaplain who filled in as a medic. Corporal Jacob Goldstein. He went AWOL in December of 1944 and fell completely off the grid. Jack's diary suggests the rabbi changed his name and has been living in Prague ever since. They've stayed in contact."

Sean's eyes widened. "Goldstein showed up on my flight to Frankfurt. He's here in Heidelberg. He wants the diary."

The hairs on the back of Briggs's neck stood at attention, yet he maintained his mask of granite. "In the diary, Goldstein and Jack had a peculiar bond. Like I said, I've only read half the story. We do have a few pieces to the puzzle." Briggs reached under the table and pulled out a computer printout. "I looked up all the missing soldiers in our database. Over half the men from Jack's platoon were never found. My gut tells me Jack and Rabbi Goldstein buried them in that graveyard. And, Sean, my gut never wrong."

Part 2

The Bone Field

There is more to war than the news can capture. What goes unseen by the public eye are the secret wars, the spy games, and the global puppet masters—both good and evil—pulling strings of puppet nations. All my life I have witnessed such secret wars, but nothing compares to the unspeakable darkness I battled in World War II. That war is long over and my Nazi enemies are either dead or dying of old age somewhere down in Argentina. I pray I'm doing the right thing by digging up my secrets.

—COLONEL JACK CHAMBERS, *WAR DIARY*

Chapter 7

Gray clouds ushered in a damp, pine-scented wind as Sean weaved through a maze of gravestones. He craned his neck, sensing vertigo. The Catholic church, with its jutting spires and massive bell tower, loomed like a medieval castle. Green ivy walls framed towering stained-glass windows. In several places, new flagstones had filled in gaps, patching up old war wounds. Ravens cackled in the wind, flapping from ledge to ledge like black-feathered angels.

Sean zipped his jacket and walked between two enormous crypts. Atop one stood a white statue of the Virgin Mary, glistening with morning dew. Her pale eyes watched as Sean's muddy shoes violated sacred ground.

A voice whispered in the wind. *Do you believe there is a spiritual presence here on earth?*

Sean felt his gut cramp. *I've been so driven to fulfill Grandpa's dying wish, I never considered asking God's advice.* Gooseflesh sprouted across his arms. *Had God sent a rabbi to intervene?*

Rabbi Goldstein's warning echoed in Sean's head. *Some bones should stay buried.*

Too late, Rabbi. The wheels are in motion.

Shovels scraping against earth echoed off the tombstones.

Ignoring the Virgin's vacant stare, Sean hurried between
the crypts. Beyond stretched a massive graveyard surrounded
by fir trees. A military forensics team gathered around a grave
where two MPs were busy digging. General Briggs, puffing a
fat cigar, stood amid the garden of tombstones. The African
American commander, dressed in his field uniform and a cap,
waved Sean over to join the digging party. "Captain Chambers, you're just in time."

Two sweat-stained MPs had burrowed five feet into a
grave. Several other MPs stood ready with shovels. The tombstone read *Helga von der Heydte, born 1880, died 1934.* Sean
saluted and stepped out of the way as grave dirt flew toward
his shoes. "Have I missed anything, sir?"

"No, we're about to exhume our first grave." Briggs motioned
for Sean to follow. He and Sean walked side by side. "How's
your stay in Germany been, Captain?"

"Longer than I expected, sir. My family thinks I've gone
AWOL."

"Well, this will be over soon." The general puffed his cigar.
"I've had to go through the ringer just to dig up one grave."

"What happens if they're buried here?"

"Then I can exhume the bodies and move them to an American cemetery."

"That's all Grandpa wants."

"Just tell Jack after this he and I are even."

Shovels thunked against solid wood.

Briggs whispered, "Okay, Sean, let's see how deep we've gotten ourselves."

By the time they reached the open grave, the entire top half
of a rotten casket had been unearthed. The two MPs stopped
work and looked up at the general. "Okay, boys, open it."

They pried open the top door, the wood creaking in protest
and wet earth dribbling into the coffin. Sean and Briggs leaned
over the grave. A skull with an unhinged jawbone stared up
at them. The skeleton, half buried in dirt, wore cloth so tattered and mildewed it was indiscernible. One of the grave
diggers reached into the casket. He brushed soil from the rib
cage and pulled out a silver chain, muddied dog tags dangling
from it.

"Give it here." The cigar wedged at the corner of his mouth, General Briggs wiped off the tags with his latex-covered hand. A name was made out: G-a-b-r-i . . . Squeezing the dog tags in his fist, Briggs nodded to the grave diggers. "Haul him out."

The MPs placed the mud-covered skeleton onto an open body bag. The skull hit the black plastic with a hollow thud and turned, facing Sean. The jaw opened in a silent scream. A grub worm coiled in one of the muddy sockets. Hot bile rose up in Sean's throat. Gagging, he covered his mouth, swallowing hard. The acids burned their way back down his chest like whisky.

Briggs chuckled. "Your first corpse?"

Sean nodded, doing his best to settle the geyser roiling inside his stomach.

"General Briggs, sir!" Major Taggert called out. "Davis found something."

Briggs and Sean leaned over the six-foot pit. A stocky corporal, wearing soil-stained coveralls, beamed a flashlight along one side of the empty casket. The rotted wood had fallen away. A hole in the earth, the length of a man's body, led down into a dark abyss.

Briggs's thick eyebrows pinched together. "What's down there?"

Corporal Davis shrugged. "Sir, I didn't look."

Briggs barked, "Well, jab some light in there."

The color drained from Davis's cheeks. He lay flat across the casket's floor. His head and shoulders disappeared as he probed the cavernous hole with his flashlight. His voice echoed, "Seems to be some sort of tunnel, sir." Davis clambered out, his cheeks smeared with soil. "It's freaking cold down there."

Briggs led Taggert under an oak tree. "Major, I want four men suited up to go down there."

"Sir?"

"Did I stutter, Major? You heard me right! We're going spelunking." Briggs stamped his cigar out against the tree. "And get me a suit, too. I'm going down there with them."

Chapter 8

Wearing coveralls, gloves, and a headlamp, General Briggs climbed down a ladder into the tunnel beneath the graveyard. He winced. The dust mask covering half his face did little to hold back the stench—a foul mixture of mud, roots, and decades of entombed death. Nor did his thick coveralls shield him against a chill so icy cold it seeped into the marrow of his bones.

The other four soldiers, looking more like miners with their glowing headlamps and soot-covered faces, stood packed together in a tunnel barely shoulder width in diameter.

Briggs hopped onto the dirt floor. The passage ran in two directions. Roots penetrated the walls and ceiling. Briggs tilted his head. The beam from his lamp spotlighted the ceiling. Grub worms nestled in a network of roots. "How stable is it?"

"Fairly solid, sir." Lieutenant Collins struck the walls with his palm. "Soil's composed mostly of clay. And check these out, sir." His headlamp beam revealed how every few feet thick wooden planks shaped like horseshoes braced the tunnel. Jack Chambers's words echoed in Briggs's head: *Beneath the graveyard burrows a tunnel built like a mine shaft. That's where my men are buried.*

"Which way, sir?" Lieutenant Collins asked.

"Follow me." Weaving through the crisscrossing roots, Briggs recalled one of the more disturbing passages from the diary: *Over the years, as my heart burned with guilt for my men, I considered breaking the pact I made with Goldstein and sharing our secret. I suggested we send a team into the tunnels to dig up the bodies, and keep the rest buried. I agree with Goldstein, the world doesn't need to know the rest. I just don't want my men to be forgotten. They have families. But Goldstein reminded me that the bodies aren't alone down there. And sending a team into the tunnels would endanger the lives of others and potentially release a horror for a new generation to battle.*

Bullshit, Jack! barked General Briggs's logical side. *There's nothing down here but the sleeping dead.* The logical side sounded less convincing now that he was actually down here probing the impenetrable darkness with his headlamp. *What if everything Jack wrote was the truth?* Breathing the tainted air became a chore. One of the men behind him kept coughing.

Twenty paces along, Briggs stepped between several half-open caskets embedded in the walls like catacombs. His beam probed the graves. Nestled inside lay skeletons wearing army uniforms. The excavation team caught up. Observing their mortified expressions, General Briggs kept his face rigid. "Okay, men. We got work to do."

◆ ◆ ◆

Above ground, ravens fluttered from the church tower as the bells tolled three times.

Sean marched along a row of body bags lined up on the grass. At the foot of each sat a box filled with relics: dirt-encrusted helmets, rifles, pistols, and boots. Thunder rumbled. Raindrops formed tiny puddles on the body bags.

Lightning crackled over the forest, as two mud-covered MPs lugged over another body bag. Major Taggert unzipped it, wincing at the pungent odor. He read the dog tags and checked off another name on his clipboard. The bag remained partially unzipped. A mummified face stared up at the gray sky. Patches of hair still clinging to the skull blew in the wind.

"Oh, God." Sean spewed hot bile over a grassy plot. The surrounding MPs looked up. Sean wiped his mouth and, feeling a second wave, he raced around crypts and tombstones, ran up a set of stone steps, and exited the cemetery at street level. Leaning against a tree, he sucked fresh air into his lungs, managing to hold down the rest of his breakfast.

A brisk wind swept through the pine branches. The tops of the conifers swayed as charcoal clouds laced with veinlike electrical flashes drifted toward the church.

A white Volkswagen cruised in front of the church, idling for a moment. Inside, a silhouette craned its head.

Sean marched across the parking lot.

The car peeled out and disappeared around a bend. But not before Sean got a clear glimpse of Rabbi Goldstein's angry face.

◆ ◆ ◆

The footsteps of Briggs and his two remaining men echoed along a hollow chamber that continued as far as the eye could see. Behind them, red flares marked their path back to the exit. The deeper they delved, the hotter the acid burned in Briggs's stomach and the more he denied the diary could be true. *The mine-shaft tunnels crisscross beneath the grave-yard like a maze. The main tunnel runs from the church's basement to another cement chamber hidden deep within the graveyard. That's where the guardian stays.*

Get your men out of here, Briggs warned himself.

No, I have to prove that Jack is delusional. His nightmares can't be real.

Lieutenant Collins probed an intersecting tunnel that branched off into two more directions. "Which way, sir?"

Briggs lit another flare and jabbed it into the earthen wall. "Keep to the main tunnel."

A few more paces and the narrow passage opened up into a cavern. Straight ahead stood a rusty iron door. Engraved on it was a circle with a swastika. *I'll be damned.*

"See something, sir?" asked Lieutenant Collins.

Briggs quickly pulled his light away from the door. The icy darkness pressed against his back as he turned to his men. "You two, head back up top. I'll be out in a minute."

The lieutenant and corporal looked at one another.

"That's an order, men."

"Yes, sir." The two soldiers hustled back toward the ladder. As their lights faded, Briggs wheeled back around, his headlamp spotlighting the iron door with the swastika. *For Christ's sake, Jack, you have to be wrong. But what if you're not?* He pulled out a .45 semiautomatic pistol. Aiming at the gloom, he stepped through the doorway on shaky knees. His boots clumped onto a cement floor. The stench of death grew unbearable. His eyes watered. The headlamp panned across an image that made his scrotum tighten. General Briggs spun in a circle, not believing his eyes.

The walls were piled from floor to ceiling with skeletons.

Struggling to breathe now, Briggs knelt. His gloved hand pushed aside skulls and German helmets. Chalked on the floor beneath was an ancient symbol surrounded by hieroglyphs. He released a nervous laugh. "Jack, you crazy son of a bitch." He pulled out his notepad. Written on it was a decoded message from Jack's diary.

Mason, walk to the back of the crypt. There you will find an altar table embedded into a brick wall. Feel for the loose bricks and remove them.

Briggs followed the instructions, his headlamp stabbing into the never-ending void. Skulls with vacant eye sockets stared back at him. He reached a back wall and found a long stone table embedded in the gray bricks. Feeling along the wall, he came across a patch of bricks that protruded slightly. He pulled them out, one by one, uncovering a secret nook. Frosty air greeted his face. He tilted his helmet, aiming the headlamp into the black portal. The depth seemed infinite, like staring into an abyss. Another room. *Damn it, Jack, if you expect me to tunnel my way in there, you're out of your—* Briggs's light illuminated a ledge just to the right of the hole. *There it is!* Reaching around the cold stones, his fingers scraped something that felt like damp leaves. He pulled out a mummified relic covered in soil and cobwebs. The object, rectangular in shape, was wrapped in olive drab fabric. The rotting material felt like it cocooned a thirty-pound brick.

A passage near the end of Jack's diary echoed in Briggs's head.

Unable to destroy the Nazi relic, Goldstein and I buried it inside the altar's brick wall. For sixty years it's remained undisturbed, waiting to be excavated. Goldstein and I disagree on whether to remove it or let it rot with the bones. We both agree on one thing—the relic must never be found by the wrong people. That's why it must be removed while we're still alive. And there's only one man I trust to find the relic and dispose of it. My close friend and ally, General Mason Briggs. May God protect him.

Water splashed off to Briggs's right.

He swept his headlamp, and it reflected off a pool just past the bones. The murky surface rippled. Mason Briggs froze as a large shadow shape rose from the pool. *The guardian!*

Briggs stumbled backward toward the door. His headlamp flickered, the light dimming.

Water splashed. Wet footfalls fell onto the concrete floor.

Briggs fired his pistol and bolted out of the chamber. He sprinted back through the flare-lit catacombs, bumping the narrow walls and knocking a red flare into a puddle. The flame snuffed out. The darkness swallowed up the tunnel behind him. He reached the ladder. Climbed toward the light. As his head broke the surface of the grave, he slipped. The ladder fell, leaving his legs dangling. Briggs gripped the coffin. "Men, pull me out!"

Two soldiers leaped into the grave and grabbed the general's shoulders.

An icy chill enveloped his legs.

"Hurry, damn it!"

With a hard tug, they birthed Briggs from the tunnel.

"Everyone out of the grave," the general barked. He climbed onto level ground, covered head to toe in dirt. "Fill in the grave, men. Fast." Several soldiers shoveled in dirt.

Thunder rumbled overhead. Rain pelted Briggs's caving helmet and splattered the mud puddles around the grave. He stared down at the rectangular hole.

It's watching me.

The hole filled with dirt.

Major Taggert approached holding an umbrella. He stared curiously at the fabric-wrapped relic tucked under Briggs's arm. "Buried treasure, general?"

"You never saw this. Make sure they pack the soil tight. I'll be back later." His granite composure crumbling, Briggs marched out of the graveyard and back up the steps to the street.

Sean chased after him. "General Briggs!"

Briggs reached his Mercedes and hit the trunk button on his key chain. He set the mummified relic inside and shut the trunk, just as Sean caught up. They stood in the rain beneath umbrellas taking a beating from the heavens. Lightning strobed above them.

"Sir, what did you find down there?"

"It's best you didn't know."

"Please, sir. He's my grandfather."

Briggs squeezed his fist and glanced down at his Masonic ring. "I've rented a cabin up the road. Follow me."

Chapter 9

Colonel Jack Chambers sat in his wheelchair at a window, watching the afternoon rain shower the golf course. Goldie, who had been curled at Jack's feet, stood and wagged her tail at the familiar sound of slippers gliding across the wood floor.

Eva hummed as she placed a record on an antique phonograph. After a few scratches and pops, the sounds of a 1930s orchestra filled the room. Glenn Miller crooned "Moonlight Serenade," with Eva singing along. Her slippers carried her toward the window. A soft hand caressed Jack's shoulder. "They're playing our song, Mule."

"Don't think I'm up for dancing."

"We could just hold each other like the good ol' days. Listen to Glenn till we fall asleep."

Jack shook his head, staring at the storm. "Another night."

Sighing, Eva turned off the phonograph. Moments later she set a glass of water and a plate of heart pills on his desk—atenolol, nitroglycerine, heparin, and aspirin. She adjusted the afghan in his lap. "Can I get you anything else, love?"

Jack swallowed his pills. "I'm fine."

"Well, if you need me, I'll be in the den watching TV."

She kissed his forehead and headed out of the war room.

Jack turned. "Sweet Tart?"

Eva stopped at the doorway. "Yes?"

He smiled weakly. "Why do you put up with a stubborn ol' mule like me?"

Her brown eyes beamed. "Because you're *my* mule. Call me if you need anything."

Jack picked up several freshly painted miniature soldiers, placing them in the model Hürtgen Forest around a battered Catholic church and graveyard.

Thunder rumbled outside. Storm flashes reflected off the miniature forest. A lone soldier blotched with red wounds lay in a ditch.

What was it that Captain Murdock used to say when the chips were down? He tapped his skull.

He wheeled his chair over to a bookshelf and retrieved a green ammo box from a cabinet. Opening the lid labeled WORLD WAR II, he sifted through black-and-white photos until he found the one of himself as a twenty-two-year-old lieutenant standing next to a captain twice his age. Captain Tom Murdock. The captain's famous speech filled his head.

Lieutenant Chambers, it's not the enemies out in the fields and trenches that drive good soldiers over the edge. It's the enemies that reside within us, like an army of shadows preying upon our sanity. If you can defeat those, you can win any battle.

Jack returned the photo to the box and wheeled back to the table displaying the model Hürtgen Forest. He placed the final soldier into the forest beside the wounded soldier, his eyes glazing over.

• • •

In the pouring rain, branches scraped against the windows of General Briggs's secluded cabin. Sean built a fire in the stone hearth, as Briggs disappeared into the bedroom with the mummified relic. Sean ached to know what the general had found down inside the tunnel. But he knew the protocol and refrained from asking. He had already stepped out of line by requesting to read the diary. After several moments passed, Briggs returned with a bottle of Chivas and two tumblers.

"Sir, I don't drink—"

"You're going to tonight." Briggs uncapped the bottle and filled both tumblers. "Trust me." Sean took a searing gulp.

The general handed Sean a thick dossier with a bound cover. The diary had been translated into English and neatly typed, the symbols and diagrams photocopied. "I just spoke with your grandfather. Jack and I agreed to let you read the diary on one condition."

"Sure, anything."

"You must vow that your grandfather's story remains top secret. That means you can never tell Meg or your grandmother. Not even your father. We clear?"

Sean hesitated, the whisky spreading like a fire in his stomach. "You have my word, General."

Briggs nodded and retired to his bedroom. Sean opened the dossier and read from the beginning . . .

Part 3

Life in the Green Hell

Nearly a month now we've been fighting in this god-forsaken forest. The Green Hell. The Meat Grinder. I hate the very sight of it. Endless fir trees. Brutal terrain. Steep hills and rugged cliffs border Germany like a great wall. My platoon and I have been reconning day and night, trying to map out enemy positions. The Hürtgen is an impossible maze. Still no idea why the hell we're attacking it. We have no armored support, no clear objective. The enemy is hidden well inside the fog and thick branches.

Every day brings rain. We fight wet. Eat wet. Sleep in muddy foxholes or damp pup tents, cold and shivering. Most days you can only see as far as the man in front of you. Mine fields are everywhere. Bouncing Betties and barbed coils wait in the pines like predators. Then there are the 88s. Artillery shells cut through the firs. An unending barrage of machine-gun fire flies out of the mist. I've gone half deaf from all the screeching.

Christ, Jack, you used to be an optimist. Forget all the lives you lost. Forget the Grim Reaper shadow that follows you. Just be a good platoon leader for the Lucky Seven. And for God's sake, get them out of this war in one piece.

—LIEUTENANT JACK CHAMBERS, *WAR DIARY*

Chapter 10

October 1944, Dawn
The Hürtgen Forest, Germany

"Fall back, men! Fall back!" Lieutenant Chambers raced through the fog, branches slapping at him. Bullets whizzed by his ear, stripping bark off the trees. Shells screeched overhead. The treetops popped like fireworks. Chambers ducked behind a fallen pine.

Ra-tat-tat! Ra-tat-tat-tat-tat!

Sparks lit up the haze, as German machine-gun bullets ripped the front line to bloody shreds. The Lucky Seven, covered in mud, blood, and pine needles, fired back from their foxholes.

"Mahoney, get over here!"

Sergeant Mahoney's colossal body emerged from the mist. He ducked behind the log beside Chambers, heaving. A mask of grime covered Mahoney's broad face. "Krauts're shooting from three sides. What now?"

Pine branches rained down on their heads. Chambers tilted his helmet over his eyes. "Get 'em out of here! Fall back!"

"Done." Mahoney belly-crawled over to the platoon. "Fall back, men! Keep low! Move, move, move!"

The gunfire let up. Chambers raced between the foxholes. "Everybody fall back!" All around, fallen GIs floated in pools of blood. A medic scrambled to assist a soldier screaming and cradling his own entrails. The lucky survivors of Baker Company scattered down the hill toward the Belgian border. Two of Chambers's men ran in the wrong direction. He chased after them. "Wrong way! Left, turn left!"

The two soldiers stepped on a chain of landmines and burst upward into a red spray of body limbs.

"Medic! Medic! Somebody help me!"

"Captain!" Chambers weaved between sharp, spiky branches. Cold rain pelted his eyes. He found Captain Murdock lying in a ditch, bleeding from multiple wounds. The captain tossed his helmet down the hill. He gripped his head, clutching knots of silver hair. Several pine shards speared upward from rips in his uniform. A rib bone was jutting out.

Oh, Jesus. Chambers leaped onto his knees, grabbing Murdock's hand. "Hang on, Captain, we're getting out of here."

Murdock coughed up blood. His icy cold hand trembled in Chambers's grasp. "I'm torn up, aren't I?"

"Nah, just a few scratches." Chambers searched the woods. "Medic! Medic!"

A symphony of gunfire surrounded them.

Blood rimmed Murdock's lips. A trembling red tongue emerged and licked them. "There's something . . . I need to give you."

Chambers squeezed his feeble hand. "Save your breath, Captain. We're getting outta here. First I gotta plug your wounds." He put a stick between Murdock's teeth. "Bite down, sir." He yanked the three largest splinters from the captain's stomach and thigh. Blood fountained. Murdock screamed through clenched teeth. Chambers ripped off his sleeves, tying tourniquets around the gushing wounds. He pressed down the exposed rib bone and Murdock groaned.

"Sorry, sir."

Out of the corner of his eye he saw a shape moving in the trees up the hill. A dark, faceless soldier was charging through the mist. The soup was too thick to tell if he was friend or foe. Chambers raised his Thompson. *Please be a medic.* The figure ran closer. A German helmet took form.

"Christ." Chambers squeezed the trigger. Bullets punched holes in the shadow soldier's gray uniform. The soldier dropped.

"Is he dead?" Captain Murdock rasped.

"I got him. He's—shit! Another one." Twenty yards up the hill a second German weaved through the trees wielding a submachine gun. *Ra-ta-ta-ta-tat!* Branches snapped just above Chambers's head. He ducked behind the log with Murdock. Mud geysers exploded upward around the log. Chambers returned rapid fire, sending the shadow soldier back up the mist-covered hill.

"He may be going for reinforcements. Let's move, sir." Chambers heaved Murdock over one shoulder. Murdock yelled when the rib bone pressed into Chambers's back. He raced awkwardly down the steep muddy slope, half running, half sliding, gripping trees to keep from tumbling.

Murdock coughed and spat. "I'm dying, Chambers."

"You're gonna make it!" He zigzagged through the labyrinth of pines with the captain bouncing over his shoulder.

"Christ, go slower."

"I'm trying, sir." Chambers's boots slipped sideways through the mud. The terrain finally flattened. He sprinted across a ravine then up another steep hill.

"Tell Mary Beth . . . I love her."

"Sir, please. Hang on."

"Set me down here."

"One more hill and we're home free."

"No . . . I have something . . ." Murdock vomited hot liquid down Chambers's back.

"Save your breath . . . almost there."

Holding Murdock tight to his shoulder, Chambers started up the next steep incline.

A turbulent wind, like a subway train screeching by, sped past his head. A blast of splinters and hot stinging metal catapulted them back. Murdock flew off. Chambers smacked the earth. He lay flat, dazed, fiery pines spinning above. A burning coal stung his upper arm. He tried to claw it out. "Damn it!" His chest heaved. The ground spun. "Medic!"

Out of the haze, a soldier sprinted toward them. A shadowy face and helmet, rimmed by the flaming treetops, leaned over them. On the helmet was a red cross. "Stay with me, Lieutenant."

"Help Murdock!" Chambers yelled.

The medic rolled the captain over. "Chambers . . ." Murdock wheezed. He now had a massive hole in his gut that gushed blood. He groaned and stretched his hand, wheezing. "Chambers . . ."

"Captain?" Chambers dragged his stunned body through the mud and gripped Murdock's hand. The captain dropped a metal object into his hand.

"Take . . . over . . . my mission . . ." Murdock's eyes suddenly rolled back white. The metal object fused their hands together. A surge of energy, like high voltage, rushed up Chambers's arm, electrifying his entire body. A brilliant flash blinded him. He rubbed his eyes. They burned with a roiling numbness—a dark, liquid chasm swirled before him. The chasm shaped itself into a nightmarish landscape. In the haze stretched a cemetery, and beyond that stood a church with a medieval tower. Shadow soldiers charged through fog. Then echoed whispering voices, clanging bells, gunfire, and screaming, filling his head like a mad symphony. Another flash and all Chambers could see was a blizzard of glowing white fireflies.

Silence.

Chambers's vision returned in soft focus, like staring through a mask of gauze.

Captain Murdock's hand went limp. Blank eyes stared back. The medic moved in slow motion, his face calm. He closed Murdock's eyelids and stood, becoming a silhouette against the bleak, gray sky. Flames reflected in his glasses. His voice echoed as if rising from a deep well. "God wants you to live, Lieutenant. Hang on."

He was pulled away from Captain Murdock's limp hand, and Chambers cursed at the medic. A needle pricked his bicep. And as a liquid darkness flooded his senses, Chambers felt his rage dissolving.

No, no, you can't take Murdock away, you can't . . .

Chapter 11

Lieutenant Chambers woke in a damp cocoon, feeling like a grenade went off inside his head. He rubbed his temple. "What the hell!"

His vision drifted in and out of an olive drab haze before coming into sharp focus. Above, green fabric rippled with the rhythm of the rain. A parka draped over two standing rifles shielded his head while his lower half remained exposed to the elements. Voices moaned all around. Gunshots and artillery boomed in the distance.

Where are my men?

Chambers's hands pressed on the cold, muddy ground. He forced his body up and drew a deep breath. The festering stench of battle and death was everywhere. *Christ, where am I?*

To his right the forest had been leveled to heaps of smoldering logs. Medics ran back and forth, carrying bloody GIs on litters. To Chambers's left a clearing in the woods served as a field hospital. Wounded soldiers wailed. One arched his back as two medics repaired the stringy muck of his stomach.

Chambers gagged and turned away, but another soldier clutching a blood-soaked rag to his neck rasped, "Help . . . me. Please. Somebody."

Dozens of other butchered GIs lay in the mud moaning for attention. Medics crisscrossed each other to get to those most in need. A chaplain blessed the bodies with glazed eyes. The entire field hospital spun like a merry-go-round.

Chambers lay back and gripped the muddy ground to stop the spinning. His temples throbbed. *Breathe, Jack. Just breathe.* He lay still, inhaling, exhaling, focusing on the steady cadence of his heartbeat.

Chambers held up a hand wrapped in gauze. He wiggled his fingers. His legs tingled. *My men. Where are my men! Got to find—* He sat up, searching the wounded. "Mahoney! Deuce!" The field of bloody bodies resumed rotating. "Hoffer! Garcia!"

A hand wrapped around Chambers's wrist. "Easy there, buddy. Just take it easy."

"Medic, where's my platoon?"

"Everything's all right—"

Chambers grabbed the medic's collar. "*Where the hell are my men!*"

"Hey, buddy, I don't got time for this." He dashed off to aid a crying young man missing a leg.

"The survivors have returned to base camp." A chaplain wearing a Red Cross helmet approached, wiping his hands on a rag. Crimson stains blotched his parka, neck, and chin. He knelt beside Chambers. Behind wire-rimmed glasses, the chaplain's chestnut brown eyes seemed oddly peaceful despite the surrounding carnage. "You'll be out of here in no time, Lieutenant. God has chosen to keep you alive."

Chambers rubbed his thighs. "I barely feel my legs."

The chaplain scrubbed his red hands in a pail of soap and water. "I gave you morphine. Your legs are fine."

"Why am I here?"

"Mild concussion—and this little nugget I carved out of your bicep." The chaplain tossed Chambers a chunk of shrapnel resembling popcorn.

"Christ, just what I needed."

The chaplain pushed his wire-rimmed glasses up his large nose. "If you'll lie back, I'll get the blood flowing back into your legs."

Chambers lay beneath the makeshift tent. Blurry images

clogged his head: lying on the ground, grasping his stinging arm . . . the sky aflame with fiery branches . . . a Red Cross helmet looming over him . . . the captain's blank stare.

Chambers sat up on his good elbow. "Captain Murdock's dead, isn't he?"

The chaplain lowered his head. "I tried to save him—"

"Christ . . ." Chambers shook his head. Across the muddy field, medics busily hauled off dead men on litters and stacked them along the road. He scanned the faces of the corpses.

"Sorry, sir, he's already gone."

Chambers sat up, feeling pinpricks up and down his legs. "Any chance my platoon's been looking for me?"

"Just one sergeant I patched up. A guy named Buck."

"Where!"

"Over there against that tree stump."

Chambers scanned the field of wounded soldiers. Buck Parker sat against a charred tree stump, a bandage around his neck. "Buck! Over here!" Chambers yelled, but the cries of the other casualties drowned out his voice. Buck's deep-set eyes were transfixed on a baseball that he rolled between his hands.

The chaplain massaged away the pinpricks. "Try your legs now, sir."

Chambers bent both legs on his own accord. "Yeah, seem to be working. Thanks, Chaplain."

"Call me Goldstein." He helped Chambers to his feet. "By the way, I'm holding a service for Captain Murdock later outside the chow barn."

"I'll be there." Throwing on his helmet, Chambers marched on shaky legs into the scalped forest and over to Sergeant Parker.

"You okay, Buck?"

"Reckon so, sir."

"Good to go another day?"

"Yep."

"Then let's see who else we can find."

Chambers and Buck hitched a jeep ride that took them five miles from the front. They rode in silence. Bodies covered in parkas lined both sides of the road as far as the eye could see.

Chapter 12

At the GI base camp five miles from the front, dozens of men wandered in the rain wearing lost expressions, searching for their units. Fewer soldiers milled about today than yesterday, far fewer than the day before. Having been stationed near the German border going on four weeks, the camp was no longer an offensive stronghold but a recovery station for battered survivors.

Chambers and Buck hopped out of the jeep and weaved through the bodies that passed them like zombies.

"Lieutenant Chambers! Buck!" The gruff voice filtering through the drizzle was music to Chambers's ears.

"Papa Bear!"

Sergeant John Mahoney, a grizzly bear of a man, parted the crowd with his thick arms and gave Chambers a hug that lifted him a foot off the ground. "Thank God you made it!"

"Easy on the arm, Papa Bear," Chambers said, patting his wound.

The six-foot-six sergeant returned his platoon leader to earth. His deep voice boomed, "Guys, get over here. I found him!"

A ragtag group of soldiers, humbled as beaten dogs, gathered around Chambers.

Pfc. Ralph Hoffer patted Chambers's shoulder. "Jeepers

creepers, you gave us a scare, Lieutenant. Finch said you were dead."

"No, you idiot," said Pfc. Gabe Finch. "I saw a body floating in a mud puddle that *might* have been the lieutenant. I wasn't sure."

Chambers admired his veteran soldiers, amazed they had all survived this last push. One member of the Lucky Seven, a hotshot from Vegas named Deuce Wilson, lingered several feet back, gnawing on a damp cigar and staring at Chambers like he was a leper. Deuce slapped a twenty into Miguel Garcia's palm. "Thought for sure ya became worm food out there, Lieutenant. Me and Garcia was about to wager on who'd get ya tent."

"Nobody's getting my tent." Chambers pushed through the small group. "Let's find a dry spot. I'm sick of being wet."

"Tell me about it." Hoffer followed in tow. "My underwear hasn't been dry since Paris."

Deuce chuckled. "Perhaps a diaper would help."

"Very funny coming from a guy who crapped his drawers in Sicily."

Sloshing through the mud, the six soldiers followed Chambers into a small Belgian village with a few buildings still standing. They walked along littered cobblestone streets, past storefronts with shattered windows, caved-in roofs, and walls that had been reduced to rubble. A passing jeep backfired, and the entire platoon flinched, raising their rifles.

Sergeant Mahoney shook his head. "Ease up, ladies. We're miles from the front."

The skittish platoon lowered their rifles, but their eyes stayed peeled.

Hoffer grimaced. "Jeepers, do we need a vacation."

On the rural side of town, they gathered in a leaky barn that offered some shelter.

Deuce asked, "Hey, Lieutenant, what's for lunch?"

"Same crap, different box." Chambers tore into his cardboard box of K rations. Today's meal included a tin of cold spaghetti, hard cheese, brittle crackers, Chesterfield cigarettes, a pack of gum, and a Hershey bar, also brittle. His men sat around him in a half circle, scratching at their tins with utensils. They occupied saddles, hay bales, whatever they could find to keep them off the cold ground. Chambers surveyed his platoon. Sergeant Mahoney, Buck, Deuce, Finch, Hoffer, and Garcia were the only veterans present.

Shaking his head, Chambers turned to Sergeant John Mahoney. "Is this all our boys, Papa Bear?"

Mahoney, who now wore a lovely gash across his cheek, stirred lemon powder into his tin of water. "Afraid so. Lost Jackson, Campbell, and Meyers. Rest were replacements. Seventeen altogether on today's push."

"Jesus." Chambers rubbed his forehead.

Deuce raised his tin cup. "A toast to Jackson, Campbell, and Meyers. They fought well from here to hell and now may they rest in heaven."

Tin cups clinked around the circle.

Hoffer raised his cup. "A toast to ourselves, the Lucky Seven, who now have forty-two combats under our belts."

"In five countries," Finch added.

The Lucky Seven raised their cups. "Here, here."

Buck spoke with a lump of tobacco in his cheek. "So, what's the brass have in store for us? We been tryin' to take that hill for weeks, but the Krauts keep hammerin' us."

Hoffer laid out chunks of cheese on the railing. A barn mouse scurried from its hole and nibbled on the closest piece. "Hopefully the brass'll pull their heads out of their asses. No way we're gonna push the Jerries out of these woods."

Deuce waved his cigar, shifting his voice from Groucho to John Wayne. "Yeah, that forest is thick as Papa Bear's chest hairs, I tell ya. I've yet to get one Kraut in my scopes."

Ducking his head under the barn's hayloft, Sergeant Mahoney returned with a second ration of spaghetti. "All right, ladies, bellyaching isn't going to get you anywhere except foxhole duty." The seasoned sergeant sat next to Chambers and nodded toward several trucks that just arrived. "Any chance those replacements are here to relieve us from duty, Lieutenant?"

"What's this?" The six looked up from their rations. "Did he say relieve us?"

"We're leaving the front!"

"Maybe." Chambers took a drag on his Camel, giving Sergeant Mahoney a disapproving sidewise glance. "I wasn't going to say anything until I knew for certain . . ."

Chattering, the platoon gathered around Lieutenant Chambers and Sergeant Mahoney.

"Come on, Lieutenant, spill the beans."

"Yeah, yeah, yeah."

Chambers gestured for the boys to calm down. They fell silent. "Three days ago I approached Captain Murdock and explained that our platoon has been doing recon missions since the first GI landed in Sicily, Papa Bear and myself since North Africa, and that I noticed other units, some as fresh as D-day, were being relieved with half as many combats. I told the captain I felt like we had served our country to the best of our ability. I laid out all our victories, every accomplishment we've achieved from Italy to France to Belgium to Germany, and asked if there were any way for us to be given leave from the war."

"Did you mention our medals?" Deuce asked. "That bridge we captured?"

"Plus all the POWs?" Buck reminded.

"Shh, let the lieutenant speak." Garcia motioned for him to continue. "What did the captain say?"

Chambers kept a stone face. "He said he'd send a formal written request to Major Powell, and that . . . based on our accomplishments . . . at the very least we should get some time off in England."

"Hello, hot showers!"

"And cold beer!"

"And warm Englishwomen!"

The six soldiers gripped shoulders and slapped hands. They laughed and poked each other's ribs.

"Let's not put on the party hats just yet." Chambers gestured them to calm down. "I have some sad news. Our beloved Captain Murdock . . . was killed today on the hill."

The members of the Lucky Seven froze in midcelebration. "Captain's dead?"

Chambers took a drag and blew smoke out his nostrils. "A chaplain's going to do a special ceremony for him later. I'd like us all to attend. Murdock deserves to be remembered."

"Uh, how's that affect our leave?" Deuce asked.

Chambers shrugged. "That's why I didn't want to say anything yet. All I can say is there's still a chance that the captain sent the letter. I need to track down the new CO, see if he'll follow up on Murdock's request." He tossed his cigarette and turned to Sergeant Mahoney. "Papa Bear, hold down the fort." He let a smile slip. "With any luck, we'll be going home to our loved ones real soon." Leaving the cheering platoon to celebrate inside the barn, Chambers's heart sunk. *That was damned foolish, Jack. What if you can't deliver?* But saying it felt good. It made the possibility of getting the Lucky Seven out of the Meat Grinder seem real.

Chapter 13

Chambers marched in the rain toward the convoy of trucks parked along the road. He found Lieutenant Paul LeBlanc and a sergeant directing replacement soldiers as they hopped off a truck. LeBlanc stared down at a clipboard. "Sergeant, take these boys to Lieutenant Wallace for billeting. Tell him we need twelve in foxholes by fifteen hundred hours."

The sergeant rounded up the kids and marched them into the village.

Lieutenant LeBlanc wore a bloodstained bandage around his head that reminded Chambers of the Japanese flag. Le-Blanc sneezed several times and pinched one nostril, draining a wad of snot.

Chambers raised his voice as cold rain pounded their helmets. "Paul, you sound like Elmer Fudd."

The lieutenant from New Orleans looked up, a smile interrupting his miserable, rain-drenched face. "Jack, I thought you'd bought your ticket out of this hellhole."

"No such luck." They gripped forearms.

LeBlanc moaned with a nasal Cajun voice, "I left the police force for this crap! Padna, do me a favor, next time you hear me volunteer for anything, slap some sense into me."

Chambers studied the line of trucks rolling in. "Any word on our new CO?"

"Right, like anyone tells me diddly-squat."

"Yeah, yeah."

The two lieutenants marched across the muddy road as jeeps and supply trucks wheeled by. Chambers tightened his poncho around his throat to keep out the rain. "So what's your casualty count?"

The round-faced lieutenant waved a damp report in his fist. "Half my platoon on this push."

Chambers's brow furrowed. "Well, I'm down to six."

LeBlanc coughed up phlegm and spat. "We never should've done another push. The Ninth's just gettin' butchered. Captain kept advising Major Powell we need to find an easier breach into Germany. But the brass . . . jeez, all they see are pushpins on a map. Murdock's dead, a number of officers. It's insanity!" LeBlanc kicked a helmet riddled with bullet holes.

Chambers gripped his arm. "Hey, get a hold of yourself. The men are watching."

LeBlanc turned as another truck ground through the puddles and parked, splashing mud across his legs. "Ah, Christ!"

The next wave of replacements barreled out of the tarp-covered truck, their eyes gleaming with naïve excitement. Remaining at the tailgate, a tall, stocky sergeant built like a linebacker yelled in a northern accent, "Let's go, warriors! That's it! On the double!"

"Hoo! Hoo! Hoo! Hoo!" The squad chanted as they hopped off the truck.

The sergeant guided them with a twirling hand. "Keep moving, men!"

"Have them line up by that building," Chambers told the sergeant.

Huddling for shelter under the awning, these replacements appeared older and more seasoned than the normal batch of teenagers. A few had mustaches and full beards. They gripped semiautomatic submachine guns and were strapped down with various pistols, spare cartridges, and magazines, and odd-looking grenades shaped like plumbs. Each man wore fancy boots with built-in slits for fighting knives.

A blunt-faced soldier with SNAKE stenciled across his helmet lit up a handful of cigarettes and passed them around. "Ceremonial smoke, boys. Corporal Otter, today's your chance to earn some hair on your balls."

Laughing and smoking cigarettes, the platoon prodded a freckle-faced kid.

"Glad to see somebody's excited to be here," LeBlanc muttered with a bemused look.

Chambers shook his head. "Paul, I'm afraid to ask if these are mine or yours."

His buddy wiped water off the clipboard. "Neither. They're listed as Special Unit X-2."

Chambers snorted. "What's so special about 'em?"

"Beats the thunder outta me, but here's something you don't see every day. Entire platoon's made up of noncoms."

Chambers scanned the crowd, observing their shoulder patches. Every soldier except the stocky sergeant was a corporal. Not one private first class among them.

"Even stranger, Jack, check out their names: Lieutenant Hawk, Sergeant Moose, Corporal Fox, Corporal Crow, Corporal Snake, Corporal Elk, Corporal Otter. It's a damned menagerie."

Chambers counted fifteen heads, each with an animal name stenciled across his helmet. The corporals chuckled as the stocky sergeant put a headlock on the baby-faced kid named Otter.

"Hey, Frick and Frack," Chambers barked, "knock it off."

The burly sergeant shoved Otter into the crowd, which in turn pushed the kid onto the muddy ground. The group erupted like playground bullies.

Chambers pointed. "Sergeant . . . yes, you. Got some kind of problem?"

"Who, me?" He smirked, attempting to shine in front of his squad. He spoke in a thick northern accent. "No sir, Lieutenant. We're just initiating Corporal Otter into the squad."

"Well, recess is over." Chambers glanced down at the clipboard. "What's your full name, sergeant?"

The muscled noncom strutted over with a big smirk on his square, Neanderthal face. He pointed to the word MOOSE stenciled across his helmet. "That's what everybody calls me."

"I mean your real name."

"Can't say, sir. That would be leaking classified information."

"Classified!" LeBlanc chuckled. "Quit pulling our chain, Sergeant."

"Hey, I'm being square with you guys. All I can tell you is we're Special Unit X-2. Our names are protected, so we go by code names." Sergeant Moose had a habit of bobbing his head and grinning back at his squad.

"What's the X-2 stand for?" Chambers asked.

"Can't divulge that either. We've all taken an oath of secrecy. Ain't that right, warriors?"

"Ho!" they yelled back in unison.

Chambers sighed. "Who's your platoon leader?"

"That'd be Lieutenant Hawk." Moose pounded on the side of the truck. "Yo, Lieutenant!"

"Quiet, I'm sleeping," another Yankee voice growled from the front cab. Although this voice sounded more educated.

"Sorry, sir, but we got two lieutenants here requesting your majesty's presence."

"Ah, Christ." The passenger door of the front cab opened, and a tall man built like a quarterback climbed out and stretched bulging arms. His back to them, he stared at the surrounding woods. "Hallelujah, another forest." He adjusted a black strap that wrapped around a predominately bald head. Blond stubble bristled over half of it. Lieutenant Hawk flicked a lighter. The air filled with the scent of cigar smoke. "Sergeant Moose, we finally reach the Hürtgen?"

"You're still in Belgium," Chambers answered. "The Hürtgen's across the border about five miles east."

"Forests all look the same after a while." The lieutenant's accent sounded oddly familiar. Just like . . . *No, it couldn't be.* A cold wave coursed through Chambers's body as Lieutenant Hawk turned around, puffing a fat cigar. The recognition hit them simultaneously.

Chambers gawked at a severely scarred visage that resembled the Phantom of the Opera. Burn scars eclipsed one side of the lieutenant's face and neck. A black patch covered his right eye. The blond stubble that grew in thick on one side of his head was sparse on the other. A long moment passed before the shock wore off. "Pierce Fallon."

"Jack Chambers." Fallon's single blue eye looked him up and down. "Still a dogface, I see."

Chambers could only stare. A year ago Pierce Fallon had a full head of blond hair and a handsome, even regal, politician's face, with steel blue eyes and perfect teeth. The teeth were still straight, but one corner of his lips drooped from the scar tissue. He half-grinned. "What, nothing to say to an old acquaintance?"

LeBlanc said, "You two know each other?"

"Fallon was my second lieutenant in North Africa." Just saying his name put an acrid taste in Chambers's mouth.

The unscarred half of Fallon's face grimaced into a lop-sided smile. "Looks like we're equals now."

Chambers stared at the single white bar on Fallon's helmet. "Ain't life a peach." The two lieutenants eyed each other for several seconds, till Chambers broke the silence. "Thought you were out of the war."

Fallon scratched his scarred cheek. "No, I just learned there's a better way to fight than shooting from a trench."

"Special forces?"

Fallon's good eye winked. "You'll learn soon enough."

Chambers felt his patience wearing thin. "So are you the brains of this special unit or is there a bigger head in charge here?"

The muscular lieutenant pointed behind them. "Our captain's in the last jeep. You want answers, he's the man."

Trucks continued to motor by, grinding through the mud, exhaust befouling the already noxious air. As the end of the convoy finally reached camp, a covered jeep rolled to a stop. Rain drenched the windshield, blurring out the faces of the driver and passenger. The windshield wipers squeaked, swishing thick-running water side to side. For a brief second Chambers saw the passenger's face. "Major Powell."

Chambers and LeBlanc marched toward the truck. Chambers opened the passenger door. "Major, sir, Lieutenants Chambers and LeBlanc here to greet you, sir."

The major looked to be in his midforties. His narrow face

was all angles. "What, you boys forgot how to salute a superior officer?"

"Sorry, sir. Here at the front we don't normally salute—"

"I didn't ask for commentary, Lieutenant, just some god-damned courtesy."

Chambers and LeBlanc snapped to attention and saluted.

"That's more like it." The major stepped out of the truck and into the downpour. His polished boots sank into three inches of mud. "I'll be your new CO." He scanned the campground. A transporter truck was stuck in the mud, causing a traffic jam on the narrow crossroads. Jeeps were parked haphazardly. Several infantrymen roamed aimlessly like lost sheep. Major Powell shook his head. "Why is this place such a madhouse?"

Chambers looked at LeBlanc. "Uh, well, sir, we just returned from a push. Still counting the wounded. Lost Captain Murdock—"

"Fine, I'll get a report later. Where's my command post?"

Chambers pointed. "Right through them woods, sir."

Major Powell turned and spoke with a soldier sitting behind the wheel. "You can park it here." The engine cut off. The driver's door opened, and a captain dressed like the other X-2 commandos hopped out, a semiautomatic machine gun hanging from his shoulder. He wore a green wool cap over his brown hair. His hands were covered with black leather gloves cut off at the knuckles, his bare fingers sticking out—a motorcyclist's gloves.

Major Powell said, "Lieutenants Chambers, LeBlanc, meet Captain Wolf."

"It is good to meet you both." Surprisingly, Wolf spoke with a Slavic accent. He had a pale, narrow, European face that looked as if it had weathered many storms. If there was anything striking about him, it was his eyes, like sparkling gray marbles. "This rain never seems stop, eh?"

"Been like this for weeks."

Wolf looked over at the X-2 squad. "I see you met my special forces unit."

"Yes, sir," LeBlanc said. "We were just trying to figure out what to do with 'em."

Major Powell barked, "Well, get them out of this rain and see to it they get a hot meal."

"Oh, and will you tell Lieutenant Hawk to come with us?" Wolf asked LeBlanc. Chambers narrowed his eyes. He'd never seen a polite captain. Maybe it was how the British lilt occasionally blended with his Slavic accent. *Is he British or Polish?*

"Yes, sir." LeBlanc saluted and jogged over to the rogue unit. He escorted Captain Wolf's soldiers down the road. Sergeant Moose yelled, "It's chow time, warriors. Will somebody give me a Ho?"

"Ho! Ho! Ho! Ho!" Their excitement echoed off the trees.

The downpour continued. Lieutenant Fallon puffed his cigar and strutted toward them. *Except for the scars, the jerk hasn't changed a bit.* As if reading Chambers's mind, Fallon glared then smirked at Captain Wolf. "How was your ride, Captain?"

"Long and bumpy. I am certain you slept the whole way."

"Like a baby." Fallon grinned.

"Let's get out of this rain." Major Powell motioned to Chambers. "Lieutenant, lead us to my CP."

Chapter 14

Chambers led the way to the command post. The four hiked through the woods to a dilapidated rock house with two walls standing as well as one corner of the roof. Soaked debris littered the floor and surrounding yard. A brick fireplace stood like a monolith, the walls around it absent. Sandbags and camouflage netting surrounded the house's cement flooring. Two soldiers manned a machine gun behind a wall of sandbags. They gave the two special forces soldiers a suspicious once-over.

"Flash!" they called out.

"Thunder," Chambers returned. "Guys, our new CO has arrived."

"Right this way, sir." The sentries quickly rotated the barrel.

Chambers, Powell, Wolf, and Fallon stomped mud from their boots onto the floor that had once been a kitchen. "Down there." Chambers pointed with his boot.

Fallon lifted a cellar door and Chambers led them down a stone staircase. "House has a three-room basement built solid as any pillbox. Captain Murdock set up his CP here."

Lanterns lit up the shadowy cellar. Black water dribbled down the walls. The room gained surprising warmth from a

coal-burning furnace and a portable gas stove brewing coffee.
The aroma made Chambers want to kick back and enjoy a
cup.

Ducking under the low ceiling, Fallon plopped his bulky
frame into one of the wood chairs that surrounded a long oak
table. Captain Wolf studied the maps and aerial photos tacked
to the brick walls.

"Hmm, not bad." Major Powell peered into two adjoining
rooms that made up an office and radio room. Another lieutenant, who was typing a letter, stood at attention and gave a
stiff salute.

Kiss ass, Chambers thought. "This is Lieutenant Smith.
He'll be your assistant."

"Good, some coffee for me and my two guests. Extra
cream." Major Powell removed his helmet and poncho.

Chambers glanced at a cot in a corner. *Can't believe Murdock slept there just last night.* On a table beside the cot sat a
typewriter and a stack of typed reports. Chambers glanced at
Powell, Fallon, and Wolf across the room. They sat at the table drinking coffee and whispering. Chambers quickly
thumbed through the stack of papers on Captain Murdock's
desk, mostly casualty reports and requests for replacement
soldiers and supplies. He came across a typed letter to Major
Powell. Chambers's heart dropped into his stomach.

```
Major William Powell
9th Infantry Division
60th Infantry
2nd Battalion
October 5, 1944


Dear Major Powell:
    This letter is a special request. I have
in my company a seasoned platoon that has
been fighting in near constant battle since
the 60th Infantry first landed in Sicily.
Their platoon leader, Lieutenant Jack Cham-
bers, and Staff Sergeant John Mahoney both
fought as far back as North Africa. Lieutenant
```

Chambers's platoon has achieved many victories for my company. They captured a key
bridge in Northern France. In Belgium they
detained over one hundred German prisoners.
They have proven to be sharp in the field
and deserving of medals for their perfor-
mance as a team. The bulk of Chambers's
veterans had survived until we reached the
Hürtgen Forest. The strikes to these woods
have proven to be hard on even my most
seasoned squads. Chambers's platoon, serving
as the company's recon squad, has suffered
the most casualties.

If there is any way to make concessions
for these seven outstanding veterans, it is
my highest request that Lieutenant Chambers
and his men be relieved from active duty.
They have served our country well and
deserve to return home with honors.

Captain Tom Murdock

Chambers's hands started shaking. *Maybe the major will still honor it. All I have to do is convince Powell to—*

"Lieutenant Chambers, a word," Major Powell barked from the table.

"Yes, sir." Clutching the letter, Chambers stepped up to the table where Powell, Wolf, and Fallon sat cozy with steaming mugs of coffee.

Major Powell's angular face remained all business. "Chambers, get this camp into order before seventeen hundred hours."

"Yes, sir."

"Also, round up all lieutenants and have them assemble here at eighteen hundred hours. We will be going over our next objective." Major Powell jotted entries into a logbook.

"Uh, sir?" Chambers, his hand trembling, offered the letter to Major Powell. "I was wondering if you could take a look at this."

Fallon, who was cleaning his fingernails with a large knife that had brass knuckles, leaned in as Powell scanned the letter.

Chambers swallowed. "As you can see, my men and I—"

Powell looked up. "What is this?"

"Sir, it's a formal letter—"

"I can see what it is, Lieutenant, but why the hell was your captain requesting that his most seasoned platoon leave the war?"

Lieutenant Fallon snorted, "That's just like you, Chambers. Always running away from the fight."

Captain Wolf elbowed him. "Hawk, stay out of this."

"Major, sir, my men and I have been fighting hard for months. We've done countless patrols and mapped out half this forest. We were the first to locate the row of pillboxes nestled in the Hürtgen. We could use some time off."

"Couldn't we all?" Fallon chuckled. "I'd like a week at Martha's Vineyard."

Chambers glowered at him.

Major Powell set the letter down. "Denied. We need every man we've got to execute our next push."

Chambers's jaw dropped. Blood boiling, he stared at the CO, who returned to writing in his logbook. "I believe I ordered you to get the camp into shape."

Chambers remained standing at the edge of the table, his hands now tight fists at his sides. "Sir, Captain Murdock was supposed to tell you about this today, and—"

Powell didn't look up. "And he was killed in action just like every goddamned captain keeps getting killed in this forest. Now we're so short on captains I'm having to do the work of two people."

"It's just that my men have gone the longest without a break. They're so whipped, they wouldn't be any use to you."

Powell continued to write. "I'll decide who's useful and who's not."

Fallon rolled the brass-knuckled knife between his palms. "Don't let him fool you, Major. Chambers doesn't give a flying flip about his platoon. He just wants to get back to England to a piece of ass."

"That's not true, sir." Chambers held back the urge to throw Fallon's coffee into his face. He turned to Major Powell. "Sir, with all due respect, I understand your situation. But please understand what my platoon has been through. We arrived here four weeks ago with thirty men. Dozens of replacements have come and gone. I've lost all but six. The same six that have been with me since we invaded Sicily last year. I'd like to get them home if I may, sir."

"Wow, six men out of what, a couple hundred over the past two years?" Fallon needled. "No wonder they call you Lieutenant Grim Reaper."

"Lieutenant Hawk, that's enough," Captain Wolf scorned.

Chambers squeezed his fists at his sides.

Fallon's single eye blazed blue fire. "Well, Reaper, I'm surprised you kept six alive. Did you teach them how to run like cowards as well?"

"You shut your trap." The words seemed to leave Chambers's mouth without his awareness.

Fallon stabbed his knife into the table and scooted his chair back. "Why don't you make me!" Rounding the table, he flexed his fists like a barfly ready to brawl.

Aware of the major's presence, Chambers grabbed the reins of his anger. "Stand down, Fallon. What's in the past is in the past."

"Maybe for you, Reaper"—Fallon pointed at the scarred half of his face—"but not for me."

"Calm down, both of you," Major Powell barked from his chair. "Captain Wolf, take your lieutenant somewhere he can cool off. Special forces or not, I won't tolerate this behavior."

"Come on, Lieutenant Hawk." Wolf escorted him to the stairs.

"Sir, sorry for my outburst, but this coward doesn't deserve any special privileges." Fallon gave Chambers one last sneer before mounting the steps.

Major Powell's sharp, angular face remained a mask of control. "Chambers, for someone asking his CO for an outlandish request, and at the worst possible time in our offensive, this is not the best display of behavior."

"But, sir, if you'll just hear me out."

"My decision's final." Powell tore Murdock's letter in half. "Now, go round up the lieutenants and organize the camp like I said. Dismissed."

Chambers stormed out of the house and into the woods. Ice-cold rivulets streamed down his poncho. Water filled his boots as he sloshed down the muddy road. "Damn that son of a bitch!"

He walked past medical trucks hauling out the day's wounded. Men covered in bloody bandages stared out at Chambers. Others lay on litters that bounced and jostled with the rocking trucks. He actually envied the wounded, headed back to England to heal in warm, dry hospitals.

He rubbed his sore arm, wishing the wound had been more serious, disabling one of his legs, perhaps. Guilt stabbed his gut. *What kind of soldier have I become? It's been weeks since I looked at myself in a mirror. Maybe I've become like Pierce Fallon, and every time I look in the mirror all I will see is a monster.*

Chapter 15

Chambers walked to a campground behind the chow barn. He turned the corner to find the Lucky Seven lying in their single-man pup tents. *Jesus, how am I gonna break it to them?* He studied them, struggling to form the speech in his head.

Snoring that sounded like a buzz saw echoed from Sergeant Mahoney's tent, his massive boots sticking out the front flap. While Papa Bear slept, the cubs played.

Deuce and Garcia lay on their stomachs with their tents inches apart. Between lay a flat, makeshift table with a deck of cards and a pile of cigars and cigarettes. Garcia stared at his cards, a cigarette dangling from his lips. "Deuce, quit dealing from the bottom of the deck. All I get are crappy hands."

"My apologies, *amigo*. Old habits never die. See?" Deuce threw down a full house, aces and kings.

"Ah, crap." Garcia flung his cards onto the table as Deuce collected a prize cigar and did his best Groucho Marx. "Anybody else wanna challenge the Poker King? I'm feeling lucky!" He clamped the cigar between his teeth.

Buck, his cheek engorged with chewing tobacco, tossed a pouch of Red Man onto the table. "I'll take a whack, you little weasel. But no fancy dealin' or I kick your scrawny ass back to Nevada."

The Poker King scowled at the tobacco. "What's this crap? Cough up something better, cowboy. How about your baseball?"

"In your wet dreams." Buck tossed a few francs on the table. "Now give me them cards. I'm dealing."

Pfc. Ralph Hoffer lay in his tent, sketching an expert storyboard on a pad of paper. Next to the artist's tent lay Pfc. Gabe Finch with his nose in a comic book. "Hoff, I got the title for our first comic book series. Whatta you say we call it *The Amazing Combats of the Lucky Seven*?"

Hoffer pressed the ink pen to his chin. "Yeah, I like that. Hey, poker boys, check this out." Grinning, Hoffer held up a remarkable drawing of the Lucky Seven.

"Not bad, Hoff," Deuce said. "How about drawing one of us riding a ship back to the States. You can call it *The Lucky Seven Finally Leaves This Hellhole*."

Watching from the corner of the barn, Chambers took a deep breath. As he stepped between their tents, Deuce grinned. "Well, speak of the devil."

Garcia looked up from his letter-writing. "Hey, Lieutenant, any word on us going home?"

They all pinned him with hopeful eyes.

"Not yet. I should know something tonight." Chambers walked over to his pup tent that he had originally set up under a canopy of fir trees to keep dry. The tent now floated in a mud puddle.

Lieutenant LeBlanc approached, carrying a bag over his shoulder, looking like Santa Claus. "Any of you ladies care for mail call?"

Miguel Garcia leaped up. "Hell, yeah!"

Chambers leaned against a tree and smiled. Finch ripped into a package like a kid on Christmas morning. He pulled out two glossy comic books, the latest issues of *The Avenger* and *The Shadow*. The dynamic duo thumbed through the pages, ogling the flashy artwork.

Hoffer whistled. "There she is, Finch, Margot Lane, the sexiest dame to ever grace the pages of *The Shadow*."

Finch kept his nose in *The Avenger*. "I'll take Nellie Gray any day. Now she's a looker."

Deuce laughed. "You two nutsacks ever consider finding real women? With real gams, real hips"—he jiggled his hands in front of his chest—"and real ta-tas. The bigger the better. Know what I'm saying?"

Hoffer snorted, "Like you would know."

"Hey, I played ride the pony with that redhead in Paris."

"I meant a classy woman, Deuce. Not a hooker."

"Hey, she spoke French. That's classy." The scent of cheap perfume wafted across the campground. Deuce fanned the air. "Oh, for the love of God, Garcia, does Maria always have to smell up our tents with those letters of hers?"

Garcia laughed. "I can't believe we might be going home soon." He fell back onto his bedroll, eyes on his letter.

"Yeah, I'm ready to see m'daddy." The Texan opened his box and pulled out fresh pouches of Red Man, a box of Cracker Jack, and a stack of St. Louis Cardinals baseball cards. The top card had a picture of Buck Parker posing in a windup pitch.

"That you?" Deuce grabbed the baseball card. "Wow, ya weren't stroking us after all."

"You mean the lucky baseball didn't give you a clue, Deuce?" Garcia ribbed.

Buck remained stoic till he pulled out a blue bandanna. His whole face went soft.

"What's that, some kind of hanky?" Deuce asked.

"Nah." Buck tied the blue bandanna around his neck. "Just somethin' between me and m'daddy."

"Ya gonna give us a clue, cowboy?"

"Nope. Here." Buck tossed the Cracker Jack box to Deuce. "Now buzz off."

Garcia laughed as he read Maria's letter. "Guys, check these out." He passed around photos of his kids—Stefan, four, and Lucilia, two. "Maria says our little girl's been talking up a storm. The other day Lucilia pointed to my picture and asked, '*Dónde está papá?*'" Garcia's glossy eyes took in a family photo.

Still leaning against the tree, Chambers ran a hand through his grubby hair and beamed like a proud father. Lieutenant LeBlanc approached, still sounding like Elmer Fudd. "Nothing like mail to boost morale, ay padna?"

Chambers nodded. "Thanks, Paul. Today was rough for them."

"Every day here makes me long for the bayou. Got a nice letter from Rose."

"Yeah?"

"She's been doing a lot of gardening since I left. Never quits, that woman." LeBlanc laughed. "Said she's been picklin' everything from cucumbers to okra. Now what am I gonna do with fifty jars of pickled okra?"

Chambers shrugged.

"Can't wait to see her, though. Two years is too damn long. Oh, by the way." LeBlanc reached into his mailbag. "Santa's got a little something in here for you, too."

Chambers narrowed his eyes.

"No bullshit." LeBlanc handed him a thick letter. "It's from Notting Hill, England." He nudged Chambers's shoulder. "Get yourself a little English hospitality while you were recuperating in London?"

As Chambers turned away, LeBlanc grabbed his arm. "Careful now, padna. If that be a Dear John letter, you know what happens to soldiers who read 'em. It's the kiss of death."

Feeling his knees wobble, Chambers crawled into his narrow pup tent onto a damp bedroll. His letter suddenly felt like a brick in his hand. He started to open it with a pocketknife but stopped as the blade reached halfway.

He lit a Camel and smoked while gazing at the letter. The cigarette burned between his fingers, a long ash hanging on by sheer will. His temples throbbed. He set down the envelope, opened his journal, and wrote till his eyelids grew heavy. Then, despite a creeping chill, he managed to fall asleep.

• • •

Chambers dreamed he was in a hospital room, lying in a soft bed with warm, dry linens. He turned to the patient sleeping next to him. The man was bandaged from head to toe like a mummy, with slits for his mouth, nostrils, and one eye. He slept fitfully, coughing, hacking up bile and swallowing it.

The door opened and rubber-soled shoes squeaked across

the floor. "Ready for tea, Lieutenant?" A porcelain tea set rattled as Nurse Winchester placed a tray on a table.

Jack's heart beat wildly. His gaze followed her smooth calves, up the curves of her hips, her narrow back, the porcelain skin of her neck. Her blond hair was pinned up beneath her nurse's hat. She turned around, catching Jack mesmerized by the sight of her.

Smiling, Nurse Winchester handed him a hot cup of tea. "Just like you like it. Two sugars and a squeeze of lemon."

"Ah, I've been dreaming about your tea all day."

Her brown eyes beamed. She reached into her pocket. "Here, Lieutenant, I also brought you this." She pulled out a book.

Jack read the cover. *A Farewell to Arms*. He flipped open the first page. There in elegant handwriting: *To the Texas lieutenant with the emerald green eyes and charming smile. A book to keep you company. Love, Nurse Winchester.*

Jack's chest tingled. For a moment he forgot how to speak. All he could do was stare at the inscription.

She broke the long silence. "Ernest Hemingway's your favorite author, is he not?"

He nodded. "Where did you find this?"

"At a bookshop near my flat in Notting Hill. Do you like it?" Her smile lit up her face.

"Yes. Here, let me pay you for it."

"Oh, rubbish, it's a gift."

"Thanks."

She took a seat on Jack's bed. "Mind if I have a look under your bandages?"

He lay on his side, and she peeled back the bandages that covered his shoulder and back. "The burns have scarred over."

"Am I hideous?"

"No, of course not. You're one of the lucky ones." Nurse Winchester wiped a wet sponge up his back. She dried him gently with a towel then resealed the bandages. "There you go, Lieutenant. Enjoy your book." As she started to leave, he grabbed her hand. "Uh, Nurse Winchester?"

"Yes?" She sat back on the bed.

He gazed into her eyes."When I get released, I'd love to take you to dinner."

She blushed. "That sounds like a lovely gesture." She stood, tucking a strand of hair behind her ear. "I'll think about it."

"Well, don't think too long. Once I'm healed, they'll send me back to the war."

Nurse Winchester left, her rubber-soled shoes squeaking down the hall. A moment later she stepped back in. "Okay, Lieutenant, I'll go to dinner with you."

Jack felt all the blood rush to his chest. "Great, I'll take you to the finest restaurant in London."

She grinned. "Sounds lovely, Lieutenant."

"Please, call me Jack. And may I ask of your first name?"

"It's Eva." Smiling, she left the room.

"Eva," Jack repeated, lying back against his pillow, a smile pasted across his face. "Eva Winchester."

The patient in the bed next to him groaned. Through a round hole in the bandage mask glared Pierce Fallon's fiery blue eye.

Chapter 16

Several dozen GIs from Baker Company attended a service in honor of the late Captain Murdock. Chambers, along with the members of the Lucky Seven, gathered around Corporal Jacob Goldstein. The chaplain, who put in double duty as a medic, wore a white wool sash around his neck and a yarmulke. He touched the Star of David that hung with his dog tags. The other hand held an open Bible. "As for man, his days are but grass; as the flower of the field, so he flourishes. For the wind passes over it and it is gone; and the place thereof shall know it no more. But the loving kindness of the Lord is from everlasting to everlasting upon them that fear him." Goldstein's voice seemed to drift away, as if Chambers were sinking down into the earth.

He stared at a small shrine of Murdock's last possessions. Among the relics was a photo of the captain sitting in a jeep. He was smiling on that sunny day. A wave of emotions flooded through Chambers. He tightened his jaw muscles, doing his best to keep his face like a wall of stone.

Goldstein's hollow voice continued, "The Lord gave and the Lord has taken away. Blessed be the name of the Lord. Amen."

"Amen," the four platoons said in unison. After a moment of silence, the soldiers dispersed and headed for the chow line.

"You coming, Lieutenant?" Sergeant Mahoney asked.

"In a minute. Go eat, Papa Bear." Chambers remained at the shrine. Captain Murdock's photo smiled back at him.

Goldstein stepped up to the shrine. "He was a good man. You close to him?"

"I've lost a lot of friends to this war, but Murdock . . ." Chambers's throat tightened. "He was more like a father."

"I understand." Goldstein nodded and dug into his pocket. "Here, I have something that belongs to you." He pulled out a small, odd-looking bronze cross. It was badly tarnished.

"That's not mine."

"You sure? As I was checking your wounds, I noticed one of your hands was balled into a fist. When I pried your fingers open, I found this cross seared into your palm. It took me half an hour to remove it. Have a look."

His brow furrowed, Chambers lifted up his bandaged right hand.

Goldstein unraveled the gauze to reveal a red scar on Chambers's palm that matched the cross. His mind flashed back to the moment he and Captain Murdock were lying on the ground: hands gripping . . . a metal object dropping into Chambers's hand . . . burning . . . then only blackness. "What the hell, Chaplain?"

"It came from Murdock, didn't it?"

He took the cross from Goldstein. "He gave it to me as he was dying. That's all I remember." Chambers's fingers traced the Star of David. The corresponding scar perplexed him. He scratched it, suddenly remembering Murdock's last words: *Take over my mission.*

What mission? Chambers suddenly felt a stab of betrayal. *Did Captain Murdock withhold my platoon's recommendation letter for a reason?* Chambers looked up at Goldstein. "You know about this?"

The chaplain smiled, adjusting his glasses. "Captain Murdock often came to me for spiritual advice. He wore that cross with his dog tags."

"I never knew he was religious."

"He was a very secretive man. When he needed to talk, he came to me. Please know you can do the same."

"I'm not into religion." Chambers's gaze shifted between the cross and the marking on his palm. "You're a rabbi, aren't you?"

The chaplain grinned. "Rabbi Jacob Goldstein at your service. But I counsel soldiers of all religions, even those like you. What matters most to me is that people connect with God through whatever path resonates with them. Sometimes just talking about God can lead you on your way."

Chambers put the cross in his pocket. "Sure, Chaplain, I'll think about it."

Lieutenant LeBlanc approached. "Ay, Jack, you better grab some chow. Our powwow with the major starts in fifteen."

Goldstein whispered to Chambers, "Perhaps later I can help you make sense of your talisman. My door is always open at the Bone Cutter."

Chapter 17

Chambers descended the steps into Major Powell's CP and sat down at the long oak table. He had too many knots in his stomach to enjoy the chili. Pushing the bowl aside, he smoked a cigarette and sipped hot coffee. It tasted like nectar from the gods. He stared into the furnace, mesmerized by the orange coals. For the first time in a week, his socks and underwear were getting dry.

A Slavic accent broke his concentration. "Enjoying the hot meal, Lieutenant?" Captain Wolf stood holding a tin bowl of chili.

"It's all right."

Wolf sat down at the table. "Mmm, do I have an appetite. This is the second decent meal I've had in weeks."

Chambers nodded, his eyes focused on the furnace.

The other six officers came down the basement steps. They gathered around the table, brooding in their own silence.

Major Powell stood at the end of the table, holding a metal pointer between his palms. "Is this all the lieutenants?"

"What's left of us, sir." Chambers glanced around at the three banged-up lieutenants staring into their bowls and mugs of coffee. His buddy, LeBlanc, constantly blew his runny nose.

Major Powell motioned to the two new squad members

sitting across from the lieutenants. "Everyone, meet Captain Wolf." Powell motioned with his pointer to the Czech man in the olive wool cap. Wolf nodded to the group. His gray eyes, once polite, now had a burning intensity to them.

Major Powell continued, "And at the far end is Lieutenant Hawk." The ex-subordinate Chambers knew as Pierce Fallon raised a finger to the group without looking up from his chili.

"Let's get down to business, shall we?" Powell paced before the wall of maps. "Baker Company is in dire need of a swift kick in the pants. You've been here over three weeks and gained barely three thousand yards of territory. And at this rate the toll of casualties will surpass Normandy if we don't make some adjustments goddamned quick."

"Now let's go over the strategy the general and I have worked up to defeat the Germans." The major approached the wall of maps and pointed his metal rod. "In two days our Sixtieth Infantry along with the Thirty-ninth Infantry will execute a widespread push through the Monschau Corridor. Baker Company will focus on this ridge system here. Our objective is to strike these two pillboxes, get over this ridge, and push the Jerries all the way back to the Roer."

Chambers rolled his eyes. "With all due respect, sir, that map doesn't do this forest justice. Terrain is impossible to fight in. It's uphill all the way, muddy, foggy. Fallen trees block major firebreaks. Krauts are dug in so deep we can't see them. We've lost hundreds of men trying to reach those pillboxes. Another assault would only lead to more unnecessary casualties, and we're undermanned as it is."

LeBlanc cleared his throat. "Sir, I agree with Chambers. We've come to the conclusion that the Monschau Corridor is deadlocked. Perhaps we could try the Stolberg Corridor."

Powell held his cup as Lieutenant Smith poured him more coffee. "No, we've already tried the Stolberg Corridor, and the Germans have held our armored units in a stalemate. The generals believe the Monschau Corridor is the best avenue of attack, and I agree. I know you men have been fighting in the dark down here, but what you don't know is the Germans are putting up a smokescreen. Their line of defense is thinner than they want you to believe. We have had other squads probing these woods." Major Powell motioned to Wolf and Fallon. "Captain Wolf and Lieutenant Hawk, who come directly from an intelligence branch, have gathered information that has given the Allies the upper hand. Captain Wolf, you have the floor."

The firelight from the furnace reflected on Captain Wolf's face. "We are at a fulcrum in the war, and the scales are about to tip in our favor." As the lieutenants crossed their arms, Wolf smiled. "I know this may sound optimistic, but it's true. The closer we get to Berlin, the deeper we see inside Hitler's fanatical mind and learn about his weaknesses. And he has many. One is that his army is too spread out. They're trying to defend multiple fronts as the Allies attack from the west and the Russians from the east. German soldiers have surrendered by the thousands." He looked at Chambers. "The problem here in the Hürtgen Forest is, if you'll pardon the cliché, you can't see the forest for the trees. You think you're fighting an entire army in there, but in reality there are only scattered German platoons who have a better vantage point. Pillboxes that probably contain fewer than ten men are holding back hundreds of GIs. Up till now you've tried to attack them with patrols and undermanned pushes. But tomorrow an elite special forces unit will take out those pillboxes and clear a path for the offensive."

Major Powell boomed from the far end of the table, "Task Force Powell is going to take one village after another, until we reach the Roer and send those Jerries fleeing back to Berlin! It's time we stopped scratching our asses around here and win this war. Prepare your units to do a push in two days. Dismissed."

Chairs scooted across the cement floor as the eight officers rose. The major charged up the steps with the bookish lieutenant Smith following him like a squire. Chambers poured himself another cup of coffee and started to leave.

"Chambers, can you stay a moment?" Captain Wolf's Slavic voice called from behind. He and Fallon had remained seated along one side of the table. "Please, have a seat." Wolf motioned to an empty chair beside Lieutenant LeBlanc.

Exchanging a glance with his buddy, Chambers dropped back into his chair.

Wolf smiled. "We were just proposing an opportunity to Lieutenant LeBlanc and thought it might be of interest to you."

LeBlanc smiled. "You might want to listen to this."

Wolf opened a file and laid a typed letter on the table. "The reason Captain Murdock never mailed your letter is because he sent this one to Washington instead."

Chambers took the letter.

```
General William Donovan
OSS
Washington, DC

October 5, 1944

Dear General Donovan:
   Two days ago a member of your agency
approached me with a mission. I hereby fully
accept the duties called upon to fulfill
such a mission. I have hand-selected two
seasoned platoons that have achieved many
victories for my company.
   The first, led by Lieutenant Jack Cham-
bers, captured a key bridge in northern
France. In Belgium his platoon detained over
one hundred German prisoners. They have
proven to be sharp in the field and perform
well as a team. Lieutenant Chambers has
demonstrated high intelligence in his
ability to map out enemy territory. He is
also the best platoon leader I have seen in
combat. The second platoon, led by Lieuten-
ant Paul LeBlanc, has shown impeccable
skills at organizing a base camp and setting
up a perimeter defense. Lieutenants Chambers
and LeBlanc have fought alongside one
```

another since Sicily and complement one
another as a team.

    Both platoons fit the profiles you asked
for. Therefore, if they agree to your offer,
Lieutenants Chambers and LeBlanc would be my
first recommendation to join me and your men
on this upcoming mission.

Captain Tom Murdock

"What offer?" said Chambers.

Wolf leaned forward. "Would you like you and your men to go home?"

Chambers gave the captain a side glance. "Well, yeah, but Major Powell dismissed it."

"He did. But I have affiliates in very high places who can override his decision." Wolf rubbed his jaw and stared at Chambers and LeBlanc. "I would be willing to work a deal with both of you in exchange for a service to my unit."

"What's that?" Chambers asked.

"Tomorrow while Task Force Powell is preparing to do a massive ground assault, my X-2 soldiers are doing a covert mission, going after key targets behind enemy lines. We need two platoons of seasoned infantrymen to volunteer to assist us."

Chambers furrowed his brow. "Why are you asking for volunteers? Why not just give us the orders?"

"Because this mission is completely off the record." Wolf glanced at Fallon. "And my X-2 platoon doesn't operate within the normal structures of the U.S. military. My sources said I could only take volunteers."

Chambers leaned back in his chair and folded his arms across his chest. "What exactly is the X-2?"

"I will explain that after you have both agreed. First, hear my proposal. If you volunteer your platoons and help us succeed in this mission, I will guarantee you both free tickets back to the states. And you each can take the men you volunteer to go home with you."

LeBlanc's face lit up. "You serious, sir?"

"You have my word."

"Then count me in, sir." LeBlanc turned to Chambers. "What do you say, padna?"

Chambers checked his gut, but all he felt was nauseated. "How about you send my six soldiers home, and I'll lead a fresh platoon on your mission? Then when that's complete, you give me an honorable discharge."

Wolf shook his head. "No, Captain Murdock recommended you. I want a platoon that is unified and has a record of success. It is either all of you or none of you. So do we have a deal?"

Chambers looked across the table at Pierce Fallon. "It sounds enticing, but I have a problem with working alongside your lieutenant Hawk. He and I have some bad blood between us. And he has a dangerous temper. Quite frankly, I don't trust him in the field."

Fallon sat upright. "Captain, we're wasting our time with him. I told you he wouldn't go for it. I say we pick a platoon leader who's more up for the challenge."

Wolf said, "No, I want Lieutenant Chambers. In order for this to work you two will just have to put aside your differences for one mission. Let bygones be bygones. After this you two never have to see each other again. Lieutenant Hawk, you know what's at stake here."

Fallon grimaced. "I suppose I can tolerate the Grim Reaper for one mission."

Wolf looked hopeful. "Chambers?"

"Will I stay in command of my platoon?"

"During maneuvers, absolutely. During combat, I'll need you to work in accordance with the X-2. We've trained for this mission. We'll be leading most of the assaults, but at times we'll need your platoons as backup."

LeBlanc said, "It's no more dangerous than going on the push in two days. Either way, we're heading back into the Meat Grinder. But with X-2 we also get our ticket out of here."

Chambers looked from his friend to Wolf. "When can we expect to go home?"

"As soon as we capture and secure our main target. If all

goes according to plan, your men can be on a ship by the end of the month."

LeBlanc said, "Come on, Chambers, this is the chance we've been waiting for."

"Okay, we'll do it."

Fallon, his scarred face in a half-grimace, pushed two contracts across the table. "Then if you gentlemen will sign here, everything will be official." As Chambers and LeBlanc scanned the pages of legal jargon, Fallon explained, "It just says you understand this is a highly classified mission. Only you two will be privy to top secret information. No details of the mission will be discussed among the others. And anything you see or hear while on this mission is considered intelligence that can affect the outcome of the war, and leaking such intelligence is considered an act of treason, punishable by death by firing squad." Fallon punctuated this last warning with a wink at Chambers.

Wolf pressed his hands into a steeple. "I need you to swear to secrecy."

"I swear." LeBlanc signed the document. Chambers held his breath, contemplating the odds of getting his men out any other way. They had patrolled behind enemy lines a dozen times without any reward for risking their lives. At least this mission had a bonus upon completion. He and his men could finally go home. Chambers signed the document. "I swear."

Captain Wolf smiled. "Good. Then consider yourselves inducted into the X-2. We can now let you in on some classified information. Even Major Powell is not privy to everything we are about to tell you." He sat forward. "Fallon and myself are not normal army intelligence. We come directly from a special clandestine division known as the OSS."

"That's the Office of Strategic Services," Fallon explained. "We're based out of DC."

Wolf nodded. "Our OSS branch, known as X-2, comprises seasoned fighters from the U.S. Army, British Special Forces, Polish, French, and Dutch Underground. We go by animal code names to conceal our nationalities. We are

highly trained to carry out covert maneuvers, so odds are in
your favor of getting your request granted. There are some
high risks, however." Wolf opened his briefcase and pulled
out a map of the Hürtgen Forest. "Two weeks ago Lieutenant
Hawk and I parachuted behind enemy lines and joined a
team of German Underground agents. We got as far as this
German town here—Richelskaul." Wolf handed Chambers
and LeBlanc some black-and-white photos of soldiers occupying a town square. "While the front line remains thin, the
Germans are building a hive of reinforcements in Richelskaul. We believe this is the head command post for the entire seventy square miles that make up the Hürtgen Forest.
We saw SS troops among Wehrmacht soldiers. They were
gathering supplies, petrol, armored vehicles, and evacuating
townspeople. My team was disguised as Wehrmacht soldiers.
We talked with other soldiers. They were mostly young boys,
fourteen to seventeen, and old men."

Fallon jumped in, "The Wehrmacht were so ready for the
war to be over, they were practically pissing their pants. But
the SS troops were a different breed altogether. We asked
them if Berlin was ready to surrender, and they laughed. Ar-
rogant assholes."

Wolf said, "They told us Hitler was only beginning and
that the Allies and Russians would fall quickly when the Nazis unleashed their secret weapons."

Chambers examined a photo of four Wehrmacht sentries
manning machine guns at the town's entrance. "Any specula-
tion about these secret weapons?"

Wolf answered, "You have all the details you need at this
point. What you and your men need to be aware of is that
while the front line is still thin, the Germans are forming a
hive in and around Richelskaul to defend the Hürtgen."

"They'll never get the chance." Fallon cracked his knuckles. "We're going to seize this command post and shut down
the entire Hürtgen campaign by cutting off the bees from the
hive."

Chambers rubbed his jaw. "My men and I ventured that
far behind enemy lines only once, and I lost over half my men
that day. Major Powell considered the mission a disaster."

Wolf put his files back in his briefcase. "Well, this time you'll be in good company. You can tell your men they will be going home soon, but there will be no mention of the OSS. As far as they are concerned, this is a routine reconnaissance patrol. Are we clear on this?"

Chambers and LeBlanc nodded.

"Good." Captain Wolf smiled. "Welcome to the OSS."

Chapter 18

The wind's icy nails raking at his neck, Chambers sauntered across camp. He passed a group of doctors trudging toward the chow line. Chambers stopped one of them, an older man with a tired-looking face. "Have you seen Corporal Goldstein?"

"Yeah, back at the Bone Cutter."

Ahead stood a hospital tent that connected to the skeletal remains of a farmhouse. Over the front porch someone had painted THE BONE CUTTER. Inside the makeshift hospital all was dark, except for a lantern where a doctor sat reading as he kept watch over the sleeping patients—mostly men who had the flu or trench foot. Chambers weaved through the shadows of the dilapidated house, his boots crunching over glass, wood, and fallen shingles. He found Goldstein in a back supply room, sitting against a wall with his legs crossed and his hands resting on an open Bible. A chain with a Star of David pendant intertwined his fingers. A shaft of moonlight shown through a hole in the ceiling, illuminating his face. His eyes were closed. He was breathing deeply, his belly expanding, then contracting. He wore the most peaceful smile.

Remaining in the shadows, Chambers beheld the chaplain. *Must be nice to tune out the war, even for a few moments*. He tried, but chattering voices filled his head—Major Powell, Captain Murdock, and a dozen others. The sound of gunfire and bombs exploding, like ghostly residues of a war that had become one with him, echoed in his mind with a hollow ringing.

Goldstein opened his eyes, the chestnut brown appearing iridescent in the moonlight, like shiny gold coins. "Lieutenant, what a pleasant surprise."

He smiled and rubbed his bicep. "Thought I'd get a fresh bandage."

"Sure, sure, there's a table in the next room."

Chambers sat on a makeshift gurney and removed his shirt. Goldstein peeled off the bandage on his bicep and cleaned the wound.

"Everything okay, Lieutenant? Your arms are trembling."

Chambers looked at the ceiling. "To be honest, I didn't just come here for my wound."

"What, you need a chaplain?"

"You said Captain Murdock used to come to you . . ."

Goldstein put away the roll of bandages. "From your lips to God's ears. You have my undivided attention."

"Okay." Chambers swallowed hard, staring at the sleeping patients.

"Just tell me what's on your mind."

Chambers focused on the dirt floor and shook his head. "Nah, this is stupid. I don't know why I brought it up." He stood and grabbed his shirt.

"If there's something bothering you, perhaps I can help. To be quite honest, I'm a better chaplain than I am a medic."

Chambers stared at Goldstein for a long pause, then sat back down. "This is just between you and me."

Goldstein held up his palm. "You have my word."

"Okay . . . When I was carrying Captain Murdock through the forest, his last words . . . well, he said some strange things to me. And . . . I thought I saw something when he pressed the cross into my hand. But I can't remember. And on top of everything, I lost the one man I could look up to . . . it's got me all tied up in knots."

"I see." Goldstein looked up at the ceiling. "Can I share

this with him? Yes, I have permission." Behind his glasses, the chaplain's eyes seemed to glass over. "When Captain Murdock came to me for consultations, he was a nervous wreck. He told me that every night since we arrived at the Hürtgen, he had nightmares. He came to believe they were visions of what was to come."

"Visions?" Chambers looked at the chaplain askance.

"How shall I put this? . . . I suppose there's no way to say it but to say it. Murdock believed the reason our forces haven't been able to penetrate the Hürtgen Forest is because we are no longer fighting just the Germans. In his visions, Murdock saw an army of dark assassins—shadow soldiers, he called them—attacking from the woods, slaughtering our GIs."

Chambers snorted. "Those were just war dreams. We all have them."

"Murdock's dreams were the same night after night. He claimed he was visited by a ghostly figure wearing a hooded robe who told him of a secret war going on, a war within the war. A battle of light and darkness. In Murdock's dream, the robed figure told him the shadow soldiers were not killing just GI soldiers but Germans as well. The robed figure handed Murdock a glowing bronze cross and said he had a mission to fulfill. God is the general, and he's recruiting soldiers of light to battle a darkness greater than Hitler."

"No offense, Goldstein, but this sounds like a bunch of hooey."

"Don't you believe in God?"

Chambers shook his head. "God and I had a falling out years ago."

"Well, maybe now he's trying to reach out to you."

"Disguised as a robed figure. Right. And maybe Hitler will surrender tomorrow and we can all go home."

"Seriously, Chambers. Maybe that's why Murdock passed on the cross to you. God has chosen you to fight this battle."

"Sorry, Goldstein, but this is more than I came to hear." He stood and grabbed his coat.

"Wait. There's something you should know about your cross."

Chambers paused at the door.

"When Murdock woke the next morning, he was still holding the cross the robed figure had given him in his dream. And it had burned the same scar into his hand."

"Chaplain, don't feed me bullshit."

"I've never been more truthful." Goldstein raised his palm. In the center was the familiar cross-shaped scar. "I had the same dream."

Feeling his knees shake, Chambers quickly turned away. "Good night, Chaplain."

"Just consider what I'm saying, Chambers," Goldstein's voice called from behind. "God may be trying to reach you."

Part 4

Into the Mist

There are moments in battle when a platoon leader has to make decisions that will affect the destinies of his soldiers. I command orders that lead to good men falling dead in the mud. I suppose these sacrifices are necessary to win the war, but in the coldest, darkest part of my being, I feel like I'm nothing but a servant to the almighty Grim Reaper.

—LIEUTENANT JACK CHAMBERS, *WAR DIARY*

Chapter 19

Chambers's body burst through the wall of pine needles. Branches slapped at him like spiked tentacles. His legs kept running, running, running. Something shimmered up ahead, floating in between the trees. Glowing like a firefly, it shaped itself into a ghostly figure wearing a hooded cloak.

What sounded like a pack of ferocious wolves approached from behind. Gasping, Chambers glanced over his shoulder. Downhill, branches slapped together. The hungry growls drew closer.

Refusing to look back, he raced after the cloaked figure, into the dense woods. A winding trail led to a spiked wrought-iron fence covered in ivy. Beyond, an enormous graveyard spread across a hillside. The mist drifted between stone crosses and tombstones like specters.

Chambers opened a rusted iron gate, its hinges squeaking, and stepped into the cemetery. He meandered between crosses and tombstones, some of which had oval photos of the sleeping dead. Hearing gunshots, he hunched behind a tombstone. At the top of the hill the vapor parted to reveal a medieval church. A war-damaged bell tower jutted upward above the fir trees. Lightning shattered the bruised sky, illuminating the church's battered, jagged roof.

"Where are my men?" He scanned the tombstones and crypts dotting the hillside up to the church. At one grave, an object stabbed up from the soil, glinting in the moonlight.

A voice echoed behind him, "Forget your men, Chambers." He whirled around to see the cloaked figure standing beside a crypt. "You have a bigger mission to fulfill."

"I don't understand. What are you talking about?"

"The cross holds all the answers."

Shadows charged from the mist, wielding submachine guns. Bullets kicked up mud around Chambers's feet as he bolted across the cemetery. Ahead the small object glowed radiantly—a metal cross sticking out of the mud.

Guns clacked. Boots splashing through mud charged up the hill.

Chambers reached for the cross. A rifle butt struck his temple. He fell face first onto the grave. Dazed, the tombstones spinning around him, blood trickled into his eyes.

The robed figure's voice whispered in his mind. "You're our only hope, Chambers."

He reached for the cross again. A boot pressed his wrist flat against the soil, cracking the bones.

Chambers wailed. His heart pounding, he looked up. A shadow soldier studied him with glowing red eyes. More shadows gathered around. Chambers stared at the bronze cross that stabbed up from the soil just inches from his face. It faded in and out of focus. Then he looked back up to see the red-eyed shadow drawing something long and silver . . .

• • •

Chambers sat up, wheezing. It took him several seconds to settle his breath and realize he'd been dreaming. He fell back on his pillow and rubbed his face. "Jesus . . ."

Boots squished in the mud outside his tent.

"Everything okay in there?" Sergeant Mahoney whispered.

"Yeah, Papa Bear. Nothing to worry about."

Mahoney knelt, peering into the tent. "Listen, I hate to ruin your beauty sleep, but my watch reads oh four-thirty. Think it's about time we get the boys up?"

Chambers yawned. "Let 'em snooze another fifteen. They're gonna need it."

"How about you?"

"Be out in a minute."

Mahoney's boots marched away and the night became filled with sounds of him rustling in his tent. Chambers lay on his pillow, staring at the shadows that clung to the drab fabric of his tent. He scratched his bandaged hand and recalled his dream, the cloaked figure, the bronze cross. Was there something to Goldstein's warnings? Was God trying to contact Chambers through the dream world just like Murdock had experienced? A more chilling thought pricked his skin. *The cloaked figure was the Grim Reaper leading me to my death.*

No, it was just a natural reaction to losing several men in combat. Chambers had had dozens of war dreams.

Then what about the shadow soldiers?

Goldstein, with all his good intentions, must have planted those thoughts in my head. Whatever the case, they weren't real.

Then why aren't you getting out of bed?

His body lay there, refusing to budge. He dozed off again and woke up to Sergeant Mahoney kicking the heels of his boots. "Rise and shine, Lieutenant. We got us another foggy day in the Meat Grinder."

• • •

Chambers stood at the edge of the trees, watching and listening. No distant gunshots disturbed the dead calm. Overnight silence had fallen across the Hürtgen Forest with the heaviness of the morning dew.

Gray light, cocooned within a damp fog, spilled over the mountain's crest like the breath of a great beast. The mist drifted down the steep incline, sifting through the Dragon's Teeth that bordered Germany.

He checked his silver watch: 0520. Ten minutes till game time.

A hand came to rest on his shoulder. He turned to see Goldstein wearing his Red Cross helmet. "Morning," the medic said, barely a whisper, and offered a steaming tin of coffee.

Chambers accepted it gratefully and stared at the fog drifting over the war-battered forest.

"Makes a lovely postcard," Goldstein whispered, adjusting his glasses. "So, you think about what I said last night?"

Chambers nodded, sipping his coffee.

"And . . ."

Chambers shrugged. "As much as I respect Captain Murdock, I believe his nightmares were just nightmares. And if he believed they were real messages, then I'm afraid he was delusional."

"Did you reconsider listening to God?"

"I hate to burst your holy bubble, Goldstein, but he's not reaching out to me."

"Well, sir, you're certainly at choice whether or not you want to listen or see the signs." Goldstein held up his palm. "I have my sign. That's why I've volunteered to be in your patrol platoon."

Chambers gave him a sideways stare. "You know Murdock went into battle believing in this hooey, and all it got him was dead."

"I'll take my chances."

Chambers sipped his coffee. "Good luck to you then."

The members of the Lucky Seven gathered around them. Chambers said, "Guys, you remember our chaplain, Corporal Goldstein. He'll be our medic on this patrol."

Hoffer said, "Good, maybe you can give us a blessing as well."

Finch thumped his helmet. "He's a rabbi, knucklehead, not a priest."

"Well, since I don't see any priests around, I'll take what I can get. Chaplain, you can accommodate other religions, can't you?"

"I'll counsel anyone who needs to speak to God." Goldstein shot Chambers a glance.

Garcia pulled out his family photo and rosary beads. "I'm glad you're coming, Chaplain. I feel like this might be the Big One."

Hoffer shook his head. "This isn't the Big One, *amigo*. Stop jinxing us."

"Feels like the Big One," Garcia muttered.

"Enough of that," Sergeant Mahoney barked. "We're all coming back. This is just another day on the job."

"Everybody ready?" Chambers asked, trying not to appear nervous.

They all nodded.

"Good, we move out in five." The stone mask of confidence he wore seemed to be holding up. *That's it. Just keep it level.*

Deuce gnawed on an unlit cigar, staring out at the fog-cloaked mountain. "Man, they ain't really gonna send us out into this soup."

"Rain or shine," Buck grumbled. "Brass don't give a rat's ass whether we can see the Krauts."

"Quit your bellyaching, boys," Mahoney said.

Chambers said, "Let's keep positive."

"Don't forget the Lucky Seven ritual," Deuce said, holding out a joker from his deck of cards. They stood in a circle. Each man held out a personal object that he considered lucky. Chambers held out his silver watch. "Everybody lives."

"Everybody lives," they repeated.

Lieutenant Pierce Fallon stepped into the circle, drawing stares from the Lucky Seven. Fallon's scarred face and slick bald cranium was painted in a black and green war mask. It punctuated the white of his fiery blue eye. "Captain Wolf needs a word with your platoon. Follow me."

They weaved through crowds of teenagers from LeBlanc's platoon. This morning there was no talking or smoking or laughing. Just silent waiting for that imminent call to battle. Wide eyes, some with nervous ticks, watched the chosen point platoon move to the rear of the crowd.

Fallon led Chambers's platoon under a tentlike shelter with camouflage netting. Wolf was leaning over a map on a table. The Czech captain still wore his olive wool cap tight over his light brown hair. He was dressed in the same commando uniform as the X-2 soldiers, complete with semiautomatic rifle and plumb-shaped grenades. The captain's face, also painted, remained expressionless, all business. "Are your men ready, Lieutenant?"

Chambers eyed the Lucky Seven. Each man was holding his breath. The fifteen X-2 mercenaries, looking fresh and excited, filled in behind them. The elite squad all had black and green paint smeared across their faces. Each commando had his code name stenciled across his helmet—HAWK, MOOSE, FOX, CROW, OTTER, RAVEN, SNAKE, and a half-dozen other animal totems. In front stood Lieutenant Fallon wearing a maniacal grin like a boxer eager for a fight bell.

I can't believe I agreed to do another mission with this lunatic. Chambers turned back to Wolf. "We're ready."

The X-2 captain offered a pleased half grin. "Good. You are first to move out. Chambers, give everyone a quick lesson on the forest we'll be fighting in." Wolf stepped out of the group and put on a radio headset.

Lieutenant Chambers approached the map table, waving the men to gather around. "The Hürtgen extends from a larger wooded region, the Ardennes here in Belgium." He pointed to the rows of stone pyramids. "On the other side of those Dragon's Teeth, the Hürtgen stretches seventy square miles in parameter and lies in a square formed by the German towns of Aachen, Düren, Heimbach, and Monschau." Chambers tapped the four points on the map. "Contained within that square is a variety of terrain. You can see from here, a ridge system, covered with thick fir trees, runs from southwest to northeast. The highest peak rises to over twenty-one hundred feet. The inclines are so steep in places they are near impossible to climb. Through the valleys run numerous creeks and rivers, such as the Roer and the Kall. The forest is one big booby trap with minefields just about everywhere you step, so follow my lead and stay in the column at all times."

Wolf stepped in. "Okay, let us go over the mission once more." His finger tapped the map and traced a red line shaped like an arrow. "This first line represents Lieutenant LeBlanc's platoon along with myself, code name Spear. Lieutenants Hawk, Chambers, your platoon makes up the spear point. We will push up through the middle along this firebreak. Reach these two pillboxes, Target 1 and Target 2, dig in. When the spear reaches this ravine, we will divide into two squads and defend your outer flanks. Chambers, your squad will engage a base fire here in the center, while Lieutenant Hawk's men circle the German bunkers both north and south and take out the pillboxes from the rear."

"It's going to take a lot of TNT to break through those pillboxes," Chambers said.

"We've brought plenty," Wolf said.

Chambers stared at Fallon and the fifteen X-2 commandos. They all looked like this was going to be a cakewalk.

"Once those bunkers are captured," Wolf continued, "the two spear columns, led by me and Lieutenant LeBlanc, will merge with the spear point. From there we will hike over this second crest, and depending on resistance, push our way to Target 3, the small town of Richelskaul. Once we capture Richelskaul, we will establish a new base camp, and I will fill you in on our next objective from there." He showed them a photograph and the X on the map that marked the town's location. "Beyond these pillboxes the front line is thin, but once we reach Richelskaul we're expecting resistance, so be sharp." Wolf clapped his hands together. "Okay, move out."

LeBlanc walked over and gripped Chambers's forearm. "A couple more days and we're going home, buddy."

"We're going home." Chambers tossed out the rest of his coffee and turned to his men. "Let's roll."

Chapter 20

The twenty-four-man point platoon, a blend of GIs and X-2 commandos, marched up the near vertical incline. They hiked around fir trees that lay in mangled heaps and where artillery shells had opened gaping wounds into the earth. Scraps of metal littered the ground: bullet shells, artillery shrapnel, exploded grenades, and shattered helmets.

From the top of the ridge stretched a dense forest. In one long column, the soldiers weaved through the giant fir trees, thin streams of gray light barely penetrating the thick canopy. Branches formed a ceiling over their heads. In several places they had to walk hunched over.

Corporal Otter got tangled in a coil of barbed wire. He yanked and kicked. "Damn it, somebody help me."

"Don't piss your pants, buddy. Hold still," Buck said as he cut him free.

"Lieutenant Hawk's gonna kick my ass!" The kid cursed at a rip in his fatigue pants.

Buck grumbled, "Welcome to the Hürtgen, buddy. Forest ain't nothing but mines and barbed teeth."

"These woods actually started out as a fir tree farm." Deuce waved his arm like a nature guide. "Notice how the trees are planted in perfect rows?"

Chambers glared at the chatting soldiers and dragged a finger across his throat.

Boots crunched over a thick carpet of pine needles. Two X-2 scouts crept ten paces ahead. Some men watched the branches for snipers, while others scanned the mist for movement. Lieutenant Chambers focused on the ground. He stopped and held up his fist. The platoon froze. Chambers knelt, signaling everyone to gather behind him. He deftly lifted a pile of leaves. Three wood prongs stabbed upward from beneath the pine needles. He whispered, "Bouncing Betty. The ones here have wood prongs and are filled with glass. They pop up about face high. They're nasty bitches, so watch your step."

After surveying his topo map, he led the platoon northeastward, gravity pulling at their legs as the forest sloped. Hiking up the steep jagged hill, Chambers's men had to use branches and tree stumps to pull themselves up.

The sky above darkened. The air grew heavy with the familiar dampness of a storm brewing. The fog thickened into white smoke, closing in around them, as if the platoon were marching straight into the clouds. As they climbed higher, the stench of rotting death began to assault Chambers's nostrils.

GI corpses littered the hill. Arms sprouted grotesquely from the mounds of fallen branches where tree bursts had scalped the trees. One man floated facedown in a puddle. The bottom half of a torso hung upside down in a tree, its leg hooked over a branch. Another soldier sat against a tree, staring straight ahead. Mouth open, lips curled back over red teeth, his face frozen in a life-ending scream. Several X-2 men gasped. Some vomited. *Welcome to the Green Hell, warriors.*

Chambers kept his gaze riveted on the fog ahead. He licked his chapped lips, the anticipation of battle flooding through his veins. The platoon advanced another hundred yards. Butterflies flapped in Chambers's stomach. Charred fir trees stood in eerie silence.

The two X-2 scouts signaled up the hill.

Chambers and Fallon ducked, waving for everyone to take cover. The twenty-four soldiers hunkered behind fallen trees and flattened into foxholes dug out from previous battles.

Chambers exchanged glances with Fallon then peered through
his binoculars. Up the hill sat two German pillboxes. Dirt
from the hillside enveloped the heavily wired and concrete-
enforced structures. Trees sprouted on top, and ivy camouflaged the front walls. The bunkers were staggered, with one
higher up the hill to cover the first one's backside. At each
bunker, high-powered MG42 machine-gun barrels jutted
outward from the dark, square apertures.

Fallon motioned for Corporal Fox to hand over the field telephone. Fallon whispered into the phone, "Sir, Spear Point's up-
town and dug in. Targets 1 and 2 spotted. Guns perched at the
ready. Presence unknown. Repeat, presence unknown. Copy."
Fallon listened to Wolf's crackling response and nodded. "Roger."

An explosion boomed downhill to their right, echoing
across the mountain.

Chambers aimed his binoculars at the two bunkers. The
four machine guns sat idle.

Fallon whispered into the mouthpiece, "Spear Point to
Spear. Explosion on right flank. Repeat, explosion on right
flank. Please advise." Chewing his bottom lip, he listened.
"Roger that." Tossing the phone back to Fox, Fallon motioned
for Chambers and Moose to crawl down the hill with him.
The three crouched down into a large foxhole.

"What's the report?" Chambers asked.

Fallon checked the magazine in his submachine gun.
"Spear 1 and Spear 2 are delayed by minefields. Captain says
secure bunkers pronto."

Sergeant Moose grinned. "About time we see some action."

Chambers studied the two concrete boxes. Four gun barrels
were aimed downhill, poised to unleash a metal storm of rapid
fire. "Wait, Fallon, our plan was to strike with two squads on
each flank."

"Well, plans have changed. You both know the drill.
Chambers, your platoon creates a base fire. Moose and I will
take out the bunkers. We strike in sixty seconds." Grinning,
Fallon whispered to his husky sergeant, "Let's see what our
warriors can do in a *real* combat situation."

Chambers asked, "How many bunkers have your men
captured?"

Fallon answered, "In training, dozens. In a real combat situation—these two will be our first." He winked at Chambers. "Trust us. Ready, Moose?"

"Does a Kraut shit in the woods?"

Fallon grinned. "Unless he shits his pants first. Let's go."

The three jumped into action. Chambers relayed the message to the Lucky Seven. They dug in, their rifles aimed at the two concrete bunkers. The forest remained deathly silent.

Fallon and Moose communicated to their squads with hand signals. Carrying the bazooka, an X-2 commando and his shell loader crawled up beside Chambers.

Wearing a two-canister flamethrower, Fallon led a three-man squad up the steep incline on the left, staying just behind the treeline. Three men advanced up the hill tree to tree in leapfrog fashion—two men always covering the advancing man. Sergeant Moose led the second three-man unit up the right side. Mist cloaked the approach of the two units. Chambers searched the thickening miasma through his binoculars. *Damn it, where are they?*

Finally, a man emerged from the fog. Another followed. The units neared the tops of the pillboxes then set themselves into position. Chambers counted all six. With that he gave the signal to fire.

Bullets cracked the silence. The Lucky Seven at the bottom of the hill laid a base fire. Chambers leaped up from his log, sprayed the hilltop with his submachine gun, and ducked back down. Beside him, the bazooka loader stuffed a shell into the pipe and ducked. *Whoof!* The gunner's shoulder-held cannon blasted Bunker One's left portal. "Bull's eye!"

The bazooka team reloaded. The Lucky Seven riflemen rotated rounds of grazing fire into the second aperture. The German machine guns at Bunker 2 had yet to return fire. Chambers watched through his binoculars. *What are you Krauts waiting for?*

The bazooka let loose with a roaring screech. Another direct hit knocked out the second machine-gun. "Bunker 1 disabled!" the gunner yelled.

"Now take out Bunker 2!" Chambers yelled back over the gunshots.

The base-fire team pounded Bunker 2 with a metal hailstorm. *Whoof!* The bazooka shell erupted in the grassy knoll in front. Still no fire from Bunker 2. Amazed, Chambers looked over at Goldstein to see if he was praying for the guns not to fire. But the chaplain was in full medic mode, poised like a cat ready to leap to the first man wounded.

The bazooka's next two blasts made direct hits on the machine-guns of Bunker 2.

Up the hill, Fallon's squad ran with their backs against the ivy wall of Bunker 1.

Chambers gave the okay signal.

The two bomb squads climbed onto the rooftops of both bunkers.

Down the hill, the rest of the platoon watched for an enemy counterattack. Chambers stared at the second hand on his watch. Ten seconds . . . fifteen . . .

Feeling his stomach rumbling, he peered through his binoculars.

Twenty seconds . . .

Fallon's squad hunkered on the rooftop of Bunker 1. Fallon dug into the escarpment with a spade and barked at his men. The commandos chained together explosives.

Thirty seconds . . .

Chambers watched the woods for approaching Germans.

Forty-five seconds . . .

The rooftop of Bunker 1 blew skyward, raining down dirt and concrete chunks. The air filled with dust.

Sixty seconds . . .

Fallon ran across the rooftop to assess the damage. He cursed at his men. His squad pulled out more explosives. They packed TNT into the holes, lit the fuse, and got the hell out of Dodge. Concrete debris blasted into the air. The entire area rocked like an earthquake.

Chambers's ears popped. He glanced at his watch.

A minute thirty seconds . . . *and no retaliation.*

Fallon shot flames into a breach at the side then disappeared into Bunker 1. Rapid submachine-gun shots came from inside.

Farther up the hill, Sergeant Moose's squad pressed against Bunker 2's front wall. The MG42 machine guns had been reduced to twisted metal. An X-2 soldier swung his body in front of the first aperture. With his flamethrower he roasted the interior. Another tossed a grenade into the second hole. Shots fired, followed by another earth-shaking explosion. Moose's squad rounded the side. Chambers rotated his binoculars down the hill to Bunker 1. Lieutenant Fallon's squad, still somewhere inside Bunker 1, had yet to surface. The shooting stopped.

Chambers felt pins and needles in his knees. Three precious minutes ticked by. "Come on, boys. Everybody lives."

Smoke from the smoldering pillboxes drifted down the hill. First platoon crouched low, each man staring ahead, yet somehow inwardly. Buck spat tobacco. Garcia bit his nails. Deuce chewed on his cigar, grinning like this was a poker game and he had pocket aces.

At Bunker 1, Fallon climbed out and gave a thumbs-up. Moose's squad at Bunker 2 did the same.

Chambers finally released his breath. "Okay, let's roll!" He led the platoon up the hill to the clearing in front of Bunker 1. He whispered to Mahoney, "Sergeant, line up sentries. We've made enough racket to wake up half of Germany."

"You got it."

Fallon stood by a steel door on the bunker's side. Gray soot covered his shoulders and some of the green of his painted face.

Chambers approached him. "Why didn't they fight back?"

Fallon wiped a sleeve across his sweaty brow, smearing the war paint. "Bunker's empty. Steel door wasn't even locked. Popped right open when we blew the roof. Looks like somebody else got here first." He removed his flame pack, his face a mask of disappointment.

Moose joined them. "Bunker 2's also empty. Lots of expended shells, but no bodies."

Chambers chewed his lip, staring into the bunker's shadowy maw. Burning ivy dangled over the entrance. Concrete chunks littered the grass. He scanned the thick woods surrounding them.

"Moose, secure the perimeter." Fallon waved at one of his soldiers. "Corporal Fox, come have a look at this."

A lanky, professorial man with dark red hair and a trimmed red beard adjusted his glasses. "Find something interesting, did you, sir?" he asked with a British accent.

"Yeah, Fox, something right up your alley. Follow me. You, too, Chambers."

Inside the bunker darkness pressed in like black oil oozing over them, choking out the light. Flashlight beams carved through the gloom as Fallon, Fox, and Chambers burrowed through barracks and storage rooms. Dirt and spider webs covered the walls. The sound of boots echoed off the concrete floor.

"It's bloody creepy in here, if I do say," Fox said.

Fallon shined his beam along a back wall pocked with bullet holes and oily crimson stains. "Here it is." Bloody handprints covered the concrete wall. A phrase had been finger-painted. Fallon sniffed like a bloodhound. "Smells like Kraut blood to me."

Chambers poked his flashlight into an adjacent room. "Where are the bodies?"

Fallon shrugged. "Never found any. Just this." He shined his beam along the smeared archaic letters.

ᚺᛗ ᛒᛁᚠᚲᚺ ᛞᛟᛗᛗᚠᛏᚺ ᚠᚱᛗᚺᚲᚱᚠᛏ
ᛚᚺᛁᛉ ᚠᛏ ᚠᛟᚱ ᛞᛟᚠᚱᛝᚠᚲᚠᚠᚺᛗᚱ
ᛋᚠᛟᛗ ᛟᚺᛝᛋᚠᛟᛗ ᛟᚺᛝ

"Bloody hell, they're runes," Fox said. "An ancient Nordic alphabet used by the Nazis. They believed that the Roman alphabet was too Christian and decided that the runes were linked to their Aryan heritage. Fascinating."

Fallon sneered. "Save the lecture, professor. Can you translate it?"

"I can translate anything." Fox shined his light along the letters. His dark brow furrowed. "Hmm, this is quite odd. 'The black demons are scratching at our door. All-Father save us. Save us . . .'" The message trailed off in a smear.

"Black demons?" Chambers asked.

"Doesn't make a bit of sense," Fox said. "Demons are mainly a Christian and Jewish concept. The Nazis are pagan. They celebrate winter solstice instead of Christmas and worship the Teutonic god they call All-Father."

"Probably some kind of code," Fallon said.

Fox grinned and adjusted his glasses. "Runic codes are my specialty."

Fallon tapped his watch. "You got thirty seconds. And spare us the historical rhetoric."

"Well, sir, it's clearly a cry for help. The ink blood indicates that the scribe was wounded or one of his men was already dead. The enemy that he refers to as 'scratching at the back door' must have been attacking from outside and trying to get in, and by the looks of it, the enemy succeeded."

"You're very astute, Fox, but what does our scribe mean about the black demons?"

The Brit rubbed his beard and shook his head. "I haven't the foggiest idea."

Chambers shone his light along the floor. Blood had pooled in several places, causing his boots to stick to the concrete. From one corner came a stench that reminded Chambers of his deer-hunting days, when he gutted his fresh kill in the field by hand. He spotlighted a pile of crimson refuse covered in flies. White fragments speckled the stained floor. He knelt for a closer look. They were teeth. The crimson refuse looked like a lower jawbone and a bulbous mass that might have been a tongue.

Chambers scratched his chin. "Who could have gotten here before us? Some of your Underground boys?"

Fallon crouched and examined dozens of empty shells that littered the puddles. "No, if our German squads had done an assault, Wolf and I'd know about it."

"The OSS has German squads?"

Fallon nodded. "We have agents all over Europe. The German partisans, the French, the Dutch, the Polish."

Chambers spun his beam around. "Any guesses then who might have done a job on these Krauts? Just yesterday these bunkers were giving my men hell."

Fox tapped his chin. "I must say, this code's got me befuddled. I've seen black demons in Christian art, but I don't have any reference for them in German lore. Perhaps the Nazis were metaphorically referring to a Christian or Masonic enemy dressed in black. Some sort of rogue assassins not tied into the network."

Fallon shrugged. "Whoever attacked this bunker snatched all the weapons from the storage rooms. Strange, though, they left a full bottle of Russian vodka sitting on a table." Fallon held up the bottle. "Straight from Moscow." He winked at Chambers.

"We should get back with our men." He hiked back down the dark passage toward the squares of light that formed the gunner windows. Climbing back out through the side door, Chambers felt the oily darkness ooze off his body as the gray morning light washed over him. His sentries surveyed the woods, while the X-2 platoon stood around looking bored.

As Fallon got on the radio with Wolf, Chambers spotted Deuce wandering off into the woods. "Stop. Where are you going?"

The Poker King whirled around. "I saw one of the X-2s disappear into the woods."

Chambers put his hands on his hips and scanned the thick forest.

A kid wailed from beyond a wall of mist.

The platoon jerked their rifles.

Lieutenant Fallon and Sergeant Moose bolted down the hill.

"Who's screaming?" Fallon asked.

Another scream echoed off the mountainside. "Help!"

"That's Corporal Otter," Moose said.

"Let's find him." Fallon and Moose set off into the woods.

"Wait. Let us lead, there could be mines." Chambers and Deuce crept single-file toward the sound of the scream. Fallon and a half dozen of his commandos followed. They found the missing X-2 corporal a hundred yards deep curled up in a ball on the ground, his pants bunched around his ankles. He blubbered, gripping a blond head covered in blood. Vomit stained his mouth and shirt.

Fallon slapped the freckle-faced kid. "Shut the hell up! You're gonna get us killed!" Spit and snot dripped from the boy's face. He now had a bloody lip as well.

The X-2 soldiers gathered around, scanning the woods with submachine guns at the ready.

Moose examined Otter's blood-soaked hair. "Where are you injured, kid?"

The baby-faced teen pulled up his pants, sniffling. "It's . . . not my blood." He pointed into a circle of trees. "It's theirs."

The X-2 soldiers crept into the brush and froze. "Jesus H. Christ . . . Sir, you gotta see this."

Fallon stepped into the clearing. "What the . . . ?"

Pushing back the branches with his rifle, Chambers stepped into the circle of trees.

Hot bile filled his throat.

Eight bare-chested German soldiers hung upside down from the branches, their ankles bound with barbed wire. Swaying in the wind, their fingers scraped the ground. Bullet holes riddled their chests. Blood streamed from the wounds, painting over bizarrely deformed faces.

"Jesus." Deuce looked to his platoon leader.

Chambers shook his head, unable to avert his eyes. The barbed wire was wrapped around the Germans' throats, mouths, and eyes so tightly the spiked bindings had dug trenches in the cheeks and punctured eyeballs. One cadaver was missing the bottom half of his face. Chambers remembered the jaw and teeth from the bunker.

Fallon spun the stiff body with the missing jaw. There was a swastika tattoo on the shoulder.

"Nazis. Young ones, too." Grinning, he poked one with his knife. "See, they barely got hair under their pits."

"Knock it off, Lieutenant Hawk." A wave of acid burned through Chambers's stomach. "Who the hell would string them up like this?"

"Don't know." Fallon nudged Moose. "But I like their style."

"Fallon, you make me sick." Shaking his head, Chambers

stepped around the dangling bodies and studied the thick woods. Suspicion pricked the back of his neck. "I feel like eyes are watching us."

Deuce started into the woods.

"Deuce, don't go in there."

"I was just—"

"Get back here. *Now*."

The Poker King whispered, "Sir, I'm getting a bad, bad feeling."

"Yeah, me too. Let's hustle back."

Crack!

Chambers whirled around. A hanging corpse swung in a circle, smashing branches off the tree. Wearing a sated grimace, Fallon wrapped something in a handkerchief and tucked it into his breast pocket.

Chambers examined the swinging corpse and noticed one of the fingers missing, clotted red tissue exposed at the knuckle. "Fallon, what the hell are you doing?"

"Just a little something to remember them by." The hawk-eyed lieutenant patted the lump in his pocket.

Chambers gritted his teeth, his stomach filling with the same acrid revulsion he had felt back in North Africa. "You haven't changed one goddamned bit."

Fallon waved his bloody knife. "Warriors, want a souvenir?"

Sergeant Moose flashed his teeth. "Hell yeah, sir. That gold ring's nice."

"This Kraut sure don't need it." Fallon grabbed the dangling hand that bore a wedding ring.

"Lieutenant, show some respect."

"Respect!" Fallon's camouflage-painted face contorted. "Listen, I'm not your second lieutenant anymore, so you better show *me* some respect. X-2 soldiers fight by a different code than you dogfaces. Moose, explain to Lieutenant Chambers our warrior code."

"Kill the enemy at all costs, sir."

"And what's our bounty?"

"Salvage, sir. We take whatever the hell we want."

Fallon lopped off the German corpse's ring finger and tossed it to Moose. "And *nobody* stands in our way."

Moose held up the bloody stub with the wedding ring and grinned. "Man, that's a fine piece. Thank you, sir."

Chambers said, "We'll address this matter with Captain Wolf."

Fallon chuckled, sliding his brass-handled knife back onto his belt. "Go right ahead. He honors the warrior code. All you have to do is mind your own business, and there won't be any trouble." He pulled out the vodka he'd found in the bunker and took a swig.

Moose grabbed the bottle and chugged it like water from a canteen. "Ah, that's the stuff. Have a victory swig, warriors." The vodka made the circuit of X-2 solders. Fallon took a second swig then offered the bottle to Chambers and Deuce. "Shall we let bygones be bygones?"

"Let's get back, Deuce." Unable to look any of them in the eye, Chambers marched back with Deuce and regrouped with the platoon.

Holding up the field telephone, Corporal Fox approached. "Captain Wolf."

Chambers snatched the phone. "Spear Point."

Wolf's voice crackled. "Report status of missing soldier. Over."

"Soldier found. Situation unstable. Copy?"

"Copy. Change of plans. Spear delayed by minefields. Push to Target 3. Copy?"

"Repeat. Situation unstable. Request to hold position till merger. Over."

"Negative, Spear Point. Push to Target 3. Copy?"

Chambers ground his teeth. He eyed the steep hill above the two bunkers. Thick fog shrouded the forest with bleak uncertainty. *The Krauts have to be close by now.*

Wolf crackled, "Spear Point, I said push to Target 3. Do you copy?"

"Roger." Chambers handed back the phone, cursing under his breath.

Fallon, Moose, and the other X-2 commandos returned with a shaken Corporal Otter. Fallon stuck an unlit cigar into his mouth. "What's the status?"

"LeBlanc's platoon is delayed." Chambers pulled a parka

over his head as the drizzle set in. "Captain wants us to push to Target 3 without 'em. My gut tells me we're better off digging in. And my gut's never wrong."

Fallon stared up at the mist-covered hill. "The plan is to reach Richelskaul at all costs. We stick with the mission."

"This is bullshit." Chambers looked back at his men watching their two lieutenants speaking in heated whispers. He lowered his voice even more. "We have no backup. Odds are we'll either get killed or captured."

Fallon squared up to him. "I am aware of the risks, Chambers. But this mission will be pivotal to ending the war. For that I am willing to risk my life. How about you?"

"Listen here, you know my situation. So don't patronize me. There's no reason to lead a good unit into a massacre. We dig in till Wolf and LeBlanc's squad arrives. I'll take the heat. We'll stand a far better chance with fifty men."

Fallon shook his head. "Captain Wolf and I spent weeks strategizing this attack. The plan is to patrol until we meet resistance or reach Richelskaul. I haven't seen any live Germans yet, have you?" Fallon waved at the men. "Let's push ahead."

The platoon fell into formation behind Lieutenant Fallon.

Chambers stood frozen in anger as each soldier passed by.

Thunder rumbled, quaking the earth beneath his boots. The gray sky darkened like water beneath a frozen lake. The air filled Chambers's mouth with a damp metallic flavor.

Bringing up the rear, Sergeant Mahoney stepped up beside him. "Everything okay, Chambers?"

He looked up at the tall sergeant. "Remind me again what the punishment is for wringing another lieutenant's neck."

"Immediate court-martial. Imprisonment if you're lucky. Execution by firing squad if you're not."

"Right. Thanks, Papa Bear. Keep reminding me."

Chapter 21

Chambers navigated the recon squad through patches of forest, farm groves, and a hazy field dotted with oak trees and bushes. The whole way a question had nagged him. *Where are the Krauts?* He pushed his exhausted legs up and down steep inclines, climbed over one ridge after another. An obstacle course of rocks, logs, coils of barbed concertina wire, and scattered minefields made the hike laborious one moment, treacherous the next. Mud swallowed his boots, filling them with slimy water, his wet socks rubbing his feet raw.

The gray sky rippled with electrical forked tongues. Scattered raindrops pelted their helmets, rolled down their pale faces. At the top of another ridge, the terrain flattened, much to the relief of Chambers's legs. The air filled with sighs from the Lucky Seven. Up here the fog closed in, allowing only ten yards of visibility. The path came to a dead end at an eight-foot-high barbed-wire fence.

"Man alive," Buck whispered. "M'daddy and I used to build barbed-wire fences on our ranch. I ain't never seen nothin' like this."

The fence towered high above their heads. Concertina wire spiraled between posts that crossed one another forming an X. The razor-sharp obstacle course weaved back into the pines twelve layers deep. Every few feet, prongs stabbed upward from a pile of leaves, a Bouncing Betty waiting for some fool to crawl over it. The fence stretched into the forest in both directions. On the other side of the barbed maze, the fog, swirling in a slight breeze, thinned out in places, revealing a cluster of one-story buildings.

Chambers motioned the men to duck down. He indicated the small town beyond the fence. "That should be Richelskaul."

Fallon nodded. "That's it, all right."

"Looks like we already bombed it." Chambers lay flat, scanning with his binoculars. Two sandbag bunkers with MG42 machine guns guarded the entrance into town. A paved road led into the downtown square. Several wooden and brick buildings with pockmarks and shattered windows stood in silence. Many had caved-in roofs. Other buildings had burned to the ground, leaving foundations covered with charred refuse. Twisted metal that was once a car blocked the main road. A ghoulish wind howled through the empty streets. Rain hit the rooftops and made waterfall splashes on the exposed floors. Chambers cocked his head, trying to hear beyond the sounds of falling water. No German voices. No boots crunching over rubble. No truck engines grinding or half-tracks rolling through mud. Not even the domestic bustle of locals. Acid burned Chambers's gut. "Okay, let's dig in right here, watch the place awhile."

"No, we're crossing through this fence," Fallon said.

Chambers shook his head. "It'll take hours to cut through."

"I know of a secret breach farther down the fence."

"What about mines?" Chambers pointed to several mounds of leaves and pine needles.

"The path we carved is clear." Fallon signaled for the field telephone and got on the receiver. Speaking to Wolf with a muffled voice, Fallon watched the village.

Deuce belly-crawled to Chambers. "Sir, guys are wondering what's going on."

"We're reconning this village."

"Yeah, but . . . we've never patrolled this far. Where are the Germans?"

"Deuce, get back with the others."

Fallon wrapped up his phone conversation.

Chambers pulled down his binoculars. "How close are Wolf and LeBlanc?"

"About a half kilometer back and closing."

"Good, they'll be here soon. I insist we recon from here till they catch up. The men are due for a break."

"Orders are to go into the village."

Chambers glanced across at his men lying flat on the grassy hillside, rain forming puddles on their parkas. Exhaling, he turned back to Fallon. "After you, then."

The platoon followed Fallon away from the road, down the fence line into the forest. The endless barbed-wire barricade continued just past the town's last demolished house. The haze thickened, sifting between the trees, clotting up visibility. Fallon crawled through an overgrown clump of evergreens to where the barbed wire had been cut just wide enough to slip through the bottom layer. He lay flat on the damp pine needles and crawled under the fence first. Ten feet in, the white smoke engulfed him completely. One after another his fifteen X-2 commandos squirmed through on their bellies. The Lucky Seven followed.

Chambers carried up the rear. *If the Krauts show up now, we're sitting ducks.* With Mahoney's boots just inches in front of his face, Chambers wormed along cold wet ground. Pine needles covered his hands. Holding the rifle in front of him, he dragged his body with his elbows inch by inch. The barbs scraped his helmet and snagged his parka, so he lowered his face to within an inch of the ground. He got through the maze with only a few minor snags. On the other side, Fallon silently separated the twenty-four soldiers into two squads. Twelve commandos huddled behind the first house that backed up against the woods. Chambers's twelve-man squad lingered behind a cluster of fir trees, aiming their rifles at the silent village.

Fallon's squad ran hunched to the first house, stopped, and

aimed their semiautomatic rifles at an empty street that curved
into the mist. The stout lieutenant searched a row of skeletal
houses—charred and hollow from air bombings—then waved
Chambers's team to advance. Chambers maneuvered his men
along the outskirts of town, past neighborhoods, every house
dark, vacant, and silent except for the hollow whistle of the
wind. The only sign of life in Richelskaul was a spindly gray
cat that darted underneath one of the houses.

The two units ducked behind parked vehicles on a main
road. Chambers searched the perimeter. Vision was good for
twenty yards before the air clotted with gray swirling wisps.
Nothing moved. The road lay deathly quiet, except for the
pitter-patter of rain pelting everything around the squad—
rooftops, parked cars, mailboxes, their helmets and rifles. A
muddy pond had formed where the street dipped, and the
raindrops strafed it with an endless *poppity, poppity.*

The barbed-wire fence opened up for a gated entrance, a
sharp, jagged mouth wide enough for a tank to pass through.
On both sides of the gate, sandbags formed bunkers containing four tripod-mounted MG42 machine guns. There were no
guards in sight.

Chambers duck-walked behind the cars to Fallon's side.
"You sure this is the town where you saw the Germans?"

Fallon nodded.

"Why aren't they manning the gate?"

Fallon shook his head, his gaze fixed on the two bunkers.
"They were here two weeks ago. Four guards posted at those
guns at all times. They let only military vehicles pass through.
We watched them argue with a farmer for a good twenty minutes, before the guards made him turn his truck around."

Chambers peered through his field glasses. "Did they set
up a guardhouse around here?"

"Yeah, that feed store across the road." Fallon pointed to a
gravel lot. "Guards must be inside, waiting out the storm." Beyond the misty curtain a sign with a cow head dangled from a
small brick building.

Chambers surveyed the store through the field glasses. The
door to the feed warehouse was wide open. The darkness within
was black as slate. "How many guards?"

"Eight, maybe ten." Fallon peered through his binoculars. "We'll have to take care of 'em." He searched around, a vein sprouting across his bald cranium. "My squad will take care of the guardhouse. Wolf has already seen the inside. Night guards will be asleep in back. Day guards will most likely be playing cards to the left of the entrance. My men can circle around, sneak through the back door. Chambers, can you handle the street if all hell breaks loose?"

Chambers stared down the main road that vanished into the mist-enshrouded town. "How many Germans are occupying Richelskaul?"

"About a hundred," Fallon answered.

"Tanks?"

"At least one. A Tiger."

Chambers looked from the road to the guardhouse. "No, too risky. You're going in blind, and any racket you make's gonna stir up the hive."

Fallon's face twisted. "Don't be such a coward."

"The plan was to attack with two full platoons, not twenty-four against a hundred men and a tank."

"You're forgetting that sixteen of us are X-2 commandos. Besides, we're following Wolf's direct orders."

"Wolf's not here to assess the situation. If the Germans pin us in here, we're all dead, mission over."

"Christ, get some balls, Chambers, you're fighting with the big boys now. If you want to earn your reward, you have to play by our rules. Rule number one—I take full command during combat. Got it?"

Chambers gritted his teeth.

Fallon screwed a bayonet onto his machine gun. "I'll leave a couple of my men with you, if that makes you feel better. I'll also set up four of my men inside those bunkers. Those MG42s still look hot." He checked his watch. "Shit, we've wasted five minutes. Okay, remain here and take out any Krauts who advance from the town. Think you can handle it?" Fallon grinned, relishing giving orders to his old platoon leader.

"We can hold our own."

"Glad to hear it. We got seconds. We'll get in, get out, then join your squad behind that hill." He pointed to a gnarled cropping of rocks and trees near the barbed fence.

Chambers hurried back to his squad to fill them in.

Fallon's X-2 commandos, all but the two who stayed with Chambers, circled through the trees along the fence. Four of them climbed behind the bulky MG42s and swiveled the gun barrels toward town. Lieutenant Fallon and nine other commandos darted across the main road and disappeared into the trees on the other side. His heart racing, Chambers eyed the feed store. Any moment he expected the German guards to come barreling out, screaming with their submachine guns. But as with the two empty pillboxes, there was nobody home.

Two minutes passed. *Where are the shots?* His fingers gripped the cold metal of his rifle. Time stood still. Chambers studied the faces of his men. Deuce's right eyebrow twitched. Buck's tobacco bulged his left cheek. Finch's eyes blinked. Garcia kissed his cross. Hoffer chewed his sketch pen. Mahoney traded glances with Chambers.

His bandaged hand tingled as if it had fallen asleep. The tingles turned into itching. He scratched his scarred palm, but the pinpricks grew worse. "Jesus."

"What's happening with your hand?" Goldstein asked.

"Nothing. Wound itches like a mother—"

Shots cracked.

Muzzle flares flashed inside the dark warehouse. High-pitched screams rippled through the clapping rain. Shadows moved frantically within the brief strobes made by the firing rifles. An X-2 soldier stumbled out, blood spurting from the stump where his arm should have been. His other arm cradled a pink ropy mess against his torn-open belly. The commando collapsed to the ground.

"Jeepers," Hoffer muttered.

Goldstein bounced up, but Chambers grabbed his elbow and pulled him back behind the car. "Not yet."

"But he's bleeding to death!"

"I said not yet!"

The gunfire inside the warehouse popped like fireworks

inside a metal barrel. It wasn't the adrenaline-charged screaming of battle, but the panicky shrieking brought out by sheer
terror. *Jesus, is that the Germans or the X-2 men!* Then Chambers saw something his mind couldn't grasp—two silver dots
floating within the darkness. They moved together like two
fireflies flying in unison. A second later they were gone, and
Chambers wondered if he'd really seen them.

"We should help them," Corporal Snake said, his knee
bouncing.

"Yeah, what are we waiting for?" said Otter.

"Hold your positions," Mahoney barked.

"Everybody keep your eyes on the road. Finch, Hoffer,
watch our backs." Chambers looked down the main road into
town. So far no sign of German reinforcements. No sounds of
running feet or roaring engines. But they had to have heard
the gunshots. The street would be crawling with Krauts in no
time.

Chambers looked at his squad. "Get ready, men."

Rapid shots within the feed store shattered windows, punctured the tin roof. A flamethrower lit up the interior with a
ten-foot flame, torching a soldier with a steel-kettle helmet. A
rippling sunburst aura outlined his entire body. The torched
German raced out of the warehouse into the downpour, flailing his arms, running toward the road. The rain extinguished
the fire. Black steam rose off his charred skin and uniform.
His eyeballs had burned out, leaving hollow pits.

The X-2 squad manning the MG42s unleashed a barrage
of machine-gun fire. Bullets sparked along the pavement,
knocking the Kraut's body forward.

"Shit, he's still running." Deuce let loose with his BAR.

The rest of Chambers's squad followed suit. Bullets pelted
the Kraut's chest, shoulders, and legs, but he turned down the
main road toward town. More bullets struck his back before
the mist swallowed him up.

"Hold your fire," Chambers said. "He's gone."

The men ceased fire, and the gunshots echoed away, replaced by the din of endless rain. Clouds of cordite smoke
drifted around them, the scent of battle heavy in the air. Empty

cartridge shells rolled off the car hoods and *chinked* to the pavement.

"Did he fall?" Deuce asked.

"Had to," Garcia muttered.

"He's dead, all right." Buck spat tobacco. "No man can survive that many hits."

"Then why'd he keep running?" Deuce asked.

Garcia shook his head. "Unbelievable."

Chambers pointed toward the feed store. "Someone's coming out."

The men turned their rifles back toward the shadows of the open warehouse door.

Two X-2 soldiers emerged. The husky one ranting and cursing appeared to be Sergeant Moose. The tall, leaner one, Fallon, leaned against a tree.

Chambers felt his guts cramp when no one else came out. "Okay, men, listen up." He pointed to the fog swirling over the main road. "Corporal Otter, Garcia, go make sure that German's dead, and then hustle back. Be wary of Krauts on the move. Everyone else follow me."

Garcia and Otter split off down the road, disappearing into the vapor. Meanwhile Chambers led his men across the main road toward the feed store. Goldstein got there first, leaping down to aid the X-2 soldier missing an arm. The soldier named Corporal Crow lay in a crimson puddle, his intestines coiled around his midsection like a pile of stillborn snakes. His eyes stared blankly at the dark gray sky. Goldstein closed the lids and mouthed a prayer.

Chambers caught up with them. "What the hell happened?"

Fallon remained against the tree, his face ashen.

Moose paced. Rainwater dribbled down the sergeant's Neanderthal face. "Is that Kraut dead! I'll burn him to fucking hell if he ain't."

Deuce shrugged. "We shot him full of holes then lost him in the fog. Gotta be dead by now."

"I don't know how he got away." Moose wiped rainwater from his face. "We shot him a dozen times ourselves."

Chambers watched the surrounding woods, his submachine gun tucked under his armpit. "Where are the others?"

Fallon motioned back to the warehouse door. A black curtain of darkness cloaked the entrance of the feed store. From within drifted the stench of blood and released bowels.

"I'll show you." Moose motioned to the corporal who had stayed with Chambers's squad. "Snake, take point."

Goldstein followed. "I'm going, too."

Corporal Snake eased toward the shadowy doorway. Moose, Chambers, and Goldstein followed. The four soldiers crossed the threshold into a gloom so foul it stung Chambers's eyes. Thick fetid air went down his throat as if someone had gagged him with a rope. His stomach retched. He concentrated on the darkness, listening for the cries of the wounded. But there were no cries—only the eerie echoing of boots off the wet, sticky concrete floor.

Flashlight beams stabbed the darkness, sweeping over feed bags that had been ripped open like gut wounds, spilling out corn and oats. Many bags were splattered with blood. Greasy reddish black puddles stained the floor.

A few paces ahead, Corporal Snake yelled, "Oh God," then puked.

They caught up with Snake, who was standing ankle deep in human refuse. First their flashlights located a severed arm, the hand still gripping the trigger of a rifle. Then a helmet came into view. Strapped inside was a head trailing red sinews and a shattered neck bone. All around lay the remains of eight of the X-2 commandos who had followed Fallon into the warehouse. They looked as if they had fallen through a fan blade. There was not one dead German among them.

Moose cursed and kicked a helmet and sent it banging against the tin walls.

"What the hell happened?" Chambers asked.

A blue flame glowed from Moose's flamethrower. "Can't say exactly. I was last to enter. The guys ahead of me started shooting. Then they were screaming, and all I could see were body parts flying."

Chambers's beam panned across the strewn bodies. "How many Germans were in here?"

"All I saw was the one I torched." Moose stepped over to a

mutilated torso. A long steel object was jutting from the rib cage. He pulled it out with a wet sucking sound. "And the only weapon that Kraut had was this." He raised a saber to the flashlight beams, the curved blade dripping with the blood of his fallen comrades.

Chapter 22

A dismal gray cloud hung over Richelskaul. Rain poured endlessly. Half the platoon hovered inside the two bunkers at the gate's entrance. Four X-2 soldiers stood behind the German MG42s aimed toward the village, alongside the bazooka team. Chambers's squad lay just outside the fence in foxholes, their rifle barrels poking through the barbed wire.

Chambers sat inside one of the bunkers, his back against a wall of sandbags. Water dripped over his parka hood, a cold spray constantly hitting his numb cheeks. His fist squeezed a ball of clay. His guts twisted into a mass of knots as he watched the fog.

Garcia, where are you? The Mexican kid and the X-2 corporal named Otter had not returned from their hunt for the maimed German. Thirty minutes had passed, and Chambers feared the worst. He glanced through the barbed wire at his men and they all looked away. Sergeant Mahoney was the only one who held his gaze. Papa Bear raised a thick eyebrow. Chambers shrugged and looked down at his hands. One hand continued to squeeze the ball of mud. The other, the one with the bandage, nagged him with a relentless itch. He peeled back the bandage, eager to scratch the scar. His fingernails stopped short. *I don't remember that.* To the left

of the Star of David was a marking that resembled the letter *H*.

He reached into his pocket and pulled out the cross Murdock had given him. Etched into the bronze surface was the same letter.

"What's that?" Fallon motioned to the cross.

"Nothing." Chambers put the pendant away and resealed the bandage.

One of the X-2 sentries whispered, "Look, someone's coming."

The clack of rifles echoed along the fence line. A lone figure carrying a rifle ran out of the mist like a wraith, moving directly toward the bunkers. The silhouette's poncho flapped in the rainstorm. A GI helmet bobbled on his head.

Chambers said, "Don't shoot. It's Garcia."

The Mexican soldier leaped over the wall of sandbags, gasping.

Lieutenant Fallon grabbed him. "Where's Corporal Otter?"

Garcia shook his head. "I . . . lost him in the fog. One minute he was right behind me, next he was gone."

"Christ, you left my man behind?"

"I tried to find him, sir. But you can't see worth shit in there. I figured maybe he backtracked here."

"God damn it!" Fallon glared at Chambers. "Don't ever send one of my men off again!"

Chambers scanned the town, hoping to see a second soldier running toward them.

Garcia lowered his head. "Sorry, guys. I screwed up."

"No, it was my mistake." Chambers crouched beside Garcia. "Did you see any Krauts?"

He shook his head. "Town's dead as a graveyard."

"What about the one we shot?" Chambers asked.

"Never found him."

"Didn't you follow his blood trail?"

"He didn't leave one, sir. I swear there was no sign of him anywhere."

Minutes passed like hours. The impenetrable skies continued to pelt the fifteen platoon members with raindrops the size of pebbles. Sitting idle made the cold dampness seep into the bones. Chambers felt as if his entire skeleton had turned to ice. His chest ached for sending Otter into the village. *Lieutenant Grim Reaper strikes again.*

A strange ululation reverberated from the opposite side of the town.

He looked up from the clay snake that he had rolled between his palms. The distant echoes sounded off in an even cadence. Heavy bells, with a deep resonating *clang . . . clang . . . clang . . . clang.*

Eleven clangs in a row. Eleven hundred hours.

As the sounds trailed back into the cadence of the falling rain, Chambers stared at the ghost town. Nothing moved within it.

Corporal Fox, sitting in a corner with the radio, came to life. "Sir, reinforcements have arrived."

"Where?"

Fox indicated the tree-dotted field on the outskirts of town. Chambers scanned the perimeter with his field glasses. The fog in that direction had cleared a bit. About fifty yards away, where thick fir trees bordered the field, GI soldiers moved within the gray gloom. First five, then ten, then more than twenty foot soldiers setting up a line of rifles, bazookas, and mortar. *About damned time.*

Fox put his hand over the radio's microphone. "Lieutenant LeBlanc wants to know if the field's clear to send over a relief unit."

"Tell them to tiptoe and stay close to the trees." *Wonder how Paul's holding up.*

Fox relayed the message in radio code. Within seconds, a squad sprinted across the field, ducking behind bushes and trees along the way. Reaching the town's gated entrance, the replacement soldiers filled in the gaps along the fence line.

A sergeant leaped into the bunker. "Captain wants to see Lieutenants Hawk and Chambers."

Chambers turned to Fallon. "After you."

◆ ◆ ◆

Chambers climbed down into a muddy crater surrounded by fallen trees. The camouflage netting thrown over the top gave the sense of being inside a spider's den. The shelter filtered out most of the rain, reducing it to sporadic drips. He joined three officers sitting around a rainproof map—Lieutenants LeBlanc and Fallon, and Captain Wolf. Shadows filled the hollows of their faces, making them look like skeletons with helmets.

Holding the German saber in his hands, the captain glared at Fallon and Chambers. "How can one German kill eight of our commandos?"

Fallon shook his head. "We're not sure how it happened. He just kept attacking from the darkness with *that . . .*"

"I only saw the aftermath," Chambers said. "The entire squad was sliced all to hell."

Wolf frowned. "There had to be more than one German."

"We only saw the one," Fallon said.

"Chambers, what was *your* squad doing while my men were getting slaughtered?"

"Defending the road in case reinforcements arrived."

"And did they?"

"No."

Wolf shook his head. "Eight X-2 soldiers dead and one missing. Well, men, this is a real mess. You were not supposed to split up." The captain pinched the bridge of his nose.

Chambers's jaw tightened. He scooped a ball of muddy clay from the escarpment and rolled it between his hands. "How many men do we have?"

"I brought thirty," LeBlanc answered. "With your platoon that makes a little over forty."

Chambers sighed. "The plan was to attack the town with two solid platoons."

"We'll just have to be efficient, won't we?" Fallon half-grinned, the scarred side of his face remaining stiff.

"There is definitely something different about Richelskaul," Captain Wolf said. "By your descriptions, it sounds like the Germans have already pulled out. Maybe they left a few guards and snipers, but I doubt there's a full company. Otherwise they would have retaliated by now."

"My gut tells me different," Chambers said. "I think they're nestled in there, waiting for us to enter the town."

"Like a trap?" LeBlanc asked.

"Yeah, the unmanned guard posts are just to lure us in."

Fallon said, "Thank you for that insightful report, Chambers, but we make decisions based on gathered intelligence, not gut feelings."

"Yeah, your decision to go into that warehouse was really intelligent."

"Fuck you."

"Enough, both of you!" Wolf pulled out an aerial photo of Richelskaul. "We need to find out if this town is still occupied. Chambers, I'm sending your platoon in to recon."

Fallon's brow furrowed. "I'm going with him, aren't I?"

"No, all X-2 soldiers are staying back here with me."

The mud ball oozed between Chambers's fingers. "Sir, I thought we were all supposed to patrol together."

"The plan has changed. You can take one of Lieutenant LeBlanc's squads with you. Lieutenants Hawk, LeBlanc, round up another eight men."

LeBlanc patted Chambers on the shoulder. "I'll send my best squad."

Left alone in the spider's den with Wolf, Chambers leaned back against the muddy escarpment and lit up a cigarette. "So what's in this for you, Captain?"

Wolf looked up from the aerial photo. "What do you mean?"

"This love affair you got going with Fallon. I know what gives him a hard-on, but why are *you* so damned eager to capture Richelskaul?"

"Just doing my duty."

"Duty, my ass."

Wolf's face shifted from a determined captain to a man on the verge of rage. "Chambers, you know all that is necessary to carry out this mission." He glanced down at the map, unable to hold eye contact. "Now, your men will follow the main stree—"

Chambers grabbed his wrist. "At least answer me this, Captain, why is a Czech mercenary from Prague working with the OSS?"

"My reasons are classified. If you're not willing to work with me, then say the word, and I will send Lieutenant Le-Blanc in your place."

Chambers took a long drag from his cigarette. "All right, Wolf. I'm in." He pressed his cigarette into the muddy wall and leaned over the aerial photo of Richelskaul.

Chapter 23

"Best of luck to you, padna," whispered Paul LeBlanc at the front gate bunkers as Chambers's platoon set off into the mist. "We got your backs." The sentries staying behind looked clearly relieved they hadn't been chosen.

Chambers's reconnaissance platoon of sixteen GIs walked single file down the main street. The buildings loomed overhead, dark, gutted-out hulks in the storm. Rain streamed off shingled roofs, turning the road into a muddy river. Chambers gave hand signals for two privates to take point. His squad, wide-eyed and wary, crept with their backs against the buildings. Soldiers jerked rifles into broken windows and open doorways. They reached the town square, where buildings bordered a park. The mist closed in around them. Pools of smoke eddied around their boots. Rumbles echoed in the distance.

Finch nudged Chambers. "Did you hear that?"

He strained to hear beyond the din of the storm. "Could be thunder."

"No, sir, that was a gunshot."

"I heard it, too," Garcia whispered. "Came from behind us."

Lieutenant LeBlanc's platoon?

From the town's entrance, gunshots grew in number, sounding like a fireworks show.

"There goes our surprise," Garcia muttered to Buck. The rancher nodded and spat tobacco.

"Any votes for coming back when it's sunny?" Deuce chuckled.

"Quiet. Everybody stay focused." With visibility reduced to a matter of feet, Chambers led his unit through the gauze-thick haze, keeping close to the building facades. His bandaged hand tingled again with a thousand tiny pinpricks. *Jesus, what's going on?* A kid yelped somewhere down the chain of soldiers.

"Papa Bear, take lead." Chambers moved down the column, each man appearing and disappearing in the fog as he passed. At the end of the line a private mumbled frantically to a sergeant.

"What's all the commotion?" Chambers asked.

"Reese disappeared." The kid's teeth chattered as if the damp air had dropped to subzero.

Chambers stared back into the mist. It swallowed up the street behind them. "Where to?"

"Don't know, sir. Reese was bringing up the tail. I heard him grunt. When I looked back he was gone."

Chambers herded his platoon around him. He had come in here with sixteen. Only thirteen were present. "Who else is missing?"

"I don't see Davis," one of LeBlanc's men said.

"Jonesy is missing, too," said another.

The gathered soldiers eyed the surrounding fog like lost lambs wary of circling wolves. Chambers looked to a stocky soldier from LeBlanc's platoon. "Sergeant, take two men, backtrack twenty paces. See if our missing boys are still on the main road. Remember the code word so you don't get mistaken for Germans. Find them and hustle back."

The sergeant grabbed two privates and disappeared into the fog.

The rest of the platoon pushed forward and soon reached an area where German military vehicles were parked haphaz-

ardly along the square. Bullet holes riddled the windshields.
One car had crashed through a store window. Chambers's men
peered into the vehicles as they passed. No signs of anyone
dead or alive. It looked as if every inhabitant had simply vanished. The fog cleared a few yards ahead, and several large
water-filled craters came into view. Aerial bombs had wreaked
havoc on the main street. What looked to be an arm was jutting up from the water of one crater, stiff fingers raking at the
mottled gray sky.

The men eased up to the crater. Raindrops rippled the dark
murky water. Chambers glanced in every direction, then back
down at the red face floating just beneath the surface.

"Another dead Kraut?" Mahoney asked.

"Naw, one of our boys." Buck dipped his hand into the water and pulled out a helmet labeled OTTER.

"No way," Garcia said.

"Pull him out," Chambers barked.

Buck and Mahoney hauled out the corpse. Corporal Otter's face and chest had been hacked away to an unrecognizable pulp. The eyes were missing.

"Jesus . . ." Garcia kissed the cross around his neck.

Goldstein stepped forward, putting a hand on Garcia's
shoulder. "It's not your fault."

The chaplain gave Chambers a suspicious look. "What do
you make of this, Lieutenant?"

"We're not alone." It felt like insects were burrowing into
his scarred hand. He gathered the platoon. "Everybody listen
up. Apparently we got Krauts hiding in here. So keep tight to
the man in front of you. Nobody wanders off."

More shots fired in the distance, *pop, pop, pop-pop-pop*,
closer this time, just beyond the barbed wire at the edge of
town.

Deuce looked back, whispered, "That's LeBlanc's platoon."

"We're under attack!" a soldier's voice cracked.

Sergeant Mahoney shook him. "Keep quiet."

"Screw this recon shit," Deuce whispered, gripping his
BAR.

Small-arms fire continued to echo at the outskirts of town.

Chambers grabbed the radio receiver from Garcia and called Wolf. "Spearhead calling Spear, what's happening? Over."

Wolf's voice crackled, "Meeting resistance. Over."

"This town is a deathtrap. We're coming back to help you. Copy?"

"Negative, situation under control. Maintain reconnaissance. Find a refuge. We will rendezvous there. Copy?"

"Roger."

"We heading back?" Deuce asked.

Chambers shook his head. "We're doing what we came here to do. Stay focused." A sudden hunger overtook his body with an intense shudder. *Stay focused yourself, Chambers.* He searched the dark, shattered windows of a hotel. "In there." He followed Deuce and Garcia into the ruins. Dust-coated rubble littered the lobby. A ceiling had fallen through, and he could see up into the second floor. They checked the first-floor rooms for Krauts.

Chambers ordered, "Fan out." Half the platoon moved into the kitchen, while Chambers led another group through the lobby and dining room. Every downstairs room came up empty. He started up the winding wood staircase, the stairs creaking beneath his boots. His hand tingled again, the pinpricks growing more intense with each step. Chambers paused midway, observing the darkness at the top of the stairs.

"Sir, I'm feeling something," Goldstein said from the bottom of the stairs. "Dear God, you have to see this."

Chambers backed down the stairs, the tingles fading as he reached the bottom. "What?"

Goldstein looked up from his palm. "When you climbed up those stairs, the cross on my hand began to glow."

"Chaplain, I don't have time for religious bull—"

From inside the kitchen came screams of gut-wrenching terror. Gunfire sounded throughout the hotel.

Heart hammering, Chambers glanced around. Several men raced out the door into the thick fog. Shots cracked along the street. Men yelled at phantom soldiers.

At the top of the stairs, muzzle flashes lit up the darkness, shredding the walls above Chambers and Goldstein. A chandelier crashed to the floor behind them.

"Move, move, move!" Chambers shoved the medic out a busted window. Outside, the storm concealed all but three men. Garcia, Deuce, and a kid from LeBlanc's platoon shot wildly. The others vanished into the smoke, including Goldstein. A man screamed and was cut off. More screams echoed from somewhere. Chambers grabbed his three visible soldiers and charged toward the battle cries. Dropped rifles and helmets littered the pavement.

Garcia stumbled over a severed arm. "Oh, Jesus."

Deuce picked up a baseball floating in a red puddle. "Buck!"

"Quiet." Chambers pulled Deuce and Garcia behind the blackened remains of a car. The blood-stained road seemed to be spinning, spinning, rain falling, choking, clotted gray air swirling around him, blinding him. *The platoon's falling apart. Just like North Africa.*

Deuce pressed up against him. He flinched with every distant explosion. "They're slaughtering us!"

The mist eddied around them.

The kid from LeBlanc's platoon sobbed. "I don't see anybody."

Garcia whispered, "What do we do, sir?"

"Follow me." The four soldiers darted across the sidewalk, crouching in a half-open doorway. Chambers nudged open the door with his rifle. It creaked on rusty hinges. Shadows draped the ruins of a tavern. Long tables with benches filled the room. A long bar with stools stretched across one wall. "Inside."

Deuce and LeBlanc's soldier entered first, followed by Garcia. The other members of the Lucky Seven were nowhere to be seen.

The fog pressed against Chambers. He jerked his rifle in every direction. His palm erupted with a burning sensation, and he ripped off the bandage. The cross-shaped scar was *glowing*. He watched incredulously as another letter, *V,* mysteriously formed on the bottom edge of the cross.

A baritone voice screamed behind the wall of smoke.

"Mahoney!" Chambers started to look for him when an unearthly shriek echoed from inside the tavern. Deuce and

Garcia screamed. Bullets shattered the windows above Chambers's head. He hit the ground. Heart slamming against his chest, he aimed his Thompson through the doorway. Halfway inside, blood began streaking the wood floor. The bloody trail led to a large German shadow dragging a body into the darkness.

Chapter 24

Chambers fired his Thompson, hitting the German silhouette dead center. The enemy stumbled back against the bar, releasing a banshee scream. His machine-gun fire arced wildly, shattering a mirror. Chambers pounded his chest with lead, and the German dropped to the floor, dead, with a heavy thud.

No, not dead!

Incredibly, the shadow rose from the ground, sweeping the room with glowing silver eyes. He shrieked and raised his machine gun. Muzzle flashes lit up the darkness in short bursts. A chain of bullets sprayed across the tavern.

Chambers flattened against the floor as slugs punched holes into the table above him.

Move your ass! He elbow-crawled between the bench tables, heart smacking his sternum. He could see only parts of the Kraut's silhouette now—knee-high jackboots, ammo belt, large gray hands gripping the gun. Muzzle flashes reflected in the German's eyes. Not eyes. *Goggles.* A gas mask covered his broad face. A steel-kettle helmet crowned his enormous head. A Nazi Frankenstein. His submachine gun sprayed a chain of fury across the tavern. Ceiling tiles and glass rained down. Lanterns crashed onto tables. Somewhere in the darkness, Chambers's soldiers wailed and returned fire. The storm of hot metal shredded tables and benches into splinters. He pulled his helmet down over his eyes.

The submachine gun clicked empty, then clacked to the wood floor. The German drew a saber from a scabbard, metal swishing the air. Chambers's skin prickled as he heard a growl that sounded like an enraged Rottweiler.

He searched the shadows for his rifle. The jackboots marched toward him, weaving between the tables. The blade tapped across the tabletops. *Tap! Tap! Tap! Tap!* Chambers scurried on hands and knees. He skidded across a slippery puddle. Froze. Ahead lay the boots of the GI dragged into the gloom. Gray slime that smelled of swamp mud covered his ankles. The ooze blotched his uniform and the bloody stump where his head should have been.

Christ! Chambers scurried backward, gagging. *Is that Deuce?* An unearthly scream echoed behind him. The saber chopped at the tables. Wood splinters shot into his neck like tiny darts. He found his Thompson beneath a bench. He leaped up and shot the German point blank in the stomach, chest, and throat. His broad body stumbled backward. He dropped his sword, arms spinning like a windmill, and crashed through a swinging back-room door. Chambers let go the trigger and caught his breath. The door swung on rusty hinges. *Squeak-squeak. Squeak-squeak.* He searched the gloom. *No other Krauts in the tavern. Just the bastard who took out three of my men.* Something growled inside the back room.

Chambers eased toward the door. Behind it came a rustling. Pots clanged. The thump of boots. A door slammed. Pushing the door inward with the barrel of his Thompson, Chambers expected to catch the boot of the dead Kraut. But the door swung open fully. The body was gone. The back door hung open. A dark, rain-drenched alley lay beyond.

At the front end of the tavern, Garcia cried, "Jesus, man! Somebody get me a medic!"

Chambers followed the moans and spotted his man leaning against a front wall. He knelt in front of Garcia. "Where were you hit?"

"Leg and hand. Bastard blew my middle finger off!" He cradled a shattered hand. "Christ, it hurts."

"Garcia, stay put. I'm getting help."

"Did ya waste him?" Deuce crawled out of the shadows. Relief flooded Chambers.

"Yeah. You hit?"

"No, got lucky."

"Stay with Garcia." Chambers ran to the door. "Medic!"

Outside gunshots ruptured the steady din of the rain. Windows shattered. Wood splintered. Rock dust rose and merged with the fog. Soldiers ran through the mist. A baritone voice yelled, "Find cover!"

"In the tavern!" Chambers hollered.

"Lieutenant!" Buck and Mahoney emerged alive from the smoke curtain to Chambers's surprise. They fired at an unseen enemy across the street. German bullets sprayed the road, whizzing by their heads, pinging off walls and doors. Mahoney zigzagged across the road.

"Get in here!"

Buck and Mahoney dashed into the tavern.

Lead hail pocked the walls.

"We stirred up a Kraut's nest!" Mahoney busted out a window, firing back.

"They're advancing from behind us."

Buck stabbed his gun barrel through a window. "They've blocked the entrance."

"Keep a steady base fire. I'll find others." Chambers peered out the entrance. A stick grenade exploded in the street. A running GI rolled flat on his back. The kid cried, squirming in a puddle of his own blood. Goldstein flew to his aid.

B-r-r-r-r-p-p-p. A burp gun's rapid burst sparked the pavement around them. Goldstein ducked while hoisting the wounded soldier off the ground.

Chambers fired at the opposite building. "In here!"

The medic lugged his human cargo across the street. Muzzle flashes lit up in the windows behind them. Bullets snaked across the pavement and punctured red holes along the injured soldier's back and chest. He slumped against Goldstein.

"Leave him!" Chambers pulled the medic out of the gun-fire.

Water beaded Goldstein's face and wire-rimmed glasses. He grabbed his chest, gasping. "I almost . . ."

"Garcia needs you." Chambers pointed to the bleeding soldier.

Boots clumped across the veranda. Bullets barraged the tavern as Finch entered with Hoffer.

"Guys, give us a hand!" Buck yelled.

The platoon fired at shadows that weaved in and out of the mist like wraiths.

Hoffer screamed, firing round after round.

An 88 screeched and blasted the building next door.

Garcia flinched. "What's happening?"

Goldstein wrapped a bandage around Garcia's hand. "Stay down!"

Chambers got on the field phone. "Spear, do you copy? . . . Spear, do you copy?"

Fallon answered. "Copy."

"Spearhead pinned by heavy resistance! Need backup! Repeat—need backup!"

"Hold your position."

Shrapnel peppered the front door. *Pop! Pop! Pop!* He ducked behind a table. "Our position's fucked! We need backup! *Now!*"

"We got our own problems." Fallon's voice grew choppy. "You—hav—t—hold—y—r—own!"

Chambers shouted, "Send a team in here now or we're dead!"

Static filled the receiver. Chambers hurled the radio. He clenched both fists. *Hold it together. You're in charge here.* He tried to remember how Murdock would act in this situation. Chambers inhaled, exhaled, and lifted his shaking wrist. The silver watch ticked away the seconds. Thirteen twenty-eight hours.

Another 88 rocketed through the air, and a deafening blast jolted the tavern's roof. Burning two-by-fours crashed down on tables. Smoke and fire spread across the tavern.

"Retreat!" Coughing, eyes burning, Chambers herded his

men toward the back. The Lucky Seven and Goldstein escaped through the back-room door into a narrow alley. Turning onto a side street, they merged with the X-2 squad running with Wolf and Fallon. LeBlanc ran farther back, barking orders at his platoon. A German half-track charged around a corner. Krauts riding in back unleashed raging machine-gun fire. The closest GIs fell over like bowling pins.

Wolf screamed. "Get off this street!"

The platoons scattered between buildings. Some men fled into the woods.

A mortar burst ignited a rooftop into flames. Gun smoke billowed through the thick mist. Rain came down in torrents, dousing the fires.

"This way!" Chambers screamed at his platoon. "Move, move, move!" He charged forward through the smoke and drizzle. Ducking behind some brick ruins, he waved his men over.

"Krauts!" Mahoney shouted.

"Take cover!" Chambers aimed his Tommy gun over the chest-high wall. *Ra-ta-ta-ta-tat!*

A dozen German silhouettes emerged from the buildings, shooting submachine guns.

Bullets strafed his platoon. Bloodied bodies littered the street. The ones who made it filled in around Chambers. "Base fire everybody! Stay sharp!" His Tommy gun spat out another round, and emptied. "Damn it!" He felt his pockets for a fresh magazine.

"Here!" Sergeant Mahoney tossed one of his. "Got a plan, sir?"

"Working on it!" Chambers slammed the fresh magazine home.

Mahoney fired over the wall. "Better hurry!"

"Where's LeBlanc's platoon?"

"Crossing now."

Chambers peered over the wall. *Come on, buddy.* Lieutenant LeBlanc's platoon raced across the street. Behind them dozens more German shadows advanced from the mist. A metal storm chopped down several of LeBlanc's men. Only half of them made it to the ruins.

"Fire! Fire! Fire!" Chambers's platoon shot from one advancing German to another. The enemy soldiers reflected bullets like armor-plated tanks.

"We might as well be tossing rocks!" Deuce spat out a damp cigar. "Screw this! I'm outta here!" He fled to the back of the group.

"Keep firing, soldiers!" Chambers spread cover fire to his right. He knocked several shadows backward, but more emerged. The enemy closed within fifty yards. A tank shell blasted a nearby wall. Dust drifted over the platoon, filling Chambers's mouths with grit. His men fired madly at the fog.

Goldstein, up to his elbows in blood, hurriedly patched the wounded.

"Chaplain, get your head down, damn it!" Chambers hovered behind the wall, his back glued to the flagstones. Metal chipped the stones above his helmet. He turned to the wounded lieutenant next to him. "LeBlanc, where's the rest of your platoon?"

"Lost 'em!" LeBlanc gripped a bleeding hand. "We got eighteen between us."

Chambers glanced at his men. Battered and bloodied, their young faces looked to him imploringly.

Artillery shells shrieked through the village. A building one street over exploded into a spray of rubble. Sergeant Mahoney screamed. "They're closing in!"

Ahead stretched the Hürtgen Forest, black pines stabbing upward through the fog. "Mahoney, get these men into the woods. We're falling back."

The bear-sized sergeant's voice boomed, "Let's roll, boys! Move, move, move!"

Chambers stayed back. *Come on. Everybody lives.*

Behind his platoon, a gas station disintegrated in a fiery *whooooosh!* The soldiers ducked to avoid fireballs of flying shrapnel. A second explosion released a dragon's breath of fire. Scorching heat knocked Lieutenant Chambers to the ground. A heavy weight crashed on top of him.

Gasping, he wiped mud and pine needles off his face. Rain drenched the blaze around him. He tried to move, but a dead

soldier pinned his torso and legs. Beside him lay another dead
GI, a charred face staring with one drooping eye. Chambers
scanned the wooded clearing at the smoldering bodies piled
on top of one another.

Jesus, they're all dead!

Chapter 25

The ground quaked beneath the mechanical roar of tank tracks. The body pinning Chambers's legs suddenly moved. A hand gripped his thigh. "Oh man," LeBlanc groaned.

"Paul, you all right?"

"My back. Christ, it burns."

The back of LeBlanc's shirt was burned away, the flesh charred. He started to rise, but Chambers held him. "Stay down."

"Jesus," LeBlanc moaned.

"Shhh." Gritting his teeth, Chambers felt around for his rifle. It lay beneath a pile of branches, out of reach. German shadows entered his peripheral vision. He froze. "Play dead." Flat on his stomach, eyelids at half-mast, he lay amid the scattered bodies. Rain pelted his face. LeBlanc's hands, clinging to Chambers's legs, trembled. *Please, Paul, just play dead like me*. Chambers's blood ran cold as shadows wearing gas masks packed around them.

A stout Nazi wearing a black uniform stepped forward, the buglike eyes of his gas mask surveying the piled up bodies. He pulled a sword from his belt. LeBlanc clutched Chambers's back and screamed in agony as the blade stabbed several times. LeBlanc fell limp. The sword released with a wet sucking sound. A boot rolled him off Chambers's legs. The stout Nazi circled, jackboots standing on either side of Chambers's head. He held his breath. A short life of twenty-two years flashed before his eyes, along with so many regrets, the biggest being he would never see Eva again. *No*, he decided in a split second. *Jack Chambers doesn't surrender to death. Especially not to these Nazi bastards.*

He watched the Nazi standing over him. The blood-dripping sword aimed up at the charcoal sky. Gunshots echoed from the woods, striking the Germans. The pack stumbled backward. Bullets zippered up the chest and throat of the Nazi and knocked him flat on his back. A second later he got back on his feet. He felt the dark, gaping holes in his chest and neck, and then, as if unaffected by his wounds, pointed his sword into the woods. The German silhouettes charged into the trees, firing their submachine guns.

The earth under Chambers spun like a mad carnival ride. He remained frozen amid the pile of dead soldiers, not sure if they were X-2s, LeBlanc's men, or part of the Lucky Seven. When the shooting faded, he opened his eyes fully and surveyed the village. Flames consumed the gas station whole. More explosions whooshed into the fir trees. A tank rumbled by, its squeaky tracks crunching over bricks and discarded weapons.

He squirmed across the pine-needle carpet to LeBlanc. The Cajun stared back with blank eyes. The pit of Chambers's stomach went hollow. He gripped his friend's shoulders as if to shake life back into him. "Damn it, you son of a bitch!" LeBlanc's head lolled to one side. Tears whelping at the corners of his eyes, Chambers dug into his best friend's shirt and pulled out the farewell letter he had written to Rose and his parents. "I'll get it to them." He sat in a daze as the drizzle formed rings in the mud puddles.

In the dark husk of a building sparks lit up. A German machine gun fired in a wild arc across the fallen bodies. Bullets kicked up the mud around Chambers. Yanking his Tommy gun loose from the fallen branches, he belly-crawled through the bodies. Strafing bullets snaked along the ground in hot pursuit. He rolled behind a tree, bark and fir branches snapping all around him. He waited for the machine-gun fire to end. Then he ran through the forest until the battle zone echoed farther and farther behind.

Chambers stumbled and collapsed onto one knee, leaning on his rifle for support. He sat back against a tree, snorting a wet sigh of relief. The Hürtgen Forest remained a dripping green cavern, quiet except for the occasional distant gunshot. The impenetrable gray fog ruled the trees. His hands trembled. *Are they all dead?*

Reaper. Reaper. Reaper.

Chambers glanced around at the shadowy trees.

You boys better hope you don't get Lieutenant Reaper's platoon. You get Grim, you're good as dead, chum. Good as dead.

"This wasn't my fault."

The branches to his left slapped together. Boots splashed through mud. Chambers pressed the butt of his Thompson against his shoulder, struggling to hold the barrel steady. He leaned against the tree for support. The branches parted. A single shadow emerged from the mist. Chambers's finger rubbed the trigger. "Flash!"

"Thunder!" The soldier wore an X-2 helmet. "Don't shoot!" Captain Wolf stopped in the clearing. "Thank God I found you."

"Back away." Chambers kept his rifle aimed. "Get out of my sight."

Wolf raised his hands. "Easy, Chambers . . . I am leading you out of here."

"Forget it."

"Look, what happened back there—"

"I think my men are dead."

Wolf knelt in front of the barrel. "No, not everybody. I found your sergeant and a few others." Lightning cracked the sky, flashing across Wolf's haggard face. "They're waiting for us."

German submachine guns fired from somewhere nearby.

"For God's sake, Chambers. Just lower your weapon and follow me."

Running feet and snapping branches echoed just beyond the trees, accompanied by the growl of something rabid.

Chambers followed Wolf along a creek littered with fallen logs and slippery rocks. Freezing water filled Chambers's boots as they ran upstream. They reached a low concrete bridge that resembled a cave in the thick foliage. Underneath huddled a dozen GI soldiers. The gloom masked their faces. Buck greeted them first. "Chambers, I'll be damned."

Mahoney bear-hugged him. "Thank God, you made it!"

Chambers lay flat against the cold culvert wall, exhaled. He pulled off his helmet and wiped water from his face. His body shivered. His ears throbbed from artillery fire and near-miss bullets.

Deuce crawled up beside him, a damp cigar wedged in his gap-toothed grin. "Chambers, I knew ya was still alive! Just knew it. Told ya those bastards can't stop the Lucky Seven."

"Everybody made it?"

"Yep, every damned one of us. Lost all of LeBlanc's men, though."

Chambers scanned the silhouettes crouched on the concrete walls that ramped up the hills on both sides of the creek. A few of the X-2 men had made it here as well. The narrow stream trickled at their feet. "Where are we?"

Mahoney answered, "I think we ran east."

Wolf crouched beside Chambers. "Southeast. Above us is a road we followed from the village. It continues farther into the woods. It's best we head along that route."

"What about the Krauts?" Chambers asked.

Mahoney wiped down his rifle. "We shook them for the moment. I got Buck watching the road."

Chambers looked up at the two-lane bridge spanning ten feet above their heads.

"The Germans aren't far behind. We should keep moving."

Wolf sat up. "We're better off staying here for now. It at least gives us a vantage point."

Chambers shook his head. "They find us under here, we're trapped. All they have to do is toss one grenade. Let's keep moving."

"No, we're staying put." Lieutenant Fallon emerged from the shadows. "Captain says when it's time to move again. Discussion over."

Chambers glared.

Hoffer pushed through the bodies. "Chambers, come quick. The medic needs you."

Chambers followed Hoffer along the slanted culvert wall to where Goldstein was fighting to save two wounded soldiers. One of the X-2 corporals appeared already dead, the victim of a nasty chest wound. The other man hit closer to home—Miguel Garcia. Blood spurted from his body, running down the wall. He hyperventilated. "M-morphine. N-need morphine."

Goldstein ripped open Garcia's pant leg. He snapped his fingers. "Chambers, get me bandages and morphine needles!"

"Where are they?"

"In my pack! Hurry!"

Chambers rummaged through the med pack. The group of soldiers hovered over them. He elbowed them back. "Give us some room here!"

Goldstein poured a canteen over Garcia's thigh. The red meaty hole filled with water, flushing out blood clots and bone fragments.

"*Dios mío,* it hurts. Oh, Maria."

"Stay with us, Garcia." Chambers handed Goldstein needles and bandages. Several items dropped into the stream.

The medic jabbed morphine needles into Garcia's good leg. "Chambers, tear off a strip from his pant leg."

Chambers's pocketknife sliced the fabric of the bloody pant leg.

Garcia stared with glossy eyes. "I don't wanna die. Maria needs me, *mis niños* . . . I never even seen my baby, Lucilia. *Jesús, no puedo morir.*" He crossed himself.

Goldstein pushed up his glasses with a bloody wrist. "You're not gonna die, Garcia."

Deuce gripped his buddy's hand. "Goldstein's gonna patch ya up good as new. You'll see little Lucilia soon enough."

"Gracias, Deuce . . ." Garcia managed a smile.

Goldstein pressed down on the kid's gushing wound with a wad of gauze.

Garcia arched his back, moaning.

"Stay with me," Goldstein said. "Look at my eyes . . . good. Just focus on me."

The medic snapped his fingers at Deuce. "Your cigar."

"What?"

"Give it to me!"

Goldstein held the cigar to Garcia's lips. "Bite down on this."

He clenched the cigar between his teeth. His facial muscles tightened around watery eyes as Goldstein cleaned the bullet hole. "Just a few more seconds, *amigo*." The medic sprinkled sulfur powder into the wound. He then took the strips of fabric from Chambers. Goldstein tied a tourniquet around the red thigh and the bleeding stopped. Garcia passed out.

Deuce's eyes widened. "Jeez, is he dead?"

The medic checked Garcia's pulse. "No, off in dreamland."

Releasing a breath, Chambers patted his shoulder. "Good work, Goldstein." He crawled back to where Mahoney paced like a distraught father. "How's Garcia?"

Chambers squatted, washing his bloody hands in the icy cold stream. "Alive, but he won't be running any marathons. What's the status up top?"

"All clear," Mahoney answered.

"Not for long, though. Germans are combing these woods. Wolf, we need to get far away from here."

"I know of a better shelter. We're heading out soon."

Chambers picked up his Tommy gun and helmet. "Forget shelter. I say we find our way back to friendly territory. Mahoney, rouse up the—"

Fallon yelled, "We're still in charge here, God damn it!"

"Your mission is FUBAR. The Germans killed Lieutenant LeBlanc and his entire platoon. I'm not losing any more men because of your damned mission."

Fallon jabbed a finger into Chambers's chest. "You aren't backing out now—"

"Quiet!" Wolf pushed between them. "Listen."

A strange vibration pulsed through Chambers's boots. He cupped his ear to the wall. The concrete hill thrummed, as if something were drilling up from beneath the ground.

The metal groaned above their heads. Fallon looked up at the bridge. "Shit."

The platoon stood, grabbing their gear.

Chambers poked his head outside. A tree-covered hill led up to the road. "Everyone hold steady. No chatter." He loaded a fresh magazine into his rifle. Beyond the rain approached a cacophonous rhythm, like the hooves of a hundred horses clopping against asphalt. His heart beat with the same pulsing rhythm.

Buck scurried down from the embankment. "Fog's pretty thick, but I hear vehicles comin' from the southeast side of the bridge."

Wrinkles bunched across Wolf's forehead. "That's the opposite direction of Richelskaul."

"Shit, we're surrounded!" shouted a frantic voice from the group.

"Oh God, we're screwed," Finch cried.

"We should surrender," said another soldier.

"Warriors don't surrender," boomed Fallon's voice.

Wolf ran into the center of the group. "Everyone shut the hell up. Fallon, cover the far side. Chambers, your men cover this side. No talking. Guns ready."

Fallon led the X-2 soldiers to the opposite side of the bridge, where the creek led away into the forest.

"Everybody hang tight." Chambers stepped back in the rain, staring up at the bridge's outer railing. Thick cords of water fell from the heavens, drenching his face. He climbed up the grassy hill. He eased his head around the wall. The double-lane bridge stretched about thirty meters. Beyond, an asphalt road curved into the pines before it was devoured by fog. An engine groaned. Metallic wheels crunched ever closer. Glowing eyes formed as a German half-track rolled around the curve. A column of German soldiers wearing rubber gas masks marched out of the mist alongside it.

Chambers leaned back against the wall, chest heaving. He checked his watch—1230 hours. The second hand made its rounds. It was then a familiar terrifying thought struck him. This was the final countdown of his life.

Chapter 26

Chambers slid down the grassy hill on his rump. The bridge rumbled, the rafters shaking. Metal half-tracks screeched and groaned.

The two squads crouched with rifles aimed at the ceiling.

Buck squeezed two grenades in his fists.

Wolf and Chambers stood side by side, their semiautomatic rifles poised at the grassy hill that sloped down to the creek.

Outside the bridge's shelter, the rain continued its downpour, covering the green forest with a gray curtain.

Chambers gripped his rifle tighter. *If the Krauts decide to search beneath the bridge . . .*

Small vehicles rolled over the crossing, engines tooting like European motorcycles. Next followed the rhythmic cadence of marching boots.

Just keep moving along. Nothing to see here.

Chambers aimed his rifle at the creek outside the hideout. His finger brushed the trigger. The storm continued to shake the pine branches.

Chambers and Wolf glanced at one another then back to the wooded creek. No German voices to be heard. No footsteps hiking through the trees. The grinding wheels and marching boots trailed down the road. Chambers peered out from his crevice, expecting to see sentries leaning over the bridge. But the railing was clear.

He tapped Wolf's shoulder and pointed outside. The two snaked up the grassy hill on their bellies, wary of the trees around them. The bridge was empty. Down the road, a column of SS troops marched toward Richelskaul. Their stiff arms and legs moved in perfect cadence, like the black-clad Nazis Chambers had seen in German propaganda films. Except these wore rubber gas masks. Submachine guns and burp guns hung from their shoulders. Others carried long rifles. Each had a saber strapped to his utility belt. Some, donning commander's hats and long coats, rode alongside on two-passenger BMW motorcycles. As the column faded into the haze, Chambers exhaled and glanced at Wolf.

They climbed back down. "All clear."

The entire platoon released their held breaths.

Mahoney crossed his head and chest. "Mother Mary, that was close."

"We've got a long hike back." Chambers stepped back into the rain. "Let's get moving."

The Lucky Seven hoisted Garcia and followed him. They didn't wait for Wolf or Fallon to object.

• • •

The platoon marched down a dirt path that ran alongside the road. Drooping fir branches offered some shelter from the drizzle. The dark gray haze ruled the hills and trees. Driveways led to rural farmhouses that sat like tombs in the rain.

Captain Wolf jogged up beside Chambers, who led the pack. "Chambers, slow down. We need to get to our shelter."

"Do what you want, Wolf. My men and I are pushing our way back to camp."

"Stop for a moment and listen to me."

Wind and rain whipped around them like a monsoon. Chambers willed his body to move against the torrents. The fog thickened into a gray soup, cutting visibility down to ten yards. He reached a crossing. Four roads led off into uncertainty. He watched the roads for movement then glanced down at his map. The others caught up, gasping and heaving.

Wolf shouted at them. "The storm is getting worse. We are finding shelter."

"We're still too close to Richelskaul." Chambers checked the compass on his silver watch. "We keep pushing south. Gain some distance."

Wolf shook his head. "If we follow this road, we will just hit another German defense post. Finding shelter is our best option."

"How about southwest?" Chambers insisted.

"Too many obstacles. Germans have set up barbed wire and minefields all throughout these woods."

"Then we follow the roads."

"Roads are blocked and heavily guarded."

Chambers glared at the X-2 captain. "Damn it, then how the hell do we get back to the line?"

Wolf pointed behind them. "The way we came."

"Ah, Christ!" Fallon moaned. "Let's get to the shelter pronto."

Chambers looked at his men. "I say we keep moving while there's still daylight."

Wolf spoke above the rain. "Listen, men, we will never find our way back in this mess. We need a dry place to hole up for the night. I will lead us to shelter. Then we can radio back to camp."

"Chambers, I vote we take shelter," Deuce said.

"Me, too," echoed Buck.

Every head in his platoon nodded, including Sergeant Mahoney and Goldstein, who held up Garcia's half-drugged body. "Garcia won't make it that far without a stretcher."

Feeling stung, Chambers glanced down the four roads that led into the endless walls of fir trees. He studied his map and compass as if either might offer some insight. Finally, he gazed into Wolf's intense hazel eyes. "Okay, we'll follow you to shelter."

The X-2 captain addressed his weary charges. "Hang with me, men. We will be out of the storm soon." He turned left on the road, heading southeast.

"Finally, a decision," Fallon muttered to Sergeant Moose.

All was quiet as they marched alongside the road. Rain

slapped the asphalt and whipped the trees back and forth. Their boots squished through mud as they entered a winding dirt road where dark, war-battered farmhouses hunkered deep into the woods on either side.

Ice-cold rain dribbled down Chambers's face. His nose and cheeks felt numb. He searched the drizzle for enemy movement, his efforts aided by an occasional flash of lightning. Thunder rumbled with such fury the ground vibrated beneath his boots.

Wolf turned up one of the long driveways, staying close to the woods. Back in the trees a sturdy barn stood beside a house that had burned to the ground. The column of foot soldiers ran haphazardly up the hill, sliding in the mud. Farther back, an injured Garcia hobbled between Goldstein and Mahoney. The three ran through the rain as if trying to win a three-legged race in which life was the trophy. The X-2 soldiers covered their rears.

Wolf signaled everyone to hold up. He stepped into the shadowy barn. It was a good five minutes before he returned, giving the platoon a thumbs-up.

As each soldier reached the barn, Chambers directed the men through the open front double doors. He counted thirteen survivors including himself. Before entering, he leaned against the threshold, holding his rifle tight against his chest. The clouds went from mottled gray to black, and a malevolent darkness descended upon the barn.

Downhill, in the liquid gray woods, he saw a dozen German shadows approaching the barn, their faces obscured by black rubber masks. Chambers jerked his rifle. Then lightning flashed and the shadow soldiers disappeared. He rubbed his eyes. The forest remained empty.

Part 5

Wolves in Sheep's Clothing

During combat the threads that hold a unit together can quickly fray. As platoon leader, my job is to make sure we don't unravel completely.
—LIEUTENANT JACK CHAMBERS, *WAR DIARY*

Chapter 27

Inside the barn the platoon collapsed onto the floor, laying down rifles, pulling off helmets, gasping for air. Buck chinked out a dirt-covered window with his rifle. Like a faithful watchdog, he scanned the area in front of the barn for any approaching enemy.

Chambers leaned against a post, cold water dripping from his face and poncho. He pulled off his helmet, wet bangs falling out, and sat down against the post, thick powdery soil and straw offering a soft cushion. He wiped a handkerchief across his face, snorted out water and mucus from his nostrils, and inhaled. The barn smelled of dust, hay, rusted metal, and old leather. The roof leaked in places, but most of the dirt floor kept dry. A ladder led up to a loft stacked with hay bales.

The barn appeared longer than it was wide, like an airplane hangar. A rusted green tractor took up most of the center. Cobwebs stretched between the two giant back tires. Beyond the tractor, the entrance light tapered off into darkness.

Chambers leaned forward on his knees and looked into the frantic eyes of his platoon huddled on the ground around him. Lightning briefly lit up their faces. The Lucky Seven had made it. Their luck had even rubbed off on Goldstein and five members of the X-2 squad—Captain Wolf, Lieutenant Fallon, Sergeant Moose, and Corporals Fox and Snake.

Out of fifty men, just thirteen remained.

Chambers's gaze bore holes into Fallon, who sat directly across from him. The X-2 lieutenant, the paint half washed from his face, returned a daggered stare.

The group sat in a circle on the dirt floor, brooding in silence. Their labored breathing echoed in the hollow barn. *What the hell can I say to them? The mission's failed and they know it.* Chambers just gulped in oxygen alongside them.

Someone in the gloom burst into a high-pitched giggle. Tired faces glared at Deuce.

Mahoney whispered, "Deuce, hold yourself together. We made it."

"You call this making it?" Deuce spoke like Groucho Marx. "I hate to break it ta ya, fellas, but our shit's hit the fan."

"He's right. What the hell happened out there?" Finch's wide eyes flitted from face to face.

Deuce's eyebrows bounced like Groucho's. "We just got a royal ass-kicking." He giggled on the edge of tears. "We shot those Jerries a hundred times. But they just kept coming. Why wouldn't they die?"

Chambers stared out at the storm that raged around the barn. He remembered the German in the tavern that he'd shot. Later he saw the Nazis with sabers stabbing survivors of the blast. He witnessed a Nazi survive several shots to the chest and throat. He had no explanation.

Finch broke the silence. "Anybody see their faces? They were wearing rubber masks."

"Gas masks," Hoffer added.

"Yeah, what the hell?" Deuce put an unlit cigar between his lips. "Can anyone explain who we was fighting? 'Cause they sure wasn't regular Germans."

Chambers looked to Wolf. The X-2 captain shook his head, signaling Chambers to keep his mouth shut. "Everybody just calm down. We're safe for the moment."

"Jeez, Louweez." Deuce snorted. "Garcia was right. This *is* the Big One."

"It's not the Big One," Chambers said. "Everybody just get that out of your heads."

"Yeah, tell that to Garcia." Deuce motioned to the Mexican soldier lying prone in the hay. "He'll never make it back with that leg wound."

Chambers said, "Deuce, we'll get everybody back. Just calm down." He turned to Wolf. "Well, you got us to shelter. What now?"

Wolf looked at each man. "We catch our breaths. We still have our radio." He snapped his fingers at the X-2 corporal named Fox. "See if you can contact base camp."

The British corporal put the receiver to his ear, turned some dials, and shook his head. "Storm."

"Well, keep trying." Wolf stood and brushed hay from his damp uniform. "Major Powell is bound to be calling. When we get a signal from base, we will decide our next move. Now everybody just hang tight. No talking above a whisper. Chambers, I want sentries watching all sides. This barn has a rear entrance. My men will cover the back." Wolf and his X-2 boys disappeared into the pitch gloom of the cavernous barn.

Chambers looked at his seven men. "All right, let's get some eyes on the forest. Hoffer, Finch, cover the barn doors. Deuce, set your BAR up beneath the tractor. Buck, still got your sharp shooter?"

"Yessir."

"Good. Take that window up in the loft. You all know the drill, so hop to." Chambers stood between the soldiers dispersing to their posts. "Now's probably your best chance to eat your Ks. So refuel." He stepped beneath the hayloft where the chaplain was sitting cross-legged with his back against the wall. Goldstein's Bible lay open in his lap, the hand curled around his Star of David necklace. His eyes were closed, a peaceful look on his face.

In the hay beside the chaplain, Miguel Garcia slept with his head on a poncho stuffed with hay. Chambers knelt, watching the kid's chest rise and fall. Garcia's helmet lay upside down in the hay. Two family photos were fastened to the banding inside the helmet. Chambers pulled them out and brought them into the gray light that filtered through the barn doors. The first photo showed Miguel at nineteen, standing in front of the Alamo, holding hands with a two-year-old boy with jet black hair and the same puppy dog eyes. Garcia's teenage wife, Maria, stood beside them. They were all eating ice-cream cones. The photo brought a smile to Chambers's face. The second photo showed Maria sitting in a hospital bed holding an infant, Lucilia, the day she was born.

Garcia's face had turned a pasty pale. His blood-soaked leg showed massive bruising around the bandages. He shivered. Chambers found a horse blanket and draped it over him. "Goldstein, how's he doing?"

The bespectacled medic opened his eyes and yawned. "Lost a lot of blood, but I think he'll make it. Needs a surgeon to get the slugs out." He put away his Bible and necklace. "I've done all I can for him."

Chambers nodded. "We'll get him back soon enough. How're you doing?"

"Fine. Just trying to make sense of what happened."

"It's pretty cut-and-dried. The Germans were waiting, and we got ambushed."

"Well, I got a bad feeling our captain knows more than he's telling us. And I don't believe we were fighting normal Germans."

"Do you have a theory, Chaplain?"

Goldstein nodded. "You remember Captain Murdock's dreams I was telling you about? The shadow soldiers? Well, last night I dreamed about them. They wore black uniforms and masks. They chased me through the woods. Then I saw this robed figure. I followed him through a deserted town that looked like Richelskaul—"

"And into a church graveyard . . ." Chambers's throat constricted.

Goldstein's eyes widened. "You had the same dream, didn't you?"

"It was just a dream."

"Not if we both had it. That, my friend, is a message. Only one of us is willing to listen."

"I'm sure there's a logical explanation."

"What's happening defies logic. You saw the shadow soldiers, didn't you? They looked just like the ones in our dreams."

"All I saw was chaos."

"I think Murdock's prophecy is coming true. The only explanation that makes sense is that we're dealing with a supernatural army."

"Let's not get into this again."

"Chambers, open your eyes." Goldstein looked down at his palm. "My scar tingled and glowed every time those soldiers came near us. And these letters kept appearing." He held up his palm.

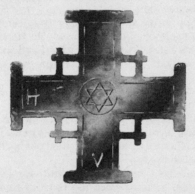

Chambers stared, speechless, and peeled back the bandage on his hand. The same two letters had formed on his palm. His spine shuddered. *What the hell's going on?*

The chaplain gazed wide-eyed at Chambers's hand. "Something is happening that's not of this earth. And you and I are being called to fight it."

"Get some rest, Goldstein, you're delirious."

"Delirious is the man who refuses to see his calling."

Chambers checked on his men. Each stood at his assigned post, eyes peeled while quietly eating the K rations. The smell of food made Chambers's stomach growl.

"Sounds like you need to eat." Mahoney tossed him a box

of rations. "Here, take a meal break. I'll look after the boys."
The eldest of the platoon by ten years, the bear-sized sergeant
looked as if he'd earned a few more white hairs in his bushy
eyebrows.

Chambers felt an overwhelming sense of gratitude that
Mahoney was among the survivors. "Thanks, Papa Bear. I'll
be upstairs." He climbed up the ladder to the hayloft and sat
against a pile of hay. He devoured his can of cold chili maca-
roni with a side of cheese and crackers. No leftovers for the
mice today.

Thunder rumbled outside. Rain clicked along the tin roof
in a steady rhythm, creating a rare moment of peace. Chambers's eyelids grew heavy.

Buck sat up in the loft, his sniper rifle leaning beside a
window that overlooked the farm road. He leaned back into
the wall of hay bales. "Now this is what I call southern com-
fort." Buck yawned. "I could just close my eyes and sleep for
a week."

"Don't get too cozy." Chambers fought to keep his own
eyes open.

Buck stuffed a plug of chewing tobacco into his cheek. "We
have a barn just like this back at m'daddy's ranch in Amarillo.
'Cept we keep horses in ours." He pulled out his baseball and
rolled it between his hands.

Chambers's lips tingled with the desire for a cigarette. To
kill the craving, he unwrapped the Hershey treat that came
with his meal. "Tell me about the cowboy life, Buck."

The rancher rubbed the blue bandana tied around his
neck. "Growing up, m'daddy and I'd go on these long cattle
drives across the panhandle, up through Kansas and Colorado. We'd sleep 'neath the stars most nights, saddles as our
pillas. Every time I returned home from a drive, I'd always
go straight to our barn and sleep in the hayloft. To me that
was heaven."

Chambers smiled. "Sounds peaceful."

"Yeah, before I moved off to play baseball with the Cards,
I used to compete in rodeos and sell livestock there. Mostly
steers and heifers." Buck spat tobacco and grinned with a

lump in his cheek. "Yeah, good ol' Fort Worth. Used to date this girl there, Ruthie Jean. Her daddy owned a big ranch in Bedford. He and m'daddy did a lot of business, so I got to see Ruthie Jean every couple months. She loved to go two-steppin' at Cowtown dance hall. Damn good dancer. We won a couple of contests."

Chambers raised his eyebrows. "Buck, I had no idea you danced."

"Nobody does. If you don't mind, sir, I prefer keeping it between you and me."

"Your secret's safe."

"Ever whirled a girl around the dance floor?"

"No, I have two left feet."

Chambers let his eyes close for one peaceful second. Buck's voice and the rhythmic rain drifted away, replaced by a moment of no sound, no sight, no thought. As if Chambers had plunged beneath a dark, watery surface. He liked floating here. Then came a *scratch-pop* like a phonograph needle touching down on a record . . . echoes of an LP spinning, spinning, became relaxing music. Slow horns, gentle strings. The soft melodies of an orchestra playing an easy tune. First distant, then growing closer, filling up the empty space around him. The silky smooth voice of Glenn Miller crooned "Moonlight Serenade."

• • •

Chambers opened his eyes. Before him stretched a room illuminated by soft candlelight.

A female voice asked, "Would you like to dance, Jack?"

His chest swelled. Eva Winchester stood by a phonograph, an album cover in her hands. "Can you believe I found a Glenn Miller record in Notting Hill?"

He leaned back on the bed. "I told you I can't dance."

"You certainly dance well beneath the sheets."

He laughed. "So do you, you tart."

"Tart!" She tossed a pillow at him. "Oh, now you have to dance with me, you stubborn mule."

They swayed to the music, his bare toes touching hers.

The musk of her glistening neck scented the air. Her heart beat against his. They held each other for three songs, and then the swaying turned into kissing, the kissing into peeling off clothing. Afterward Eva lay on his bare chest, and they stared at the open window, watching the lightning of an approaching storm crackle across the night sky. Thunder rumbled. And then the rain fell, clicking across the roof.

• • •

"Lieutenant?" echoed a hollow voice. "Chambers?" Someone shook his shoulder.

He opened his eyes to a blurry gray world. "What? Huh?"

Buck's face came into focus. "You dozed off on me."

"Oh, man." Chambers rubbed his eyes. "How long was I out?"

"Hour or so." Buck rolled the baseball between his palms. "I was telling you about the time I got to pitch in the World Series. I looked over and you were snoozing. Didn't have the heart to wake you."

"Thanks. Guess I needed it. I'll take a rain check on that story." Chambers rose, brushing hay from his uniform. "I should check on the others." He started down the ladder.

"Sir?"

Chambers stopped at the top of the ladder. "Yeah, Buck?"

"You think we're gonna make it back?"

"We'll find a way out. We always do."

Chapter 28

Chambers marched between several stalls that smelled of horses and old leather. The long barn opened up again at the rear. Gray afternoon light filtered through cracks at the back double doors. As he rounded a large tilling machine, five silhouettes stopped whispering and turned their heads in his direction.

Fallon stood, his face hidden in shadow. "What can we do for you, Chambers?"

"You can shed some light on what the hell kind of Germans we were fighting."

"The less you know, the better."

Chambers turned to Captain Wolf. "If we're going to defend ourselves, then my men should know about the enemy."

"Perhaps you should." Light from a window flickered across the Czech mercenary's face. "The Germans we fought are not normal Wehrmacht soldiers. They are *Einsatzkommandos*. A Nazi Special Forces unit of highly trained killers. The fact that the SS are this close to the front signifies that Hitler and Himmler are getting desperate."

Chambers glared at Wolf. "Why didn't our bullets stop them?"

"They must have been wearing some kind of protective

shielding beneath their uniforms, like armor to deflect bullets."

"Armor!" Chambers squeezed his fists. "You never mentioned anything about bulletproof uniforms! How're we supposed to kill them?"

Wolf shook his head. "This surprised us all. They may be bulletproof, but we can still kill them."

"Hell yeah." Moose grinned and patted his backpack. "Next time we just hit 'em with good ol' American TNT."

The captain smiled. "We do have some good news, Chambers. We got a signal out on the radio twenty minutes ago. Reinforcements are on the way."

A wave of relief flooded Chambers's body. "Good. So we just lie low till they get here."

"Not exactly," Wolf said. "The reinforcements are meeting us at our final target."

A vein sprouted across Chambers's temple.

"The Nazi command post." Wolf turned on a small penlight, dug into a black leather satchel, and handed him a photo of four guards with Rottweilers standing in front of a church.

Chambers snorted. "You can't be serious."

"*Einsatzkommandos* under the command of SS-Hauptsturmführer Manfred von Streicher—Himmler's handpicked monsters—have converted this abandoned church into a base to carry out an operation called Eisen Sarg." Wolf walked back to the bench with the map. "Our mission is to sabotage all communication and steal any intelligence. Capturing this base will weaken the Nazis' hold on the Hürtgen. The blow will be so huge Hitler and Himmler will feel it in Berlin."

Fallon grinned. "This is the moment of truth, warriors."

"Time to exterminate the Nazi hive." Sergeant Moose knocked fists with Fallon.

"Let's kick some ass," Snake said from his post at the back door.

Chambers shook his head. "Have you lost your minds? You saw what we're up against. For Christ's sake, these *Einsatzkommandos* annihilated our platoons in a matter of minutes. Hell, one took out eight of your men with just a saber."

"They had the element of surprise," Fallon said. "Now we have it."

Chambers paced. "We need the strength of a company to carry off a mission like this."

"Christ, Chambers, you're forgetting we're X-2s. We're used to being outnumbered. That's why we go in covert."

Chambers gave him a sideways glance.

Fallon released a breath of frustration. "Let me draw you the big picture. We're not assaulting their headquarters like a bunch of half-cocked kamikazes. We're going in disguised as Germans, just like Captain Wolf and I did before. We'll mingle with the Nazis, gain their full trust, then"—his Nazi knife stabbed into the wood table—"cut their balls off when they least expect it."

Chambers paced, playing out the scenario in his head.

Fallon smoothed out the dirt floor, revealing a trap door. The floor opened into an underground storage space three feet deep. Entombed there like dusty relics were Nazi uniforms, steel helmets, gas masks, maps, and dozens of German weapons—MP40 machine guns, burp guns, Lugers, potato-masher grenades, and a flamethrower. Fallon handed out uniforms. "This barn was once owned by agents of the German Underground working as a branch of X-2. Captain Wolf and I assisted them on their last mission."

"What happened to them?" Chambers asked.

Wolf shook his head. "We lost contact with them two weeks ago. Their last message warned that the Nazis had implemented Operation Eisen Sarg. They went to have one more look and never reported back. We were hoping to find them hiding here."

"I told you they'd be dead," Fallon muttered, putting on a steel helmet. "Either that or they fled. You can't trust a Kraut."

While the five commandos slipped into German uniforms, Chambers paced. "So this mission is about finding your lost agents."

"No, the agents are expendable," Fallon said. "Sabotaging Operation Eisen Sarg and stealing records are the main objectives. At all costs."

Chambers studied the photo of the church's arching double-door entryway. Four Waffen SS guards stood stiffly in their black uniforms. The Rottweilers flanked them like the mythical hounds of hell. "You said the Nazis set up this base to carry out Operation Eisen Sarg? What is it?"

Wolf buttoned his black coat. "Corporal Fox, explain it to him."

The British commando took off his radio headphones. "Right, sir. *Eisen Sarg* translates as "iron coffin.'" He handed Chambers a photo of SS soldiers loading what looked like metal coffins into a long cargo truck. "The trunks are built solid from iron. We're still unsure what's in them, but the Nazis claimed they contain some sort of weapons no army has ever seen."

Wolf said, "When I asked the guards if they had seen the weapons, they said only the highest SS ranks knew the secrets of Operation Eisen Sarg."

Fox added, "By the looks of all the *Einsatzkommandos* with gas masks, we believe it may be chemical warfare."

Each X-2 commando hooked a gas mask onto his uniform. Moose put a bug-eyed rubber mask to his face and made a ghoulish sound to Snake. This brought a round of chuckles.

"Stop clowning around." Wolf adjusted the straps of his mask. "Last word from our German contacts was the Nazis are strategically setting these iron coffins throughout the Hürtgen."

"Just setting them out in the woods and leaving them," Fox added. "One of the SS soldiers we interviewed said the coffins are some kind of Pandora's box. When the Allies open them, all hell's supposed to break loose."

"Jesus," Chambers breathed.

"You are starting to get the picture, yes?" Wolf said. "We do not know how many coffins the Nazis have placed in the Hürtgen, if any. But we know they plan to place one every mile for the entire length of the Siegfried Line. Since the Allies have been pushing against the German borders, the SS troops have tripled their productivity in Richelskaul. That is why our mission is so urgent."

Chambers rubbed his hand through his hair. "So you five

are going to just waltz right into the Nazi headquarters as SS soldiers?"

"That's the plan," Fallon grinned. "Like wolves in sheep's clothing."

"They won't know what hit 'em." Moose tested the flame nozzle of a German flamethrower. It spat a bluish orange plume.

Fallon strapped his brass-knuckled knife onto a belt that wrapped around his black tunic.

Chambers took a deep breath. "So what role does my platoon play in all this?"

"Oh, it's a biggie." Fallon smirked. The slick bald commando, now fully suited up as an SS officer, hooked stick grenades to his belt.

"The plan is simple," Wolf explained. "Nine of us will go. Three of your men will hide out here with your wounded man till we come back for them. We will march straight to the church. Your men will pretend to be our prisoners."

"Whoa, you never said anything about my men walking into the lion's den as prisoners."

"This was always part of the plan. LeBlanc and his men were supposed to do it."

"Guess you're the lucky ones," Fallon jabbed.

Hearing LeBlanc's name stung Chambers's chest. "Forget it. I won't subject my men to this."

Fallon wiped the war paint off his face with a damp rag. "You signed a contract, Chambers. Backing out would be an act of treason."

"This is bullshit! We put our lives on the line. We got you this far."

"The deal's to assist us in capturing *all* targets. The church is our main target."

Chambers sighed and looked up at Wolf. "Okay, what about weapons for my men?"

"We will bring extra. Once we decide to attack, we will toss each of you a weapon."

"You make this sound like a cakewalk."

"Chambers, no X-2 operation is a cakewalk." The captain loaded a submachine gun. "We know this mission is dangerous. But the stakes are too high not to take action."

Chewing a cigar, Fallon cocked his MP40. "Christ, lighten up, Chambers. What's the fun of combat if the odds aren't stacked against you?"

• • •

The Lucky Seven gazed at the floor, the ceiling, outside, at anything other than looking Chambers directly in the eye. Even Mahoney appeared shaken.

"Buck, Deuce, Finch, and myself will go as prisoners. The rest of you will stay behind with Garcia."

Deuce paced in front of the tractor, his cigar rolling between his fingers. "Odds are hundred to one against us." He stopped abruptly. "No, thousand to one. We're digging our own graves if we go anywhere near that Nazi base camp."

"Nobody's dying," Chambers said.

"Yeah!" Deuce's voice switched to James Cagney. "Tell that to the other forty GIs who started this harebrained mission."

"All right, enough bitching, Deuce," Mahoney whispered, looking back over his shoulder. "This is just another recon job, same shit, different day. So everybody put on your game face and listen to your lieutenant."

"Hang tough, guys," Chambers said. "We'll get through this like we always do."

"We're not only getting through this, we're gonna change the fucking course of history." Fallon emerged from the shadows fully decked in an SS lieutenant's uniform. Next followed Moose, Fox, and Snake dressed in black and loaded down with weapons. They stood behind Fallon like henchmen.

Captain Wolf followed in tow, sharply dressed as an SS captain, complete with an officer's cap and three Iron Crosses on his chest. A black strap hung across his chest, a leather satchel resting at his hip. "Get your gear on, men. We move out in five."

The Lucky Seven threw on helmets and parkas. Goldstein pulled Chambers aside. "Sir, I feel like I should be going with you."

Chambers smiled. "I need you to remain here, Chaplain. Look after Garcia. Mahoney and Hoffer will keep you company."

"Why do they get to stay behind?" Deuce asked. "How about I stay and you take Hoffer instead?"

"Yeah, let me go." Hoffer's eyes pleaded with him. "You can't attack the Nazi lair without the Shadow."

"This is no comic book, Hoffer."

"I know it's dangerous, but I want to help."

"All right, Hoff, gear up. Papa Bear, Deuce, there's a lot of materials in this barn. Find a way to make a stretcher."

Mahoney nodded. "We'll have it ready when you return."

"Deuce, this isn't a time to play poker."

"Thank you, sir." The Poker King shook hands with Buck, Finch, and Hoffer. "Good luck, fellas. Everybody lives, okay?"

"Everybody lives," the Lucky Seven repeated.

Fallon peered out the barn doors. "Storm's finally passing."

"Let me tell you something, men." Wolf stepped in the center of the group, looking each man in the eye. "When we pull this off, it will be a huge strategic win for the Allied forces. President Roosevelt will know your name. All I ask is that you bring your belief in success of all your previous missions to this one. We get through this and I promise every one of you gets to go home a hero. Are you with me?"

"Yes, sir," the group chanted in unison.

Chambers studied his men. *Maybe we can pull this off.* His hand felt the thick unopened letter inside his jacket. *And maybe, just maybe, a lovely English nurse will be waiting for me in Notting Hill.*

Chapter 29

The mist sifted between the fir trees and along the empty farm road.

Chambers marched third in a column of nine soldiers—five dressed as SS troops, four as American POWs. Weaving through a maze of branches, Wolf led the soldiers along a firebreak that sloped through a thick network of fir trees.

Fallon followed second, a Schmeisser clacking at his hip. With his stout upper body and thick neck, he looked the picture of a German prison guard. He occasionally glanced back at his four prisoners—Chambers, Buck, Finch, and Hoffer—who walked in silence with their hands on their heads. At the rear of the column, Moose, Fox, and Snake watched the thick woods on either side of the road.

Chambers carefully stepped into every impression Wolf and Fallon left in the mud. Gravity tugged heavily at Chambers's legs. Breathing became a chore. Thick fir branches, still wet from the storm, dripped onto helmets and ponchos. At several points along the trail, a three-pronged Bouncing Betty stabbed up from the pine needles. He pointed the mines out to Buck, who in turn pointed them out to Finch.

Finch whispered to Hoffer, "Watch your step, buddy."

Snake slammed Finch in the back with a rifle. *"Sprechen Verboten!"*

"Hey, easy, you big goon."

"Halt's Maul!" Snake gave him another shove.

Finch gave him the finger.

They marched upward in silence. The only forest sounds were light rain sprinkling the evergreen canopy and their boots squishing along the muddy trail. Chambers glanced down at the helmeted heads bobbing up the trail, each soldier laboriously stepping from one deep boot impression to another.

The farther they carved through the Hürtgen, the more disoriented Chambers felt. He studied the compass on his silver watch. The trail curved south, southeast, at some points even due east. *Where are we going?* He stared up at Wolf and Fallon as they whispered in German.

The trail led to a spiked wrought-iron fence covered in ivy. Chambers's neck hairs stood on end. Beyond the fence an enormous graveyard ascended up a muddy hill. The mist drifted between stone crosses and tombstones like specters. His nightmare flashed in his mind, merging with the real-life images before him.

Wolf opened a rusted iron gate, its hinges squeaking, and stepped into the cemetery. Chambers hesitated a moment until Fallon shoved him through the gate. The nine soldiers meandered between crosses and tombstones, some of which had oval photos of the sleeping dead, their eyes watching them pass.

Wolf guided them into a crypt that had been fractured open by a blast. The stone door lay on the ground like a pale plank. The men crossed it, squeezing into a chamber half the size of a cellar. The smell of century-old mildew filled the airspace.

"What are we doing in here?" Chambers asked.

"Assessing the situation." Wolf motioned to several cracks in the crypt's wall.

Chambers put his eye to a crack, peering outside. Again a sense of unease shuddered down his spine. At the top of the hill, the vapor parted to reveal the backside of a stone church. Sharp spires and a massive bell tower jutted upward above the fir trees. On one side stood a garden of unkempt hedges.

Wolf peered through a scope. "No guards in sight."

"Let me see." Fallon pushed his way to one of the cracks. "Shit, where are they?"

"This isn't right. They usually have four guards with dogs manning that back door."

Chambers looked from his peephole to Wolf. "Have you ever seen that door without guards?"

"Never." Wolf's marble eyes glazed over briefly. Then he peered back out the crack.

"Maybe they pulled out already," Chambers offered.

"They've got to be lurking somewhere," Fallon said.

Wolf gripped his MP40. "Chambers, you and your men stay quiet from this point forth. Follow our lead. When we're ready to strike, we'll say the code word *Blitzkrieg* then toss you weapons."

The nine soldiers stepped out of the crypt and hiked up the hill through the cemetery. As Chambers walked, hands on his head, he scanned the church windows. Bullet holes riddled the stained glass. If there were German snipers posted at those windows, they were completely camouflaged against the darkness. Walking straight toward the church made them easy targets. Chambers just hoped the POW ruse held up.

At the top of the hill, Wolf led them through a labyrinth of hedges to a swampy clearing behind the church. Mud-covered debris littered the area. They stepped over German helmets, boots, uniforms, belts, flashlights, glasses, even rifles that had been discarded in the grass.

Fallon picked up an Iron Cross medal, pulled off the grass and dirt, and pinned it on his uniform.

Exchanging a suspicious look with Chambers, Wolf stopped everyone then stepped into an archway and tested the back double doors. Locked. He scrutinized the church windows and surrounding hedge garden, then back down at a trail of bare footprints in the mud. A few boot prints marched on either side of the barefoot trail, curving around the corner. Damp wind carried a swampy odor, like rotten fish. Birds cawed in the distance.

The nine soldiers followed the footprints on a twisting, turning path through the hedge garden. The bird cawing grew louder. The maze opened up again to a long rectangular pool with green water and lily pads. A broken fountain with three dancing cherubs stood in the center. The swampy stench stung Chambers's nose and filled his mouth with a briny taste he couldn't spit out. Bile rushed up the back of his throat. He choked it down. The soldiers around him coughed and spat. Rubbing his eyes, Chambers followed Wolf and Fallon around the pool. Everyone froze midway.

In the green water, intertwined with the lily pads, floated dozens of pale, naked corpses. Arms and feet and moss-covered heads rose barely out of the water. Ravens fed off the swollen bodies. The black birds cawed at one another, beaks sparring for the meat inside a dead man's skull.

"Oh God!" Finch sprinted to the hedges and vomited.

The X-2 commandos tightened their grips on their machine guns, watching the surrounding hedges. Fallon whispered an order in German.

Moose shoved Finch in line with the POWs. Fallon and Wolf whispered as they studied the vacant church windows looming over them. Chambers and Corporal Fox traded glances then looked at the pool. The pale faces beneath the green water looked like souls of the damned peering through a window separating earth and hell.

The captain barked something in German. The X-2 soldiers shoved the POWs past the macabre pool. The air became breathable again. The cawing of the ravens faded as they meandered through another maze of hedges. They mounted a set of stone steps to the top of a hill and stepped through a brick archway. They walked onto a gravel parking lot in front of the church. No vehicles were parked in front. A hollow wind blew through the broken windows and rattled the front doors.

Corporal Snake walked up the front steps. Peering into the open doors, he knocked. *"Guten Tag!"* He knocked again, the sounds echoing through the church. *"Wir haben amerikanische Gefangene. Ist hier jemand?"* With perplexed eyes, he looked back at the squad.

Captain Wolf motioned the corporal to enter.

Snake pushed open the double doors with his submachine

gun. The hinges creaked as the doors swung inward. One by one they entered the gloomy vestibule, boots clumping onto hardwood floors. The place smelled like a damp cellar. Embedded in one wall was a fountain of holy water. On an opposite wall stretched a table with unlit votive candles covered in cobwebs. Moose pushed open a side door. A dark stairwell wound upward to the bell tower.

Submachine guns poised, the five X-2 commandos gathered at the edge of the vestibule. Beyond stretched a cavernous nave where shadows worshiped a superior darkness. Pews and columns faded into oblivion. The only light came from the pocked stained-glass windows where storm flashes danced in kaleidoscopes of reds, blues, greens, and yellows.

Wolf yelled, *"Hallo! Keiner da?"* His voice echoed back.

"Shit, what happened here?" Moose asked.

Corporal Fox said, "Didn't you see? They're all floating in the pool."

"Ruhe!" Fallon growled, maintaining his German accent. He barked at Snake. *"Klaus, pass auf die Gefangenen auf!"* Snake shoved Chambers and his men into a corner.

Moose, his flamethrower aimed, led Wolf and Fallon into the nave. The darkness swallowed them, their heated German whispers echoing off the high ceiling.

Buck, Hoffer, and Finch gave Chambers a questioning look. He shrugged and looked back at Snake. He watched the four prisoners like a Doberman. Fox kept his rifle aimed at the nave.

After several moments, the others returned. Fallon whispered, "All right, listen up. We don't know what the hell went on here, but there doesn't seem to be any survivors, so we can drop the Nazi charade." Fallon pulled a Thompson off his shoulder and handed it to Chambers. "Guys, give them their weapons."

Receiving rifles, Buck, Finch, and Hoffer glared at the X-2 commandos. Snake flashed them a reptilian grin. "No hard feelings, boys."

"What now?" Chambers asked.

Wolf pulled out a flashlight and screwed on a red lens.

"My men and I are going to explore. See if we can gather any intelligence the Nazis might have left behind. The rest of you stay here and watch the windows. Chambers, if you see any movement out there, come get us."

Chapter 30

A light show crackled across the sky as another storm moved in. Buck and Chambers watched the road from the doorway while Finch and Hoffer peered out the side windows at the forest. Chambers glanced down at his watch: 1700 hours. "Our X-2 boys haven't made a sound in over an hour."

Buck walked to the edge of the vestibule, peering into the pitch-dark nave. "Any idea when they'll be back?"

"They didn't say."

The sergeant shrugged and lumbered back to his post.

Ten feet down, Finch whispered, "Guys, we've got some amazing combat missions under our belts, but this one tops them all."

"The Lucky Seven battles bulletproof Germans behind enemy lines," Hoffer said. "This creepy church makes a great setting for our next issue."

"Keep it down, you two," Chambers whispered.

"Sorry." Finch took it down a notch. "I wonder who executed those Germans out there." He turned to Chambers. "Sir, you got any clues why the Nazis set up headquarters in this church?"

"You know as much as I do."

"Come on, Captain Wolf had to give you something. What's really going on here?"

"And who the hell are these X-2 jokers?" Hoffer asked.

"Not regular army, that's for sure," Finch said.

"How did we get chosen for such a risky mission?"

"Bad luck, I guess." Chambers's stomach went into knots. "Let's talk about something else. What do you guys plan to do when you get back home?"

Hoffer said, "Finch and I are going straight to Atomic Comics with our stories. *The Amazing Combats of the Lucky Seven* will be right up there with *Superman* and *Doc Savage.*"

Chambers shook his head. "How about you, Buck? Got any big plans when you get back to Amarillo?"

The rancher tugged at the blue bandanna around his throat. "Part of me wants to return to baseball, while another part wants to help m'daddy run cattle drives. I reckon it'll come to me when I get home." Buck stared out the window, rolling his lucky baseball in his hands.

Chambers glanced at his watch again: 1715 hours. "Where are they?" He peered back into the dark nave.

Finch said, "It's gonna be nightfall in a couple of hours. I'd sure hate to go looking for that barn in the dar—"

A sonic boom echoed beneath the church. Chambers's ears popped. The floorboards pushed him upward. He fell against a wall, one elbow plunging into a vat of holy water. The double doors swung open. A window behind Hoffer shattered. "What the hell?"

Finch's hand gripped his chest. "I think a bomb went off."

Chambers shook his soaked elbow. "That was dynamite."

Buck closed the front doors. "It came from beneath the church."

Gripping his Tommy gun, Chambers stepped between the last rows of pews. "All right, Buck, you and Finch watch the road. Hoffer, let's find out what's happened to our X-2 boys."

Walking down the center aisle, Hoffer whispered, "It's pitch dark in here."

Chambers pulled out his flashlight. "Use your red lens. And don't aim it at the windows."

Twin red beams swished across the nave like lighthouse beacons. Mammoth-sized columns divided the space into two open corridors with a wide aisle running down the center. Empty pews stretched fifty yards to the pulpit and sanctuary. Many of the pews had been upended, some shredded to pieces. Muddy boot prints, traveling in both directions, covered the wood floor. Chambers stepped over a pile of strewn hymnbooks. "Wolf, are you guys back here?"

Hoffer shined his light upward. Dark wings flapped in the red glow as the light passed over the vaulted ceiling. Nests of bats clotted an enormous pipe organ. "Jeepers, look at that. Nazis picked a real winner of a hideout."

They reached the pulpit, shining their lights along velvet knee rests. Chambers climbed a few steps, entering a dome-shaped sanctuary lined with confessional closets. He craned his head at the murals decorating the dome ceiling. The damp cellar smell intensified into a rotting stench. At the rear, a raised platform led up to the high altar. They eased up the wood steps, their footfalls echoing off the dome ceiling.

Chambers called out, "Hey, Wolf, Hawk, where are you? Moose? Fox?"

"Over here," came a familiar British accent.

The red lights uncovered Corporal Fox sitting on an organ bench, hugging his rifle.

"Where are the others?"

Fox pointed at the floor. "Downstairs somewhere. Captain told me to stand guard."

"What was that explosion?"

"Don't know. I was taking a whiz in a corner when the explosion knocked me sideways. Bloody pissed all over myself."

Chambers shone his light around the altar. "Wolf tell you he'd be using explosives?"

"No, sir. I hadn't the foggiest."

Hoffer kicked something metal that rolled across the floor. "Look, the floor's covered in empty shells."

"Yeah, some kind of battle went on in here." Fox shone his flashlight upon a dozen cartridges scattered along the blood-stained floor. "These expended from an MP40."

Chambers swished his light around the altar. In back stood a wood post as thick as a railroad plank. His light followed the dark post up to a twelve-foot-high cross draped with a giant red flag with a black swastika. Ivory hands and feet stuck out from beneath the flag.

"Somebody's going to hell for this." Hoffer gesticulated. "Why would the Nazis cover up Jesus?"

Fox adjusted his glasses. "Because they hate the Catholics nearly as much as they hate Jews, Freemasons, and Bolsheviks. Nazis are pretty much anti everything that isn't *völkish* or pagan. In fact, my theory about Hitler's Thousand Year Reich is that once the Nazis wipe the planet clean of Jews and communists, they're going after the Catholics."

"Well, they're going to hell for sure."

"I don't think they bloody give a damn. Nazis worship Lucifer and believe that heaven is a world made completely of ice."

Hoffer's eyes widened. "For real?"

"They call it Thule. That's why the SS have been making expeditions to Iceland."

"You need to tell this to my buddy Finch. He's a writer."

"Hoffer, can we stay focused?" Chambers spotlighted the bespectacled X-2 commando. "Fox, show us the stairway to the basement."

They followed the blood trail to a passageway. A stone staircase spiraled downward into the shadows. The stench rising from below burned Chambers's nostrils.

Hollow banging echoed from the stairwell. The clamoring sounded muddled and distant, as if reverberating from the pit of a well. Then came a metallic rattling, like chains being dragged. "Wolf! Hawk! Everybody okay down there?" Only Chambers's voice echoed back.

Hoffer leaned past him. "Think maybe they're dead?"

"No, they're ignoring us." Chambers started down the stairs, his flashlight beam pushing back one layer of black after another. "Okay, let's find them."

Fox hesitated. "Captain's going to get upset if we leave our posts."

"We're just making sure they're okay. Any idea what's down there?"

Fox followed second. "The church's undercroft."

Hoffer said, "I've been down in an undercroft once before, back at my cathedral in Erie, Pennsylvania. Gave me the heebie-jeebies. How about I just stand guard up top?"

Chambers motioned with his flashlight. "Hoffer, come on. And keep quiet."

Down below, the banging stopped.

Chambers paused. A long silence made his jaw tighten. The banging continued, sporadically. "We're coming down, Captain!"

Why aren't they answering?

He removed the red lens from his flashlight. The white beam revealed muddy boot prints and walls smeared with dried gray mud. As he descended the winding stairs, the air grew stale and breathing became a chore. At the bottom steps his flashlight shined upon a red, gnarled face. "Christ, we got a corpse."

Fox hurried down. "Dear heavens, one of our guys?"

"No, a Nazi!" Chambers traced the misshapen body with his flashlight beam. Clad in a black uniform pinned with medals, the dead German lay splayed across the bottom steps. Chambers picked up a rumpled commander's hat. "SS captain."

"Jeepers." Hoffer's rifle poked the body's torso. "Look at his face."

Chambers knelt over the body. The scarlet face was a mask of shredded sinews gnawed to the bone, the jaw open, an expression of sheer terror. The eyeballs had been plucked or chewed from the sockets. His skeletal arm jutted upward, the hand frozen in a claw as if pleading for mercy.

Fox breathed, "Jesus."

Chambers stepped over the corpse. "Let's keep moving."

The British commando grabbed his wrist. "Sir, maybe we shouldn't." He stared at the pitch black passage that lay ahead. "Ever since we found that rune message at the bunker, we've encountered nothing but dead Nazis. I've been racking my brain trying to decipher who the runes were referring to as black demons."

"Runes! Black demons!" Hoffer said. "Lieutenant, you never mentioned this."

"It's classified. That means don't repeat this conversation."

Fox said, "What if the assassins who killed the Nazis in the German bunker also came here? That would explain the bodies we found floating in the pool outside and why this place is deserted."

"What if it's not deserted?" Hoffer gulped. "The assassins could still be down here."

Chambers checked his palm. It didn't tingle. "No, they would have attacked us by now. Fox, my gut feeling tells me your X-2 squad is down here and they may need our help. Be ready for anything." He pressed farther into the darkness—more cautiously now.

The brick passage beyond reeked of war gone sour, as if death had been pickled in a jar. Chambers felt his throat clenching. It took all his willpower to keep from vomiting. They explored the dank passage with their flashlights: a broken chair . . . scattered papers . . . a shattered lamp . . . more empty cartridge shells . . . bullet holes that snaked along the floor and brick wall.

Fox picked up some of the dusty papers, whispered, "German documents. There's an SS emblem at the top."

"Anything important?"

"No, just inventory lists of food supplies and uniforms." He pointed to the SS emblem. "There's a prime example that the Nazis worship runes. The twin thunderbolts derived from the ancient *Sowelu* rune, also known as the *Sigel* rune, which means "sun." The rune was redesigned by Walter Heck, *Stürmfuhrer* in the SS, and became the menacing double *Sig* runes, marking the insignia of the Schutzstaffel. The Nazis are a fascinating lot when you start to delve into their philosophies, don't you think?"

"No, Corporal, I don't share your fascination. Neither do my Jewish friends." The hallway opened into a wider passage that stretched into a boundless void. Chambers had the gut-gnawing feeling they had left behind the church's sacred precinct, and at the end of the tunnel awaited the grinning face of eternal damnation.

They passed a series of rooms on either side of the hallway—
offices with filing cabinets, desks, chairs, and walls still adorned
with paintings. Flags with German swastikas hung in every
room. Fox entered a mess hall and jiggled the light switch. "Everything here's dead. Hey, Lieutenants Hawk, Moose, you
around here?"

"Jeepers, check this out." Hoffer's beam passed over
three dead Nazis sitting around a dinner table. One corpse
leaned back in his chair, his face a reddish gray mess. He
still held a fork in his fist. The other two slumped over their
plates. Rats crawled across the table and the dead men's
backs. The beady-eyed creatures had already picked clean
the dead soldiers and eyed Chambers, Hoffer, and Fox as if
hungry for more. Rats on the counter sent tin bowls clanging
to the floor.

Chambers stepped into the kitchen. "We just found the
source of the banging."

"This doesn't put me at ease—" Hoffer jumped back with
a rat on his shoulder. "Holy Moses!" He threw it down, kicking at it.

Chambers shook his head and returned to the hallway.
"Wolf! Hawk! Moose! If you're down here, show yourselves." His own hollow voice echoed back as if the church's
undercroft were an endless chasm. "Christ almighty." Chambers led them farther down the central corridor, swishing
the beam from one room to the next, illuminating bunk
beds, a shower room with dark-stained tiles that reflected
his flashlight, and an office. He spotlighted a mahogany
desk with a blotter and nameplate titled SS-Hauptsturmführer
Manfred von Streicher. Behind the desk sat a dead Nazi
dressed in a black officer's tunic with a red swastika band
wrapped around one bicep. SS medals covered the left breast
pocket.

Must be the Von Streicher the X-2 men are looking for.

The commander slumped in his winged-back leather chair.
His decayed face was unrecognizable. The eyes had sunken
inward and rotted into a grayish mush. A spider's web of
dried blood covered one side of his head where a bullet had

entered, blowing a gaping hole out the other side. Judging by the Luger in his black-gloved hand, the fatal wound was self-inflicted.

Chambers's light passed over a bookshelf that featured a framed photo of Nazi officers. In the center stood Von Streicher. In the photo he looked more like a bookish professor than a Nazi elite. Beady eyes stared through tiny oval spectacles. The bookshelves displayed a dozen other photos, a visual tapestry of the Nazi life. "Hey, guys, come have a look at this. Hoffer? Fox?"

The darkness behind Chambers was deathly silent. An acid snake coiled in the pit of his stomach. "Guys, where are you?" He shone his light back down the hallway. "Hoffer!" Chambers stepped into a room across the hall, swishing his beam across rubble. He breathed air thick with the residue of explosives. Gray soot covered the walls and ceiling. On the back wall was a charred world map. In the back corner stood a tall safe, the thick door hanging open on one hinge. He stepped over the debris of what appeared to have been a conference table and leather chairs. On the floor near the safe sat several duffel bags, the tops open. His flashlight spotlighted thick stacks of money and shiny gold bars. "What the—?"

"Stop right there." A soldier wearing a gas mask shoved a Luger barrel into his face. From behind, a hand wrapped around Chambers's mouth and a knife blade pressed against his throat. A second soldier pulled him against a wall. Pierce Fallon's muffled voice spoke from beneath the rubber mask. "You aren't supposed to be down here."

Another masked soldier stepped into the light. Wolf said, "Lower your pistol, Snake. Hawk, let him go."

Fallon held the knife against Chambers's throat. "No, I don't trust him."

"Damn it, let him go. That's an order, Hawk."

The blade released, and Chambers rubbed a nick on his Adam's apple. In the singular beam from his flashlight he saw Moose, also wearing a gas mask, standing with Fox and Hoffer.

"Captain, what's going on here?"

"We're gathering intelligence."

Chambers pointed to the duffel bags filled with money and gold. "You call this intelligence!"

"That's none of your business." Fallon's goggle-eyed mask loomed over him. "Why aren't you at your posts?"

"We heard the explosion. We came to make sure—"

"This bunker is off limits to anyone other than X-2 soldiers."

Chambers's face burned with a heat rash. "Perhaps you can explain this—"

A sudden *ka-whump* sounded behind them in the hallway.

Everyone whirled. In the glow of flashlight beams, a dark shape raced past the doorway.

"Christ, did you bring others down here?"

"No."

Wolf ran to the door. "Then who the hell was *that*?"

Echoes of running feet trailed off in the distance.

Moose fired his flamethrower down the hallway. A door at the end slammed shut.

"What's back there?" Fox asked.

"We haven't explored that far," Moose answered.

"Well, we got ourselves a survivor," Fallon said. "Go get him, warriors."

Three of the X-2 commandos charged down the corridor. Chambers and Hoffer, remaining in the hallway, traded glances.

"Uh, sir, I think we should go back upstairs," Hoffer said.

"Not a bad idea," Chambers said.

"No, we may need everyone." Wolf's flashlight motioned to follow.

"I'll stay and guard our salvage." Fallon remained at the conference room door. "You boys enjoy the hunt."

Chambers and Hoffer followed Wolf down the dark passage.

"Sir, I don't like this."

"This is no picnic for me either, Hoffer." Every room they passed reeked of death. They caught up with the X-2 commandos where the hallway ended. Flashlight beams shined along the edges of a warped metal door with peeling gray paint.

Hoffer's lips quivered. "I got a bad feeling . . ."

"Be ready for anything." Wolf nodded. "Okay, Snake."

Corporal Snake twisted the marble knob, and the door creaked open.

Chapter 31

The heavy door rattled against the wall. Six rifles aimed at the impenetrable black void.

Chambers flattened against the wall, waiting for the onslaught of gunfire. Arctic air wafted from the antechamber, carrying with it the stench of damnation.

"Jesus." Fox slipped on his gas mask.

Moose offered to toss in a grenade. Wolf shook his head and gave his three commandos hand signals. They nodded and stormed through the doorway. Moose blasted the flamethrower, pushing back the darkness. A low cement ceiling hung over their heads.

Chambers whipped his rifle left and right. His heart jackhammered against his sternum. Hoffer followed last, hovering close behind.

The six-man unit spread about the deep subchamber, guns aimed like snipers. Flashlight beams probed the void. Moose shot out a burst of flames, lighting up some kind of large undercroft chamber that stretched the width of the church. Its depth seemed boundless. A labyrinth of red brick columns offered dozens of places to hide. Above their heads hung crossbeams and planks that made up the nave's floor. Dust and cobwebs clung to everything.

The commandos weaved between the columns, whipping around rifles and flashlight beams. Wolf stopped them. Their lights panned across several dozen wood crates spread out across the antechamber like coffins in a funeral parlor.

"S-Sir, this looks like a vampire's lair." Hoffer walked elbow to elbow with Chambers.

"Shhh."

They crept between the wood crates. German words were inked on the tops. Military cargo. Two X-2 commandos tried to open them. "We need a crowbar."

Wolf said, "We will deal with these later. First, find our survivor."

A dozen yards into the antechamber, a third commando waved them over. An unearthly stench burned Chambers's nose and twisted his stomach into knots.

"Get a load of this." Snake pointed to severed limbs on the ground and the decapitated torso of a brutally slain Nazi soldier. The clothes were shredded, the flesh gnawed to the bone.

"Please tell me the rats ate him," Hoffer muttered.

A bloody trail led to a dozen more Nazi corpses that lay twisted and clumped together as if they had been flung into a pile. The flesh of their faces appeared desiccated. A plump rat skittered over the pile and burrowed into a hollow rib cage. Beyond the bodies, the antechamber trailed off into darkness.

The four masked X-2 commandos looked at one another.

Moose backed away. "Captain, I recommend we get our asses back upstairs."

"I second that," Fox said.

"Not until we secure the area. Keep searching."

"I saw movement." Snake swished his flashlight.

Everyone jerked their rifles. "Where?"

"In the pile of bodies. I saw a finger move." Snake's barrel poked a corpse in the ribs.

The human refuse exploded upward, severed arms and legs and entrails flying. A Nazi corpse leaped up, wailing. "Hyaaaaaaaahhh!" Wild eyes stared from a crimson mask. The corpse charged them, flapping his arms. "Hyaaaaaaaahhh!"

The commandos machine-gunned him point blank. The German spun with a dozen red holes, blood splattering, and fell backward.

Chambers's heart beat wildly. He barely caught his breath before the pile of bodies began *moving*. The mound of flesh and bone writhed like some alien creature out of one of Hoffer's comic books. Heads and arms jutted upward. "No shoot! No shoot!" Frightened eyes squinted in the flashlight beams. "No shoot! Please no shoot!"

"Hold your fire!"

The frantic platoon began screaming in unison. Their rifles aimed at three Nazi soldiers, alive and covered in blood and filth.

"Get down!"

"On the ground. Now!"

"Move, move!"

"Hands up!"

"You, too. On your knees!"

The three Germans clad in black uniforms fell to their knees with arms raised. One yelled in broken English, "*Nein* shoot! *Geben auf!* Ve surrender. Please, *nein* shoot! Ve are unarmed."

"Everybody hold your fire." Wolf's boot shoved the old man's chest. "No talking." He shined his light across the pile of dead soldiers. "Check for more, shoot anybody who moves."

The commandos kicked at the corpses, puffing up human dust and a horrible stink that tested Chambers's gag reflex.

"Don't make a move, you fucking Krauts." Corporal Snake shoved each prisoner, patting their every pocket. "What are you hiding here?" He retrieved a Luger pistol from the older German's lower back. Snake's muffled voice said, "Here, Moose, souvenir."

"Thanks, I've been wanting one of these."

"That's it," Fox said. "Rest are all dead."

Wolf shoved his flashlight into each soot-covered Nazi face. The oldest German had a shaggy white beard. The other two captives, Nazi youths, had only patches of facial hair. Their eyes squinted at the light beams.

Moose kept his flamethrower aimed at their faces. "Why aren't we shooting them?"

"Because I said not to!" Wolf spotlighted the oldest man. "This one looks like an officer." The X-2 lieutenant kneeled, pressing his mask into the SS officer's face. *"Sind noch mehr von euch da unten?"*

The old German's pale eyes stared straight ahead.

"Fox, bind the prisoners," Wolf commanded. "Everybody else secure the area. Fan out in pairs."

Moose's flamethrower barbecued a dozen feeding rats. Hoffer stayed close to Chambers's side as they crept into the shadowy void. Together they swished their flashlight beams between brick columns, drawing closer to a side brick wall.

Someone moaned off to the left. Hoffer and Chambers jerked their beams to a stained mattress propped up against a far corner. The mattress moved.

Hoffer's mouth fell open. "Jeepers." He raised his rifle.

"Hold your fire." As they approached, the mattress continued to shake. A chittering noise resonated from behind it. Chambers motioned with his flashlight. Hoffer dragged the mattress away. Inside a nook, glaring with panicked eyes, was a teenaged girl.

Chapter 32

Hoffer whistled. "Well, call me Margot Lane."

Chambers shone his flashlight in the girl's eyes. Her face was covered in filth, her brown hair long and stringy. Large dark eyes darted from Chambers to Hoffer like a rabbit cornered by coyotes. She kept clambering back against the nook, which was only a couple of feet deep, as if some trap door would open to offer an escape.

"Easy there." Kneeling, Chambers reached for her. "We're here to help." The girl's panicked eyes grew feral. She growled and kicked at his hand. Chambers backed away, the knuckles stinging.

"Ay, what have we got here?" Snake emerged from the darkness. His flashlight probed the girl, blinding her eyes. Her shirt was torn, exposing part of her bra and milky white breast. "Ooh, she's ripe. Who is she?"

"Probably some Nazi's mistress," Hoffer said.

"A Nazi whore, ay." Snake grabbed his crotch. "How 'bout spreading them pretty legs. I'll show you right here why they call me Snake."

The girl growled and kicked him in the groin.

He buckled over. "You bitch!"

"Snake, quit harassing her." Chambers surveyed the

darkness that pressed against their backs. Forty yards down the brick wall three flashlights bobbed and weaved. "Corporal, go get your captain."

"How 'bout you get him yourself."

"Now, Corporal!"

"Fine. But Snake's gonna get him some."

When the X-2 corporal was out of earshot, Hoffer muttered, "What a goon."

Chambers stared at the girl. Her dark trousers and shirt had no Nazi markings. She looked to be sixteen or seventeen, her face at the turning point from girl to woman. She was slim, undernourished. Through her ripped blouse, Chambers could see her ribs. The girl watched his every move. When he ventured forward, she coiled in the corner like a viper ready to strike.

A commando wearing a gas mask entered the glow of flashlights. Wolf's muffled voice spoke with urgency. "Snake said you found a girl."

"Yeah, be careful, she's got a wild streak."

Removing his mask, Wolf knelt, keeping a safe distance from the girl's kicking leg. *"Guten Tag, Fraulein. Wir wollen dir helfen."*

She pressed against the nook.

"She's wounded." Chambers spotlighted her bleeding arm. "One of our stray bullets."

"Was she armed?"

"Not that I could see. She won't let anyone near her."

Wolf chewed his bottom lip. "We have to take her with us."

"Be my guest."

Wolf turned back to her. *"Sprechen Sie Englisch, Fraulein?"*

Slowly she nodded.

"We wish to rescue you." He reached out his hand to her. "Will you go with us?"

She shook her head and looked away.

"Here, *Fraulein,* you must be hungry." He reached into a black leather satchel that was part of his Nazi disguise. He pulled out a small brown bag and unraveled the paper, revealing a thick chocolate bar. *"Schokolade?"*

The girl looked at the chocolate with large hungry eyes.

Wolf broke off a chunk and tossed it into his mouth. "Mmmm. *Köstlich, ya*." He smiled. "*Von* Switzerland."

Releasing a desperate moan, she grabbed several chunks, devouring them.

He handed her the bag. "*Essen. Essen*." Wolf stood, dusting off his knees, smiling at Chambers. "I do not know about America, but in Europe no girl can resist chocolate."

Chambers could feel time slipping away. "Captain, we've burned ten minutes with her. Can you persuade her to go or not?"

"Patience, Chambers. She is clearly in shock."

"Well, keep working your charm."

Wolf sat against the wall next to the girl. She nibbled at the chocolate, her eyes wary of his every move. He drank from his canteen. "Ahhh, good, ya. *Wasser*?" He offered his canteen. As she snatched it, a stream of blood dripped onto the concrete floor.

"May I examine your wound?" Wolf reached for her bleeding arm and the girl slapped at him. "Easy there, *Fraulein*. I am trying to help."

She lowered her guard.

He reached again and she flinched at the touch of his fingers. "I will be gentle." He pulled her arm into the light. Dribbling blood plowed red trails in the soot that covered her skin. "The shoulder wound is a bullet wound—just grazed her. A little cleaning and a bandage will patch her right up." Wolf turned her arm over, examined it. "Dear God . . ."

"What?" Chambers said.

"See here?" Amid numerous rat bites, a seven-digit number was tattooed on her forearm. "That's how the Nazis mark Jewish people at prison camps."

Hoffer leaned over Wolf's shoulder. "What's a Jewish girl doing in a Nazi command post?"

"Probably a servant. The pretty ones get chosen to serve in the officers' quarters." Wolf rolled up his sleeve, revealing a tattoo similar to the girl's. "I understand the horrors you have been through, *Fraulein*."

She looked up at him with shocked eyes.

"Treblinka . . ." Wolf's eyes watered. "Everyone in my family was murdered in the gas chambers. Several of us broke out and escaped to England."

The Jewish girl's eyes glazed over.

"I have joined the Allies to defeat Hitler." He motioned to Chambers and Hoffer. "Did you know the American soldiers have entered Germany? It is true. I swear it on the Torah. We have pushed the Nazis out of France and Belgium. Soon we will end the war and free all Jews."

For a long moment she and Wolf gazed at one another. The girl's beautiful brown eyes were tarnished by so much anger and fear. The horrors she must have seen. How she survived down here with the rats and decaying bodies Chambers couldn't fathom.

"*Fraulein,* we want to get you somewhere safe. Will you come with us?"

She looked away with tears dripping down her cheeks. Her eyes transfixed on the shadows behind them.

Wolf glanced over his shoulder. "What is it?"

An X-2 commando approached, still wearing his gas mask. Fallon's muffled voice said, "Where's the Nazi whore Snake was talking about?"

Wolf answered, "She is not a Nazi. She is a Jewish prisoner. Show her some respect."

Chambers said, "We're trying to get her to come with us."

Fallon shone his light in her eyes. "Shit, we don't have time to mess with her."

"We will make time. Give her a few minutes to adjust to us," Wolf said. "She can provide information." The captain glanced back to where Fox's flashlight was spotlighting the three bound Nazi prisoners. "Bring them over here."

They shoved the prisoners to the wall a few feet down from the nook where the girl remained crouched. Fox and Fallon pushed the three prisoners onto their knees and muttered something in German that sounded like a threat. The old Nazi and the teenaged boys faced forward.

Chambers turned to Fallon. "We need to head back. We're burning daylight down here."

"What's your hurry?"

"I promised my men at the barn we'd get back before nightfall, which according to my watch is less than two hours away."

"They can wait. We've got more important things to deal with right now." Fallon turned to a stout silhouette walking toward them. "Moose, what's the status?"

"Man, what a slaughterhouse." The sergeant pulled off his gas mask and ran a hand across the stubble on his head. Sweat covered his face. "I must have found thirty dead Nazis down here. Most cut to pieces."

Fallon pealed off his mask. "Where's Snake?"

"Back where I left him. Sir, we found something . . . You gotta come see this shit."

As they approached, Snake called from the corner, "Guys, take a sweet look at this." He stabbed his flashlight into a crevice. "A mine shaft."

The five soldiers gathered around the gaping maw.

"Listen." Snake cupped his hands around his mouth and called out, "Anybody in there?" His voice echoed back several times. "This place goes on for fucking ever."

Moose shot a ten-foot flame into the burrow. Every few feet thick planks braced the earthen walls and ceiling.

Snake's beam probed the narrow shaft.

Chambers turned to Wolf. "What's a mine shaft doing beneath a church?"

The captain shrugged and looked at Moose and Snake. "Either of you explore it?"

"You crazy?"

"I'm with Moose," Snake said. "Who knows what's in there?"

Fallon nudged them. "Stop being such pansies."

Snake stepped into the mine shaft, ducking beneath roots that hung from the ceiling. "Appears to go beneath the graveyard. Christ, I think I see part of a coffin. Looks like it's been opened."

The chill that turned Chambers's skin to gooseflesh seemed to emanate from that passage. His bandaged hand tingled. He backed away. "We need to get out of here. Snake, come back."

"No," Fallon said. "Explore another ten feet."

"We should listen to Chambers," Moose said.

"Christ, you of all people—"

A high-pitched scream echoed from the passage.

Twenty feet down, machine-gun bursts lit up the passage, revealing the shape of Snake struggling. His body tossed violently from side to side, smacking the dirt walls. His rifle fell to the ground, and he vanished into the gloom, his high-pitched scream turning primal. A snapping sound echoed, followed by a liquid splatter. Then a head rolled out, landing at Moose's boots.

The sergeant's eyes grew wide. "Snake!" He lifted his flamethrower. In a near-imperceptible blur, a giant shadow lunged from the shaft. It smacked Moose across the chest, slamming him against the wall.

Chambers and Wolf fired at the movements. Snake's killer dashed into the gloom beyond their flashlights.

"Where the hell did he go?"

"Over there!"

"Shoot him!"

Running boots echoed off the concrete.

Shots reverberated in the chamber.

"Lost him!"

"Shit!"

"There he is!"

Flashlights located a large gray shape moving toward them. They shot at it in a frantic rage. Bullets pounded holes in the shadow's broad chest. He stumbled back into the pile of dead Nazis with a crunching sound, like someone diving into a pile of dried leaves. Chambers, Wolf, and Fallon advanced, rifles shouldered. The killer rose again, hurled severed legs and arms at them, and disappeared behind a brick column. The clump of his jackboots faded down the corridor.

Hoffer caught up to them. "Who was that?"

"A crazed Nazi. He killed Snake."

"Christ, he's getting away!" Fallon yelled. "Get him!"

Chambers, Wolf, Fallon, and Hoffer raced between the columns. Reaching the undercroft's center, the four stood back to back, whipping their flashlights and weapons side to side. Movement to their left. Chambers rattled off rounds from his Thompson. Bullets tore across the bricks. The shadow dashed in and out of beams. A phantom shape charged. Bullets knocked him back into the void. Footfalls echoed, circling them.

"Bastard's not human," Hoffer chuckled hysterically.

"Where is he?" Fallon screamed.

Running boots charged from behind. Rifles clacked against shoulders, aiming at a purple flame bouncing toward them.

"Don't shoot! It's me!" Moose joined the circle. He had a torn shirt and three bleeding cuts above his eye. "Let me torch the bastard!" His flamethrower blasted a dragon's breath of flames, lighting up the undercroft. A shirtless figure with mottled gray muscles disappeared behind a column.

"Hoffer, he's headed your way."

"Where—"

Claws dug into Hoffer's shoulder. He went down. "Helllllp-pppp!" The attacker pounded him against the floor. A monstrous hand rose to shred him to bloody ribbons. Chambers swung his rifle like a baseball bat, knocking the assailant back. The shadow bounced back to his feet. Something flashed silver in the light as he charged, a blur of clawing hands.

Chambers, screaming like a madman, fired into the towering silhouette until the rifle turned hot in his hands. *Click! Click! Click! Click! Click! Click!*

Cordite smoke billowed from Chambers's rifle and stung his nose. His flashlight probed the darkness. The body slumped on the floor against a column, a massive bald head lolled toward the shadows. The Nazi wasn't breathing.

Fallon appeared, gripping a knife in one hand, a Luger in the other. "Is he dead?"

"Shoot him again to make sure."

The X-2 lieutenant fired his pistol into the slumped body, making it flop with the rapid session of bullets. The body fell limp again. Fallon nodded. "He's dead now."

Wolf stepped up beside them. "Everyone keep your distance."

Moose limped into the circle, rubbing his bleeding head. "What the hell is it?"

Their flashlights traced the Nazi's muscular back and neck. The skin was a mottled gray, as if the man had covered himself in mud.

Chambers looked at Wolf. "That one of the *Einsatzkommandos*?"

Dozens of fissures pocked the Nazi's flesh. Bullet holes had riddled his black pants and jackboots. Something glinted silver at the hands. Claws. Metallic and razor sharp. Something about his corpse made the hairs at the back of Chambers's neck twitch. *Where's the blood?* The floor should have been pooling with it. Yet there was not a drop anywhere. A sucking sound echoed in the antechamber, like water flowing down a drain. The wounds on the Nazi's back began closing, the gray flesh mending itself until all the bullet holes vanished.

Chambers's hand burned as if caught on fire. He ripped off the bandage. The Star of David cross now had several symbols that glowed with white light.

The Nazi craned his head. Flashlights lit up eye sockets filled with mud.

"What the hell?" Chambers muttered.

The mottled gray face was like something out of a nightmare . . .

The Nazi-thing charged them, razor talons slashing the air.

Wolf emptied his machine gun into the creature. "Shit!" The thing knocked the captain back several feet.

Chambers batted its head with a rifle. Fallon, roaring like a linebacker, tackled the killer and drove his knife into its chest. The shadow wriggled beneath Fallon. He pinned down one flailing arm. "Pin the other!"

Chambers grabbed the attacker's wrist, pinning it down with a knee. Wolf held down the legs. Fallon stabbed into the killer's chest, hacking, hacking, hacking, but the Nazi-thing continued to twist and buck beneath them.

"Shit!"

"Stay down!"

The thing clawed at their arms. Fallon, Wolf, and Chambers grappled to hold it down.

Moose appeared. "Move! I'll torch his ass!"

The three soldiers leaped off.

"Burn in hell, you son of a bitch!" Moose blasted it with the flamethrower. The shadow-thing fell back. The pants caught fire. The flesh melted. The air reeked of burning sulfur. The thing stood, towering over Moose. It backhanded him sideways. The X-2 sergeant skidded across the concrete floor. Fallon and Chambers backed away. The shadow charged forward, its pants rippling with flames. A gooey hand grabbed the closest man—Wolf—lifting him by the throat. The captain's boots dangled off the ground.

"Nein! Nein!" The teenaged girl ran into the glow of Chambers's flashlight. She held up her glowing palm to the creature's face. *"Nein!"* she commanded. *"Er ist ein Freund."*

The thing lowered Wolf to the ground and backed away, its face and upper body fading into the shadows. Then, with heavy footfalls, the orange glowing embers walked away.

Chambers backed against a column, gasping, his face dripping with sweat. Hoffer leaned beside him, his dark hair a rat's nest of sweat and mud. They exchanged looks of disbelief.

Several yards behind them, the footfalls echoed back toward the rear of the antechamber, where the mine shaft tunneled into the earth like a gateway to hell.

Chapter 33

The grays of twilight filtered in through the windows, casting deeper shadows within the church. At the corner window, Finch stared with his mouth gaping as Hoffer whispered with wild hand gestures.

Chambers stared down at the wood floor.

What the hell were we fighting down there?

He couldn't shake the image. The Nazi had walked upright like a man and wore pants and jackboots. But the hollow eyes, gray skin, and indestructibility defied any kind of logic.

Chambers jerked when Fallon's shouts echoed from the nave. "Damn it, Kraut, answer me!" Moose joined in on the shouting and shoved a pew.

Chambers arose wearing a determined look. "That's it." He charged around the corner. In an alcove near the back of the nave, silhouettes shoved and kicked the submissive German prisoners. Lightning lit up the alcove. The three captives, bruised and bloodied, were bound with ropes. They glanced at Chambers wearing looks of supplication. Fallon smacked one Nazi youth so hard he fell over.

Chambers whispered, "Fallon, shut the hell up! You're gonna alert every Kraut within ten miles."

Fox looked up with a grim face. Moose snarled, "Snake's

dead because of them." He kicked the other teenager's stomach.

Fallon paced like an enraged tiger, shaking blood off his knuckles. "This isn't your business, Chambers. Get back to the front."

"We need to get the hell out of here."

"We're not going anywhere. Fox, escort Chambers to the front."

Chambers pointed at the X-2 corporal, who backed off. "Where's your captain?"

Fox motioned with his head. "Over there."

Searching the gloom, Chambers found Wolf sitting with the girl a few pews down. The Czech mercenary stared down at his gloved hands.

"Captain, you need to talk some sense into your soldiers."

Wolf looked up, his marble eyes swirling with turmoil. "Interrogating prisoners is Fallon's area, not mine."

Moose brought the three prisoners back up to their knees.

Fallon drew his brass-knuckled knife and traced the blade across each of their chests, stopping with the old SS officer. "I'm done playing nice. Now I want some answers." He grabbed the old man's hand and pressed the knife against his thumb. "Every question you ignore, I cut off a finger. Now what was that *thing* that killed one of my men?"

The eldest Nazi's pale eyes glared at Fallon. "I do not know."

"Don't fucking lie, Kraut." Fallon sliced the old German's thumb, drawing blood. "The next one snaps the bone."

The Nazi winced. "Please, do not hurt us. I vill tell you all I know."

Fallon got in the officer's face. "Then start talking."

"My name is SS-Obersturmführer Helmut Eichman. Fritz and Hans are corporals. They know nothing."

"Know nothing, ay." Moose grabbed a knot of the Nazi teen's hair and yanked his head back. "Can I slit their throats?"

"Hold off, Moose." Fallon focused back on the SS officer. "I don't give a fuck about your names. Tell us why the hell every Nazi except you three is dead."

Eichman swallowed some blood that dribbled from his busted lip. "I vas commander of our camp in Richelskaul. This church vas headquarters for another SS division led by SS-Hauptsturmführer Von Streicher. I received a distress call from him. The soldiers here vere under attack. I heard screaming and gunshots on the radio. When my soldiers got here . . ." The SS officer stared at the wood floor. "Ve found every soldier downstairs just like you found them, torn to pieces. Everybody except *her*." He pointed to the girl sitting on a pew with a velvet curtain wrapped around her. "That *Ungeheuer* that killed your soldier . . . there vere several of them downstairs, waiting in the dark. They ambushed us. Ve didn't know what to do. The enemy vas dressed in black like us, as SS *Einsatzkommandos,* but they vere something else. *Ungeheuer.* No matter how much ve shot, they would not die."

Moose leaned in. "Kraut, tell us something we don't know."

Fallon said, "Those men floating in the pool. Yours?"

Eichman nodded. "I brought forty *Einsatzkommandos*— the Reich's finest. Those *Ungeheuer* killed most of them in a matter of moments. The men who surrendered vere stripped naked, marched to the outside pool, and executed."

"Mmm-hmm. Sound familiar, Jew-killer?" Wolf stepped into the gray glow of the window.

Eichman looked at the boys bound next to him. "A few of us managed to survive. Ve hid in the bell tower until they left the church. Ve tried escaping, but those *Ungeheuer* are roaming the woods, killing every soldier in sight. They killed all my men in Richelskaul."

"When did all this happen?" Wolf asked.

"Two veeks ago."

Chambers looked out a broken window. The woods outside grew thick with fog and twilight shadows. "How many of these *Ungeheuer* are out there?"

"Forty, fifty." The Nazi shrugged. "It vas too dark to see."

"Are there any more hiding beneath the church?" Fallon asked.

"Just the one you fought. It is *der Vormund*."

"The guardian," Wolf translated.

Chambers glanced back at the darkness that cloaked the altar stairway.

"What is it guarding?" Wolf asked.

"Whatever is down that passage. That is where it stays most of the time."

Captain Wolf paced. "SS-Hauptsturmführer Von Streicher was implementing Operation Eisen Sarg, a Nazi plan to unleash a new kind of weapon."

Eichman nodded.

Wolf pulled out the photo of SS soldiers loading iron trunks into a covered cargo truck. "What kind of weapons are in these trunks?"

"I vas not privileged to such information. All Von Streicher told me vas he developed a new weapon that would stop the Allies and Russians from invading. I saw a cargo truck pass through Richelskaul carrying these coffins, but I never knew what vas in them."

Fallon grabbed his hand again, poised to cut off a finger. "Bullshit."

Eichman's intense pale eyes looked at Wolf. "I swear. Only Von Streicher and his officers knew the truth about Operation Eisen Sarg. I have told you all—"

Fallon stuffed a gag into the SS officer's mouth. "We'll have some more fun later."

Wolf said, "Fallon, take the radio and see if you can contact our reinforcements. Moose, keep an eye on the prisoners. Fox, guard our backs in case that *Ungeheuer* decides to come up here. Chambers, I need your men to keep watching the front windows."

"Where are you going?" Chambers asked.

"To see if the girl can tell us more about this *Ungeheuer*."

"Captain, what does *Ungeheuer* mean?"

Wolf shook his head skeptically. "It means 'monster.'"

Chapter 34

Chambers returned to the vestibule. "Everybody back to your posts."

His men stared as Moose and Fox shoved the German prisoners against a column. Buck shook his head. "Unbelievable."

"It was a damn horror show down there, Buck." Hoffer sketched a monster on his pad of paper. "You should have seen this thing. It was as big as Frankenstein. Had these sharp claws."

Buck's brow furrowed. "Hoffer, you're letting your imagination run wild again."

"Well, I didn't imagine it clawing me." Hoffer lifted up a flap of his torn shirt, exposing parallel wounds across his shoulder and biceps. "I was attacked by some kind of walking dead thing with claws."

"Like a zombie?" Finch asked.

"Yeah, tell him, guys. You saw the claws."

Moose pointed to a gash above his eye. "It clawed the hell outta me, too. Thing must have crawled up from the pits of hell . . ."

Buck looked at Chambers. "You see a zombie, too, Lieutenant?"

"It happened so quick, I'm not sure what it was." Chambers reloaded cartridges into his magazine, wincing at the pain caused by his every move.

"It sure as hell wasn't a man," Moose said. "He didn't bleed. Like he was already dead."

Hoffer's eyes lit up. "That explains why our bullets wouldn't kill the ones back in Richelskaul. The Nazis are already dead. Freaking zombie soldiers."

"Yeah, that makes sense," Finch said. "I noticed them walking kind of stiff. Jesus, you know what this means?"

Hoffer nodded. "Our weapons are useless."

Buck rolled his eyes. "You guys should hear yourselves."

Moose threw out his chest. "Hey man, you weren't there to see it tear Snake's head clean off. With its bare hands. Shit, I never seen anything like it."

"Bullets don't kill vampires either," Hoffer offered. "There were crates down there that looked like coffins. Maybe we're dealing with vampires."

Moose turned to the redheaded commando. "Professor, what's your take on this?"

Fox adjusted his glasses. "The zombie theory has more validity. Although not in the way you might think. I once did an anthropological expedition on Haiti. My fascination with these dark-skinned islanders was their practice of *voudon*, or what's more commonly known as voodoo. I was privileged to study some of their rituals. A local witch doctor, called a *loa*, told me he could turn people into zombies by giving them a potion that contained a highly strong nerve poison called tetrodotoxin, which comes from the puffer fish."

Hoffer and Finch grinned at one another. "Zombies really exist?"

Fox nodded. "This toxin severely damages a person's neurological system, mainly the left side of the brain, which controls their reasoning. The victim becomes lethargic, and his pulse slows to the point that he appears dead even to a physician. These zombies are, however, physically alive, just brain dead, and they are easily controlled by the *loa* who poisoned them. Although I never actually saw a zombie, I heard rumors

that Haiti has a black market for selling zombies to planta-
tions. They use them as slave labor." The British corporal
smiled. "Interesting enough, their penal system has actually
made zombie making illegal."

"You suggesting the Nazis have played with voodoo?"
Chambers asked.

"I wouldn't put it past them. The SS have been known to
travel as far abroad as South America to quench their thirst
for the occult. Several of the men in Hitler's inner circle are
occultists, including the head of the SS, Heinrich Himmler,
himself. His SS is also notorious for its scientific experiments. That thing down there could be one of their subjects.
The fact that they've excavated a tunnel beneath the graveyard arouses my suspicion even more."

Hoffer chewed on his thumbnail. "Every story I've ever
read about zombies, whoever got scratched or bitten by one,
became one."

"That's werewolves," Finch said.

"Zombies, too."

Chambers said, "Okay, enough talk about monsters. We
need to keep our heads straight."

Lightning flashed in the stained-glass windows. Damp
tempest winds howled through the church's pocked structure.
Chambers stepped up beside Buck, who eyed the forest intently, like a watchdog that could smell danger coming. A
large hole in the window offered a view of the gravel parking
lot and road. Rain tossed the conifers from side to side. The
ghostly fog swirled with the changing winds. "Buck, any
movement out there?"

"Nada."

"You holding up okay?"

The Texas rancher kept his eyes trained on the road. "Yep,
don't worry about me."

"Good. I need you to stay rock solid."

Buck nodded and stuffed another plug of tobacco into his
cheek.

Chambers slouched against a column and pulled his helmet over his eyes, pretending to catch a few winks. He remained vigilant, though, watching Wolf sitting on a pew with

the Jewish girl. She was looking down at her hands, playing with a hole in her sleeve. Dust covered her grimy face, except for the area around her eyes where tears had washed away the dirt. Her long hair hung disheveled.

The X-2 captain examined the gash in her shoulder. Blood had clotted and stained the white fabric. "I need to dress your wound before it gets infected."

The girl shook her head.

Wolf sighed. "Well, at least let me look at it." He touched her arm. She didn't flinch this time. The bullet had torn a hole in the upper arm of her blouse, exposing the tender flesh. "I just want to get a closer look." Wolf pulled open the sleeve. "Ah, you are lucky, *Fraulein*. The bullet just grazed you. Please, may I clean it?" He swabbed the gash with water. Her big catlike eyes watched his face. The tension in her cheeks softened.

Good, Chambers thought. *Wolf's gaining her trust.* Chambers felt a deep gnawing in his gut about this girl. *How did she survive such a massacre? And how did she stop that thing from killing Wolf?*

Wolf leaned back. "All done, *Fraulein*." He offered his canteen. "Thirsty?"

She gulped too fast and water dribbled down her chin. When she lowered the canteen, wet filth streamed around her mouth. She mumbled something in German.

Wolf mumbled something back then handed her a handkerchief. She poured water on it and wiped away the mask of grime.

Wolf smiled when she was finished. "You have the face of an angel."

She looked away.

For a moment Wolf's mercenary features softened, growing gently paternal. He held her hands, caressing her delicate fingers. "Will you speak to me?"

The girl kept her face in the shadows.

"Okay, can you at least tell me your name?"

She hesitated then mumbled something under her breath.

"What was that?"

"An-na."

"Anna. That is a beautiful name. I am Izak Wolfowitcz. Call me Wolf." He opened his satchel. "Here, this is what Americans call a K ration special. *Käse mit Schinken*." He gave her a small can of dried cheese with ham flecks. "Your wine has been aged to perfection, selected from a vintage year for grapes." He sprinkled a packet of grape powder into her canteen. "*Essen*. We will talk later, *ya*!"

Wolf stood and walked over to a side window. He rubbed the back of his neck. Chambers ended his sleeping charade and joined him. "You never cease to amaze me."

"I don't know. I felt like I was running out of options. I was this close to singing my Yiddish favorite, 'Papirosen.'" He smiled. The unexpected humor made Chambers chuckle.

Fallon returned from the shadows, wiping blood off his knuckles. "What's the status on the girl?"

"I got her name—Anna."

"Well, we need more than her name and ASAP."

"It will take some time. She's traumatized."

"You have news for us, Fallon?" Chambers asked.

"Yeah, just spoke with the captain of Charlie Company. An all-out push is still scheduled for dawn. I told them we cleared a path to Richelskaul. They should be here by tomorrow afternoon."

"Tomorrow afternoon!" Chambers rubbed his jaw. "What the hell are we gonna do till then?"

Wolf answered, "We have decided to stay the night here. Make sure the Germans don't try to recapture their command post."

Chambers frowned. "Are you nuts? The last thing we should do is spend the night in this hellhole."

Fallon said, "It's the most defensible shelter in the area."

Wolf motioned back to the altar stairway. "And we have a lot more intelligence to gather before reinforcements arrive."

"What about my men back at the barn?"

Fallon answered, "We'll get them tomorrow."

"No," Chambers insisted. "I promised I'd come back for them. Besides, we should keep everyone together."

Wolf nodded. "He's right, we could use the extra manpower. We can be there and back within the hour."

Fallon walked over to a shattered stained-glass window, his eye darting as he thought. "No way, too dangerous. Those Nazi-things are out there. Besides, Wolf, I need you here to fulfill our mission. We still have to go back for our salvage."

Chambers recalled the duffel bags filled with gold and cash from the safe. The X-2 commandos had left the undercroft in such a panic that they left it behind.

"So this whole mission is about stealing Nazi gold."

Fallon stuffed a fat cigar between his teeth. "You got your reward, we got ours. And we aren't leaving till we get paid."

Chambers glared at Wolf. "I risked my men for you."

"Don't give us that bullshit," Fallon said. "You risked your men so you could go home to a piece of pussy."

Chambers shoved Fallon into a pillar. In a blur of motion Chambers was flipped onto his back, a blade pressed against his throat. "I told you he'd turn on us," Fallon growled. "He's nothing but a liability."

"Let him go." Wolf grabbed Fallon's wrist and pulled the blade away. "Compose yourself, Lieutenant, before the men see you."

"He attacked *me*."

"Go take a walk." Wolf got in his face. "*Now.*"

Fallon pointed his brass-knuckled knife at Chambers. "You ever touch me again, Reaper, and I'll be wearing your balls as a necklace."

Wolf helped Chambers up. "I'll give you directions to the barn. Take two men and go get the rest of your platoon. And when you return, you goddamned better have cooled off."

Chapter 35

Chambers, Buck, and Finch ran across the gravel parking lot. They hunkered under a clump of trees, watching the farm road and forest. Chambers checked his compass. The road wound through the forest north to south. Dense woods stood straight ahead to the east. To the west loomed the Gothic church with its bell-tower facade. He pointed down the road that curved farther south through the woods. "Barn's a couple miles. Should get there within the hour. Stick close and don't make a sound."

Buck and Finch nodded, their eyes alert.

The three bolted down the swampy road, their boots sinking into the mud. They stayed close to the tree line in case a vehicle drove around the dead-man's curve. The green-gray fog had lifted to the tops of the conifers, allowing visibility up to forty yards. Brown water trickled in the ditch alongside the road. Every tree dripped with dampness. Buzzards circled overhead like a squadron of enemy planes. On both sides of the road, long driveways stretched up hills to lifeless farmhouses staring from the trees with vacant window eyes. Front doors hung wide open. Up ahead a charred German cargo truck with a long enclosed trailer had careened into the ditch. The windshield was pocked with holes.

The three soldiers ducked behind the cargo truck's front grill. Chambers crept along the passenger side and peered into a shattered window. Flies buzzed. Blood and human matter fouled the windshield. Two Germans in gray uniforms sat slumped across one another, both bodies riddled with bullet holes. Chambers winced at the smell.

From across the cab, Buck peered in through the driver's side window. He raised an eyebrow. Rounding the truck, they found the back tailgate down. Inside the cargo trailer were several iron trunks, the lids standing open. Signaling Buck and Finch to watch the road, Chambers climbed into the back of the truck. He stepped between the coffin-sized trunks. Large rivets sealed every edge. All sides were emblazoned with a white skull and bones—the Nazi death's head—along with the jagged thunderbolts of the SS. Broken locks littered the floor. Each trunk Chambers passed was empty. Except . . . there was something peculiar about them—the cold iron interior of each trunk was covered with a gray residue. *Is this some kind of mercury?* It didn't shimmer like mercury. Whatever the substance was, it made the truck's interior smell like a swamp.

"Spsssssd." Buck stood just outside the tailgate, tapping his watch.

Chambers held up a finger then hastened his reconnaissance. He passed dozens of iron trunks stacked in pairs. *Wonder what's in the ones beneath.* Toward the front of the truck the interior grew pitch black. Chambers switched on his flashlight. The lid on the farthest trunk had been popped open on one corner. A crow bar was left sticking out. He shone his light along the seam, trying to see inside. A lump of fabric . . . a steel helmet.

His hand began to itch. *Oh, Jesus Chri—*

Something slammed against the lid from inside.

Chambers fell back against a trunk, his heart hammering. The corner of the opposite trunk popped up an inch. Gray fingers jutted from the crack. Silver eyes peered out. The thing inside growled and banged against the coffin walls, nudging the corner up another inch.

Terror scuttled down Chambers's back like an army of

cockroaches. He stumbled back down the trailer. Banging echoed from other trunks. He leaped out the back. "Move! Move! Move!"

Buck and Finch chased after him. "What the hell?"

"Just keep running."

Chambers sprinted full speed through the rain, not looking back until the last of the banging had faded. He checked his palm. The Star of David cross no longer itched. Still, he picked up speed. Buck, the star athlete, kept up stride for stride. Finch huffed and puffed ten feet behind them.

Twilight painted the forest in deep grays and ink blacks as the light steadily drained from the sky. Chambers stopped and knelt at a muddy driveway that wound up a tree-dotted hill. Beyond the scattered firs, a familiar barn sat beside a house that had burned down to its foundation. He glanced at the surrounding landmarks. *This has to be it.*

Buck knelt beside him. "Chambers, I didn't know you could run that fast."

Finch gasped, his face a mask of panic. "Jesus, what the hell happened back there?"

Chambers peered through his binoculars. Up the hill the barn doors were open, the blackness within impenetrable.

Watching their backs, Buck rolled his baseball between his hands. "Sir, what was inside that cargo truck?"

"More of those things."

"Zombie soldiers!" Finch whined. "We're toast."

Chambers grabbed him by the collar. "Keep your voice down, soldier. Hold yourself together. No mention of zombies till we get back to the church, *comprende*?"

The kid nodded, wide-eyed.

Chambers aimed a flashlight toward the barn and flashed the light three times. The barn's entry remained dark as slate. "Come on, guys, where are you?" He flashed again.

When a light flashed back four times, relief flooded his chest. "Let's move."

At the top of the hill, Sergeant Mahoney guided them into the barn.

"Thank God." Goldstein and Deuce gathered around them.

"Everybody okay?" Chambers asked.

"We've just been waiting," Goldstein answered.

"Where are the others?" Deuce asked, his voice on edge.

"Safe. We've got a new hideout. I'll explain later." Chambers scanned the gloom for Garcia. He was still lying in the hay covered by a horse blanket. "Did you make the stretcher?"

"Yeah," Mahoney said proudly. "Out of yard tools and horse blankets. Pretty sturdy."

Chambers nodded. "Nice work. Let's transport Garcia. We move out in five." He noticed Buck checking his pockets. "What is it?"

"Sir, I dropped my lucky baseball down by the road." He started toward the entrance.

"No, stay inside the barn."

"Come on, Chambers, I can get there and back in a flash."

"Forget it. It's too risky."

Buck stared at the roadway. "I gotta get my ball back."

"What's so damned important about that baseball?"

"It was the first ball m'daddy gave me. I was five. He never talked much 'cept when I pitched to him." Buck looked back with eyes like a wounded puppy. "My baseball's kinda like your lucky watch, sir."

Chambers sighed. "You can get it on our way back. Just stay put." He stepped under the loft. "How we doing, Goldstein?"

The medic and Deuce hoisted Garcia onto the makeshift litter. "Just need to strap him in. Another minute."

Dusk steadily transformed into night. The shadows within the barn grew gloomier. Endless rain pecked against the roof. Private Finch's silhouette sniffled as he gathered up packs. Chambers put a hand on the teenager's shoulder. "Hold strong, Finch. We're almost out of this."

"I'm sorry, sir." He wiped his damp cheeks. "For the first time in months, I feel . . . you know, like we're doomed."

"Is that something the Avenger would ever think?"

Finch straightened his shoulders. "No, sir, the Avenger's fearless in the face of danger."

"Well, that's the way I need you to be. We're invincible,

remember?" The hand clamped on Finch's shoulder began to tingle with pinpricks. Finch looked up, shock in his eyes. "Jesus, what's with your hand?"

Chambers stared down at the bandage wrapped around his palm. The tingling intensified, turning into an irritating itch. "It's nothing. Keep gathering those packs." He walked behind the tractor, scratching his palm. His heartbeat quickened.

"They're coming," Goldstein said. The chaplain held up his palm. The cross-shaped scar glowed with tiny electrical sparks that reflected in his glasses. "God's warning us."

Trembling, Chambers looked back down at his bandaged hand. He peeled back one of the corners. A light glowed from beneath.

"We have to get out of here."

"Shhh!" Sergeant Mahoney called from the front of the barn. "Everybody listen."

Chambers and Goldstein bolted to the open doors where Mahoney stood watch. Deuce and Finch hovered behind them. Outside, the rain had turned to a light drizzle. Beyond the pitter-patter playing on the tin roof came a muffled reverberation.

Mahoney cocked his ear to the doorway. "Hear that?"

Chambers frowned. "I don't hear . . ."

The distant reverberation grew into a distinctive *whah-oom, whah-oom, whah-oom*, softly at first, but grinding louder with each passing second.

"Buck, got anything in your sights?"

At the window, the rancher stared into his riflescope. "Not yet, sir. Too many trees. Hear a vehicle coming, though."

Chambers whispered, "We got company. Move Garcia to the back of the barn, then I want everyone back here in double time, rifles locked and loaded."

The squad scooped up Garcia's litter and dispersed into the shadows. Fifteen seconds later, they returned ready for combat. Buck scurried back up the loft to the window. Finch took the downstairs window. Deuce lay prone between the tractor's giant tires and set up his BAR on its legs. Goldstein, armed with Garcia's M1 rifle, climbed behind a pile of haystacks.

Outside, the chattering motor grew closer.

Chambers and Mahoney watched the road through cracks in the barn wall.

An engine growled over the hill like an approaching predator. A single glowing headlight peered through the haze. Wheels sloshed through mud as a BMW motorcycle with sidecar stopped in the road, fifty yards downhill from the barn. A lump formed in Chambers's throat. Through his field glasses, he saw the outlines of two SS soldiers. They sat idle for a moment, searching the perimeter. Their masks with goggled eyes, making them look like insects, scanned the farmhouses tucked into the woods. The passenger climbed out of the sidecar, kneeled down, and picked up something white and spherical. A baseball. The Nazi examined the boot impressions leading up the muddy driveway.

"I got my sights on 'em," Buck whispered from the hayloft window.

"Hold your fire," Chambers whispered.

Both Nazis turned their heads in unison. Reflective goggles transfixed on the barn.

An icy river flooded through Chambers's veins.

The crouched Nazi dropped the baseball and climbed back into his sidecar. The motorcycle whipped around and roared up the muddy driveway. The single headlight beam lanced from the smoke and spotlighted the barn. Chambers ducked as light filtered through the cracks. The cycle rumbled to a stop, tires splashing a puddle. The motorbike purred like a hungry tiger.

Chambers gripped his rifle and peered through the cracks. Beyond the bright headlight, the two Germans remained seated on the motorcycle, staring intently in Chambers's direction. He felt like a rabbit spotted by wolves.

The driver gripped the handlebars. The other soldier sat in the sidecar holding a submachine gun. Both wore black uniforms, steel helmets, goggles, and what appeared to be masks of gray mud. The passenger in the sidecar stepped out, his knee-high jackboots splashing into the mud. The Nazi approached the wide-open barn doors, the submachine gun clacking at his hip.

Chambers braced himself against the wall, looked to Mahoney. Bright light and shadows painted stripes on the sergeant's face as he raised his eyebrows and nodded. Showtime.

Between the tractor's tires, Deuce gripped his BAR. His eyes flitted from Chambers to the barn door.

The clacking submachine gun drew closer.

Chambers and Mahoney backed away from the entrance in opposite directions, searching for cover.

A warped shadow stretched across the dirt floor like a spreading pool of oil. The Nazi's face and steel helmet pierced the entrance. The head turned, goggled eyes locking on Chambers. The Nazi charged. Chambers fired into his face. The man's head snapped back. His steel helmet fell to the dirt. The Nazi shook his slick bald cranium, rubbed the bullet hole in his cheek, and ripped the goggles off his face. Silver fire blazed in his eye sockets. The thing roared, jerking the submachine gun. The muzzle flashed. Bullets arced across the corner. Chambers dove behind a post as ricocheting metal popped like firecrackers behind him. Tools fell off the walls, crashing and clanging.

Screaming, men fired repeatedly into the Nazi's chest, knocking him back outside.

From the motorcycle, a burp gun fired several short bursts.

B-r-r-r-p-p-p!

Chambers hit the ground as bullets riddled the barn walls.

Barrel flames lit up faces in the gloom. Deuce unleashed his BAR. Finch screamed like a lunatic as he fired wildly out the window. Up in the loft, Buck took steadily aimed shots at the motorcycle. Cordite smoke singed the air.

Chambers plucked a grenade off his chest and belly-crawled beneath the metal storm. Dust and splinters rained down on his neck and back. He reached the open barn door, pulled the pin, and tossed the grenade out the entrance. An explosion pelted the barn walls with shrapnel. Chambers pulled his helmet over his head as the boards above snapped inward. Metal hornets punctured a dozen large holes in the clapboards and pinged off the tractor.

Glass shattered. Finch screamed from the window. "I'm hit!"

When the dust and debris settled, Chambers peered outside. One Nazi lay on the ground. Bullets fired into the Kraut's back and buttocks as he crawled away. The driver leaped off the cycle and shot back with the burp gun. Unfazed by bullets ripping into his jacket, he scooped up his maimed comrade and placed him in the sidecar. Then the driver hopped back on the bike and revved the engine. The motorcycle whipped around and growled down the hill, its red taillight disappearing into the mist.

Buck continued to shoot.

Mahoney peered out the barn doors. "They're gone, Buck. Save your bullets."

Chambers stood, dusting off splinters. "Everybody okay?"

The soldiers emerged from the shadows, their expressions a mix of horror and relief. Finch curled up in a ball. "I can't see! I can't see!"

Goldstein pushed past Chambers and pried apart Finch's hands to reveal a face streaming with blood. "You're gonna be okay, kid." Goldstein plucked glass shards from his cheeks and forehead. "Sit still. I'll have you cleaned up in a jiff."

Buck hopped down from the loft's ladder. "Did you guys see that? Our bullets didn't do diddly squat."

"No, but grenades sure's hell gave them a wallop," Mahoney said.

Chambers stared at the road. "Krauts know we're here now."

Deuce whined, "Jeez, those things will be coming after us."

"We won't be here when they do." Chambers snapped fresh cartridges into his Thompson. "Buck, watch the front. Everybody else to the back of the barn."

Chambers hustled through the stalls and pushed open the back doors. Beyond lay a field of knee-high grass. A dozen bundles of hay stood like tepees. A tall barbed-wire fence and thick fir trees bordered the field. "We'll route across the field and through that forest. Thirty seconds, men."

Mahoney barked, "Goldstein, Finch, grab Garcia's litter."

The wounded soldier squinted at his comrades. "What's going on?"

"Nazi zombies are hunting us," Finch whined. His eyebrows were stained with blood, but he could see again.

Mahoney slapped him. "Finch, shut up. Don't listen to him, Garcia. We're just changing scenery. Hang tight." The sergeant turned to Chambers. "We're ready to roll, sir."

"I'll get Buck." He ran back through the stalls to the front of the barn. "Let's roll."

No answer.

"Buck?" Chambers looked up in the loft. Empty. He searched the gloom around the tractor. "Buck, we're going." His hand tingled again. He raced to the front entrance and spotted Buck running down the hill toward the road. "Buck!"

He stopped and turned around. Chambers waved him back.

The tingling hand burned like a rash.

"My baseball!" Buck pointed down at the road. "I see it."

An engine grumbled. Down the hill a German troop transporter shrieked to a stop.

"Holy sh—!" Buck bolted back up the hill as a dozen black shapes leaped out. They scattered between the trees, charging up toward the barn, firing madly at Buck.

Chapter 36

Gunshots cracked from down the hill.

Buck hurled a grenade. A geyser of mud and smoke knocked the front Nazis on their backs. The other black shapes fanned out, attacking from three sides.

Chambers yanked Buck through the entrance as bullets shredded the barn walls. "Back of the barn. Now!"

Buck high-stepped past the tractor.

"Let's move, everybody!" Chambers bolted through the back door. Bullets rattled the barn behind them. The platoon raced out behind him, into the fog and drizzle.

Lightning split the heavens with a thundering crack.

Barreling into the torrents, his Thompson held tight against his chest, Chambers sprinted across the grassy field. He glanced back. The two men carrying the stretcher raced in the middle of the pack. Goldstein ran closest. "There could be mines in this field."

"We'll take our chances."

Buck and Deuce carried the rear. They stopped behind a tepee of hay, fired at the Nazis charging out of the barn. MP40 bullets strafed the field. The Krauts ran slower, their gaits stiff and lumbering, as if fearless of getting shot. Buck and Deuce hurled grenades and continued running.

Chambers leaped down into an irrigation ditch. He fended off the pursuers with a base fire as the others worked their way into the ditch. Bullets pelted the embankment and whizzed over their heads. "Set Garcia down for a second. There's too many of them."

All six of them fired from the trench, knocking down several Nazis in the high grass. But a dozen more shadows sifted from the trees on both sides of the barn. The soldiers they shot kept getting back up.

"We can't stop 'em!" Finch yelled.

Chambers yelled, "Everybody! Grenades!"

The six men yanked pineapples off their chest, pulled the pins, and hurled them across the field. Several geysers sent the front Nazis flying. Smoke drifted over the field. Bullets continued to crack the air above their heads.

Buck plucked off two more grenades. "Keep running! I'll hold 'em off."

Chambers ran through the irrigation ditch, his boots splashing through ankle-deep water. Picking up the stretcher, the other four followed their platoon leader around a corner, sprinted down a shoot for twenty yards, and rounded another turn. Ahead a barbed-wire fence spanned a ravine that fed cold trickling water into the trench. Chambers felt beneath the surface, finding a one-foot gap between the ground and the jagged bottom wires.

A soldier screamed behind them. Shots fired.

"Buck!" Deuce turned toward his buddy's scream.

Mahoney yelled, "Deuce, get back here!"

Machine-gun shots echoed closer.

"Hurry, under the fence!" Chambers dove flat on his stomach, submerging beneath the murky water. He squirmed through the narrow gap beneath the fence. Barbs snagged his parka and legs. He surfaced, spitting out muddy water. On the other side the ravine snaked through a forest of dark fir trees. "Come on! Everybody under!"

Soldiers plunged under the water, crawling through one at a time. Chambers covered them. Mahoney surfaced, then Deuce.

"Get Garcia through!" Chambers commanded.

On the other side, Goldstein and Finch wrestled to push the stretcher through the gap.

"It won't fit!" Goldstein screamed.

Chambers leaped in, water now up to his chest. His hands plunged, gripping the bottom of the fence. Sharp barbs stung his hands as he lifted. "Okay, now!"

"Hold your breath, Garcia." Goldstein dove his head under water, pulling the Mexican soldier with him. Chambers held up the wires as Mahoney pulled Goldstein and Garcia through.

"Hurry!" Finch pushed on the back end of the stretcher from the other side.

Splashing echoed from the trenches behind him.

"Hurry, damn it!" Finch shoved Garcia's legs through then dove for the gap. Halfway across, Finch surfaced with a panicked squeal.

"Come on!" Chambers yelled.

"My canteen's hooked!" Finch twisted and splashed, becoming more entangled. "Help!"

"Hold steady." Chambers worked to cut him free.

Behind the kid, several Nazi shadows rounded the corner of the trench.

"Hurry!" Deuce and Mahoney fired rapidly into the advancing horde. Bullets knocked off steel helmets. Battered away guns. Ripped off rubber masks. Silver eyes blazed in the darkness. The front Nazis fell. But others trampled them, sloshing through the quagmire.

Chambers rushed to cut Finch free.

A creature with glowing eyes pulled out a saber.

Finch screamed and kicked at it.

Chambers's muddy fingers gripped Finch by the armpits, but the fence had him in its teeth. The thing grabbed Finch's boots, resulting in a deadly tug-of-war. Chambers felt his grip slipping. Two more Nazis joined the game, yanking Finch back under the fence. "No!" Chambers fell back beneath the water. Muffled screams and gunshots echoed above. He resurfaced. "Finch!" Through the barbed wires, he watched helplessly as the kid released a guttural cry before being swallowed by the ravaging mob.

"Finch!" Chambers fired point blank at the creatures just

beyond the fence. More glowing eyes joined their numbers. He emptied his submachine gun on the pack then battered at the mottled gray hands jutting between the barbed wires.

Several groping hands gripped Chambers and pulled him against the fence. He screamed as gray fingers clawed at his mouth and throat, tore at his parka. Mahoney and Goldstein ripped him free as several blades stabbed through the fence.

Deuce shot into them with his BAR. "Die, God damn it!"

"Behind those trees!" Mahoney and Goldstein dragged Chambers into the woods. He collapsed beside Garcia's litter. Chambers's heart hammered his chest. He gasped and coughed muddy water.

Mahoney screamed, "Deuce, get over here!"

The Poker King fired off a few more rounds, then leaped behind a thick log beside Chambers.

The Nazi-things pressed against the thick barbed fence. The barrier bowed outward, testing the metal posts, but held. Several soldiers became snagged on the barbs. Finch's bloody, tangled body clogged the only gap. The things continued to hack and rip at him as if death wasn't enough.

Chambers plucked off his last two grenades. "Give 'em hell."

They barraged the entangled Nazis with six grenades. Smoke filled the ravine. Chambers didn't wait for it to clear. "Let's get the hell outta here!"

Chapter 37

The rescue team pushed nonstop for half an hour. Chambers felt his way through the pitch-dark forest, unseen tree branches grating his flesh. The gunshots following them faded off until the dominant sounds became the swish of their uniforms and the squish of their boots over mud and pine needles.

Exhaustion burning his legs, Chambers glanced back at his men. Deuce's lanky silhouette, holding up the stretcher's front end, stumbled awkwardly but kept moving. Mahoney and Goldstein, carrying the back end of the stretcher, hiked too far behind the night's curtain to be seen. But their huffing and puffing remained within earshot.

"Just a little farther, guys," Chambers assured them.

In time the path turned into a slight decline, much to the relief of the men. Gravity became their ally. They weaved between thicket after thicket of spiky pines. Chambers was beginning to doubt his navigational instincts when the trees finally gave way to a grassy field. A half-moon through the clouds offered enough light for nocturnal vision. The electrical storm had passed. Water dripped from the pine needles.

Chambers signaled everyone to stop. Running hunched over, he crossed the rest of the field on his own. As he neared a muddy farm road a motor growled. Headlights, like gleaming predator eyes, charged toward Chambers. He dropped flat in the tall grass. A half-track vehicle trundled down the road and stopped, its engine grumbling just twenty yards away. A spotlight panned across the field, lighting up the grass around Chambers with blazing white intensity. He remained frozen. *I'm invisible. I'm invisible.* German soldiers swished through the high grass, their boots crunching all around him. The profiles of two SS soldiers stood a few feet away, their steel helmets and gas masks silhouetted against the moon. Chambers's heart pounded so loudly he feared they could hear it. He held his breath. The spotlight weaved back and forth. The Nazis lingered a few more seconds, then wordlessly headed back. Chambers released a breath as the half-track continued down the road.

He found his men hovering behind a thicket of bushes. "Everybody okay?"

"We were more concerned about you," Goldstein said.

"That was close," Mahoney said, watching the road. The half-track echoed in the distance. "You can't keep pushing your luck like that."

Chambers kneeled beside Garcia. "How're you holding up, *amigo*?"

Strapped on the stretcher, the Mexican gave a thumbs-up.

"Okay, let's roll." The rescue team marched less than a hundred yards down the dirt road before a loud racket sent them ducking for cover.

Clang . . . clang . . . clang . . .

Eight of them sounded off—2000 hours. *Music to my ears.*

"Almost there." Chambers followed the treeline. The woods parted, and the silhouette of a massive bell tower appeared above the treetops. He grinned. The war-battered church's dark facade loomed before them, a still and quiet fortress.

Goldstein stared up at the sharp spires and bell tower. "The same as my dream."

Despite the pocked stone and several broken stained-glass windows, the church offered sanctuary from the cold night and the forest creatures that lurked in the dark. Chambers hoped his men were still in there. "Let's make sure it's secure." Huddling the unit behind a clump of trees, he studied the gravel parking lot and surrounding woods to make sure no Krauts were on the move. Satisfied, Chambers flashed three quick signals toward the church. In the dark front windows came two white flashes, a pause, then two more flashes.

"Let's go." The team ran across the gravel lot carrying the stretcher.

Hoffer opened the front door and waved them through, grinning. "Man, am I glad to see you guys. I was beginning to worry when we saw that half-track drive by." The rescue team set Garcia's stretcher on the floor. Goldstein checked his vitals while Chambers, Mahoney, and Deuce collapsed on the floor, breathing heavily.

Fox shoved a pew toward the door. "Any others?"

"This is it," Chambers gasped, feeling a sharp pain in his side.

Hoffer's grin dropped. "Where's Buck and Finch?"

Chambers shook his head.

"What! No . . ."

"I'm sorry, Hoff. They fought bravely."

"No!" Hoffer screamed, his face turning red. "No! No! Nooooo!"

Mahoney barked, "Quiet, Hoffer, get a hold of yourself."

"No, man! We're all dead!" He ran into the nave, the darkness swallowing him up.

"Hoffer, get back here!" Mahoney yelled.

"Leave him." Chambers scanned the dark vestibule. The three prisoners were still tied together against the column. "Fox, where are the others?"

The X-2 corporal, gripping his German MP40, stared out the front window. "Downstairs doing reconnaissance."

"Go get them."

"My orders are to watch the prisoners."

"We'll watch them, Corporal. Now go tell Wolf we need them up here on the double!"

Grumbling, Fox dashed off into the dark nave. Chambers

paced. He patted his chest for a cigarette then remembered his own rule: no smoking in the dark. Spotting Fox's radio sitting on a pew, Chambers picked up the receiver and tried to get a signal. "This is Spear Patrol. Anybody there? Copy."

Static.

"Come on. Hello, this is Spear Patrol. Does anybody copy?"

He slammed down the phone.

Part 6

Revelations

I know how to kill an enemy soldier. He's flesh and blood like me, and where I tear open, he tears open. A bullet to the head or through the heart will surely kill him, or at least take the fight out of him. But an enemy who defies these human limitations . . . what flesh is he made of? How do I kill him?

—LIEUTENANT JACK CHAMBERS, *WAR DIARY*

Chapter 38

Collapsing into a pew before the altar, Chambers fought back the tears. *Never let anyone see you cry,* came the voice of a man who had mastered the art of wearing a stone mask—his father. *A boy who cries becomes a man who is easily weakened by his emotions. The emotional become the puppets to the puppet masters. Always remember that.*

Captain Murdock only strengthened this motto. *Lieutenant, crying is for the privates who miss their mommies, not for platoon leaders. You have to lead like a man built of granite, or they'll lose faith in you.* Chambers felt like the stone armor he had built his whole life was crumbling. He ached for the men he'd lost today—first LeBlanc, now Buck and Finch. *I failed them. Fallon is right. I am the Grim Reaper.*

He felt eyes watching him and looked up. Storm light shimmered at the back of the altar, where a giant crucifix loomed. The Nazi flag had been removed. The ivory Jesus looked iridescent against the dark wooden planks. It had been carved with painstaking detail, the flesh sinking inward, causing the skeleton to rise out in relief. Bright red droplets dripped around the thorny crown and oozed down from the arrow wound in his side. Chambers felt an eerie sensation, as if the painted eyes were analyzing every detail about him, as well. He had to look away.

Goldstein approached. "You praying, Chambers?"

His face hardened back into stone. "Just catching some quiet time."

"Shall I leave you alone, sir?"

"No, Chaplain." Chambers patted the pew. "Have a seat."

The bespectacled rabbi sat down. Chambers glanced back at his men. Mahoney, Deuce, and Hoffer were spread out along the windows, watching the woods. "What's Garcia's status?"

"Patched up. The barbed fence tore some of his bandages. He's sleeping like a baby now. I dressed Hoffer's wounds as well. Nasty scratches."

They both sat forward, elbows on their knees like two men sitting together on a park bench. Goldstein broke the silence. "We've gotten ourselves into a real pickle, haven't we?"

Chambers nodded.

"Well, Lieutenant, I've been praying for us. I keep looking for signs that God's gonna show us the way to fight our shadow soldiers."

"Goldstein, be honest. Has God ever truly answered your prayers?"

"Every day, sir."

"In what way?"

"Through small miracles. When we were escaping from that village, I prayed for a refuge, and he has led us to three: the bridge, the barn, and now this church."

"Getting here was a damn stroke of luck. I lost two of my best men . . ." Inside his mind he saw the Nazis with the glowing silver eyes, their blades slashing and hacking at Finch's body. "Where was God when we needed him?"

"He was there, making sure you, me, and the others got back to safety."

"But if God exists, why would he let Buck and Finch, two God-loving men, be killed in battle after surviving so long? Why not kill me instead?"

Goldstein adjusted his glasses. "Why God chooses to spare one man over another is a timeless mystery. I believe he honors free will and empowers us to cocreate with him. We can choose a path that enhances life or destroys it. If we choose to fight one another, God steps back and leaves us to our own fate. Then when we leave our earth-bound bodies he decides what's next for us in the afterlife."

"That's all religious people ever talk about. Life only gets good after we're dead."

"I disagree. You can experience a connection with God right now through meditation and prayer. When you ask God's help, he's right here waiting to assist. And his help shows up in small miracles. All you have to do is look for them."

"I'm trying to see the world like you do. I just can't."

Goldstein grabbed Chambers's hand and peeled off the bandage. "*This*, my good friend, is a miracle."

Chambers stared down at the pink welts on his palm. "I must be going crazy, Rabbi, because yesterday I swear there were no letters. Same with the cross." Chambers pulled out the bronze cross. "Seems like they've appeared out of thin air."

"Astonishing, isn't it? The way God works never ceases to amaze me."

"Okay, Chaplain, you got my attention. What the hell do these letters mean, HVHY?"

Goldstein shook his head. "You're reading it wrong. If you start from the top, it reads . . ." He pointed to the letters YHVH.

Chambers's throat tightened. He looked up at Goldstein with wide eyes.

The chaplain nodded. "So you've seen his sacred name before."

Chambers struggled to speak. "Yes . . . a few times . . . during my childhood. But I don't remember much about it. Only that I wasn't supposed to speak it."

Goldstein traced the letters on his palm. "That is because these four are the most divine grouping of letters that make up the incommunicable name of the Supreme Being. It is not pronounced except with the vowels of *adonia* or *elohim*. In Exodus 3, Moses ascended Mount Horeb, and God spoke from the burning bush, 'Tell your people Jehovah—YHVH—has sent me.' He later tells Moses, 'Put my name on the sons of Israel and I will bless them.' This Hebrew tetragrammaton is also called Shem HaMeforesh or Brilliant Name of Fire." Goldstein gazed at his palm. "What more proof do you need that God is trying to speak to us?"

"But why me? I've never believed in any of this."

Goldstein faced him. "Sir, may I ask why you don't believe in God?"

Chambers sighed, shifting in his seat. He stared off at the stained-glass windows, the colors going blurry, spinning like a kaleidoscope. He saw a ten-year-old boy with light brown hair helping his mother and father set the table for dinner. "I grew up confused about religion. My mother was Jewish and did her best to instill Jewish values and beliefs in me. She taught me Hebrew, and we celebrated all the Jewish holidays. My father, who was raised as a fire-and-brimstone Christian, didn't trust religious dogma of any kind. He saw it as mind control. He taught me to respect my mother's Judaism, but to keep my guard up. He viewed the world as having two sides. The side we see and the side we don't. The side we see is life with our families, our friends, our nation's politics, and the wars as depicted by propaganda. What we don't see are the secret men behind everything, pulling the strings of society, deciding our governments, our religions, our wars, the fates of our countries. Dad called them puppet masters. They've been controlling our fates since the beginning of man. There are evil ones and good ones, and behind the cloak of everything we see happening in our lives, these puppet masters are constantly battling a secret war."

"No man can pull the strings without God's hand," Goldstein said. "I see these puppet masters not as mortal men, but as angels and demons. The ones who bring war, death, and destruction to our consciousness are the dark angels or demons. But there are also angels of light who counter the forces of evil. The world, as I see it, is always in balance between these polar forces of good and evil. And we are at choice whether we follow the guidance of the angels or the demons. Free will is God's greatest gift to man."

"Before today I never would have bought into the existence of demons. Now, I don't know . . ." Chambers rubbed his jaw, swallowed. "I'm not an atheist. My father did teach me to believe in God, just not religion. I used to find him praying and meditating. My father once told me that God for him was a personal spiritual devotion. And that I should follow my own path. Three days later my parents were in a car accident. My mother was killed instantly. My father survived for a week. Just before he died, he gave me this." Chambers held up his silver wristwatch with the compass built into the faceplate. "Dad's last words to me were, 'Wear this always, buddy boy. It will guide you in the right direction.' "

Goldstein stared with glazed eyes. "Chambers, I'm . . . sorry. I understand your misery."

"Do you, Chaplain? Can you possibly fathom how betrayed I felt? At age ten, God made me an orphan." Chambers's hands gripped the pew, his being once again filled with a boy's rage. "After the accident I hated God. When I got older, I decided that if there is a God as the almighty puppet master, he's unreliable. And if I was going to survive, I had to rely on myself."

The medic pushed his glasses up the hump of his nose. "I

understand how you feel, Chambers. I was thirteen and had just completed my bar mitzvah. My father, who was rabbi of our synagogue in Brooklyn, was murdered that same day by a street gang because he was Jewish. My world was shattered. There was no man more holy than my father. My mother, who was a doctor, dealt with my father's loss by taking me to Africa to do mission work, delivering supplies to sick people in the villages. The diseases were rampant, and Mother contracted one of them. She withered away on a cot in a filthy room swarming with flies. There were no other doctors, and I was the only one in the village with any medical skills. Still there was nothing I could do but sit there, holding her hand and praying. She told me not to be sad. That she could see angels in the room with us. I looked around and all I could see were the buzzing flies. She said that my father was one of the angels. He was telling her that she was needed elsewhere. And that it was time for her to go with him to the next place."

Chambers blinked several times, keeping tears at bay.

"I begged Mother to take me with her," Goldstein continued. "But she looked at me with the most peaceful eyes and said God needed me here on earth. My mission work wasn't done. Then she rubbed my chin like she always did and said, 'God is with you always, Jacob, and so are the angels. Now, I'll be one of them. So keep looking for those miracles.'" Goldstein's eyes were teary, yet not sad. He was smiling. "Chambers, I swear I see them. Even amid all this war, I see them."

Chambers released a breath that might have been a laugh. "What a miserable pair we are. Not exactly hero material." His finger traced the cross on his palm. "Goldstein, when you were having that dream about the shadow soldiers chasing you, you followed a cloaked figure into the woods, right?"

"Yes, he led me to this church."

"You think that was an angel?"

"I'm gambling my life on it."

Chambers remembered the figure cloaked in black robes leading him through the woods. "But how do we know if we followed an angel and not a demon?"

Chapter 39

As Chambers and Goldstein sat on the front pews, gazing up at the crucified Jesus, the X-2 squad emerged from the stairway beside the altar. Their faces were covered in dust and their arms weighed down with files.

"Thank God you made it back." Coming down the altar steps, Wolf entered the nave first. The Jewish girl, Anna, followed like a shadow. Her long hair appeared to have made peace with a brush. She kept her eyes on the floor.

Fallon set down two large duffel bags that clinked against the wood floor. "Put the crate over there," he ordered the two surviving members of his squad.

"Man, am I glad to be back up top," Moose grumbled as he and Fox set a heavy wood crate on the floor. It kicked up clouds of dust. "If I never see another goddamned rat in my life it'll be too soon."

Chambers studied the darkness behind them. "You guys actually went back down there with that thing still roaming the tunnels?"

"We didn't go anywhere near that mine shaft," Moose said. "No way in hell."

"Besides, we had our mighty protector." Wolf smiled at the Jewish girl.

Fallon sat against the communion rail, his muscular arms folded across his chest. He grimaced at Chambers. "So your little rescue mission didn't go so well."

"Hawk, show some respect." Wolf sat on the pew beside Goldstein and Chambers. "Tell us what happened."

Chambers told them about the abandoned cargo truck. "It was filled with iron coffins. Most were empty, but a few contained those Nazi-things." The encaged prisoners' pounding from within still echoed in Chambers's head and sent rashes of gooseflesh along his forearms. He described the patrols that had happened upon the barn, and the Lucky Seven's narrow escape. The image of those Nazi-things jamming up against the barbed-wire fence haunted Chambers's mind. He painfully described the loss of Buck and Finch.

Wolf's marble eyes gleamed with understanding. "I'm sorry about your men."

Chambers nodded, giving it all he had to hold himself together.

Goldstein broke the awkward silence. "Those things that attacked us . . . we got a good look at them. They were dressed like Nazis, but they weren't human. Their faces looked monstrous."

"How many did you see?" Fallon asked.

"At least a dozen," Chambers answered. "We maimed a few with grenades. That's the only thing that seems to slow them down." He looked at the stack of files beside Wolf. "You got any idea what we're dealing with?"

The Czech mercenary rubbed his soiled face. "We're still sifting through the records. We've got a few more rooms to explore."

Chambers frowned. "Captain, there's something else. A half-track is patrolling the roads. They know we're out here, and it won't be long before they find this place." He stood, staring at all the shattered windows. "If we're going to hole up here for the night, we've got to make this church defensible."

"That's a waste of time," Fallon said. "We're better off pushing ahead with our search. If a patrol unit comes, there are plenty of places to hide down below."

"I'd rather not let them in at all," Chambers said. "There are enough pews to barricade the doors. If we spread out along the windows, we can hold them back."

Fallon snorted. "You think this timber's gonna hold them back?"

"It'll buy us some time. Maybe till reinforcements arrive tomorrow."

"Chambers is right," Wolf said. "Fortifying this church is our next priority. We can use the weapons we found below."

Chambers's brow furrowed. "You found weapons?"

Wolf nodded. "Remember those wood crates we found in the antechamber?" He motioned to the wood crate on the floor. "Moose, open it up."

The husky sergeant pried the crate's lid off with a crowbar. Inside lay an MG42 machine gun with bipod and several chains of ammunition.

"There's a whole arsenal down below," Wolf said.

Chambers nodded to the Jewish girl staring at the floor. "What has Anna told you?" At the sound of her name, she looked at Chambers, her eyes now sharp.

"Nothing yet." Wolf's hard features softened. He rubbed Anna's hand. "She's still adjusting to everything. Goldstein, I need you to dress her wound."

"Yes, sir."

The girl recoiled against Wolf's shoulder. He smiled. "Anna, it is okay. Rabbi Goldstein is our medic. He will fix your arm."

"Hello, Anna." Goldstein grinned and adjusted his glasses. "I promise to be gentle." She tensed up but let him examine the bullet wound in her arm.

Fallon leaned in and whispered, "Captain, I need a word with you."

"I will join you as soon as Anna is patched up."

"No, now, Captain." The X-2 lieutenant led Wolf to the windows. Chambers followed.

Fallon frowned. "Take a hike, Chambers. This is between me and the captain."

"No, you two aren't keeping me in the dark."

Wolf exhaled. "Just say your mind, Hawk."

"You're spending too much time fawning over that girl. I need you focused on this mission."

"I am focused. She may help us find what we are looking for."

"Well, get her talking or I do it my way."

Wolf glared up at his lieutenant, and the captain's voice suddenly filled with rage. "Hawk, you lay a hand on her, and I'll . . ."

The X-2 lieutenant raised his hands. "Easy, Captain, I'm on your side, remember?"

"Leave Anna to me. Let's get this church defensible. We have a long night ahead of us."

• • •

An hour later the church was nearly fortified. Chambers's men barricaded the front and back doors with pews, altar tables, desks, even the organ.

Chambers watched the soldiers upend the long pews at each window, leaving a slat for a rifleman to shoot out. The captain stepped up beside him, wearing an impressed half-grin. "Not bad, Lieutenant. They teach you this in the army?"

"No, I got the idea from a history book about the Alamo."

Wolf's eyebrows knitted. "The Alamo?"

"When thousands of Mexican soldiers invaded Texas, one hundred and eighty-nine Texas volunteers barricaded a Spanish mission called the Alamo and held back the Mexicans for thirteen days."

"Did the Texans achieve victory?"

"No, every man in the Alamo was killed."

"Let us hope we have a better outcome. Come, I will show you what my men have been doing." Wolf led Chambers to one of the nave's side windows. Outside in the graveyard, Fallon was standing watch. The silhouettes of Fox and Moose crawled through the muck between the tombstones, dragging a bag of equipment with them. Wolf said, "They made a dozen trip wires by running shoestrings from the boots of dead soldiers through grenade pins. They are stretching these between the tombstones and along the front and back gates."

Chambers held his breath. It was delicate work, one false

move could blow their heads off, but Fox and Moose at last succeeded. Thunder cracked and rain began to drizzle again. The two muddy commandos hustled back with Fallon toward the front entrance, giving Chambers and Wolf a thumbs-up.

Chambers turned to his captain. "Impressive. They teach you this in the OSS?"

"No. I fought in a Jewish resistance group, the ZOB. I led a unit that did covert missions and smuggled guns to all our branches. I eventually fled to Poland and joined the Jewish uprising in Warsaw. Ever hear of it?"

"Yeah, read all about it. The Nazis had your ghetto surrounded, but the Jews held them off for months using guerilla war tactics. A number of Nazis were killed."

"Even more Jews were killed in that battle. The rest of us were captured."

"That how you got that number on your forearm?"

Wolf nodded and motioned out the window. "The booby-trapped graveyard serves a twofold purpose. First, since there are too many doors and windows to defend, the trip wires will have to work as our rear and side defense. The explosions will also alarm us that the enemy is moving in."

"Maybe we can hold them off. All we need is twenty-four hours." Chambers studied the thick stone walls and pew-covered windows. "The fortress isn't impenetrable, but at least it's more defensible. Fortunately the side and back windows are ten feet off the ground. As long as the Nazis don't bring ladders, we're okay. I'm concentrating our men at the weakest area—the front vestibule—where the windows meet at ground level. The double-doorway is the most likely target for assault. If we have any advantage it's that there's very little tree cover in the front parking lot. Vision is decent with enough moonlight to see twenty yards away. Any German infantry trying to cross that lot's gonna be welcomed with a gauntlet of gunfire."

Chambers and Wolf walked from post to post, checking on their sentries. Mahoney manned the window nearest the barricaded double doors. His M1 cartridge shells stood lined up in the sill like miniature brass soldiers. Mahoney picked them up one at a time, genuflected the cartridge across his body, and loaded it into his rifle. When the old sergeant realized his lieutenant and captain were observing this ritual, Mahoney whispered, "I'm done relying on luck."

Chambers stepped up to a couple of crates the X-2 boys had hauled up. One was full of unopened Vodka bottles. "Planning on throwing a party, Captain?"

"Yeah, if any guests arrive, I thought we might serve Molotov cocktails."

"I like your thinking. And what's in this crate?"

Wolf slid off the lid, revealing three metal tubes with what looked like iron bowling pins sticking out one end. He picked one up. "Ah, now this was a treasure find. Panzerfaust 60 rocket launcher." He balanced the metal tube on his shoulder like a bazooka. "It's a single shot, disposable anti-tank weapon. Shoots effectively up to sixty meters. Punches a nice hole through armor."

"Yeah, I think I've seen the bad end of a few of these." Chambers tried it on his shoulder. It felt light, easy to aim. "These will come in handy."

"There's just three launchers, so we have to use them wisely."

Chambers set the Panzerfaust back into its crate.

Ten feet down stood Deuce, who was wearing a chain of machine-gun cartridges around his neck. His BAR leaned against the window. He gnawed on a damp cigar and kept his gaze on the forest road. Hoffer sat on the floor next to him. His face intense, the combat artist was doing what he often did during idle moments—inking a figure on his sketchpad. Hoffer's good hand pressed hard into the paper. Black ink filled the white space in quick arcs. Chambers leaned over his shoulder, observing the drawing of a GI swinging a saber and lopping off the head of a Nazi with electric eyes. Hoffer had barely spoken since he lost his best friend and comic book collaborator, Gabe Finch. Chambers tried to think of something uplifting to say, but settled for a pat on the shoulder.

Wolf motioned to the drawing of the Nazi-creature. "What is that on his forehead?" Chambers looked at the cartoon more closely. The creature's severed head, floating inches above the stump of its neck, had strange symbols just above the glowing eyes.

Hoffer shrugged. "Some kind of engraving. I noticed it on the creature down below."

The blood seemed to drain from Wolf's face.

"What is it?" Chambers asked.

"Finish securing the church. I will be back." The Czech mercenary disappeared into the blackness.

At the far window Fox assembled the MG42 machine gun. He loaded a turret and snapped it just to the side of the pistol-grip handle.

Beneath the fountain of holy water, Garcia sat up against the wall, now wide awake. The heavily bandaged soldier motioned Chambers over. "Sir, will you do me a favor?"

"What's that, *amigo*?"

"I was wondering if I could spend some time in the confession booth. It's been a long time."

"I don't see any harm in that." Throwing Garcia's arm over his shoulder, Chambers escorted the soldier to the back of the nave, where several confession closets lined a wall near the altar. Being careful with Garcia's wounded leg and hand, Chambers set the teen down inside the booth.

"Any chance the chaplain's free to come talk with me?" Garcia asked.

Chambers glanced across the nave. Goldstein's silhouette was in an animated discussion with Wolf and Anna. "Looks like he's occupied."

"Guess I'll just have to confess straight to Dios."

"Looks that way. I'll check on you later."

"Wait, sir." Jaw trembling, Garcia whispered, "I've got a bad feeling in the pit of my stomach . . . I . . . was wondering if you could deliver this to *mi familia*." Clutched in his hand was an addressed envelope.

Chambers recalled Eva's unread letter in his breast pocket. "Give it to her yourself."

"But, sir—"

"No buts, Garcia. You'll see Maria and your *niños* again if I have to escort your ass to El Paso myself."

Garcia nodded and tucked the letter into his coat pocket. "Sorry, sir."

Chambers tried to smile. "Just have faith that we'll find a way out of this."

Garcia kissed the cross and rosary that hung with his dog tags.

Chambers closed the confession booth and returned to the vestibule at the front of the church. The three bound and gagged Nazis watched as Fallon and Moose loaded their uniforms down with weapons. Fallon wiped boot polish across his face and over his bald head, looking like a black-faced Mephisto. He had torn off both sleeves of his black tunic all the way up to his shoulders, exposing his bulging muscles. Celtic tattoos banded around both biceps along with a dozen smaller tattoos.

Chambers shook his head and looked around for Wolf. The captain had disappeared with the Jewish girl and Goldstein. Chambers searched the shadowy nave. The storm flashed outside, lighting up the stained-glass windows depicting angels flying across a golden sky with swords in their hands. The bloodlust of war burned in their eyes. They seemed to be flying downward toward an enemy that was unseen due to the bottom half of the window being shattered. Chambers clumped toward the shards of colored glass that littered the wood floor. He picked up one the size of his boot and held it up to the faint moonlight in the window. He could barely make out two shadow figures on it. *Come on, storm, give me some light.*

The sky responded with a lightning bolt, causing the eyes of the two shadow figures to glow silver. Chambers dropped the glass and it shattered at his boot.

"Everything okay, Chambers?" Three silhouettes approached, materializing into the shapes of Wolf, Goldstein, and Anna.

"Dandy. I've been looking for you. Wolf, what the hell did you see in Hoffer's drawing that made you run off?"

"I think there's a way to stop our enemy. Anna says she can take us to a hidden antechamber where the Nazis hold the secrets to Operation Eisen Sarg."

"You're not actually going back down there!"

"We have to," Wolf insisted. "Our bullets can't stop these creatures. Our only hope is to figure another way. Anna thinks the answers lie somewhere inside that mine shaft."

Chambers's skin prickled. "What about the guardian?"

"*Der Vormund* is not like the others," Anna said, shocking Chambers. They were the first words he'd heard her utter since she said her name. "*Der Vormund* vill protect the chosen." She raised her palm, showing a cross-shaped symbol with a Star of David. "You are one of us, ya?"

"Yes, he's one of us," Goldstein answered for him. "Chambers, we need to explore that mine shaft."

"No way in hell am I going back down there."

Wolf said, "Chambers, it's time I shared something that may shed some light as to why you've been chosen for this mission."

"I'm listening."

"How shall I put this?" Wolf pointed to Chambers's wrist. "May I see that?"

Chambers hesitated then slipped off his silver watch.

The Jewish captain studied the *G* emblem on the faceplate. "Where did you get this?"

"My father. It was a gift from one of his social clubs."

"It was more than just a social club, Chambers. Your father was a Freemason."

He looked at Wolf with a sideways glance.

"Your father was part of a secret society that not only built the American government but also runs a massive spy network across the globe secretly fighting for democracy."

"You're saying my father was a spy?"

Wolf nodded. "He gathered foreign intelligence for the Masons. His focus was Munich. After the Great War, he reported information on the political rise of a secret society known as the Thule Society. Thulists were Anti-Semitic Germans who hated everything that wasn't *völkish*, or pure German. They hated Jews, Bolsheviks, Gypsies, and Freemasons. They were especially anti-Masonry because of the Masonic lodge's Jewish origins and their building of democratic governments. The last thing these pagan Germans wanted was for Germany to become a Democratic or Communist country. After pushing the Communist regime out of Munich, the Thule Society formed the German Workers' Party, which put Adolf Hitler into power. This party later became the National Socialist German Workers' Party. The Nazi Party. After taking the control of Germany away from the Soviets, the Nazis went after their other enemies, Jews and the lodges of Freemasonry. Your father, Chambers, was fighting this secret war as a Freemason."

"How the hell do you know this?"

"Because Captain Murdock was also a Freemason tied into this network. Before the war he worked with your father."

Chambers slumped back against a pillar as the floor began to spin. Memories swirled around him: the auto accident that killed his parents . . . his father, lying on his deathbed, giving him the watch with a built-in compass. *Wear this always, buddy boy. It will guide you in the right direction.* Then the war flashed before Chambers's eyes: North Africa, 1943, losing his platoon to a recon mission that ended in a raging fire . . . recovering in England with Fallon's mummified body lying in the next bed, the bandaged face watching him with a single, hateful eye . . . Captain Murdock taking Chambers under his wing, guiding him like a father . . . Murdock dying in the Hürtgen battle, passing the Star of David cross on to Chambers. *I need you to complete my mission.* His last image was of an OSS captain showing him a letter from Murdock recommending Chambers for this covert mission.

He gazed at Wolf. "You're part of this, too."

Nodding, Wolf pulled off one of his fingerless motorcycle gloves, exposing a palm with a cross-shaped scar on it that was more developed than Chambers's and Goldstein's.

"This cross is a symbol of a secret Kabbalah order within the Freemasons. This order has protected the world's most sacred secrets since the Knights Templar first discovered the treasures beneath Solomon's Temple. Your father and Murdock were both working alongside that order. And they shared my passion for stopping Hitler's madness. Chambers, Captain Murdock chose you for this mission because you are a legacy, and he believed you were highly capable of succeeding if he didn't."

Chambers was speechless. He watched lightning crackle outside the windows as his brief childhood with his secretive father flashed before his eyes.

Wolf continued, "I know this must come as a shock to you. But I felt you should know. You are one of the chosen. We are all on the same divine mission."

Goldstein pointed to the symbol on Wolf's hand. "Murdock received that symbol from a cloaked visitor in his dreams. So did I. Is that how you got it?"

Wolf's voice became filled with emotion. "The cloaked figure first appeared in my dreams in the summer of 1943. I was a prisoner at a Jewish death camp in Treblinka. The symbol materializing on my hand saved my life. While the Nazi prison guards marched everyone in my barracks to be murdered in the gas chambers, I was pulled out of line by guards who noticed my hand glowing. They escorted me to the back corner of the camp. The guards kept calling me Jewish sorcerer and said it was their duty to rid the earth of sorcerers. They were about to shoot me when I saw the robed figure moving behind them." Izak Wolfowitcz's marble eyes dilated. He rubbed his chin. "I never believed in angels, but I swear I witnessed one that day. The guards turned and saw it, too, for they yelled and stumbled backward. That's when I grabbed one of their guns and shot them both. The cloaked figure motioned me to follow. I raced between the barracks, shooting guards and freeing as many prisoners as I could. My mutiny turned into a major uprising, but only seventy of us made it out alive. I took refuge with one of X-2's German Underground units. The cloaked figure continued to visit my dreams, directing me to this church. My mission was to stop whatever evil force the Nazis created." Wolf put a hand on Chambers's shoulder. "I thought I was called to carry out this holy mission alone."

"Me, too," Goldstein said. "Till I met Captain Murdock and then you, Chambers."

Chambers felt an incredible weight on his shoulders. "Murdock was supposed to be the chosen one, not me."

Goldstein said, "But he chose you, which means God chose you to take his place."

Wolf said, "Chambers, may I see the bronze cross Murdock gave you?"

He pulled it out of his pocket.

"It's exactly like mine." The captain turned it over in his hands, rubbed the etched symbols. "A fascinating piece of work. Have you figured out what it does yet?"

"I have no idea."

"Watch this." Wolf pressed the Star of David inward. *Snick!* A three-inch blade shot out. "Makes a handy secret weapon."

Chambers took back the cross, tested the double-edged blade's release. It snicked in and out. "Do all your X-2 commandos have one of these?"

Wolf shook his head. "No, just me. Only Lieutenant Hawk is aware that my mission is a holy one. He saw the opportunity to salvage any Nazi treasure we might find, so he offered to supply me with a commando squad in exchange for secrecy. I thought charging in here with a commando force would be a success. I had no idea what kind of enemy we'd be facing. Now, I feel our only hope is finding out what in God's name the Nazis created."

"So what do you have in mind, Captain?" It was Fallon. His black-painted face and eye patch materialized in a shaft of window light. Moose stood beside him, weighed down with weapons.

Wolf brushed past his commandos. "Be ready for anything, men. We're going into the mine shaft."

Chapter 40

Chambers along with Goldstein, Anna, and three X-2 soldiers eased toward the crevice in the brick wall, their weapons aimed. Flashlight beams penetrated a narrow tunnel that burrowed into the earth. Roots stabbed out from the ceiling and walls. The tall horseshoe-planks, placed every few feet, held the mine shaft in place. Water dripped into muddy puddles. The air reeked of wet soil, rotted wood, and centuries of death.

Wolf released a breath. "Everybody ready?"

Chambers nodded, gripping his Tommy gun.

Fallon screwed a bayonet onto the end of his rifle. "Let's do it."

The captain motioned toward the crevice. "Okay, Moose, you first."

"Yo, why me?"

Fallon growled, "Because you got the flamethrower."

Moose motioned to Anna. "I thought she was leading."

"Well, if you need *her* to save your ass, she'll be right behind you." Fallon kicked Moose in the pants. "Now, give us some light."

"There's no amount of gold worth this shit." The husky sergeant entered the tunnel first, spitting out flames every few feet. Anna followed quietly. Then Wolf, Fallon, and Goldstein entered the passage. Chambers carried the rear, the darkness once again chilling the marrow of his bones.

They weaved through the jungle of burning roots. The tunnel walls and ceiling squeezed around them, barely wider than their bodies, the snug spots catching Chambers's shoulders. In some places, he had to sidestep. The smell of scorched mud and roots filled his nose. Clumps of dirt, flaming twigs, and dripping water rained down on his head and shoulders. Above, the din of the storm seeped into the passage like a choir of lost souls.

Twenty feet deep the sergeant stopped and looked back. Sweat dripped over his blunt, Neanderthal face. "I can see Snake's body. It's covered in rats."

Chambers's flashlight shone upon several dozen beady eyes around Corporal Snake's decapitated corpse. The blood-soaked mud clung to Chambers's boots as he squished through it, kicking the rats to the side. As he stepped over the body, he suddenly remembered Hoffer's zombie theory. Something about a person killed by a zombie always rises up from the dead. Was that possible? He suddenly imagined Corporal Snake rising up from the ground, a headless body covered in rats walking the tunnel with them. Feeling his skin crawl, Chambers whirled, shining his beam back on the dead soldier. The bloody neck stump glistened. Snake's body remained stiff, motionless, as the furry carrion eaters ate their fill.

Moose reached an intersection and blasted a flame in three directions. "It's a damn maze under here."

Chambers aimed his light down two adjoining passages. Tunnels crisscrossed between rows of graves. Flashlights shined upon caskets embedded in the walls like catacombs. The clay soil had been excavated until one side of the wood was visible. Most of the coffins had been shattered open. Every grave they passed was empty.

Why on earth would the Nazis gut out a graveyard? The question hung in Chambers's mind. Part of him hungered for answers, while another part—one that tightened the flesh along his spine—urged Chambers to get the hell out of here. But his own curiosity won this battle, as his legs pushed him deeper beneath the graveyard.

Moose stopped at another intersection to wipe sweat from his brow. "Okay, which way?"

"That vay." Anna motioned straight ahead.

They walked another fifty feet then paused where the passage opened up into a cavern. A burst from Moose's flamethrower lit up the wide chamber. At the far end was a concrete wall. A tall iron door stood open. Wolf put a finger to his lips. Stepping around puddles, the explorers eased their way to the entrance. As Chambers drew closer, his nostrils burned. The stench of death escaped from the subterranean antechamber like a lethal gas. The air grew colder, too, as if they approached an open freezer.

Captain Wolf hand-signaled his squad. They gathered three and three on either side of the door. The antechamber was deathly silent. Dark as midnight. Chambers's breathing quickened. A hundred doubts flapped through his mind like winged bats.

His palm tingled and glowed. The symbols on the hands of Anna, Goldstein, and Wolf did the same, illuminating their faces. Anna's eyes held no fear. Goldstein looked nervous. Wolf remained stoic as he looked at his men then nodded. They stormed into the antechamber. Moose blasted the flamethrower, lighting up a hallway that had rooms on either side. The squad entered with their guns at the ready. The first room they passed was stocked with excavation tools. Goldstein and Chambers traded glances as they stepped into a second room, this one stocked with Nazi uniforms along with weapons that could have been the arsenal of medieval knights. Chambers shone his light on a wall lined with sabers. Farther down the hall, Anna grew frantic. The third room contained a single iron chair in the middle surrounded by trays of sharp instruments. In the corner sat a machine used for shock treatment. Anna's face twisted into a mask of horror. She barreled into Wolf's arms, sobbing.

"It's okay," the captain said, leading her away from the torture room.

They entered the final room at the end of the hallway. Skeletons sat side by side along the walls, their dusty heads fused together by spider webs. Tattered clothing hung on their bones. *Sweet Jesus.* Chambers's palm continued to burn. *The guardian's down here, waiting for us.* He remembered the unholy thing that had attacked them earlier. It had torn off Corporal Snake's head with its bare hands and slashed Hoffer's shoulder with tigerlike claws. Its flesh had absorbed their bullets. No amount of men could have stopped it. If it weren't for the Jewish girl, they would have all been turned to rat food. Chambers studied her now as she walked silently, her face consumed with terror. *Anna, you better be right about the guardian. Because it's a long sprint back.*

Rifles poised like snipers, the soldiers stepped through the rows of skeletons, pressing farther into the dark ocean of the subterranean chamber. Goldstein and Anna walked between them, their illuminated palms guiding the way. Along another wall, they found blocks of clay stacked to the ceiling. Moose shot a blast into the abyss, and in that flash of light, Chambers swore he saw a human shape standing in the center of the room.

Fallon's flashlight whipped across the darkness and located a hideous face. "There it is!"

Moose fired away. The creature didn't move or scream, and it took Chambers a moment to realize the Nazi was a lifeless mannequin propped up by a pole. Its uniform, burning like a torch, pushed the shadows back to the walls, where they danced along the piles of human bones.

"Jesus . . ." Moose said.

The six explorers gathered together, staring in amazement. In the center of the room, twenty skeletal figures stood propped up by poles that ran from floor to ceiling. Five of them were completely clad in Nazi uniforms and German steel helmets. Clay was molded onto their skulls. The others were unfinished clay sculptures in various stages of assembly. One remained half a human skeleton with sculpted clay legs. The bones had been reinforced by steel rods and, at the hands, steel claws protruded from the clay fingertips. All stared with hollow eyes.

"Everybody stay back," Wolf ordered.

"What in God's name is going on here?" Fallon asked, stopping short of the sculptures.

"This is madness," Chambers breathed.

Goldstein said, "These must have been the sculptors." He located two dead men in black robes. "Their hands are covered in clay."

Chambers studied the intricate handiwork. They hadn't just slapped clay onto bones. The Germans had skillfully shaped the clay into muscles to mimic the human body. The only exceptions were the sculptures' faces. They lacked detail, and all had the same hollow eyes, modest noses, and a slit for a mouth—scarecrows made of clay.

"What do you make of this, Captain?" Fallon nudged him. "Wolf?"

The Czech mercenary gazed at the clay bricks. His face had turned ashen. "Make sure none of them are alive."

They rattled off rounds, making the sculptures dance like marionettes in some horrific puppet show. When the shooting ceased, the clay-covered skeletons dangled on their poles.

Fallon weaved between the sculptures. "Whatever the Nazis were doing to give them life, they never completed these."

Chambers studied the unexplored shadows to their right. "Where the hell's the guardian?"

"I was just wondering the same thing," Wolf said, staring down at his glowing hand. "Anna, can you sense him?"

"He is watching us."

Flickering light cast their shadows on the wall. From the far end of the antechamber, Moose yelled, "Holy frigging canolies! Guys, check this out." The sergeant was standing in a circle of burning candles.

Everyone hurried toward the ring of fire. Chambers's boots crunched over bones and dried clumps of clay. Every sound reverberated off the brick walls. Flashlight beams passed over a wall with hieroglyphs and a Nazi crucified to the large swastika on the wall. Goldstein craned his neck. "What in God's name?"

Moose's dark eyes dilated. "Get a load of this mumbo jumbo." Six red candles formed a circle ten feet in diameter. Inside the circle a strange symbol—a series of concentric circles with hieroglyphs and runes—had been chalked onto the concrete floor. The inner core contained a spine-shaped drawing surrounded by Hebrew words and a symbol that matched the glowing scars on the palms of the four chosen ones—Chambers, Goldstein, Wolf, and Anna. "What the hell is this?"

"Evidence that the Nazis were trying to play with the devil." Corporal Moose held up a handful of bone fragments. "Some sort of voodoo magic. This is how they brought their zombie soldiers to life."

"It's not voodoo." Wolf kneeled, studying the chalked symbol. His eyes sparked with a dark realization. He traded conspiratorial glances with Goldstein and Anna.

"This can't be happening," Goldstein whispered, falling to his knees.

Chambers kneeled on the opposite side of the circle. "You two know what this is?"

Goldstein remained frozen, as if seeing the ancient symbol had turned him to stone.

"Parts of it." Wolf pulled out a miniature camera and snapped photos. Chambers noticed sweat beading on the Czech mercenary's upper lip.

"Moose may be onto something." Fallon picked up one of the red candles and lit his cigar, puffing smoke. "Sure looks like voodoo to me."

"Nein!" Anna shook her head, her eyes wide with terror.

"Put that back," Wolf barked at Fallon. "This is a sacred space of incredible power. It's not to be tampered with. These symbols aren't voodoo. They're a mixture of Hebrew and runes. Our Nazis appear to have been performing Kabbalah."

"What the hell is Kabbalah?" Fallon asked, stepping out of the shadows.

"Jewish sorcery," Wolf answered. "It's how rabbis who practice Kabbalah perform magic."

Fallon snorted. "Now I've heard everything."

"What makes you so sure?" Moose asked.

"I recognize many of these words," Wolf said. "See this one, *Adonai*? It means 'Lord.' So does this one." He pointed to a symbol marked YHVH. *"Atzilut* means 'emanation.' *Chokhma* is 'wisdom.' I can't read the scripture in runes. We'll need to have Fox take a look at this." The X-2 captain pulled out a knife and pointed to the chalk drawing that looked like a spine with branches, an energy sphere at the tip of each. "This is the cosmic tree of life. It is a map Kabbalists use to guide themselves through God consciousness."

"You've lost me," Chambers said.

Wolf said, "Perhaps our rabbi can better explain."

Goldstein broke from his trance. "Kabbalists believe that God is one with everything, and everything is linked to everything else. Kabbalists use the cosmic tree as a map of how to connect with God and the energies of the planet through meditation. Rabbis who practice Kabbalah have been known to tap into this God source and use the earth's energies to perform magic." Goldstein looked frantic now. "My father practiced Kabbalah. He taught me how to use some of the meditations myself." He looked at Wolf with haunted eyes. "There's something I don't understand, Captain. Kabbalah's supposed to be used for good, not evil."

"Magic is magic, Goldstein. It is the intent behind the magic that makes it good or evil."

Chambers rubbed his jaw. "Captain, why on earth would the Nazis have any interest in a Jewish ritual? They loathe everything about Jews."

Wolf's face remained grim. "Evidently they've discovered one of our greatest secrets: how to bring clay sculptures to life through magic. In essence, we are standing in a factory for indestructible soldiers. Nazi golems."

Chapter 41

Candlelight flickered across Pierce Fallon's black-painted face. He chewed on his cigar, staring down at the chalked symbol. "What the hell are golems?"

Wolf stared into the ring of fire. "Human-shaped figures made from the earth. Usually mud or clay. Then given life through the magic of Jewish mysticism. Golems have superhuman strength and are virtually unstoppable. They are meant to be spiritual bodyguards to the rabbis who create them. Now they're the enemy."

Chambers shone his light on the twenty sculptures propped up against poles. The steel-enforced skeletons had been the structure, the clay the flesh. Then they were dressed in black SS uniforms and armed with guns and sabers and menacing steel claws. "Captain, let me get this straight. You're telling us that the Nazis tapped into some kind of earth energy to raise these things from the dead."

Wolf stood, dusting off his knees. "As crazy as that sounds, yes, only golems are generally composed completely of clay or river mud. The use of the graveyard skeletons was a deadly twist added by the Nazis." The Czech mercenary looked into the eyes of the other five. "In Prague there is a legend of a Rabbi Judah Loew ben Bezalel—a famous mystic known as the Maharal, who made the legendary golem come to life in the fifteen hundreds. The golem protected Rabbi Loew's village. No matter how hard enemies tried, they couldn't kill the golem. It was indestructible."

Chambers said, "When I was a kid I saw a silent film about the Golem of Prague."

Wolf nodded. "*Der Golem*. I saw it, too. I thought it depicted the Jews poorly and made Rabbi Loew look like a madman. He wasn't. He was a genius. And he created the golem with good intent."

"But the golem legend is supposed to be a myth."

"The golem is real. I would find it hard to believe, too, if I hadn't seen something like this before." Izak Wolfowitcz's marble eyes reflected inward. "Before the war, I attended Altneuschul Synagogue in Prague where legend says Rabbi Loew disassembled his golem and stored it inside the attic. My grandfather was a rabbi at Altneuschul. He was also a Kabbalist who belonged to a very secret order. They were the guardians of the Old-New Synagogue. When I was a teen, my grandfather initiated me into the order. They took me up to the attic and showed me the enormous crate where the golem was stored. We watched over it until the Nazis invaded Prague. Then we moved it to a secret place in Poland. Many of our rabbis were captured and their magic books stolen. The Nazis must have figured out a way to form their own versions of the golem."

A sound, like stone scraping against stone, echoed in the darkness.

Anna's wild brown eyes looked past them. "*Der Vormund*!"

An uncanny feeling wormed through Chambers's gut. He spun around with his flashlight. Somewhere beyond the beam's reach, rocks tumbled into water.

"Jesus, it's in here with us!" Moose jerked his flashlight. A rat with a long knobby tail skittered past a pool of murky water that reflected the light.

Beyond the pool, the antechamber disappeared into a dark abyss.

Fallon whispered, "Fire your flame in that direction."

Moose torched the darkness. The orange-blue flames hissed. An army of plump rats splashed into the pool, clambering over one another to escape the flames. Chambers caught a glimpse of something beyond the pool.

"Flame that whole area," Fallon ordered.

"Nein! Nein!" Anna cried and scurried deeper into the antechamber, her body disappearing into the pitch darkness. The only sign of her whereabouts was her glowing hand.

"Anna, wait!" Wolf chased after her. The others followed more cautiously, especially Goldstein, who steered as far away from the swimming rats as the wall would allow.

As the team crept around the pool, Chambers realized the murky water was not an underground swimming pool, as he had first suspected, but a jagged crater roughly ten feet in diameter. The horde of rats splashing across sent waves against the edges.

When Anna reached a brick wall at the far end of the antechamber, she froze.

"What is it?" Wolf's flashlight lit up a monstrous clay face that towered above him. Flashlights spotlighted broad shoulders, thick muscular arms, and hands the size of bear paws with steel talons that could shred a man to ribbons. The golem stared down at the captain with vacant eye sockets, its face devoid of emotion. Engraved on its forehead was a Hebrew word, *emet*.

Fallon and Moose raised their weapons.

"Don't shoot!" Wolf yelled. He set down his rifle and, holding up his palm with the iridescent Kabbalah cross, approached the golem. Cocking its enormous head, the clay giant stepped forward, stirring up an odor like swamp mud. It raised a daggered hand. A talon touched the symbol on Wolf's palm, gently, tracing the Star of David.

Chambers held his breath.

Wolf said, "I have been called to be your master, Golem. We are your friends. Now back away." It took a few steps back. The only sounds it made were the heavy footfalls. "Show me I am in command. Kill that rat." The clay giant followed Wolf's flashlight beam toward a rat perched at the edge of the pool and crushed it beneath its heavy stone foot. "Good, now stand over there against that wall." The golem did as ordered, standing still as a tomb statue.

"Amazing," Goldstein whispered.

Chambers released his breath. "That was damned crazy, Captain."

Wolf smiled. "Anna told me the golem didn't harm her because she wore this symbol. I had to know if the same went for all of us."

"That doesn't make *me* feel any safer," Fallon said, keeping his submachine gun aimed at the creature. "Not all of us are Jewish."

"Don't worry. A golem is built to take commands. Rabbi Loew used to command his golem to do whatever task he requested. I won't let him harm anyone."

Goldstein said, "But didn't the Golem of Prague go on a rampage? That's why Rabbi Loew eventually had to destroy his creation."

"We can kill it if we choose."

"How?" Moose asked.

"The golem was given life by magic, which means it can be destroyed by magic." Wolf pointed to its broad forehead. "See the symbol engraved on its forehead? That's the Hebrew word *emet*. It means 'life.' All we have to do is scratch off the first *e* and that leaves *met*, which means 'death.' That's how Rabbi Loew of Prague killed his golem in the legend."

"Then what are you waiting for, Captain?" Fallon said. "Destroy the mutherfucker."

"Not yet. We may have use for it."

"Take a look over here, guys. We got another corpse." Moose spotlighted the remains of an old man with a ratty beard lying near a cot, his chest riddled with holes. Shackles on his ankles chained him to the wall. His face, the flesh dusty and brittle, had sunken until it rested against the skull. The old man wore a black robe with a hood.

Chambers and Goldstein glanced at one another with secret knowing. *The cloaked figure from our dreams.*

"Must have been the Nazi's black magician," Moose muttered.

"No," Wolf said. "He's a rabbi."

Anna kneeled beside the corpse, sobbing.

Wolf put a hand on her shoulder. "Was he someone close to you?"

The girl nodded, her face grief-stricken, eyes leaking in continuous streams. "He vas my *zayde*—my grandfather."

"What was his name?"

"Yosef Klein."

Wolf's eyes widened. "*Rabbi* Yosef Klein from Prague?"

Anna nodded.

"You knew him!" Chambers said.

"Oh, God." Wolf sat down on the dusty cot, looking as if he'd just been sucker-punched. "Rabbi Klein was part of the Altneuschul Synagogue's secret order. He was captured, and I never knew what happened to him."

"Looks like he was helping the Nazis," Fallon suggested.

"No," Anna said, sniffling. "They brought us here against our will. The Nazis tortured me until my *zayde* agreed to build them golems." She pointed to the clay giant still standing at the wall. "He built *der Vormund* to protect me."

Wolf shone his light across the rat-infested pool. "I imagine at one time that was Rabbi Klein's *mikvah*."

"What's a *mikvah*?" Fallon asked.

"A ritual bath. It is traditional to cleanse before performing a ritual."

"This must have been his spell book." Moose lit more candles, illuminating a long stone altar table against the back wall. On top lay a thick book covered in dust and cobwebs.

"Move aside." Wolf flipped through the pages, stirring up clouds of filth. His eyes roiled with gray intensity as he scanned what appeared to be an ancient Bible scribed with a quill. Thick papyrus paper contained archaic text and elaborate drawings. "What is this?" Chambers asked.

"A book on Kabbalah." Wolf snapped the book shut and dropped it into his black leather satchel. "This is what we've been looking for. Let's head back up."

"Wait," Fallon pointed toward the golem. "We're not leaving that thing alive down here. Remember what it did to Snake."

Wolf exhaled and stepped over to the clay giant. "Golem, kneel before me." It moved away from the wall and got on one knee. Its broad gray face stared mindlessly. "Such a powerful ally you would be if you were not so unpredictable." Wolf rubbed the *e* off its forehead. The golem crumbled to dust and bones.

Chapter 42

When the six returned to the church's altar, they were met by a frantic Private Hoffer. "Thank God! We need your help."

"What's the problem?" Chambers asked.

"We have visitors. Come quick."

They followed Hoffer down the nave to the vestibule. Mahoney, Deuce, and Fox had their guns aimed out the windows toward the front parking lot.

"It's about time ya guys got here," Deuce said. "I'm this close to having a coronary."

Everyone filled in the gaps between the sentries. In the moon glow, thirty yards across the gravel lot, three Nazi silhouettes stood motionless in front of a parked convertible. Lightning crackled across the sky behind them. A damp wind flapped their long black coats.

Wolf turned to Fox. "How long have they been there?"

The British mercenary kept his MG42 machine gun locked on the three targets. "About twenty minutes. They haven't budged since they climbed out of their car."

"Did you fire any rounds?"

Fox shook his head. "Bloody hell! We didn't want to piss them off."

"Christ," Fallon said. "This is all we need."

"It was only a matter of time," Wolf said. "We need to take care of them quickly."

"What do you suggest?" Chambers asked. "We can't shoot them."

"No, I have another idea." Wolf pointed to Chambers, Goldstein, and Anna. "You three come with me. Rest of you, keep watch. Do not, under any circumstances, fire your weapons. If the golems start approaching, come get us."

"Golems!" Deuce said. "What the hell are golems?"

"Moose can explain." The chosen went around the corner for a private meeting. Fallon followed on his own accord.

Wolf whispered, "I realize now why Rabbi Klein visited each of us in our dreams. He's used Kabbalah to pass his magic to the four of us. Our mission is to destroy the golems the Nazis created."

"There must be over thirty of them," Chambers said.

"More like fifty," Anna corrected.

"How the hell are we going to destroy fifty golems?"

Wolf answered, "Based on what I know, we have two options. Option A is the four of us approach them one by one and rub the first letter of the sacred word off their foreheads. It would be a time-consuming process, and there's no way to be sure we got them all."

"I'm hoping Option B is better," Goldstein said.

Wolf pulled the large black spell book out of his satchel. "Our second option is we read through this and see if Rabbi Klein left us some kind of spell that would destroy them all at once."

"I vote for option B," Chambers said.

"Both will take time."

"Which we don't have a lot of," Fallon intervened. "Especially if those three out there decide to get curious. There must be an Option C. We still have some explosives. Can't we pound them with good ol' American TNT?"

Captain Wolf shook his head. "You might maim a few, but the reality is golems are virtually indestructible. While walking back from the graveyard tunnel, I realized why the Nazis behind Operation Eisen Sarg planned to place iron coffins up

and down the Siegfried Line. When the Allied forces opened
the coffins, it would be no contest. One golem can take out a
single platoon; two together can take out a company. There is
more at stake here than our own lives. We have to stop them,
and I'm afraid our ammo and explosives will only slow them
down."

"We have to fight magic with magic," Goldstein said.

Wolf nodded. "And fortunately for us, we have four among
us who have been granted Klein's power to control and destroy them."

"So what's our plan?" Chambers asked.

"We are going to take care of these three golems right
away. We can't afford to let them get away, or worse, barge in
here shooting." Wolf handed the Kabbalah book to Goldstein.
"Rabbi, how familiar are you with Kabbalah?"

"I just know a few meditations." The chaplain held the
book with reverence. "I've never performed any mysticism,
though."

"How about you, Anna?"

"*Nein,* my *zayde* never show me."

"Well, I need you both to get with Fox and start going
through this text. See if you can decipher it. Part of it is in
Hebrew and part in runes. We're looking for any kind of re-
versal spell. When the time comes, I can perform the ritual
necessary to end this madness."

Goldstein looked at the book. "Wait a minute. This isn't
any Hebrew I've ever seen."

Wolf leaned over his shoulder. "You're right, I should have
known Rabbi Klein would use the Atbash cipher."

Goldstein wrinkled his brow. "What's an Atbash cipher?"

"It's an ancient code using the letters from the Hebrew alphabet. Here it so happens you have a code breaker. Hand me
your Kabbalah cross." Wolf accepted Goldstein's bronze
cross and pushed the letters YHVH along the outside edges.
The cross opened like a locket. Engraved on one interior side
were the twenty-two letters of the Hebrew alphabet. Engraved
on the other side was a column of the same Hebrew letters in
reverse.

ת	א
ש	ב
ר	ג
ק	ד
צ	ה
פ	ו
ע	ז
ס	ח
נ	ט
מ	י
ל	כ
כ	ל
י	מ
ט	נ
ח	ס
ז	ע
ו	פ
ה	צ
ד	ק
ג	ר
ב	ש
א	ת

"Just substitute *aleph* (the first letter) for *tav* (the last), *beth* (the second) for *shin* (one before last), and so on, reversing the alphabet."

Goldstein glanced at Anna. "*Oy*, looks tedious."

"It is, that's why in the meantime, we'll have to do things the hard way." Wolf put a hand on Chambers's shoulder. "My good friend, it's time you and I tested our faith."

• • •

The three golems remained statue still in the gravel lot outside the church. Their faces were hidden in shadow as the storm light flashed behind them.

"This is your plan!" Sergeant Mahoney stared at Chambers and Wolf like they were crazy.

"It's the best one we got for now." Chambers put on his

parka at the front entrance. He tried to hide the fact that his knees were shaking.

"We can do this." Wolf buttoned up his Nazi coat. "You saw how I commanded the golem. The symbols on our palms act as shields. Just trust in the magic Rabbi Klein has given you."

Chambers stared down at his palm. Yellow light outlined the cross, the Star of David, and all the letters within. The Lucky Seven survivors looked at him like he was from outer space.

"Jeepers," whispered Hoffer. "You're gonna make one hell of a comic book hero."

"You two ready?" Fallon said. He had taken position at one of the windows. This was the first mission the X-2 lieutenant looked relieved he was not taking part in.

Wolf stepped up to the front doors. "We're ready."

Mahoney slid the barricade away. As Chambers stepped up to the threshold, feeling the brisk damp wind blowing against his face, Mahoney offered his canteen. "Here, take this. It's filled with holy water." The old sergeant raised a thick eyebrow. "It can't hurt."

"Thanks, Papa Bear." Chambers looked at the front windows at the row of men covering them with rifles. They each gave a salute.

Wasting no time, Wolf and Chambers stepped out into the rainy night armed with only their heated palms, a canteen full of holy water, blind hope, and a prayer. Boots crunching over gravel, they marched toward the enemy. The three Nazi shadows stood so still, Chambers wondered if by some grace of God the magic had left them, like a battery running down. None of the golems were armed with guns. Their iron-claw hands hung at their sides. As the two holy mercenaries closed the distance from thirty yards to fifteen, Chambers's heart hammered faster and faster till it echoed inside his head. Captain Wolf's face remained a mask of granite, his marble eyes burning with intensity. He raised his glowing palm. "I'll take the one on the left. You get the one on the right. First one to kill the center golem gets a cigarette break."

"You're on." Chambers and Wolf split up, walking in wide arcs, coming at the golems from opposite sides. When they got

within ten feet, the three golems slowly craned their heads—
two facing Wolf, one facing Chambers. The nearest golem
stared with hollow eyes, the sacred word *emet* partially hidden
by its steel helmet. Chambers stretched his trembling hand toward the nearest creature. The glowing palm now tingled painfully. *Christ, I can't believe we're doing this. Just have faith in
the magic.* The golem's eye sockets filled with silver light.

Chambers froze.

Wolf walked straight up to the one on his side. "I am your
master, golem. Take off your helmet and kneel before—" The
golem roared like something out of hell as it raked its talons
across Wolf's throat. Blood gushed down his chest. The captain spat blood as the clawed hand burrowed into his chest
and lifted him off the ground.

The next moment passed in slow, dreamlike motion.

Chambers screamed, "Nooooo!" The captain stared down
in shocked defeat. Other screams echoed from behind as gunshots cracked the night air. Bullets riddled the chest of the
creature impaling Wolf's chest. The two fell backward.

The other two golems, eyes blazing silver, growled at
Chambers.

Everything moved at full speed. Chambers backpedaled.
The clay soldiers advanced. Claws swiped the air. Machine-
gun bullets fired. Another golem collapsed while the one that
had fallen regained its footing. Chambers stumbled, falling
backward onto his rump. The nearest golem charged. Bullets
pelted its head, knocking off its helmet. The monster leaned
into the metal storm, its fiery gaze directed toward Chambers. Relying on instinct, he opened his canteen and slung
the holy water into its face. The clay flesh sizzled. Shrieking,
the golem grabbed its face and stumbled backward. Chambers barely got to his feet before the next creature attacked—
the one that had killed Captain Wolf. Chambers screamed
like a madman and doused it with holy water. The golem
fell to the ground, its face melting down to the skull. The
word *emet* dissolved with the clay. The silver eyes winked
out and the clay turned to dust. A Nazi skeleton crumpled at
his feet. The other golem he'd splashed had fallen and was
crawling away on its stomach. Chambers pounced on its back

and raked his nails across its slimy forehead. Mud and bones collapsed beneath him. The third golem jumped into the German convertible.

Chambers leaped to his feet. "Come back here, you bastard!"

The headlights came on and the car roared toward Chambers. He leaped and rolled across the gravel as the front fender missed striking him by inches. The tires screeched. Bullets pelted the side of the convertible, shattering the windshield and taillights as the car swerved back onto the farm road and disappeared into the fog.

Cradling the canteen, Chambers stood above Captain Wolf's body. The bitter moon reflected in the Czech mercenary's vacant eyes. Men shouted from the church. Running boots crunched over gravel. Chambers didn't bother to look behind him. He was too busy cursing at the night sky.

Part 7

Chaos

There was in times of old,
where Ymir dwelt,
nor sand nor sea,
nor gelid waves;
earth existed not,
nor heaven above,
'twas a chaotic chasm,
and grass nowhere.
                    —*THE EDDAS*

Chapter 43

Inside the church, the platoon was silent, still in shock from losing Captain Wolf. His body lay in the far corner draped with a wet parka. Anna, who had grown close to the Czech mercenary, sobbed quietly in the shadows, as if she were trying to hide her sadness. Goldstein touched the girl's arm, but she brushed his hand away.

Chambers leaned against a column. His right hand trembled. He held it with his left till it stopped.

Mahoney put a hand on his shoulder. "You okay, Lieutenant?"

"Yeah, round up as much holy water as you can find. It took care of two of those golems."

"I'm on it."

Chambers marched along the front windows. His sentries stared down at their boots, their faces portents of inescapable doom. Deuce flinched at the crack of lightning. Hoffer scribbled frantically into his artist's pad. Moose slumped beside his machine gun. "Hang in there, everybody. We're going to find a way to stop them."

"The hell we are!" Deuce said. "We have to get the hell out of here! Soon we'll have a whole army of those things shooting down our throats."

"Stay calm. I'm working on a plan."

Sounding like Fallon, Deuce said, "Death's the only fate in the platoon of the Grim Reaper."

"Can it, Deuce!" Mahoney barked.

The bells inside the tower clanged, reverberating throughout the church.

Twelve tolls. The witching hour.

Chambers paced, struggling for words that would inspire his platoon to victory. But the odds were so stacked against them. *We're dead if we leave, dead if we stay.*

The two bound and gagged Nazi youths stared hopelessly. The eldest Nazi, Major Eichman, kept his pale gaze fixed on Chambers. He pulled out the German officer's gag. "You got any ideas?"

Eichman grinned. "Hell is coming. Ve are all doomed."

"Taking advice from the enemy now, Chambers?" Fallon marched out of the shadows, carrying two heavy duffel bags. He set them near the door, the clink of Nazi gold hitting the wood floor. "Moose, get the other bags. Everybody else, get your gear together. We're repositioning down below."

Chambers stomped across the vestibule. "The hell we are! We'll be trapped down there."

"Better we hide where they can't see us than stay here. I said move it, men."

"Everybody stay put," Chambers ordered. "Up here we can still escape if we have to."

The platoon stayed at their posts.

"I gave you an order!" Fallon screamed at his two commandos. "Now, go get the duffel bags." Fallon shoved Moose into action, and the sergeant ran into the nave.

Corporal Fox, flipping through the Kabbalah book, looked to Chambers.

"Stay where you are, Fox. I need you to decipher those runes. Goldstein, Anna, I'm depending on you two to find a way to reverse the rabbi's magic."

Goldstein glanced at Anna and Fox. "We'll do our best."

"I need you to do more than your best, Chaplain. I need you to work miracles."

Fallon said, "Your Jewish magic won't work. Look where it got Wolf."

The memory of the captain's death stung Chambers's heart. "The holy water kills them if you pour it on their forehead."

"Then let's all fill up our canteens and move below ground. We stand a better chance barricading ourselves in the antechamber."

"There could be more of them down there hiding. We're staying up here where we can see them coming."

Fallon rubbed a hand across his black-painted face. "Christ, Chambers, what do you intend to do when that golem comes back with a dozen more? Two dozen!"

"Lieutenant Hawk's right," Deuce said. "We're toast if we stay up here."

"What we need to do now, men, is put up our best defense and hold the enemy back long enough for us to reverse the spell."

"This is ridiculous," Fallon said. "Chambers is telling you to gamble your lives on a hunch that there's some magic remedy. Get a fucking clue!"

Chambers glared at Fallon. "Now looks who's running like a damned coward. Let's put up one hell of a stand. It's going to take all of us."

"Well, you can count the X-2 men out. Moose, Fox, let's move." Fallon opened one of the duffel bags and held up a gold bar. "Anybody else who goes with us gets to share the reward. The rest of you are shit out of luck."

Deuce stepped into the nave. "I'll carry a bag."

"Deuce, get back here!" Chambers felt the sting of betrayal.

"Sorry, Lieutenant, I ain't got a death wish. Come on, fellas, our luck's better hiding below."

"Who else is coming?" Fallon's fiery blue eye glared from his black-painted face. The rest of the platoon stayed at their posts, including Fox.

"No way, man," Hoffer said. "No amount of gold's worth going back down there. If you saw all the slaughtered bodies, you'd stay up here, too."

Mahoney said, "Deuce, you leave the Lucky Seven and you got no odds of surviving."

"Ah, screw it." The Poker King set down the duffel bag and returned to his post.

Chambers crossed his arms. "Fallon, looks like you and Moose are on your own."

Moose's face twisted with rage. "Screw every one of you!"

Fallon marched over to Corporal Fox. "You can forget your reward! And the rest of you can fucking forget going home!" Fallon and Moose disappeared into the nave with their salvage.

Chapter 44

Chambers ascended the stone steps that wound up the dark tower. Using a handrail for guidance, he felt his way through the blackness, a shadow rising out of an abyss. Gray moonlight seeped in high above him. His footsteps echoed off the circular walls. A hollow wind swirled through the passage as if the tower were an immense air valve. It fluttered his hair, chilled his face and neck. He tried lighting a cigarette, but the wind kept snuffing out his lighter.

Halfway up he reached a landing and stepped through a door. To his left the organ's brass pipes rose to the vaulted ceiling, where a horde of bats nested in the spires. He moved to the edge of the choir's loft, overlooking the entire multicolumned nave. Below stretched a black pit rimmed with eerie slivers of light. Pews stood upright against the stained-glass windows, leaving slits large enough for rifle barrels. In several of those glowing slivers stood sentries who Chambers had assigned watch duty. He started to turn away when he spotted three silhouettes sitting in the moonlight beside a window. Fox's hands gestured as he described something to Anna and Goldstein. The chaplain looked up, locking gazes with Chambers.

Godspeed, Rabbi. Show me we still have hope. Chambers

gave a thumbs-up and stepped back onto the landing. The hollow wind embraced him. He continued up the shaft toward the sphere of gray light. The steps ended, and he climbed an iron-rung ladder past thick ropes that hung from the rafters. He reached the top of the tower, where massive bronze bells hung from the ceiling. They operated by some medieval timer but could be rung manually by pulling the ropes. A doughnut-shaped stone floor circled the shaft. Moonlight poured in through four portals that offered a bird's-eye view of the forest. The back portal overlooked the church's jagged roof and the holes where bombs had chipped the spires and broken through the elaborate stone facade.

Chambers propped his rifle in a corner, then sat down and looked out the front portal. Beyond the farm road and parking lot, acres of mist-enshrouded forest stretched in every direction. In the distance, mountain ridges rose up through the haze. *If I were hunting elk in Colorado, this would be a beautiful view.* He smiled as he recalled when he used to hunt with his father. An image filled his mind of the two of them sitting in a cold tower overlooking a field, waiting for a prize buck to gallop into their scopes.

Jack, age seven, noisily opened a bag of butterscotch candies.

His father, wearing a black wool cap, put a finger to his lips. *I need you to stay quiet, son. Deer can hear for miles, and any noise will scare them off. We've got to think like hunters now.*

Are we really gonna kill a deer, Daddy?

You betcha. Soon as we get one in our scopes. This is what Chambers men learn to do. Now put away the candy and sit still.

Yes, sir.

Chambers had never felt safer than when sitting beside his father in that deer tower. Now, years later, a hollow feeling in the pit of his stomach gave him the shakes.

Those days are long gone, Dad. Now I'm the one being hunted.

The shakes spread through his entire body as he was overcome by an incredible hunger. He tore into his last box of rations and devoured a can of cold spaghetti and a package of cheese and crackers.

Sitting back, thinking about all he'd been through since dawn, Chambers pulled out his journal. He recounted the events of the day, reliving every moment—finding the Kabbalah cross again, surviving the slaughter at Richelskaul, the men he'd lost along the way, confronting the Nazi shadow soldiers, and most perplexing of all, learning that his father had been a U.S. spy gathering intelligence for the Freemasons. Putting it to paper was overwhelming. His journaling ended with a letter to the woman who conjured his hope.

Dear Eva,
Well, sweetheart, I'm in a really fine mess again. Lost behind enemy lines somewhere. Don't know when I'll be coming home, or if. The odds are stacked against me. I'm no longer in control of my destiny or the lives of my platoon. Absurd for me to think that I ever was.
I feel so lost, Eva. So utterly helpless. I miss you. But I understand that a year and a half is a long time to wait for someone. Especially a man you only shared three weeks with. Who am I to expect you to carry a torch for me so long? I'm sure you've moved on to someone else. Probably for the best. I'll be gone by tomorrow anyway. Another casualty to Hitler's madness. I suppose it's time I read your letter and take it like a man.

Exhaling a deep breath, he retrieved the thick letter from his jacket pocket. His finger traced along Eva Winchester's handwriting, feeling the indentations made thousands of miles away when she pressed ink to paper. Curiosity burning his forehead, Chambers popped out the blade from his Masonic cross and opened the envelope. He pulled out three pages with elegant handwriting on front and back. He unfolded them, and a stack of photographs fell onto the floor facedown. Taking in another breath, he raised the photos to the gray moonlight. There was Eva standing on her front porch, the wind blowing her honey-blond hair sideways. She held a toddler against her hip, a boy with brown hair, green eyes, plump cheeks . . . the same boy sitting in a highchair with a messy chin . . . the boy standing, dressed like a cowboy, holding up a sign that read, "Happy Birthday, Daddy."

Chambers's lower jaw quivered.

Lieutenant Jack Chambers
9th Infantry Division
60th Infantry
2nd Battalion

September 1, 1944

My dear Jack,
    I sure hope this letter finds you. I've written so many bloody letters since you left, I've lost count. I'm worried that you might not be getting them. Or worse. I keep telling myself that you're busy fighting the war, but I wish you would write me back.
    I miss you. Our son misses you. That's right, Jack. I named him Thomas, although the nurses and I call him Tommy. I hope you like the name. He has your eyes and my nose. Today he's nine months old. Tommy was born on New Year's Day, 1944. I swear when I first held him I felt like you were here with me. And I must say Tommy is a very stubborn baby. My little mule. I long for the day you get to hold him.

The letter went on to describe Tommy's first tooth, first sounds, his love of horses, and the day he called her Mum. The last half of the letter was an outpouring of how much Eva loved and missed Jack. How many nights she stood on her balcony awaiting his return.

    Please come home soon, Jack. I'm ready for us to be a family, if you'll still have me. I miss holding you in my arms and dancing with you in my flat. We'll be here await-ing your return.

All our love,
Eva and Tommy

His chest clenched. The nerves that held him together un-raveled until he shook with emotion. Chambers read the letter again word for word. Then he stared at the photos for what seemed like an hour.

He heard footsteps down inside the passage, then someone climbing up the iron-rung ladder. Chambers scooped up the photos and letter and tucked them back inside his breast pocket.

Hands poked up from the round hole in the floor followed by a head with dark curly hair.

"Hey, Chap."

Goldstein crouched beneath the bells and peered out the four portals. "Wow, you can see half the forest from up here."

Chambers nodded, staring out the window.

Goldstein sat down beside him. "Everything okay?"

"Peachy. How's the research going?"

"Fox is translating the runes. That Brit's got a mind like an encyclopedia."

"How about you, any leads on how to perform the Kab-balah?"

"I deciphered a few paragraphs using the Atbash scale, but it's a tedious process. There are at least a hundred pages en-crypted. I'm afraid it could take days."

Chambers rubbed his face. "We got at best two hours. You two need to figure a faster way."

"We got even bigger problems. Fox and I agree there's something about these golems that doesn't match up to the legendary Golem of Prague."

"How so?"

"The use of human skeletons for one. The original golem was a sculpture made entirely of clay. And the leg-end mentions nothing about the golem having the ability to growl or having eyes that glowed silver. It was just a large, dumb automaton that followed the orders of Rabbi Loew. But the golems the Nazis built are cunning, demonic in nature."

"And our Kabbalah shields are useless against them."

"Fox thinks the answer is encrypted in the runic passages."

Chambers started to rise. "Let's see what he's found out."

"Wait, Chambers, I need to talk to you."

He sat back down. "Everything okay, Chaplain? You're shaking."

"Just precombat jitters."

"I know the feeling."

Goldstein exhaled and looked up at the bells for a long beat.

Chambers said, "Just tell me what's on your mind."

"Remember when I described this war as a battle between angels and demons?"

"Yeah. You've turned me into a true believer."

"When the figure in my dreams chose me for this mission, I had this feeling that I was invincible. That the angels were shielding me from death." Tears streamed down the rabbi's face. "But after what happened to Captain Wolf . . . I'm afraid we're up against something even the angels can't defeat."

Chambers put a hand on his shoulder. "Hey, Chap, you said yourself that God brought us together to be his soldiers of light. He wouldn't have gone to all this effort if there wasn't hope that good would prevail over evil. Until I met you, I saw only the dark side of war. I never believed that I might actually have angels on my side."

"You're right. We're not alone. Forgive me, God, for doubting." Goldstein sniffled and wiped his eyes. "Some chaplain I am, blubbering about my fears."

"It happens to the best of us. Let's keep the faith. You and I are gonna need enough for everyone."

Goldstein nodded. "Especially when you hear what Fox has discovered about our Nazis."

Part 8

The Black Order

Then went all the powers
to their judgment-seats,
the all-holy gods,
and thereon held council,
who should of the dwarfs
the race create,
from the sea-giant's blood
and livid bones.
—*THE EDDAS*

Chapter 45

Chambers spotted the silhouettes of Corporal Fox and Anna along the side windows. The British X-2 corporal paced, whispering frantically. His hand traced runic symbols in the condensation of the stained-glass windows.

Anna held open her grandfather's Kabbalah book. She shook her head. "No, no. My *zayde* would never be a part of something like this."

Fox said, "Your grandfather did it for your protection, Anna. The Nazis tortured you. They made him watch."

Anna threw down the book and growled. "I hate them! I want them dead!" Then she burst into tears.

Goldstein put his arm around her shoulders. "It's okay. It's okay." He sat Anna down on a pew.

Chambers pulled Fox over to the window. "Goldstein said you figured out the runes."

"Have I ever!" He picked up the book and paced. "The ramifications are outlandish, yet brilliant. Absolutely brilliant!" He flipped the pages. "For one, this spell book is more than just a doctrine of Kabbalah and how to build golems. Rabbi Klein's incantations from the *Sefirot* make up only a portion of the mysticism recorded." Fox rubbed his hand along the thick black binding. "We have found what the Nazis titled *Das Buch Vom Schwarzen Orden—The Book of the Black Order*. It's a monumental compilation of the archaeological research gathered by the Ahnenerbe-SS."

Chambers stared at the rune-filled pages illuminated with archaic drawings. "I've never heard of them."

"The Ahnenerbe is a bizarre experimental science division of the SS that funds expeditions all over the world, studying runes and ancient occults in an effort to prove the Germans came from a mythical Nordic race—the blond-haired, blue-eyed 'Master Race.' The Aryans." Fox flipped to a page handwritten in German. "See here, this is an excerpt from Madame Helena Petrovna Blavatsky's famous theosophical writings called *The Secret Doctrine* published in 1888. I've read her book myself. In a time when science and religion were in great conflict, Blavatsky invented theosophy, which blended science and spirituality. She theorized that man descended not from the ape, as Darwin proposed, but from vanished races of people. Some races were inferior and imperfect and others superior and pure. According to Blavatsky, the master, dominant race of all other races were the Aryans. These theories fueled the flame of the anti-Semitic Germans, in particular Hitler and his inner circle.

"The Ahnenerbe-SS was instituted by these elite Nazis— all obsessed with proving that pure-blooded Germans and Austrians were direct descendants from the Aryans and are destined to return to being this pure, dominant race within the next thousand years. Hence Hitler's Thousand Year Reich. His inner circle calls itself the Black Order. I found this in one of the offices below." Fox pulled a photo out of his black tunic—seven black-clad Nazi officials posing in front of a giant fireplace. "These are just a few disciples of the Black Order. The photo was taken at their secret headquarters in a medieval castle called Wewelsburg. The man in the center is none other than the leader of the entire SS, Reichsführer-SS Heinrich Himmler. On either side of him are two occultists who made up an ominous team—Reichsleiter Alfred Rosenberg and Soil-Mystic Richard Walther Darré."

"I have heard of Rosenberg," Anna said, joining them at the window. The tears were gone, her resolve once again evident. "He is notorious for writing articles that smear the Jews."

"Right," Fox said. "And he smears the Freemasons as well. Rosenberg promoted an anti-Semitic manuscript called *The Protocols of the Elders of Zion*. This document is a forgery claiming that a Jewish-Masonic cult was responsible for the American and French Revolutions and is currently conspiring to overthrow Christian monarchies. The Third Reich uses *The Protocols* as an anti-Semitic platform from which they must stop the Jewish-Masonic cult from world domination. Once the Nazis started occupying territories around Europe, Rosenberg ordered *Einsatzkommandos* to raid the Masonic lodges and steal their sacred secrets. This, I believe, is what convinced the United States and England to finally get involved. Not only were the Nazis attacking Jews, the bloodline of many American people, but they were attacking the brotherhood for democracy and spreading Hitler's madness across Europe like a black plague."

Chambers's mind spun as he tried to piece it all together. "So you're saying that this Masonic brotherhood, which my father was a part of, was involved with influencing our government to go to war."

"Were you aware that President Roosevelt, Vice President Truman, and Prime Minister Churchill are all Masons?"

"No, I knew very little about the Masons before today."

Fox scratched his trimmed red beard. "Isn't it interesting that all the Allied officials leading the fight against Hitler are Freemasons?"

Chambers said nothing.

Goldstein said, "He's too skeptical to take your word for it, Fox. Show him what you showed me and Anna."

"Right, right. Your entire government was built upon the principles of Freemasonry." Fox pulled out a dollar bill. "You can see the Jewish-Masonic roots in your own currency." He pointed out two places where he had marked the bill with a Star of David.

"Notice the circled letters at the tip of each point spell out ANOMS, an anagram for MASON. The pyramid is an obvious symbol of masonry, and the eye at the top is the all-seeing eye, a common Masonic symbol, as well. And on the eagle's wing are thirty-two feathers, which represent the thirty-two degrees of Masonry. Above the eagle's head the thirteen stars form another Star of David. Pretty nifty, huh?"

"Amazing," Chambers breathed.

"I could show you more, but I think I proved my point." Fox tucked the bill back into his pocket. "It is my belief that at the core of this war between the Allies and Axis powers lies a secret battle between the Nazis and the Freemasons."

Chambers thought of his father working as a spy in Germany, and his connections with Captain Murdock and Captain Wolf. "That would explain why the Masons arranged this mission."

"Precisely, because the Nazis had captured some of their most sacred Kabbalah secrets, like how to construct a golem. And because the Nazis were performing another, more threatening form of mysticism—rune magic." Fox moved his finger to the next man in the circle. "Soil-Mystic Rich Walther Darré, Rosenberg's partner in crime, actually came from Argentina. Darré is one of the Black Order's experts on performing runic mysticism and contributed several passages to this book. Beside him sits SS-Obersturmführer Otto Rahn, a seeker of the Holy Grail and author of *Lucifer's Servants*.

Rahn's interest was in South America and Aztec legends that told of a white god that came from a land of ice called Tulla— to the Nazis, more evidence that the legendary Aryans existed in an arctic land called Thule. The book also contains documentation from Otto Rahn's medical experiments performed at Dachau."

"He was experimenting on Jews?" Goldstein asked.

Fox's face turned grim. "I couldn't bear to read much of it. Otto Rahn's research in the name of science was by far the most disturbing. Fortunately he died an early death in 1939."

"Who is that?" Anna pointed to a studious-looking man.

"SS-Hauptsturmführer Dr. Ernst Schäfer. He leads the Tibetan expeditions for the Ahnenerbe. His findings on Tibetanology are also found here. So these are the Ahnenerbe masterminds who conceived this book."

Chambers tapped the officer with beady eyes and oval spectacles. "I saw a photo of this man when exploring the underground offices."

"Then you stumbled upon the office of SS-Hauptsturmführer Manfred von Streicher. He was in charge of implementing Operation Eisen Sarg."

"The Nazi golems," Goldstein said.

"Yes, Von Streicher's team sculpted the golem soldiers, performed Kabbalah to give them life, armed them with weapons, and put them into iron coffins to be placed along the borders of Germany. *Das Buch Vom Schwarzen Orden* contains all the methods needed to resurrect a golem army." Fox flipped through the pages, showing German text, Hebrew, runes, swastikas, and drawings of soldiers with swords.

Goldstein said, "So all we have to do is find the Kabbalah incantations that will reverse the spell that gave them life."

The mirth drained from Fox's eyes. "I'm afraid it won't be that easy."

"Why not?" Chambers asked.

"Because the magic we're up against is more than just Kabbalah. The reason Captain Wolf's Masonic shield failed is because the resurrected golems are only a foundation for the monsters the Nazis created. The golem exterior provides the armor. It's what the rune magicians filled these clay vessels with that scares the living Jesus out of me."

"So what exactly are we dealing with, Fox?" Goldstein asked.

Chambers looked out the window at the forest. "And more importantly, how do we stop them?"

"I think we should ask the rune master who coauthored this book." Fox pointed to the seventh Nazi in the photo. A clean-shaven officer with cropped white hair and pale blue eyes. "SS-Obersturmführer Helmut Eichman."

Chapter 46

Corporal Fox cut Helmut Eichman loose and shoved him against a column. Chambers double-checked the ropes that bound the two Nazi youths together. "Anna, you sure you can handle this?"

She held a Luger with both fists. "Don't worry about me. I watched the Gestapo shoot my papa and brother in an alley. I have no problem shooting these two bastards if they try anything."

Chambers nodded. *The girl's tough as nails.* He checked in with the three sentries at the vestibule windows—Mahoney, Deuce, and Hoffer. "All quiet?"

Deuce yawned. "So quiet it's putting me to sleep."

Hoffer said, "It's been an hour. Think maybe that golem forgot about us?"

Chambers offered a hopeful smile. "Maybe. I hadn't considered that those things might not have any kind of memory."

"Then again," Deuce said, "maybe they're sharp as tacks and hordes of them are maneuvering through the trees as we speak."

Hoffer said, "Don't jinx us, you idiot."

"Hey, I'm just throwing out possibilities. I still say our

odds are better hiding down below with the X-2 commandos."

"Can it, Deuce," Mahoney barked. "Lieutenant, may I have a word with you?"

Chambers followed the sergeant into the bell tower's stairwell.

Mahoney asked, "So what's the word?"

"Our prisoner, Helmut Eichman, has been lying to us. Turns out he's one of the guys who created this mess."

"Well, if you need somebody to beat some answers out of him . . ."

"Thanks, Papa Bear, but I need you to man the front and keep Deuce in line."

"Right, I'll be happy to beat him as well." Mahoney chuckled briefly, then turned serious again. "Listen, we never talked much about our lives back home, but . . . I got a wife and four little girls back in Denver who think their daddy might be coming home soon. I know I shouldn't have promised them, but when you said Captain Murdock was sending that recommendation letter, I couldn't help but mention it."

Chambers nodded, secretly regretting that he had volunteered his seasoned sergeant for this mission. "I'll do everything I can to find a way out of this."

"I know you will, Lieutenant. You always do."

Chambers smiled up at the giant sergeant. *My rock. God, if you're listening, please protect him.*

Leaving the stairwell, Chambers joined his two book translators, Fox and Goldstein. "Okay, guys, what's the latest?"

Corporal Fox kept his Luger aimed at the Nazi officer. "We're very close. Eichman says he has something to show us."

"All right, where are we going?"

Eichman answered. "Von Streicher's office."

Chambers eyed the Nazi suspiciously.

"I vill cooperate. I am just as eager to stop this madness as you are."

Chambers raised his Thompson. "Then lead the way. And no sudden moves."

Reaching the altar, the rune mystic entered the stairway that wound down to the undercroft. Fox and Goldstein followed, their flashlights sketching circles on the curving walls.

Suddenly feeling uneasy, Chambers stopped at the top of the stairs and spun around. The expansive nave was a nocturnal tapestry of moonlight, colorful stained-glass kaleidoscopes, and impenetrable darkness. He scanned the altar along the confessional closets and remembered he left Miguel Garcia in there hours ago. *God, I hope he's all right.* Chambers tromped along the array of closets, trying to remember which one. At the far end came a rasping sound. He put his ear to the closet door. Garcia was snoring.

Again feeling the pinpricks in his neck, like tiny darts shooting from the shadows, Chambers turned back toward the nave and challenged with his own daggered stare. *I don't know where you are, Fallon. But I can feel you watching me.*

• • •

Down in the church's undercroft an oil lamp flickered inside Manfred von Streicher's office. The SS commander's corpse had been removed, but the stench of death still hung in the fetid air. Now Helmut Eichman sat in the winged-back chair with *The Book of the Black Order* open on the desk. He leaned on his elbows, his bound wrists and gloved hands resting on the book. "Can you please untie me? It is difficult to turn the pages."

"You can manage." Corporal Fox stood over the rune mystic's shoulder, a Luger aimed at his head. Goldstein leaned against a leather couch with his arms crossed.

Chambers checked his watch. "Okay, Fox, let's make this quick."

"Right, sir." The British commando motioned with his pistol toward Eichman. "SS-Obersturmführer, we know you were working as Von Streicher's rune magician." He tossed a photo onto the desk. "We know about the Black Order and about Ahnenerbe. If you wish to survive tonight, tell us everything you know about these monstrosities you created."

Eichman's pale blue eyes gazed at the photo. The oil lamp's

dancing flame flickered across the sinister faces of those gathered in front of the fireplace at Wewelsburg Castle. "It vas Heinrich Himmler's vision. At one of our meetings, he asked, 'Why wait a thousand years for the Apocalypse that will return northern Europe to its Teutonic kingdom? Why not start the Apocalypse now?'

"'What are you suggesting, Herr Himmler?' I asked.

"And he responded, 'We, as the Brotherhood of Odin, are to make it our quest to study the world's mysticisms and raise from the dead our own Teutonic Knights. An invincible army to expand our borders, exterminate the Jewish vermin, and stop our enemies from invading the Fatherland.' Himmler slammed his fist onto the round table. 'Let the Apocalypse begin with Ahnenerbe!' We all agreed to the quest.

"When Alfred Rosenberg captured sacred secrets from the Masonic lodges, we had the first mystical ingredient to build our supersoldiers—*the Golem*. Their clay bodies can absorb bullets and shrapnel. Fire does nothing. They follow orders and can live an eternity without food or water. But the ones we built under the guidance of Rabbi Klein turned out to be problematic. For one, they were dumb beasts that could not shoot a gun or operate a vehicle. They had no warrior mentality. They lacked passion for the Reich. And worst of all, Rabbi Klein was encoding them to protect the Jews. So turning golems into soldiers was not enough to achieve our master army."

Chambers studied a bookshelf covered with framed photographs. He held up one of explorers dressed in thick winter coats and standing in a snowfield. "So the quest continued."

"Yes. That was the Ahnenerbe's expedition to Iceland," Eichman said. "We studied everything we could find that had been written in runes. I translated an ancient Nordic text called *The Eddas*. These poems paint a vivid picture of Teutonic life and the great World Tree known as Yggdrasil. It was in Iceland, in Thule, our ancestral homeland, that we discovered the second mystical ingredient to completing our invincible soldiers. The runes." Eichman smiled, his icy blue eyes gleaming. "The Icelandic legends also provided proof that we are indeed descendants of the master race. And it is our destiny to return to Thule as Aryans."

Goldstein rolled his eyes.

Fox said, "So how did you use the runes?"

"I performed rituals based on Odinism. The Nordic god Odin was the inventor of poetry and the rune alphabet. *The Eddas* come from his divine inspirations. He could transform himself into all shapes and raise the dead. And he filled the runes with magic known as Necromancy, giving man his godlike powers to speak to the spirits and raise the dead. So when we returned from our expedition, we had our divine inspiration. Use human bones to build the golems. The clay made a perfect conduit to divine energy. And the skeletons made perfect sacrifices." Eichman squeezed his black gloves into fists. "Then I, as Necromancer, performed a runic ritual to Odin, calling into the clay vessels the warrior spirits of our Teutonic ancestors."

"Bloody hell," Fox breathed.

Chambers stared at the next photo on the shelf. This one showed Von Streicher and Eichman commanding a team of *Einsatzkommandos* in front of the church. "But things went terribly wrong, didn't they, Eichman? You raised your own damnation."

The Nazi Necromancer nodded. "The first fifty resurrections were a success. We had a unit of the most deadly soldiers to ever walk the planet packed into iron coffins, ready to be transported. But the next batch was different. I resurrected a spirit-filled golem whose clay turned solid white. Its eyes were different than the others, bright red instead of silver. It had a mind of its own, and the next thing we knew our Teutonic Knights were turning on us, slaughtering every soldier in sight. I still don't know what went wrong, but I fear I may have resurrected Odin himself."

"That's what you get for bloody playing with the dead." Fox flipped through the book to a drawing that looked identical to the chalked circle they found within the six red candles. "Is this the ritual you used?"

"Yes, it is actually two rituals combined." Eichman pointed with his bound hands. "The cosmic tree here is the Kabbalistic *Sefirot*. Traced around it is the great World Tree Yggdrasil and the runic incantations."

Fox's eyes lit up. "Gentlemen, I think we may have our solution!"

Goldstein and Chambers leaned over the desk. "You can reverse the spell?"

The British commando scratched his red whiskers as he studied the drawing. "Yes, this makes sense now. Goldstein, you'll perform the Kabbalah ritual in reverse. Being a rabbi, you're much more qualified than I. Eichman, you and I will perform the rune ritual. We're going to need to go down to the crypt and prepare the ritual . . ."

Eichman started laughing.

"What's so bloody funny?" Fox asked.

"Your ritual von't work. It requires an entirely different spell to destroy our Teutonic warriors." He sat back in the chair. "And I am the only one who holds that secret."

Fox pointed his pistol.

"Nein." Eichman grimaced. "The apocalypse is the world's destiny, and only those born from true Aryan blood will survive."

"Rubbish! I'll shoot you on the spot."

"Not yet, Fox." Chambers's attention was pulled to a framed photo higher up on the bookshelf, an expedition photo marked *Iceland, 1939.* A group of men in arctic coats sat at a table inside a cabin, Manfred von Streicher and Helmut Eichman among them. Most of them had beards. They raised their beer steins over a book lying on a table. Also there was another familiar face. Chambers's blood ran cold. The explorer had thick blond hair, fiery blue eyes, and a regal face not yet tainted by burn scars.

"Pretty handsome in those days, wasn't I, Reaper?"

Chambers dropped the picture and whirled around.

Pierce Fallon and Sergeant Moose stood in the doorway, grinning madly and aiming their guns. "History lesson's over, boys."

Chapter 47

His jaw hanging open, Corporal Fox stared at the barrel end of Fallon's Luger. "Dear God, what are you doing, sir?"

"Helping out an old friend. Good day, Professor." Fallon fired and a bullet punched a hole in Corporal Fox's forehead. Red mist sprayed the back wall. The Brit's eyes sparked with the sudden shock of death, and he collapsed onto a credenza, knocking over a stack of books.

"You son of a bitch!" Chambers reached for his Thompson in the corner. A second shot exploded in the room, the bullet's heat whizzing past his hand.

"Don't even think about it, Reaper. You either, Goldstein. Untie Herr Eichman."

Gloved hands free, Eichman gripped Fox's Luger. He pointed the barrel at Goldstein. "Back away, you filthy Jew." The Necromancer's lips parted in a reptilian smile. "Fallon, it is about time you two got down here. What vas taking so long?"

Wearing a half-cocked grimace, the X-2 lieutenant with the eye patch stepped into the office. "Moose and I had to tie up a few loose ends." He pulled out his brass-knuckled knife. Blood dripped down the blade. "Don't worry, Herr Eichman, everybody's been taken care of."

Chambers's stomach knotted. "What did you do to my men!"

"Silence!" Fallon screamed, rotating the Luger toward Chambers's forehead.

Eichman kept his pistol aimed at Goldstein. "Jew, kneel before me on both knees."

The chaplain's lips trembled as he kneeled. His eyes fluttered closed as the gun barrel pressed into Goldstein's forehead. "Jew, you are hereby my new apprentice. You vill help me raise more golems."

Goldstein said, "Go to hell."

Eichman chuckled. "Perhaps she will persuade you." Sergeant Moose stepped into the room and threw Anna on the floor. She crawled and wrapped her arms around Goldstein. He held her head against his chest.

Chambers stared at Moose and Fallon in shock. *This isn't happening.*

Eichman said, "Jew, you vill do what I say or she and Dietrich here vill have a party in our torture room."

Moose grimaced. "It'll be my pleasure."

Goldstein's face twisted with rage. "You hurt her, and I swear . . ."

Eichman backhanded the chaplain. "Shut up, Jew! If you want to live a few more hours and save that bitch from Dietrich, all you have to do is serve the Nazi cause."

"Ein Volk, ein Reich, ein Führer." Fallon pointed to a swastika on the wall. *"Heil, Hitler!"*

Eichman and Moose did the same. *"Heil, Hitler!"*

Chambers's face burned with anger. "You're all going to fucking hell."

"I am sick of listening to this svine." The SS Necromancer rubbed his wrists. "Silence him."

Moose grabbed Chambers from behind, pinning both arms.

"I've been waiting a long time to do this." His single blue eye sparkling with glee, Fallon stomped over, the long black blade jutting from his fist.

"No! Don't!" Chambers braced himself as the brass knuckles smacked his jaw. The room spun and went black.

Chapter 48

The sweltering darkness wrapped around Chambers like a spider feeding on its web-spun prey. Beady sweat dripped off his forehead and stung his eyes. His jaw ached, the flesh around it swollen. The eight-legged blackness sucked out the marrow of his sanity. Walls closed inward like a vise, the pressure unrelenting. He hyperventilated beneath a filthy cloth that gagged his throat. His shoulders rammed the walls. He kicked a door. *Damn it! Where the hell am I?*

Captain Murdock's voice echoed in his head. *Breathe. Just breathe.* Chambers sucked air through his nostrils, slow and deep. Blood and sweat-tainted saliva rolled down his throat. He willed back the bile rising up his chest. His night vision adjusted, making out speckled moonlight on his knees. An outline of his fingers stuck out of ropes coiled around his arms and thighs. His right hand wriggled between the cords, chafing his knuckles, until all five fingers were free. The palm remained pinned to his side. He bent forward as far as the bindings would allow. His free hand stretched toward his side pocket. He could still feel the bronze cross pressing into his thigh. But his fingers couldn't reach it. *Damn it!* He sat back against the wall, his nostrils flaring, the gag pressing deeper into his gullet.

His night vision crystallized. Just inches from his knees was a wood door that filtered moonlight. *I'm in some kind of closet.* Then he remembered the confessionals. Somebody bumped the wooden wall to his right. A muffled whimper. *Somebody's alive!* Farther down he heard banging and moaning.

Boots stomped outside the closet. Someone kicked the door farther down. A German accent yelled, "Stay quiet!" The boots stomped away. *"Dummheit Amerikaneisch."*

The person in the closet to Chambers's right fell silent. In the closet to Chambers's left, somebody moved. "Spppt." The confession window slid open. There was a slight tearing sound, and the screen between the two booths peeled back, revealing a shadowy face. A voice, barely audible, whispered, "It's me—Garcia." An arm stretched through the window and pulled out Chambers's gag. He released a breath and spat. Garcia's finger pressed against his lips. "They don't know I'm here. I've got a gun." He held up a pistol.

"Don't do anything, Garcia."

"We have to. I overheard them talking. They're gonna kill us."

Chambers's mouth tasted like an oily cloth. "Okay . . . I'll create a diversion."

Garcia's shadowy head nodded then retreated back into the gloom of his closet. The window divider slid closed.

Chambers reached for his cross again. Got a few inches closer. He took a deep breath then kicked at the door. "Fallon, you son of a bitch, get me out of here!" He slammed against the walls, kicking and screaming. He stopped, out of breath.

Jackboots clumped outside. From several feet down metal scraped against wood, dragging across one closet door after the other. "Eenie, meenie, miney, moe. Catch Lieutenant Reaper by the toe." The blade scraped closer. "Eenie . . . meenie . . . miney . . . *moe*." The scraping ended at Chambers's door.

"Fallon, let me out of here!"

The eight-inch blade stabbed through the thin wood, narrowly missing Chambers's right eye. His heart threatened to burst.

Fallon pulled the knife back out. A blue eye peered through the slash in the door, winked. "Make some more noise again, Chambers, I dare you." Chuckling, Fallon vanished from the slash and paced along the closets. "Boys, while you all sit there, crying in your own misery, contemplating exactly how and when you're going to die tonight, wondering will it be quick, a bullet through the back of the head, or will it be a slow, torturous death? While you're pondering your fates, you can thank your Lieutenant Reaper for getting you into this situation." Fallon laughed. "Your platoon leader's got a confession to make. Go ahead, Reaper, tell them why they're here."

"Eat shit, you Nazi asshole."

"Not ready to confess, huh? Well, I guess I'll purify your sins for you. See boys, funny thing is you didn't have to come on this mission. Chambers volunteered you. Traded your expendable lives for a way out of the war, just so he could get back to a piece of ass. Not very fair to you, but such is life. Or in your cases, death."

In the next closet, Hoffer released a muffled cry.

"Don't listen to him! Fallon's a Nazi agent." Chambers clawed into his pocket, touching the tip of the cross. "You've been planning to screw us over all along, haven't you?"

"Quiet, Reaper! I'm trying to have a heart to heart with your platoon before we kill them." The jackboots clumped along the floor. "You boys ever wonder how your lieutenant earned his nickname? It goes back to his days in North Africa. Remember those days, Reaper! Good times. That is, until our last mission together. Your lieutenant and I led a platoon much like yours . . ."

A cold sweat broke out across Chambers's face. The speckled moonlight in front of him transformed into desert terrain. Horrific visions bubbled up from dark cesspools in his mind: his recon platoon attacking a German fuel dump . . . gunshots, explosions . . . dismembered men . . . Chambers running through the black fog, flinching with each blast as he walked through the quagmire of scorched soldiers. Fallon's torched body raced out of the smoke, collapsed. Chambers extinguished the fire and dragged his second lieutenant out of the inferno. Fallon strangled him. Chambers clawed at Fallon's blackened face, one eye squishing, the charred flesh around it scraping off like slime.

"The Reaper abandoned us, saving his own ass, while the rest of his men died in the blaze. Just like he was going to abandon you, if he got the chance."

Chambers's jaw tightened, the muscles forming sharp cords around his swollen cheekbones. His fingers grasped hold of the cross, pulling it out. His hands trembled with such rage he nearly dropped it. He kicked his door, cracking it.

A deep guttural laugh echoed outside the door. "And the prize goes to the hostage in closet number two." The fiery blue eye peered back through the slash. "Ain't it funny how history repeats itself."

Several boots stomped over. Eichman's voice said, "Stop playing games, Fallon. You are wasting precious time. Pull them out and execute them."

"Where are you going?"

"Dietrich and I are taking the Jews down to the crypt. Meet us there when you are finished."

Chambers squeezed his fist around the cross. The door swung open. Hands grabbed his boots and dragged him across the floor. He was slammed against a pew in the nave's center aisle. Three Nazi shadows stood around him, including Fallon and the two youths. Moose, the double agent referred to as Dietrich, had left with Eichman.

One of the Nazi youths placed a Luger to Chambers's head.

"No!" Fallon shoved the teen's pistol upward, and it fired into the ceiling. "*Nein,* Fritz. I want him to watch the others die."

Fritz hissed and marched off with the other teen, whom he referred to as Hans. While they dragged another soldier from the confessional closets, Fallon leaned in toward Chambers. "You see these?" His lighter lit up dozens of tattooed daggers that covered both arms. "There's one for every GI I've killed for the Reich." He flexed his bicep. "I've saved a spot right here for a very special Grim Reaper." The lighter flicked off, and the gloom swallowed up Fallon's muscular form. Chambers strained against the ropes that bound his arms against his thighs.

A sudden crash came from the rear of the church. Shots fired. German shouts.

The Nazi youths returned dragging two soldiers. Deuce, still bound and gagged, was slammed to his knees. The other GI lay flat on the floor facedown.

"This one thought he vas clever." Hans grabbed a knot of black hair and lifted the GI's face off the floor. Miguel Garcia's bloody mouth hung open, the eyes rolled back.

Chambers pressed the Star of David button. The blade snicked out. He sawed at the ropes.

Fritz aimed the Luger at Deuce's head.

"No! Wait!" Chambers said.

Fallon said, "Be patient, Reaper, you'll get your turn."

"What about the golems? You need us to help fight them."

"Oh, we have no intention of fighting them. We have our very own Necromancer to protect us. In fact, when your reinforcements finally arrive tomorrow, we're going to have a big surprise waiting for them."

Fritz and Hans laughed.

"Now sit back and watch the show." Fallon grabbed Chambers's head, forcing him to watch.

Fritz pressed the Luger against Deuce's temple. A gunshot fired. Blood sprayed Deuce's face. Fritz, gazing at his comrades, grabbed a wet hole in his chest and fell backward.

Hans jerked his submachine gun at the shadows around them.

Fallon screamed. "Who did that?"

An object flew out of the darkness, smashing the X-2 lieutenant in the face. Fallon's nose exploded. He fell against a column. The object rolled across the wood floor. Hans grabbed it. *"Was ist diese!"* He held up a baseball stained with blood. Another shot fired, bursting the Nazi youth's head.

Fallon dashed for cover, firing at a phantom sniper. *Ra-tat-tat! Ratatatatat!*

Chambers's knife sliced the ropes. He wriggled out and crawled between the pews. Shots rang out across the nave. Muzzle flashes lit up the scope of a GI sniper perched in the choir balcony. Submachine-gun bullets ripped across the balcony. The sniper vanished.

"Where do you think you're going, Reaper?" Fallon's silhouette stood at the end of the pew, the brass-knuckled knife in his hand. He stomped between the pews.

Chambers rolled under a pew.

Jackboots sprinted after him. "I'm gonna bleed you like a hog."

Chambers belly-crawled from one row to the next.

Fallon's shadow leaped from pew to pew. Cackles echoed overhead.

The pews ended. Chambers jumped to his feet in the vestibule. Fallon tackled him. They rolled into a wall, a scratching, grappling wad of limbs. Fallon straddled his chest. Chambers tore away the eye patch. A monstrous face with one blue eye and a pus gray orb glared with furious wrath.

The Nazi knife stabbed downward.

Chambers caught the wrist, the blade an inch from his chest.

"Your Judgment Day has arrived, Reaper!"

He held the dagger back with all his might. "No, yours has." He rammed the cross blade into Fallon's groin. The X-2 lieutenant screamed and fell sideways, grabbing his bleeding crotch. Chambers kicked the knife farther in. Then, roaring, he lunged the Nazi dagger between Fallon's ribs. The monster coughed up blood. Chambers straddled the beast's stomach, hacking away into the black pit of its heart.

A GI soldier pulled him off. "It's over, Chambers." Buck Parker kneeled with his sniper rifle, gripping the wrist that hungered to keep hacking. "He's dead."

Part 9

Immortal Combat

The sun darkens,
earth in ocean sinks,
fall from heaven
the bright stars,
fire's breath assails
the all-nourishing tree,
towering fire plays
against heaven itself.
—*THE EDDAS*

Chapter 49

Chambers hung his bloody hands out the window. Rain trick-led over them as cold as the blood flowing through his heart. The thunderclouds roared like a malevolent Medusa, their torrential heads flickering with electric snakes. Wind tossed the fir trees about as they strained to hold their ground. An endless deluge pelted the roof and windows, splashing a cold spray on Chambers's face. Bats of fear flapped inside his rib-cage. He craved a cigarette and a double whisky. He squeezed his tingling hand into a fist. Amber light glowed through his fingers.

They're coming.

He opened his hand, beholding the Kabbalah cross that was now complete.

What do I do now, God? What hope is there left?

He stared out the broken stained glass as if the storm might provide answers.

The iridescent cross shimmered. A voice resonated within: *Lieutenant, you are the last hope. Keep yourself and your men together. Fear trickles down the chain of command. If you panic, your platoon will fray at the seams. You must hold together like a stone. The lives of thousands are riding on your shoulders. Make wise decisions. Take action as if you are not alone. And whenever you reach that pinnacle of self-doubt, keep believing in miracles.*

Miracles.

Chambers cupped the icy water in his hands and splashed his face.

My men need me. Goldstein and Anna need me. If today is my day to die in battle, I'll die fighting.

He pumped his fists and grabbed one of the Nazi's submachine guns. "Men, where are you?"

"Over here," Buck called.

Chambers found his four remaining men slouched on the altar steps. Mahoney, Buck, Deuce, and Hoffer all wore expressions of defeat. Hoffer was trembling. Mahoney's face was black and blue with cuts above his thick eyebrows. Deuce cried beside Garcia's lifeless body.

Garcia's loss pained Chambers as well, but he couldn't show it. "Hand me his letter."

Buck reached into the GI's shirt and pulled out his final letter to his family. "We'll get it to them, *amigo.*" He handed the blood-stained letter to Chambers.

He spoke in an even tone, "Men, I know we've just been through an unspeakable ordeal, but we need to shake it off. Goldstein and Anna need us." Chambers held up his glowing palm. "And the golems are almost here. Let's get back to our posts."

"What's the point?" Deuce sniffled. "There's only five of us. Our luck's run out."

"He's right, Chambers," Mahoney said. "I don't see any way of stopping them."

"We have the bottles of holy water."

"They won't be enough."

"We're all dead," Hoffer said. "They're going to come in here and kill every one of us."

"I'll kill myself first," Deuce said.

Chambers threw up his hands. "So this is it, huh! You're all just going to give up." No longer containing his rage, he shouted, "God damn it, have I ever quit on you? Has there ever been a day that I quit on you?" He moved in closer, face to face, so they could see the intensity in his eyes. "Hoffer, what happened to the invincible Shadow? Deuce, what happened to the Poker King who always comes up aces?" Jaw clenched, Chambers lined up eye to eye with his master sergeant. "Papa Bear, you're the veteran who's survived dozens of battles that seemed hopeless. You've got a wife and four girls at home counting on you to come through this one." Mahoney's rock solid face crumbled.

"And you, Buck," Chambers said, grabbing the rancher's attention. "You survived out there on your own for hours. Did you make your way back to the church just to quit?"

Buck spat tobacco. "Hell no!"

"Well then, come on, men! The Lucky Seven never give up! We fight to the bloody end!"

Each of their eyes lit up with the passion he'd seen before in so many combat missions.

Papa Bear stood. "Fuck it, I'm going back to the front. You coming, men?"

"You can count on me, sir." Buck followed Mahoney toward the vestibule.

Hoffer threw out his chest. "They can't do this without the Shadow." He grabbed his rifle and chased after the two sergeants.

Deuce remained on the steps. "Lieutenant, since when did you get all gung ho on fighting?"

Chambers sat on the steps next to him. "Since I learned I got loved ones waiting for me. Today, I received a letter from the woman I left behind." Chambers reached into his chest pocket and pulled out the photograph of Eva Winchester holding up a toddler. The sight of them brought all his emotions to the surface. "I have a son. Tommy." The boy's green eyes stared back at him. Chambers bit his bottom lip. "I don't know what it feels like to hold him, or hear the sound of his laugh, but more than anything in this world I want to meet my baby boy before I die."

Deuce looked down at his hands. "I have no family waiting home for me. The Lucky Seven was my family."

"Well, your brothers need you now more than ever. You're our wild card, Deuce. Our ace in the hole. We can't get through this without you. Now, can I count on you?"

"Okay, okay, I'll do it. As long as ya stop with the bad poker puns."

"Right. Forgive me. Now let's join the others."

"Just a minute." Deuce reached into his pocket and pulled out a cigar still in the wrapper. "I been saving this for just the right occasion. Congratulations on ya little boy."

• • •

The five soldiers prepared for battle inside the vestibule. At every post they placed their arsenal of guns, ammo, and vodka bottles half-filled with holy water. They also positioned spare weapons up in the tower's choir balcony and back at the altar.

The bells up in the bell tower clanged twice: 0200 hours.

Storm light flashed at all the windows. Thunder clapped overhead. The farm road and front parking lot remained empty, but Chambers's palm continued to glow, the tingles intensifying. He set his three Panzerfaust rocket launchers beside his window slot and motioned his men to gather around. "Everybody locked and loaded?"

"Yes, sir."

"Good. Now everybody use your weapons wisely. Forget trying to kill the golems with bullets. I want you to shoot the weapons out of their hands. Maybe that will send them running. If not, we stand a better chance if they charge us empty-handed. The bottles of holy water are for close combat only." Borrowing Hoffer's sketchpad, Chambers drew a face with the word *emet* on the forehead. "The object is to explode the bottles across this symbol. The holy water works like acid. Melt the sacred word and the golem turns to dust."

"Hallelujah," Hoffer said.

"We have no idea how many are coming. Maybe only a handful. If that's the case then the odds are in our favor. Our main objective is to kill the ones that reach the windows and hold back the rest. Then we'll focus on taking out our two Nazis downstairs. Everybody got it?"

"Yes, sir."

Buck wiped the scope of his sniper rifle. "Chambers, that

symbol on their foreheads is a perfect bull's-eye for me. You reckon if it got hit, that'd kill the golem?"

"You know, it just may. If scratching it off with a finger works, I don't see why a perfectly placed bullet wouldn't do the same." Chambers put his lucky watch into the circle. "Everybody lives."

Buck held out his baseball. Deuce, his poker deck, joker facing up. Hoffer, his Blue Coal matchbook advertising *The Shadow* radio show. And Mahoney, his rosary. "Everybody lives," they repeated.

"Let's roll."

Four of them returned to the vestibule windows where pews, standing upright, left narrow slots through which to fire a rifle. *Remember the Alamo.* Buck dashed up the tower steps to his high perch in the bell room.

"What if they attack from behind?" Deuce asked.

"Remember the trip wires the X-2 commandos set between the tombstones. That should at least warn us. The back door is heavily barricaded, and the side windows are too high off the ground. The golems' best chance of getting in is through the front door and windows."

"They gotta get past us first," Hoffer said with a grin.

Chambers said, "Papa Bear, I need a word with you."

Mahoney set his flamethrower next to his rifle and followed Chambers to an alcove hidden from the vestibule. Chambers flicked his lighter and lit two Camel cigarettes, offering one to the bear-sized sergeant.

Mahoney grinned. "God, I been craving one all day. You really know how to boost a man's morale."

Chambers drew on his cigarette. "I figured you were gonna need it when I told you about my sudden-death plan."

"Sudden death?"

Chambers pulled ten sticks of dynamite out of a leather satchel. "Something our X-2 boys left behind. Still got your lighter?"

In the lower half of Mahoney's silhouetted face a glowing orange dot bobbed when he spoke. "I already don't like where this is leading."

Chambers began strapping the dynamite sticks on his belt. "We got five each. If the golems get inside the church, you and I will lure them down into the graveyard tunnels. Then when we get to the crypt—"

"Yeah, I get it. Sudden death."

"Are you in?"

"Do I got a choice?"

"Not really."

Quickly tying five sticks around each of their belts, they stamped out their cigarettes and returned to the vestibule.

Buck's voice echoed from the top of the tower shaft. "Guys, I see movement. Holy moley! There's a shitload of 'em, and they're headed right for us!"

Chapter 50

Chambers returned to his slot.

Up the road a column of soldiers advanced out of the mist like a giant black serpent with dozens of silver eyes glowing down its spine. Boots splashed through mud as Nazi golems marched toward the church in perfect unison.

Chambers lugged a Panzerfaust rocket launcher onto his shoulder. "This is it, men. Our chance to show them what the Lucky Seven's made of."

"Let's kick some ass, brothers," Deuce cheered from behind the MG42 machine gun.

"Wait till I give the order. Remember, stay calm, focus on one soldier at a time. Take out their weapons first." Chambers yelled up the tower shaft, "You hear me, cowboy?"

"Loud and clear, sir."

Chambers watched the endless column of soldiers advancing from the road. They marched across the gravel parking lot. "Hold steady . . . steady . . . FIRE!"

Rifle fire split the silence. Machine-gun bullets arced across the open lot, chopping down the front line.

Chambers fired the Panzerfaust. A rocket whooshed across the parking lot, blasting the center of the column. The black serpent divided into tentacles as the golems dispersed. The front soldiers charged, firing submachine guns, eyes blazing silver against the gloom.

GI bullets barraged the front line, knocking submachine guns out of their hands. Buck fired from the watchtower above. A few golems fell down and stayed down.

Deuce and Mahoney spun with their machine guns, howling as the wave of golems charged against the onslaught.

Explosions came from the side of the church. Chambers picked up his MP40 and raced to the windows. Golems triggered trip wires, disappeared in geysers of mud and pulverized tombstones. Another squad opened the booby-trapped front gate, and the grenade explosion sent the gate door slicing through the line like a propeller blade. Throughout the graveyard, trip wires pummeled the entire first wave of attackers.

Directly below, Nazi golems charged around the courtyard pool. Chambers unleashed a wrath of fury, feeling the electric thrill of battle coursing through his body. One creature reached the wall. Its iron claws tried to climb toward the twelve-foot-high window. *Oh, no you don't!* Chambers hurled a holy bottle down. It exploded across the golem's face. The clay smoked. The creature wailed and stumbled back into the pool of lily pads.

"Need some help?" Hoffer leaned his rifle over the windowsill, shooting at golems as they ran through the smoke like confused ants. Several crawled out of the graveyard. Hoffer laughed maniacally. "This is working! Chambers, you're a genius!"

At the side vestibule windows, the machine-gunners tossed grenades then ducked as bursts of shrapnel rained down upon the windows. The dust cleared. The graveyard was a mire of broken tombstones and destroyed hedges. The golems fled into the trees.

Everyone in the platoon looked at one another, heaving.

Deuce released his hyena laugh. "Holy crap! They're retreating."

"We kicked their asses!" Hoffer said.

Chambers, breathing heavily, said, "Let's not uncork the champagne just yet. Is anyone hurt?"

The other three men along the windows shook their heads.

"Those bastards barely even got a shot at us," Mahoney said.

Chambers released a breath. "Okay, good, this is working. Everybody just keep doing what you're doing. We may have figured a way to hold them back."

The lieutenant stepped back into the stairwell, looked up at the bell tower's shaft. "Buck, everything golden up there?"

The Texan poked his head over the doughnut-shaped floor. "Just like target practice."

"I like your attitude, cowboy. Keep it up." Chambers returned to his window beside Mahoney. "How's it look out there?"

"All clear for now. They're roaming the forest. I don't think they're used to losing."

Deuce lit a cigar and spoke like John Wayne. "They'll be back."

Occasional bodies maneuvered through the fir trees as the golems reconnoitered the church, but none attacked. The front gravel lot remained vacated. Six golems had fallen and burst to dust, leaving behind crumpled black uniforms. "Man, that Buck's some shot."

"I imagine we took out about ten of them," Mahoney said.

"That's not near enough. We used up our first wall of defense in the graveyard. Now, there's nothing stopping them from coming right up to the church."

"I see one," Deuce said.

A lone golem stepped into the clearing in front of the church about forty yards away. While the other golems had gray skin, this one was bone white with a face sculpted to resemble a skull. The leader. The clay vessel that housed the Nordic god Odin. Like a deadly djinn inside a bottle. The beast had turned against his disciples. And now it challenged Chambers's men with malevolent red eyes.

"Buck, you got a target?"

"Got my crosshairs on him, but I don't see any symbol."

"Shoot him anyway."

A shot cracked from the bell tower. The leader's head snapped back. The steel-kettle helmet clunked to the ground. The white golem raised its head. Crimson fire blazed in its eye sockets. The leader drew a saber and pointed it toward the church. The skeletal mouth opened impossibly wide, releasing the war cry of a thousand damned souls.

A giant thunderbolt split the sky behind it. White smoke spread through the nocturnal forest, devouring the fir trees. Then the farm road. The mist moved across the open lot and swallowed up the white golem.

"Jeez, what's happening?" Deuce asked.

"Stay calm, everybody." Chambers raced to the side windows. The fog sifted through the wrought-iron fence, turning the graveyard into a soupy haze. Visibility diminished to twenty yards. Ten yards. The cold mist drifted into the windows. The shadows within the nave and vestibule thickened, turning Chambers's men into mere shadow shapes themselves.

Hoffer said, "Jeepers, I can't see a th—"

They heard a crash behind them and every head jerked around.

"They're coming from the rear," Deuce said.

"No way in hell," Mahoney said. "It's completely barricaded."

Boots clumped through the darkness of the nave.

Mahoney picked up the flamethrower and burst a twenty-foot flame to illuminate the church, but it only lit up the first few columns and pews. The altar remained hidden behind a veil of darkness and oozing fog. Then two nocturnal silver eyes winked open. Then four. Then six. What looked like silver fireflies floated toward them in the gloom, and what sounded like bloodthirsty Rottweilers growled with a guttural hunger.

Hoffer whispered, "Oh, Jesus, they're coming from down below."

Chapter 51

Suddenly the six glowing eyes winked out. The growling stopped. The impenetrable blackness became silent except for the thunderstorm raging outside. Lightning lit up the fog pressing against every window.

"Hold steady," Chambers commanded. "Mahoney, Hoffer, grab your bottles. Deuce, cover us." He called up the stairwell, "Buck, come down to the balcony. We need back up."

The Texan's boots echoed in the bell tower. He reached the choir balcony and aimed his sniper rifle at the nave. "Man, it's dark in here."

Chambers and Mahoney crept down the center aisle between the columns. Hoffer followed last, carrying four bottles filled with holy water. Chambers gripped one in each hand. *Come on, where are you?*

Mahoney lit up the nave with repeated flame bursts. Storm light flickered the stained-glass windows. Beyond the front pews, the altar remained a pitch-dark cavern. The flamethrower lit up the altar, illuminating the ivory Jesus. Below the crucifix, a shirtless golem roared. This one had a roughly sculpted body with a misshapen head. Behind it another misshapen golem lumbered from the altar stairway.

Christ, the Necromancer's making more of them.

Like demonic samurai, they sliced the air with sabers. Then something amazing happened. The newly arrived golem swung its saber, decapitating the black demon standing beneath the crucifix. Swinging its blade, the rogue golem faced Chambers, Mahoney, and Hoffer. Its eye sockets remained black. Across its blunt forehead golden light traced a symbol shaped like a cross. In the center formed the Star of David.

The Kabbalah cross. But how . . . Goldstein!

Chambers released a nervous laugh. "I think this one's on our side."

Growls came from their left. Their right. Silver eyes lit up the darkness on either side.

Mahoney engulfed the nearest clay demon in flames. A human-shaped inferno charged them, shrieking. From his balcony perch, Buck shot the other assailant, knocking it to the floor. The silver-eyed demon jumped back up, snarling, swooping its saber.

Chambers ran down the nave. "To the altar!"

"You're crazy!"

"Trust me!" The third golem, bearing the glowing Kabbalah cross, stood at the altar, wielding its saber like a knight ready to slay a dragon.

Have faith, have faith. Chambers raced up the steps. The golem, looming above, didn't behead him. Instead it gently picked Chambers up and put him down behind the altar railing. Just as he had hoped. Another guardian. The golem then aimed its sword at the two clay demons chasing Mahoney and Hoffer. They reached the altar.

"Bottles!" Chambers screamed.

Together they exploded three bottles against the first demon's fiery head. It burst into dust and bones. The guardian slammed swords with the second growling, silver-eyed beast. Metal swooshed and clashed like medieval warriors in fierce combat. The guardian spun. Its sword swung upward, slicing off the sparring arm of its enemy. The black demon stumbled back, staring down at the stump at its elbow. It raised a hand with iron talons. Hissed. The guardian drove its sword into the demon's eye.

"Holy crap," Hoffer breathed.

The guardian turned around, facing the three stunned soldiers on the altar steps. Lowering its saber, the golem stepped up to Chambers and knelt before him. The Kabbalah cross glowed in gold on its forehead. "Thank you," Chambers said. "We could use a soldier like you."

Chambers hurried up the center aisle, followed by Mahoney, Hoffer, and the guardian.

Deuce rotated his machine gun back out the window. "Guys, hurry. We got engines rolling right for us!"

"Please, let that be the cavalry." Mahoney returned to his slot and grabbed his BAR.

Chambers ushered the platoon's guardian to a slot along the side windows. He handed it a submachine gun. The golem stared at him a beat, its blunt face devoid of emotion. It tossed the gun and raised the sword.

"Okay, have it your way." Chambers marched back to his post, grabbed the second Panzerfaust rocket launcher.

Rain fell outside the window like a chain curtain. He peered into the wall of smoke.

Engines grinded. Tires and armor tracks rolled over gravel. *Please be our reinforcements.*

The fog lit up with a convoy of glowing headlights.

"I see two German half-tracks!" Buck screamed from the tower.

No such luck.

Chambers rested the anti-tank gun on his shoulder. "Let's give 'em hell, men."

Deuce gripped the MG42 machine gun, the cigar clamped between his gapped teeth.

Retrieving vodka bottles from the crate, Hoffer raced from window to window, placing holy grenades at the foot of each sentry. "These are the last, fellas. Make them count."

Mahoney, keeping the flame pack strapped to his back, dropped the nozzle and gripped his BAR machine gun. "Chambers, without getting too mushy, I want you to know you're the best damned leader I ever had the privilege of fighting with."

"Likewise, Papa Bear." He nodded to the seasoned sergeant. "Remember our sudden-death plan."

Mahoney glanced down at his belt. "How could I forget?"

The convoy headlights rolled closer. Chambers aimed the rocket launcher. The mist swirled and eddied, thinning in places. Two half-tracks took form. Gunners stood in back behind mounted machine guns.

Chambers drew first blood. His rocket blasted the center of the first half-track. The golems in back burst up in the air like burning embers. The driver fled the cab, its flaming body lighting up the woods.

Bullets cut across the night. The soldiers at the windows ducked as the half-track gunners strafed the sides of the church.

Chambers shot bursts out the window with a German submachine gun. An engine roared.

The second armored vehicle barreled straight for the front door, followed by a rolling wave of infantry.

Chapter 52

The fog brightened.

The second half-track roared from the mist like a prehistoric beast. Mahoney's machine gun blew out the front tires. The armored vehicle rammed into the front door. The front grill crashed through, slamming to a halt when the front cab hit the arched ceiling. The walls and floor shuddered. Rock, wood, and dust exploded into the vestibule. The driver smashed through the windshield and rolled across the wood floor. It started to get up.

"Oh, no you don't." Mahoney picked up his flame nozzle and torched the driver.

Hoffer smashed a holy bottle over the wailing demon's face. "One more down, another forty to go."

Sweat soaking his brow, Chambers fired his MP40. A dozen Nazi infantry walked stiffly in the mist like zombies. Only these walking dead carried submachine guns, spraying the windows with rapid fire.

The men ducked beneath the bullet storm, all except Deuce, who fired like a madman with his machine gun. "Die, you fuckers! Die—" Enemy bullets riddled his face and body. He did a wild dance backward before flipping over a pew.

"Deuce!" Chambers ran to him. The Poker King's shredded

body floated in a pool of blood, his poker cards scattered around him.

"Oh, God." Chambers's ears popped. The war zone went eerily silent. The pews against the windows shook. Bullets chipped the wood into flying splinters. Colored glass fragments showered down. Mahoney and Hoffer returned fire. Their eyes raged, mouths screaming, but Chambers couldn't hear them. He remained seated against the wall. His right hand trembled. Brick dust blended with the mist, fogging the vestibule. Fogging his mind.

At the pinnacle of self-doubt, you must believe in miracles.

A gray hand reached down to him. The guardian. The Kabbalah cross shimmered on its forehead. Chambers's palm tingled. The hand pulled him to his feet. The guardian returned to a window, his saber slicing at arms and heads trying to squeeze through.

Chambers shot out the front windows. Mahoney and Hoffer defended the entrance, where the smoking grill of the half-track was wedged into the door frame. Golems crawled through an opening and were met by Mahoney's flamethrower. Hoffer hurled holy water grenades at the creatures' heads. Clay bodies burst into fragments.

"The side windows!" Mahoney torched golem arms stabbing through the slots of the barricade. The wooden pews took flame. Smoke filled the foyer.

Chambers shoved the guardian. "Stop them!" The golem's sword stabbed into the arms and heads penetrating the windows.

The demons withdrew their frontal assault, stepping backward into the mist. Chambers caught his breath.

Mahoney and Hoffer returned to the front. "Hey, they've retreated."

A third armored vehicle trundled through the haze. "Jesus Christ, what now?"

From the tower Buck screamed, "Tiger tank!"

"Christ!" Chambers looked out his slot. The barrel of a Tiger tank jutted from the mist. In the turret stood a golem dressed like a commander.

The turret rotated with a metallic clacking. The golem pointed toward the bell tower. The massive barrel tilted upward. *Clackety-clack-clack-clack.*

Chambers bolted into the stairwell. "Buck, get down here!"

"Shit! Shit! Shit!" Buck's voice echoed in the hollow shaft. He slid down the iron ladder to the top landing. Bolted down the winding staircase. A sonic boom echoed. The bell room exploded. Chambers leaped out of the stairwell as rocks and bell shrapnel rained down. A falling scream echoed.

"Buck!" When the dust cleared, Chambers and Mahoney raced into the debris-filled stairwell. The explosion had blown off half the tower's roof. Rain poured down the shaft. Halfway up, Buck sat on a landing. His face bloody, he lay pinned under a bell.

Mahoney ran up the steps, climbing over debris. "You okay, cowboy?"

The Texan wiped dust off his face. "I can't feel my leg. Damn it!"

"Hang tight! We're coming for you." Mahoney stared down at Chambers and Hoffer. "I've got him. You two keep that tank busy."

Chambers raced back to his slot. The Tiger tank slowly lowered its barrel, the turret rotating. *Clackety-clack-clack-clack.*

The second blast deafened him. One corner of the church imploded. The impact slammed Chambers and Hoffer to the ground. Debris clouded the air. Chambers spat out grit. "Okay?"

Hoffer stared frantically, his face a mask of soot. "Yep."

The dust settled. The vestibule corner now had a gaping hole large enough to drive a car through. Hoffer shook his head. "Jeepers, that can't be good, sir."

The guardian stepped up to the breach, shielding them from the night demons.

Chambers felt along the floor for his arsenal. His fingers found expended shells and shattered holy grenades. "Where is it?"

"What are you looking for?"

"The satchel charge."

"I got it." Hoffer twisted. The charge was strapped to his back like a parachute.

Chambers snapped his fingers. "Give it to me."

"Let me take out that tank."

"No, stay here. Help Mahoney and Buck."

"Sir, you're forgetting I'm the Shadow. I can blend with the mist and become invisible to my enemies."

A clash of swords echoed at the breach. The guardian was besieged by a horde of golems trying to climb up the wall.

"Shit, we're too late."

"No, we're not." Hoffer crawled under the half-track lodged at the entrance.

"Hoffer, no!"

"Cover me!" The Shadow disappeared under the truck.

"Christ!" Chambers found two unbroken bottles of holy water and marched toward the breach. The guardian slashed its saber down at a mob of golems clawing their way up the wall. Chambers smashed his bottle over one that had nearly climbed into the church. The creature's flesh sizzled, and it fell back into the frenzy of metal claws below. He hurled the second bottle down into the crowd, turning two to dust with one shot. The guardian hacked at the hands that reached upward.

"Keep holding them back!" Chambers raced to a front window, searching the mist-enshrouded parking lot for Hoffer. Twenty feet ahead sat the Tiger tank, the largest and most formidable of the Panzers. Its commander stood in high profile on the perch, rotating with the turret as it aimed for the opposite corner of the church. Hoffer materialized, like a wraith taking form. He crawled under the tank, hiding just inside the tracks. A lighter flicked. A fuse sparked.

The golem scanned the church with binoculars. It stopped at Chambers's window, then pointed. The turret rotated.

Oh shit! "Hurry, Hoffer!" Chambers fired shots from his rifle, hitting the commanding golem in the chest.

The Shadow scaled the front side of the tank. The monster growled as Hoffer yelled, "This is for Finch, you asshole!"

The turret erupted into flames, and the golem burst upward into the night. The Shadow vanished into thin air.

◆ ◆ ◆

"Hoffer . . . " Chambers breathed. Tank shrapnel flung toward the windows. He hit the floor as metal pelted the front of the church. The front barricades collapsed inward. Golems burst through the windows, knocking pews to the ground.

Chambers stumbled backward, falling over a pew. Hovering there, he tried to fire. *Click, click, click.* Empty. He tossed the gun, glanced around. Out of weapons.

The guardian slashed at the invaders. They ganged around the rogue golem, drawing their own sabers. The guardian backed toward the blown-out corner. The horde of demons climbed up the breach. Arms grabbed it from behind. It swung the sword. Chopped hands. Lopped off heads. But the frenzied mob swallowed him whole. The demons poured in through the breach, hissing, growling, silver orbs floating across the gloomy vestibule. Swords swished through the air. Submachine guns arced bullets across the pews and columns.

Chambers ran hunched, hid behind a column. *Gotta get my men out of the tower.*

But when he looked back, his heart sank. The demon army filled the entire front of the church, fighting like hungry animals to get to the prey hiding inside the tower's stairwell.

Everything went silent—except for the *ka-thump, ka-thump* of Chambers's heart. He watched helplessly. Mahoney carried Buck onto the choir balcony. Dozens of golems scratched at the walls below. The Texan leaned against the railing, shooting down into them, his face twisted as if screaming, though no sound emerged. Mahoney, still wearing his flamethrower, shot fiery bursts down the tower's shaft. Then he returned to Buck's side. Machine-gun bullets strafed the balcony, hitting them both. Buck slumped over the rail, his rifle falling below. Mahoney stumbled back into the shadows.

They're dead! Jesus, they're dead!

A candle flared in the balcony's gloom, then another, then another . . .

God, he's lighting the dynamite.

Mahoney lit up like a human sparkler. He stood at the edge of the balcony.

Golems poured onto the landing.

Mahoney faced them, arms stretched outward, embracing his fate. The mob engulfed him. Chambers screamed, "Nooooo!" as the entire balcony exploded into a rippling orange-blue ring that fanned out across the nave. The concussion threw Chambers back. He slid across the floor. Burning embers rained down. Heat singed his skin. He regained his wits, only to encounter a scene that ripped his heart out.

The nave burned like Dante's inferno. Demons wearing torched uniforms hissed and screamed within the bonfires. But they didn't die. The hellish army just kept advancing. A few feet away Chambers spotted the photo of Eva and Tommy. He reached out for it, the heat stinging his hand. The photo caught flame and crumpled to ash.

The crowd of shadows parted, and the Odin-golem stepped through. Glowing red eyes scanned the burning pews. The predators herded around their leader, searching the fiery carnage.

They want prey. I'll give 'em prey.

Chambers stood at the altar. Firelight shimmered across the crucified ivory Jesus. The Messiah's pale flesh bubbled. The face melted.

The demons have won this battle.

Chambers felt the five Roman candles around his belt. *Only one thing left to do.*

He stood at the top of the altar, spreading his arms. "Come on, you fucking demons. Come get me." Then he ran down into the bunker stairwell, the flame of his lighter showing the way.

Hellish roars echoed across the altar. Insanity parted Chambers's lips with a smile.

The demons took the bait.

Chapter 53

Chambers burrowed through the mine shaft. The earthen ceiling quaked. Water trickled down. An underground quagmire sucked at his boots. From behind, nightmarish things hissed and snarled in the antechamber. He glanced over his shoulder. Silver fireflies swarmed around the mine shaft's entrance. They parted as two fiery red dots formed in the center.

A painful, ear-splitting shriek echoed, like a rabid wolf that's just spotted prey.

The pack howled with it.

"In here! Come get me!"

The fireflies swarmed inward.

Ferocious growls filled the mine shaft.

Chambers scurried further. His palm tingled. It became his light source. Boots splashed through the tunnel—*ahead* of him. Giant lumbering shadows. Golden crosses with Star of David symbols traced across the darkness, floating toward Chambers. He ducked into an intersecting tunnel as two more guardian golems passed by. Each carried a saber. Heavy footfalls charged toward the approaching growls.

Christ, Goldstein, you're slowing down our sudden death.

Behind him, the graveyard tunnel erupted with hellacious

roars. Swords clashed. *The guardians can't hold them back for long. Just enough time to prepare for the Big One.*

Giggling like a lunatic, Chambers pulled two dynamite sticks off his belt and entered the underground bunker. The shadowy hallway stretched ahead. Light shimmered in the far room. The crypt. Leaving the bunker's main door open, he crept down the passage.

This will be our tomb. My demons and I. Goldstein and Anna will die down here, too. Such is the fate of this mission. Captain Wolf, Corporal Fox, the Lucky Seven, and now us. Blood sacrifices in the eternal fight between angels and demons. But we'll take those Nazi assholes with us—Eichman and Dietrich. And we'll invite the golems to party with us inside this crypt. There'll be lots of fireworks.

Chambers reached the crypt where the skeletons lined the walls. Candles flickered throughout the concrete room. Four figures in black hooded robes worked hastily at separate stations. Two slapped handfuls of clay over skeletons mounted on the poles. The other two figures performed a ritual, a petite one at the altar with the open spell book—Anna—and the other kneeling within the sacred circle of burning red candles—Goldstein?

Eichman and Dietrich must be the sculptors.

The robed figure in the sacred circle who had to be Goldstein leaned over a lifeless golem, whispered an incantation, and breathed into its nostrils. The clay soldier sat up. Its face, a rush job of sculpting, appeared obtuse. The sorcerer stepped out of the ring of fire and called the sculptors over. The robed figure built like a linebacker—Moose, aka Dietrich—picked up a submachine gun and motioned Goldstein to stand back near Anna.

Eichman—the Necromancer—stepped into the sacred circle behind the seated golem. The dark sorcerer chanted to the ceiling and waved his fingers downward. He drew invisible runic symbols on its cranium. The empty sockets flashed with silver light. The smudged lips parted and the creature wailed like a newborn demon. Goldstein and Anna covered their ears as the high-pitched shriek echoed throughout the crypt.

Chambers squeezed the TNT sticks. *Got birthday candles for you.*

The demon-golem rose. Eichman gave it a saber, said something in German, and led the warrior beast out of the circle, toward the door, toward Chambers. He ducked into a dark side room. The demon passed by, belching a deep guttural moan. *Definitely not a guardian.* It disappeared into the graveyard tunnel.

Chambers watched and listened. Still no sight or sound from the pursuing predators.

Knock, knock, Nazis, the Grim Reaper's at your door.

Eichman and Dietrich returned to the pole-mounted clay sculptures. The husky monk leaned his MP40 against the wall and assisted the Necromancer in unhooking the next stiff golem from the pole. They turned their backs.

Party time. Chambers lit one of the dynamite sticks and walked straight toward them.

Goldstein's eyes widened. He waved his hands, shaking his head. Chambers gave him a thumbs-up and marched toward the Nazis.

"Your work's been getting pretty sloppy."

Eichman and Dietrich spun around, their hands and faces smeared with gray mud. They stared at the lit fuse.

"The look on your butt-ugly faces is priceless."

Dietrich made a move toward his submachine gun.

"Stop or I light the other one." Chambers held the second wick over the burning fuse.

The Nazi with the Neanderthal face froze. "Man, what the . . . ?"

Eichman glared at his henchman. "Kill him."

The fuse burned down to three inches. "Here, have a party favor." Chambers tossed the stick a foot behind Dietrich. The commando chased after it and scooped the stick off the floor while Chambers grabbed the MP40. Dietrich snubbed out the fuse.

"Thanks, Moose." Chambers grinned, aiming the gun. "That was a close one." He opened the sergeant's chest with a dozen red holes.

Eichman pulled out a Luger and fired. A hot slug burned into Chambers's left shoulder. He fell back against the wall. The room spun.

"You cannot stop the apocalypse, Herr Chambers." Eichman fired again.

A slug burst through Chambers's other shoulder, cracking bone. His eyeballs sparked, his chest went numb.

Standing over Chambers, Eichman cocked the pistol at his forehead. "Thule will rise again. The earth will be cold and pure. And the Aryans shall be the only standing race." He laughed. "Good-bye, Herr Chamb—"

Something smacked Eichman over the shoulder. He turned as Anna Klein growled and struck his jaw with the hardbound spell book. The Nazi sorcerer dropped his Luger and stumbled back. Blood stained his lips. "You bitch!"

Dropping the book, she snatched the MP40 and opened fire. The submachine gun rattled Anna's tiny frame like she was gripping a jackhammer. A wild snake of bullets chipped the concrete at Eichman's boots. His black-cloaked form fled the room.

Anna kept her gun aimed at the doorway. "If he comes back, I vill kill him."

"Let the demons have him," Chambers spoke, immediately regretting the effort. Blood oozed from his shoulders. He slid down the wall.

"Chambers!" Goldstein rushed to his aid.

"I'll live, Chap. Few more moments at least."

Goldstein flung off his robe, tearing it into strips, tying tourniquets around each shoulder.

"Chappy . . . you and I gotta stop meeting like this."

"That's it, just keep talking. This may hurt a little." He pulled the tourniquets tight. White novas of pain exploded in Chambers's shoulders. He winced. Then his upper body went numb again.

"We need to get you up." Goldstein helped him stand. They hobbled toward the sacred circle.

"I got a plan to fix our demon problem."

"You call that a plan? You almost blew us all to smithereens."

"I took out the bad guys, didn't I?" Chambers coughed, tasting blood in his mouth.

"And nearly died in the process."

They passed the reflective pool of water. The ritual bath. The *mikvah*.

"Didn't matter. The demons are in the tunnels."

"I've sent guardians."

Candles flickered around the chalked drawings of the two cosmic trees of life—the Kabbalah's *Sefirot* and the Nordic World Tree, Yggdrasil.

"They won't last long. Too many of the others. We're moments from dying, Chap. This really is the Big One."

"There's always hope for a miracle."

They stepped into the sacred circle. Hebrew text. Runic symbols. Six red candles.

Goldstein set him down on the chalked drawing. Chambers exhaled, "We got five dynamite sticks. Soon as the demons get here, you two light the fuses. And we can all go out in a blaze of glory."

"I got a better plan. Stay put." Goldstein left, returning a moment later with the sacred spell book. "How about instead we send our demons back to whatever hell they came from? Anna, get in the circle with me."

She crouched at the front, her machine gun aimed at the doorway. The ten-foot radius held them easily. Holding the book open, Goldstein hurried from candle to candle, whispering an incantation. The candle flames changed from orange to white.

Chambers sat helpless, his blood-stained arms dangling in his lap. "I thought you couldn't read that book."

"I couldn't a few hours ago." The glasses slid down the hump of the rabbi's nose as he flipped to the back of the book. "Then I discovered something quite amazing about the bronze cross Rabbi Klein gave us."

"Something other than the Atbash code breaker?"

"Who needs a tedious code breaker when you can do this?" Goldstein waved the cross like a magnifying glass over a page filled with runes. The Star of David glowed. A light spotlighted the page. The mystical Nordic letters arranged themselves into

Hebrew words. "Simple to read, isn't it?" As Goldstein moved the cross down the page, the previous letters flipped back to runes. The rabbi smiled. "Works the same with the Atbash cipher. While Eichman was busy sculpting golems, Anna and I were taking turns deciphering the spell book."

"You're kidding me."

"Rabbi Klein wrote a great many Kabbalah spells, many of which he encoded with Atbash. First we found the incantations to make golems that would protect us. Then we found these pages." Goldstein tore pages from the back of the book and laid six sheets around the circle. "The ritual is designed to close Pandora's box. Each page represents a point in the Star of David. The runes and Kabbalah text are layered into the spell."

Gratitude flooded through Chambers. "Anna, your grandfather was a brilliant rabbi."

This caused her to smile. Her large brown eyes turned glossy. "Thank you. He was a great man."

The moment was broken when a German voice called out, "Yosef Klein vas a filthy Jew." Eichman's hooded face peered around the doorway. "He should have burned in an oven like your grandmother." Anna opened fire, the MP40 kicking her delicate shoulders. The Necromancer's head disappeared as slugs drilled holes around the threshold. The submachine gun clicked empty.

"Ah, is the Jewish princess out of bullets?"

Eichman stepped back into the room, chuckling, the Luger barrel jutting from his robe.

"Rabbi Klein vas nothing but a fool. Just like you three *Dummköpfe*."

Goldstein stood, holding the spell book. "He outwitted you, Eichman."

The Necromancer stepped closer, pulled down his hood. Pale blue eyes beamed over a smug grin. "How so? Please, enlighten me, Jew."

"While you were sculpting, Rabbi Klein was studying your runic spells. When he learned what you were channeling into the golems, Klein began conjuring spells that would sabotage your operation. Remember your white golem?"

"Yes, the spirit of the great god Odin. My finest summoning."

Goldstein grinned. "No, Herr Eichman. Rabbi Klein created the white golem. He's responsible for slaughtering many Nazis."

Muffled howls echoed through the subterranean tunnels.

"Nein!" The Necromancer jerked his pistol arm. "These creatures are works of brilliance. *Mine!*" He fired repeatedly at Goldstein. The bullets were absorbed by an invisible wall at the edge of the candles, the air in front of the rabbi rupturing into liquid circles before dissipating.

"Jesus Christ!" Chambers stared in amazement.

Goldstein smiled. "Sorry, Eichman, but once again, you've been outwitted by a Jew."

In the hallway boots clumped across stone. Claws scraped against walls. The hellish cries of vengeful demons shrieked and gibbered.

Eichman glanced back at the door. *"Nein . . ."*

Dozens of Nazi golems poured into the crypt. The hissing mob circled around Eichman and the three crouched inside the sacred ring of fire. Feeling woozy, Chambers turned his head in all directions. The shadows extinguished all light except that coming from the six candles. The pack growled like hungry wolves circling a herd of sheep. Demonic silver eyes blazed in their sockets. Claws scraped at the invisible force field, receiving punishing shocks.

The Necromancer yelled German commands. The horde stopped within five feet of the circle. Grinning, Eichman turned to Goldstein, Chambers, and Anna. "See, *I* am their master. Not Klein, not you, not even Odin! *I* am the All-Father. The Reich's messiah. And *I* am going to break whatever spell is shielding you. Then I will enjoy watching my legion rip you Jews to bloody shreds."

Goldstein opened the spell book. "Give it your best shot, Eichman. By then it will be too late. Anna, Chambers, let's finish this."

The Necromancer yelled more commands. Again, the demons attacked the circle. An electric whoosh knocked the mob back. Cursing, the Nazi priest shot at the circle to no avail.

Chambers grinned, dizzy and delirious. "Eichman, you might want to spare your bullets. In case you decide to exit like your buddy Von Streicher." He formed his hand into a pistol and pointed to his temple.

The Necromancer threw his pistol and tried kicking the candles over. The force field zapped his boot. Gritting his teeth, Eichman held his clay-stained hands a foot from the circle. The rune tattoos covering his palms and fingers began to glow. His eyes rolled back white, his lips moved rapidly. The candles flared.

"Can he break the shield?" Chambers asked.

"I don't know, let's move fast." Goldstein and Anna spread the pages around the circle. The rabbi lipped a Hebrew phrase and burned the page in the first candle. A bright red light whooshed upward. Air began whirling around them. The demons growled.

"One down." Goldstein jumped to the second page. He lipped an incantation, burned the second page. An orange flame. The horde of silver-eyed shadows backed away.

Chambers said, "Looks like you got company, Eichman."

The Necromancer's eyes snapped open. Behind him the sea of shadows parted. Red orbs blazed in the gloom. A ghostly moan sprouted gooseflesh across Chambers's body.

The bone white golem walked between the shadows. Its skeletal face grinned at Eichman. Red flames blazed in its sockets.

The Necromancer knelt. "Lord Odin . . ."

Goldstein looked up. "No, Eichman, that's not your Lord Odin."

The white knight raised a hand with razor-sharp talons. A Star of David cross took shape across its forehead.

The Necromancer stumbled back. *Nein!*

Goldstein stood at the edge of the circle. "Rabbi Klein filled this golem with his rage."

The bone white hand gripped Eichman by the throat, lifting him. His face turned purple, pale eyes bulging. His jackboots kicked at the air as he dangled inches from the sacred circle.

Goldstein spoke to the back of his head. "But this golem

holds more than Klein's hatred. He channeled the rage of thousands of other Jews, especially those ghosts still haunting the extermination camps. Time to meet your maker, Herr Eichman."

The Necromancer kicked and screamed as the white golem carried him through the crowd. The growling horde clawed at his robes, shredding them, opening up red slashes in his flesh.

Goldstein burned a third page in a flash of yellow fire. "Three down." He moved to the next. Some demons stayed, circling them, searching for a way into the ring of fire. Some got brave again and swatted at the candles.

"Keep going, Chap," Chambers watched from the center of the circle, too weak to assist. "I got faith in you."

Goldstein picked up his pace and chanted, "Merge, Raphael, angel of air." He lit the fourth page, and a beautiful green flame went up. "Two more."

A man's tortured cries filled the room now. The dark legion raised Eichman to a giant swastika on the wall. He screamed in agony as sabers crucified his hands and feet.

"Merge, Gabriel, angel of water." Goldstein sent the fifth page into a blue flare.

The demons stepped back, shielding their eyes.

Chambers screamed, "It's working, Chap. It's working."

Eichman, crucified to the swastika, wailed as the red-eyed golem grabbed his head with both alabaster clay hands. The golem's mouth unhinged, opened impossibly wide. The cries of a thousand suffering souls roared from its throat. Red light flooded into the Necromancer's mouth. He shuddered, his face and hands glowing red. His throat expanded. His head snapped left and right wildly, then swelled, the bones cracking, flesh stretching, tearing, body spasming against the wall until Eichman exploded in a burst of red embers.

Goldstein grabbed the final page and froze. "Dear God."

Anna gasped. Tears filled her eyes.

The demons backed away as the white golem approached in an ethereal aura. The once skeletal face was now covered in flesh. Chambers also wept as he stared into eyes of purest white. The White One nodded for Goldstein to continue.

Igniting the last page into a bright violet flame, the rabbi chanted the final Hebrew passage. The Kabbalah cross glowed on his hand. Tears streamed down his cheeks. "Merge, Michael, angel of fire. Free the angels and destroy the demons of earth."

White fire *whoooooooshed*!

The room glowed like a gateway to heaven. The demon-golems, packed in as tight as corpses in a mass grave, shrieked like banshees, their jawbones cracking open as they released a deafening chorus of the damned. The undead soldiers shook with tremors, their bodies vibrating from head to toe as if connected to high voltage. Their mottled clay skin cracked and crumbled, falling away from skulls and bony hands. Silver light sucked out of their empty eye sockets and wailing throats, swirling around them like wraiths. The iron claws melted. The skeletons, wearing rumpled Nazi uniforms, collapsed upon one another, dropping to the floor in heaps around the ring of candles. The shrieks faded away, replaced by a chorus of chanting bells. A warm energy swept through Chambers. He felt wrought with emotion as he stared into the blinding white light that was somehow gentle on the eyes. A gateway of pure loving energy opened before him. Chambers felt drawn to step through the gate and be instantly home.

The force field rippled with each vibration of the chanting bells. The silver and white essence blended and formed into the shapes of celestial figures who stood before them in a half circle, transparent beings of pure radiant light. At the center stood the man who had embodied the white golem. Rabbi Klein. Smiling, he turned toward the gateway.

The silver-white beings followed him into the light.

The white fire fizzled out.

Part 10

The Pact

Still to this day, I cannot explain what I witnessed down inside that graveyard crypt. My rational mind argues that my near-fatal gunshot wounds sent me into a state of delirium. Soldiers often claim to see crazy things when on their death bed. And maybe I went mad myself, because a part of me believes that I crossed over into another realm and briefly peered through the gates of heaven.

—LIEUTENANT JACK CHAMBERS, *WAR DIARY*

Chapter 54

Half consciousness returned. The movements changed. Up and down. Side to side. Metal groaning. Water splashing. He awoke in a cocoon that swung with the motion of a greater vessel.

A familiar face was talking to him. Chestnut brown eyes beamed through a pair of glasses. A hand gripped his. "Thank God, I was afraid I lost you, Chambers."

"Still here, Chap. Still here." He took in the hazy surroundings that never stopped moving. "Where is here?"

"Hospital ship. We're sailing across the English Channel."

This brought to his face a lazy smile. "Ah, England." He sank back into the murky waters of eternity.

"Hey." A hand shook him back to consciousness. The rabbi's face looked serious now. "Before you drift off again, I need to tell you something."

Chambers smacked his lips, his mouth dry as cotton. "Thirsty."

Goldstein sat him up, poured a cup of water into his mouth. "I need you to promise you can keep a secret."

"I can keep a secret."

"Promise."

"Scout's honor."

"Okay, I'm going to hold you to it." Goldstein set down the cup. "Anna and I made a decision that we hope you can honor."

Chambers leaned back against his pillow. "I'm listening."

The chaplain adjusted his glasses and cleared his throat. "What happened inside that church was a grave tragedy . . . and something none of us will ever forget. But it is more than the world is ready to face. Especially for those who pull the strings. You know the ones."

"The puppet masters."

"Yes, we tried destroying the Nazi spell book, but it wouldn't burn. So I wrapped it in my army shirt and hid it inside the crypt." Goldstein exhaled. "The thought of that book getting into the wrong hands scares the living daylights out of me. So Anna and I decided to make sure man never gets another chance to raise an apocalypse."

Chambers sat up. "You did what?"

"We resurrected one last guardian. It helped us remove all evidence of what happened. We buried every fallen soldier inside the graveyard. We buried the gold, everything that would draw suspicion. Then we blew up the entrance to the mine shaft."

"You lied about my men?" Chambers's eyes squeezed shut. The faces of the Lucky Seven flashed through his mind— Sergeant Mahoney, Buck, Deuce, Finch, Hoffer, and Garcia.

"I'm sorry, Chambers. It was the only way. When the reinforcements found us, we were a mile away from the church. I told them that your men had been captured, but you and I survived along with one Jewish refugee. Anna's sleeping in the next room. She promised to never tell a soul."

"You're willing to live a lie? What about my men's honor? They left behind families."

"This was a holy mission, Chambers, and they fought bravely. God will honor them. As will their families. Let them rest in peace. Let this battle never happen again. We take the secret to our graves. Promise me." He held out his hand.

Chambers stared out the porthole. The murky waters splashed at the glass. The memory of every battle raced through his mind, every tragedy, every miracle. The white golem's angelic face turning into Rabbi Klein's. Who could ever grasp such a story?

Goldstein was right. The world, still deep into war in Europe and the Pacific, wasn't ready. Nor could man be trusted with such holy powers. Not yet at least. Maybe one day.

"You have my word, Chap. To our graves." He shook the rabbi's hand. "Hey, your scar is gone."

Goldstein held up his palm. "Yours, too. The symbols vanished when we ended Klein's spell." He pulled the blanket over Chambers's bandaged shoulders. "Sleep tight, my good friend. The war's over for us. You'll be in England before you know it."

His head sank into the pillow. "Chap?"

"Yes, Chambers?"

"The last golem you resurrected . . . you did destroy it, didn't you?"

Goldstein flipped off the light. "Sweet dreams, Chambers."

Memorial

I awoke in a bed with warm, dry linens. My vision was still hazy. Sunlight filtered through window blinds. Outside I saw a blue sky. The first in months. Rubber soles squeaked across the floor. My bleary eyes strained to focus on a slender nurse setting a tray on a table. She hummed to herself, lifting what looked to be a pot. I smelled hot tea and lemons.

My heart rose to my throat. "Eva!"

The tea set rattled. The nurse turned, putting her hand on her chest. "Lieutenant, you're awake."

The voice was all wrong. Too deep. The face came into sharp focus. An English nurse I'd never met. My heart sank.

"I see you decided to join the living, sir." She felt my forehead. "You've been comatose ever since they rolled you in here. Thought maybe you were going to stay in dreamland."

"Hmpf."

"Why the gloomy face?"

I shook my head, sinking deeper into my pillow.

"Hang on," the nurse said. "I have something that just might cheer you up." Her rubber shoes squeaked out of the room.

A moment later they squeaked back in.

I looked up. Eva stood in the doorway. Hair longer than I remembered. Face radiant.

She rushed to my bed. Kissed my face. "Oh, love, I've missed you so much."

I kissed her lips, tears whelping in my eyes. "I've missed you more."

We laughed and kissed, unable to find words, just gazing at each other in amazement. Eva wiped her eyes, pouting at the sight of my bandaged shoulders. "Oh, you poor thing."

"Don't worry, Eva, the wounds will heal. And when they do, I'm going to throw my arms around you and never let go."

"I know someone else you'll want to hug." She looked back at the door. "Tommy."

A toddler wearing a white cowboy hat peeked coyly around the corner.

My entire face trembled, my eyes so watery I could barely see him.

"Come see Daddy," Eva ushered.

Giggling, the boy ran toward the bed, his tiny cowboy boots clumping across the tile. He disappeared behind his mother. She laughed. "Our little mule. Come on, up you go." Eva hefted him onto her lap. "Jack, meet Tommy."

I smiled. "Hey, cowboy."

The toddler's green eyes stared, full of wonder. A tiny hand touched my cheek. I wanted so badly to hold him, but I couldn't. Not now, at least. But soon. Soon my wounds would heal. On the outside, I laughed and cried tears of joy. On the inside, I made a pact with myself.

I promise to always be here for you guys, and when times get rough, when we reach that pinnacle of self-doubt that makes most people surrender, I'll show you miracles do exist.

With God as my witness, they do.

• • •

Over sixty years later, inside the log cabin, the fire in the hearth had dwindled down to embers. Sean Chambers closed the dossier of his grandfather's diary, held it against his chest. He wiped his eyes before any tears could spill down his face. A shaky hand poured a tumbler of whisky. He took a small sip before having to set down the tumbler. *Not going to cry.*

The stone face so characteristic of Chambers men crumbled.
The tears won over.

General Briggs stepped into the room and squeezed Sean's
shoulder. "Your grandfather and Goldstein did what they had
to do." He pulled the diary from Sean's grip. "Now we must
do the same."

Briggs threw the dossier into the fireplace. The pages curled
in orange and blue flames. Then he sat on the couch and re-
filled both tumblers with whisky. They drank Chivas in silence, watching a secret part of history turn to glowing embers
and smolder to ash.

• • •

Two months later, a large crowd sat in white foldout chairs on
a manicured lawn, among them photographers and reporters
from every media. Hundreds of white crosses lined the hills.
Colonel Jack Chambers, his army uniform adorned with medals, sat at the front of the crowd surrounded by family. Sean,
wearing his air force uniform, sat with Meg and the kids to
Jack's left, while Jack's wife, Eva, sat to his right alongside
their son, Tom, and Sean's mother. Behind them sat all the rela-
tives of Jack's platoon. An elderly widow, Mrs. Mahoney, held
a tissue to her nose. Around her sat her four daughters with
their husbands and children. Behind them the Garcia family
filled the white seats. One elderly woman kissed a cross and
held up a blowup of the Mexican soldier's army portrait.

Sean noticed an old man with a cane taking a seat in the
back row. Rabbi Jacob Goldstein lowered his bifocal sunglasses
and winked. Sean saluted him.

Chambers became an emotional basket case when the
pallbearers brought out six caskets covered in American flags.
Soldiers dressed in formal uniforms stood with firm salutes.

General Mason Briggs stood at a podium, eulogizing into a
microphone. His booming voice echoed off the white stone
crosses. "Sometimes the past remains a mystery . . . and sometimes the past gets unearthed so that we can remember and
possibly learn from those who came before us. Today, we are
here to honor six men who fought with uncommon valor in
World War II.

"Master Sergeant John Mahoney . . . Sergeant Buck Parker . . . Corporal Bobby 'Deuce' Wilson . . . Pfc. Gabriel Finch . . . Pfc. Raphael Hoffer . . . and Pfc. Miguel Garcia." Briggs looked down at the flag-draped coffins. "These six soldiers fought and gave their lives in the battle of the Hürtgen Forest so that today we could have peace between nations. They all deserve to be remembered as heroes."

A squad leader shouted orders. The two rows of soldiers lifted their rifles in the air and fired six times, a round of shots for each soldier. When they were done, a trumpeter played "Taps," while the six caskets sank down into the ground.

Sean grabbed his grandfather's hand. Chambers squeezed it tight.

• • •

When the ceremony was over and the crowd rose to its feet, Jack Chambers's family helped him with his walker. Jack gripped the handles and stood wobbly, still shaken.

General Briggs walked over. "Colonel Chambers . . ."

Everyone paused to look at the highly decorated officer. Sean hushed his son and daughter.

Jack said, "Yes, General?"

Briggs said, "I just wanted to say, Colonel, I know that in war it's tough to make the right decisions. But as long as I've known you, you've always followed your heart. You did the best you could to save these men. That's the most the army can ask of any soldier. It is truly an honor to stand before a living hero." He stood at a firm salute.

Jack returned the salute. "Thank you, General. And you have served my platoon by bringing them home. For that I am eternally grateful."

After Briggs walked away, Jack pushed the walker toward the freshly plotted graves with white crosses. His family chased after him, trying to help him walk.

"No, please, let me do this," Jack told them. "I need to be alone with my men."

His family let him go and watched Jack struggle with the walker across the grass. He stood at the graves a long while, the wind blowing his white hair. He stared at each grave for several moments before moving to the next.

Jack's family walked to the reception with all the other families. The media and military personnel left as well. Jack looked back to see Sean and Rabbi Goldstein sitting in the white chairs on the lawn. He returned his gaze to the sea of white crosses. Sean and Goldstein stepped up on either side of him.

The three stared down at the fresh graves.

Goldstein broke the silence. "Jack, I'm curious . . . Sean told me you sent General Briggs down into the crypt and he retrieved the spell book. That was my biggest concern. The book getting into the wrong hands. Where did he deliver it?"

"I can't say exactly." Jack tapped his Freemasonry ring. "Let's just say it's stored away with the rest of life's mysteries."

Jack scratched his jaw. "Chap, as long as we're sharing secrets, whatever happened with those duffel bags of Nazi gold?"

"Sorry, Jack, that's classified information." Goldstein grinned mischievously. "However, if you were to research the 1948 accounting records of the Old-New Synagogue in Prague, you might find a generous donation in memory of Izak Wolfowitcz and Rabbi Yosef Klein."

The wind flapped their uniforms. Just then movement caught Jack's eyes. Far in the distance, against a backdrop of shimmering, sun-baked air, he saw a white figure leading a ghost platoon across the rolling green hills of the cemetery. They all turned, and Jack swore he made out the faces of the Lucky Seven. And they were smiling. *I told you I'd bring you boys home one way or another.* His misty lashes blinked and the platoon vanished.

Jack smiled to himself. *Maybe it was a mirage.* But the tingling in his heart convinced him to believe the unbelievable.

clandestine adj *(1528) : marked by, held in, or conducted with secrecy: SURREPTITIOUS*
                              —Merriam-Webster's Collegiate Dictionary

The Shadows of World War II

While the story of Jack Chambers and the Lucky Seven is purely a work of fiction, many of the events in this novel were inspired by historical facts. As I delved into researching the famous battles fought between the Allies and the Germans, I discovered the Allies operated several secret missions to gather intelligence in Europe.

When the United States needed a dangerous mission carried out, it often turned to the OSS (Office of Strategic Services) led by General William Donovan based in Washington, DC. In 1943 Donovan created a counterintelligence branch called X-2. As the war escalated, the OSS stationed teams of elite X-2 commandos all across Europe that carried out clandestine operations, often behind enemy lines. Using Ultra and Magic code breaking, the X-2 mercenaries also decrypted enemy messages and passed information along to British intelligence. The OSS was notorious for having weak security, and overseas operations were often infiltrated by Nazi spies. After WWII, the OSS became the present-day CIA.

In Berlin, the Nazis were operating their own spy networks in addition to researching the occult through the Ahnenerbe-SS. Their numerous trips to Iceland and Tibet kept the Aryan fantasy alive, while the reality of an enraged world was closing in on Germany like a vise. As they hit desperate times, Himmler and Hitler wanted to make sure their research remained secret. On April 2, 1945, two days before U.S. forces reached Wewelsburg, the SS blew up the castle, leaving only the outer walls standing. The castle has been rebuilt and stands today in Westphalia, Germany.

Whether the Black Order had any interest in building golem soldiers remains a mystery. But I came across one story that made me wonder. When the Nazis occupied Prague, Czechoslovakia, they burned down numerous synagogues and, following Hitler's direct orders, left the Old-New Synagogue standing. During their entire occupation of Prague, the Nazis never entered the Old-New Synagogue's attic, where, as the legend goes, Rabbi Loew hid his famous golem.

* * *